LORDS OF
LAS VEGAS

LORDS OF LAS VEGAS

KURT DIVICH

STEPHENS PRESS • LAS VEGAS

Editor: Geoff Schumacher

Cover and book designer: Sue Campbell

9781-932173-963 (print book)

9781-932173-710 (e-book)

STEPHENS PRESS, LLC
A Stephens Media Company

Post Office Box 1600

Las Vegas, NV 89125-1600

www.stephenspress.com

Printed in United States of America

For Tami, who always believes in me.
And for my father, Ken, who believed in everyone.

Acknowledgements

Thanks to Geoff Schumacher for making *Lords* a better book. Thanks to Carolyn Hayes Uber for never giving up on this project or herself. Thanks to Sue Campbell for helping me find the title of the book. Thanks to Mary Hausch for letting me know I could do this. Thanks to Paul J. Henry for giving me a hero. And thanks to Riley, Trystyn, Kyra and Quinn for loaning their daddy to this project for years at a time

CHAPTER 1

August 2004

The little girl never heard the fatal gunshot. Not because it didn't sound with the usual ferocity of a firing handgun, but because the blare of a bullet penetrating her daddy's skull was muted by the considerable distance from his bathroom to her seat in the family room. She reached for an oversized handful of dry Cheerios just a moment after he fell from a shaking vertical stance, fleeing the return of his image in the mirror. She wouldn't think to look for him until after her DVD ended.

As she found her way to the closed bathroom door, she stood unknowingly in a trickle of his room temperature blood making its way from her father's head as he lay awkwardly against the other side. She called to him, gently at first, then whining lightly in beginner sentences that the movie was over, as if it were his fault. Waiting a half-second for his reply, she raised her pitch, imploring him to sit with her as he'd promised. Turning the knob and pushing the door, his sedentary weight precluded entry. She hit the door with the palm of her hand, calling her father and beginning to cry at his perceived rebuff.

Giving up, she sat down in frustration, her back against the door and her cotton pajamas soaking up the edges of puddled blood. His body slumped in nearly the same position on the other side, the door all that separated her life and his death. A new gun lay just beyond his right hand, a sealed letter below his left.

His suicide would be seen by most as the unlikely demise of a talented man tortured by the mistakes he'd made and the consequences they created. He couldn't see any way to keep her now or to withstand his impossible future. Ending his life would be best for everyone.

Soon, his wife would return home, pushing her way through the bathroom door and finding her husband on the floor, motionless for the first time since she'd met him. She ran her fingers through thick hair stiffened by clotted blood, whispering "I love you" with a sincerity that hadn't accompanied those words in months.

She wanted to feel surprised, to be answerless when friends and neighbors curiously asked "Why?" in the days ahead. But she couldn't. She had feared this dark end and wondered if he would flee the terminal uneasiness between them as they endured public disgrace and a grim future.

Even still, she'd entertained the hopeful notion just today that their troubles might actually bring them together, giving them an "Us against the world" evolution in their broken marriage and the resolve to fix the schism. It was a fleeting thought, poisoned with doubt as she considered a bridge to elsewhere, but it told her that she would always harbor affection for the gifted man for whom she'd fallen.

Now it was over, really over, and tragedy no longer loomed on the path ahead. As she cradled her daughter in her arms, unable to explain what had just happened, she exhaled a long, deep, and cleansing sigh. He was gone and their life would never be the same. She considered the axiom that for every action there is an equal and opposite reaction, and wondered what form that might take.

Maybe she could take her daughter and go somewhere where her name was not written in headlines and scarlet letters, leaving the misery of 2004 behind. Maybe she could start over, find someone to love her and the dark-eyed little girl. Someplace where no one knows the embarrassing truth everyone here already does.

She'd do that as soon as possible, she promised herself, once she decided where to live beyond the past. Before she did, she had her husband's bloodstained letter to deliver.

CHAPTER 2

July 2000

Daniel Madison drove toward the Mandalay Bay hotel-casino, passing houses and businesses that had been undeveloped desert lots for most of his youth in Las Vegas. The city had grown as he had, and now the once desert outpost was a burgeoning metropolis of urban and suburban dwellers, power brokers and politicians.

Today would be his coming-out party, he prayed, the display of his first real writing gig since graduating from college a year before. Daniel hadn't been able to complete an internship that might lead to employment in journalism or advertising during his senior year, working after school instead to pay his tuition. He continued to hear how lesser-skilled classmates had taken paying jobs at the firms where they previously interned and consoled himself that they weren't really writing, they were fetching coffee and cutting clips. Still, it topped his own tasks during the dinner rush at Applebee's while he waited for the right opportunity.

After eight opportunity-free months waiting tables, at last good fortune had allowed him to write a speech for a real political candidate. The opportunity had been pure happenstance as Daniel saw it, his presence at a charity event where he was volunteering leading to a conversation with another man his own age. The well-dressed attendee had struck up a casual conversation with a chair-stacking Daniel about the abundance of "MILFs" at the event, segueing to a sports dialogue and eventually introducing himself as Julian Correa, candidate for Clark County Commission.

Daniel had heard of the young Hispanic candidate and he'd seen the "Correa for Commission" signs distributed liberally in the district near his small apartment. He'd wondered how guys like Correa got so far so fast, running for an office that men normally labored into their forties before attempting. It made him consider why he was still serving riblets this long after graduation.

Now, as he drove to an event Julian called essential to his campaign, Daniel stopped to pick up a newspaper, intent on surveying the classifieds for something that paid better. The opportunity to write a speech for a candidate like Correa—young, handsome, articulate, and demographically appealing—and to have his speech read in front of some of the most important businesswomen in the city was indeed important and encouraging. His car insurance premium had just jumped again and the student loan payments would start in a month. He'd have to find more than Applebee's tips to make the monthly nut, and the speech for Julian provided an at-bat he couldn't blow … even if everything with Julian was moving a little faster than he was comfortable with.

They were only twenty minutes into their initial conversation when Julian discovered that Daniel was a writer and asked him if he wanted to draft a speech on the importance of women in society, tailoring the message to the powerful members of Working Women who were hosting a candidates' showcase for the 2000 election year. The offer had come so quickly, so easily, that Daniel at first doubted its validity, whether Correa would really accept the work of a near-stranger for what he described as a "critical moment" in his candidacy. Daniel knew immediately that Julian was gambling on his speechwriting skills as a bonus to friendship, that this fast-rising phenom was missing something that he saw in another his own age. Julian's haste wasn't unnerving, but it was incongruent with Julian's strident demeanor.

• • •

Daniel had written and rewritten Julian's speech a dozen times, wanting it to be perfect. If Julian was successful with his oration, Daniel knew he could leverage that in the job world, or even better, become integral to the campaign.

When Julian read the first draft, he knew that his first impression of

Daniel Madison was correct, that he was talented and eager. Better yet, unlike the rest of his so-called advisers, a guy his own age would be unlikely to try to handle him as the others did, as if he were a petulant child at the political toy store. His campaign was but a few months old and already a team of consultants, handpicked by Frank Hayes of Summit Communications, was wearing him out with constant advice and criticisms laced into helpful suggestions.

Julian had given the criticisms purchase by continuing to lead a single man's life without regard for his candidacy, this suave bachelor with a light Cuban accent. Stories were circulating well above a whisper of Julian's carnal conquests of all varieties, including those of wealthy wives in his district. As Julian saw it, his dalliances were part of the charm that made him a good candidate in the first place, and even a man like Hayes, who staked the campaign with dollars and credibility, recognized that Julian's nocturnal efforts helped keep the campaign funds flowing.

Nonetheless, Julian had been surprised when Michael Martin informed him that despite what appeared to be a promising campaign well on its way, he was still polling poorly in one section of his commission district where his opponent owned a restaurant. They would need to hit the neighborhoods harder with more signs and a mailer, Martin suggested. With his budget already planned to the last nickel, Martin advised Julian that a friend-winning speech in front of the powerful businesswomen and wives of the elite local gentry would be important to capturing much-needed new donations. Martin was right, Julian agreed, and he appreciated how a man like Martin, with all the connections of Frank Hayes, spoke *to* him, not *at* him. *Thank God the Madison kid can write*, Julian thought, realizing the risk he'd taken with a political neophyte.

Julian leapt from the car of last night's companion and entered through the shimmering entrance of the massive hotel. Daniel's speech danced through his head as the words lay on a few sheets of paper in his breast pocket, ready for use. Daniel parked his 1965 Mustang deep in the caverns of the parking garage, unable to gamble on his mercurial carburetor refusing duty for a Mandalay Bay valet. He grabbed the ticket Julian had given him for the event and headed toward the coffee shop where they'd agreed to meet.

Daniel's hands were sweating as he speed-walked through the casino. He thought about the unique elements from Julian's life that he'd used to make it poignant, wondering if Julian had taken any of them out of the speech as they became increasingly personal. As he walked into the coffee shop and saw Julian sipping a Pellegrino with lime, an ambient confidence in bloom, he realized how different their individual emotions were right now. And Julian was the one giving the speech.

Julian rose and greeted Daniel with a warm hug, the same as he had each time since their first meeting. "Daniel, it's just about showtime, eh?" Julian offered, looking down at his cell phone as it began to vibrate.

"Screw him," Julian said as if Daniel knew to whom he was referring, returning the phone to his suit pocket. "Frank Hayes I don't need right now."

"Who's that?" Daniel asked on cue.

"I guess you could call him my campaign manager, though I've got another guy who has that title on his business cards. But Hayes runs my show … everybody's show, I guess. The man has boundary issues, though. He's on my ass like a pregnant chick."

Daniel smiled at Julian's disdain and metaphor. He liked that Julian spoke to him like one of the guys, not the hot shot candidate the news was constantly calling "Nevada's rising star." Growing up in a middle-class neighborhood that had deteriorated into something less than that as he hit high school, it was comforting to be around a guy like Correa who acted more like the friends with whom he'd gone to high school.

"You look good, man," Daniel said, admiring the perfectly fitting suit and wanting to steer the conversation away from any subject that might irk the man who would be speaking to five hundred potential donors in a few minutes. "Let's go over a couple parts of the speech, all right?"

"Nah, I got it," Julian answered. "We're good, bro. I won't mess it up."

"You sure?" Daniel replied. "We've got time. We can work a little on the pacing or ..."

"Danny," Julian interrupted. "I know this is important to you. I'll nail it, man. This is what I do ... what I'm good at. We're golden."

"No problem," Daniel acquiesced, realizing he hadn't shared with Julian his financial plight or his self-serving hopes for the speech. "Let's get over there."

Julian stood up quickly and led the way out of the coffee shop, ignoring the bill for his water. Daniel threw five dollars on the table and turned to catch up. As he drew closer, Julian paused to retrieve his cell phone once more and his expression confirmed that Hayes had hit redial. Julian turned the phone off, buried it deep into his pocket, and looked back at Daniel.

"I'm glad we met, Danny," he began. "I just feel like everyone else I'm working with is pulling me in directions I don't want to go. As much as I want to win this thing, parts of it are getting old fast. I think you're the first normal person I've talked to in a month."

"Happy to serve," Daniel said with a jest that covered for the fact he was unsure how to actually respond. "You just let me know what I can do to help. I'm with you."

"That's good to hear," Julian said, using eye contact that would win him donors and votes and Daniel. He nodded in agreement, thinking the very same thing, that they could really help each other professionally and build a friendship in the process. They shook hands in parting, neither aware that their seemingly chance meeting was the inception of a relationship that would eventually cause one of them to put a gun against his head and pull the trigger.

CHAPTER 3

"Thank you, Senator Davis. It seems I too often have the misfortune of following your formidable lead." Julian smiled as he placed his notes on the dais, adjusting the microphone to account for the height difference between the senator and himself. His blue pinstriped suit seemed even more vibrant to Daniel under the flattering stage lights trained on the podium.

"First, I'd like to thank Working Women for letting me share a few minutes with you all. I truly appreciate it. An organization like this certainly represents the best of what Las Vegas has to offer ... wives, mothers, business people congregating as a blended unit, their collective strength a potent force in our community.

"As most of you know, I am running for the County Commission and I am young. Your eyes do not deceive you. I stand here today in many ways the same as women did not so long ago, a minority of color and young age, breaking many unwritten social rules in seeking this important office. Just as women were discouraged from campaigns and elections ... leadership, really ... so too have I been told that I am too young or too Latino for this job. But I believe those narrow voices are the real minority—not me. This is a different time, an era of unbridled opportunity for all of us, where merit transcends superficialities and linear dates. Yes, there is more work to be done. We must turn glass ceilings into vertical elevators for women, and minorities, and persons of different sexual orientation."

Daniel watched the crowd for reactions and found a contented expression on the face of Annie Halpern, his journalism teacher in college whom he thought of as his mentor. She had been the editor of the city's largest newspaper before trading the editor's desk for a professor's office. Annie had a reputation for "call 'em like I see 'em" remarks, and her husband held the elected office of university regent, the assorted experiences giving her a strong understanding of Las Vegas politics. Next to her stood Mike Martin, his large frame and big shoulders contained in a smart navy blue blazer that had been a favorite since his early days in Boston. He seemed pleased as well.

Julian continued, his hands gripping the edges of the glass lectern, a gentle lean toward the crowd a subtle display of his comfort in the spotlight. "Today we ponder the once unheard of, the possibility that a woman may soon set up shop in the mighty Oval Office. Not so long ago, a woman's loftiest aspiration was to redecorate the White House in her husband's term and to stay out of the way when things got serious.

"Well, thanks to women like you—and the good men who do not stand in your way—it is no longer possibility. It is inevitability," Julian continued, making more eye contact with the audience than Daniel had ever seen a candidate manage.

He isn't reading, Daniel noted to himself. *He has memorized the whole speech ... ten minutes' worth.* The note cards remained stacked, untouched. To Daniel's right a waitress had stopped her path of servitude, standing among the attendees. She was riveted, beaming like a proud parent at a beauty pageant, as if Julian were speaking only to her. She wasn't alone. Heads were nodding like stoners at a rock concert. Julian's presence was beyond engaging ... it was powerful, yet tender and convincing, as if he'd personally authored the potent words he uttered. This was one of the reasons Mike Martin and Frank Hayes figured he'd be viable as a candidate despite his age, agreeing on something for once. He could woo a crowd in a way that grizzled state legislators couldn't.

Correa's appeal was no mystery. Aesthetically, Julian was a female fantasy incarnate: articulate, handsome, dangerous. Perhaps it was the latter that made some women behave like they were at a Chippendale's show even at highbrow events like this. In his fitted suit, exalted above the crowd, and most obviously the star of the proverbial show, Julian surpassed the senator, rich businessmen, and devoted husbands. It was Julian's crowd.

"And while we shall all share in the glory of a nation that has reached the collective maturity, decency, and common sense to consider a woman for its highest office, that is not the most important achievement of the modern woman," Julian said, his dark eyes surveying the room, methodically making eye contact with guest after guest like an optical game of tag.

"No, I believe what is indeed more important than that lofty post is the impact we have on the small girls we call our sisters and daughters. Our greatest accomplishment, exemplified by each of you dynamic, capable women, is that we instill in these little girls the expectation that *they* can now be president." Julian paused and stepped back from the lectern like a veteran comic, allowing the break of silence to usher the applause. He reached for a water glass and gently sipped its contents, expertly letting the applause extend.

"As many of you know, my expectant mother fled the persecution of Cuba where no man or woman has the right to pursue their dreams. She nearly died, *we* nearly died, on that liberating boat ride to this country just so her son could be born an American. I arrogantly suggest that no one understands the importance of women better than I. And it is from this deep and real understanding that I recognize the contributions of women who have nurtured this city from dusty rail town to a bastion of tourism and commerce, culture and opportunity.

"Ladies, strong women, as I thank you for making this the kind of place where I can someday raise *my* little girl, I issue you this solemn pledge, this promise: I will remember the battles that you and my own mother have won. I will tread upon the road you've made mindful of the sacrifices and I will endeavor in that good way. With the blessing of your support, we can make an assemblage of female leaders in Southern Nevada an event to be held in a stadium, not a banquet room."

With that he stepped backward, as if triumphant. He then stood solemnly—almost humble—as the crowd applauded enthusiastically. Senator Davis returned from somewhere in the offing, looking to bask in Julian's benevolent glow, holding Correa's hand high like a prize fighter. If Julian hadn't secured every vote in the room, someone had been in the bathroom during his speech.

Annie and Mike Martin had moved behind Daniel sometime during the oration, and she now placed both hands on his shoulders. "That was unbelievable," she said into his ear in a powerful whisper, suppressing the shrill tenor of a voice that was second in intensity only to her flamered hair. "Un-freaking-believable. It'll look like a telethon tomorrow at Julian's headquarters there'll be so much money coming in."

"He did a wonderful job," Daniel offered modestly. "Does it get better than Julian?"

"At doing that? No. No one's better. Best I've ever seen," Mike Martin answered before lowering his voice so only Annie could hear. "His problem isn't standing at a podium. It's lying on a mattress."

Annie returned her focus to Daniel as she digested Martin's mixed remarks. "I'd have known that was your speech if it had been given by a warlord in Nigeria. You have this incredible way of being expressive without being gushy, Dan. Nice, nice, nice."

"Let me introduce you two," Annie said, realizing the men hadn't met. "This is Daniel Madison, the best young writer I've ever worked with ... even if he won't take a job at any of the PR firms around town."

Annie had stumbled upon Daniel waiting tables one day after her son's soccer game, chastising him loudly for "wasting his gift" and pledged to place him in an agency the next day. Wanting the lecture to end, Daniel had acquiesced at the Applebee's, but had since declined her multiple interview offers, telling her he was going to wait for the right moment rather than get caught up doing the grunt work of a beginning staffer.

"And this fella is Michael Martin," Annie continued with a grin. "Mike is a lobbyist and one of the good guys. Counting my husband there are two now."

Daniel and Mike shook hands, and Martin looked at Daniel. "That was your speech, eh? Very nicely done." He removed a business card with just his name and phone number from a long leather wallet in his coat pocket and handed it to Daniel. "I think I have a few candidates who can use speeches and copywriting from time to time. You interested?"

"Absolutely," Daniel replied. "This is what I want to be doing, sir."

"Well, knock off the 'sir' stuff and let's go get a drink," Martin shot back with a Boston accent as they watched Julian exit the stage, shaking hands like the paint-mixing machine at Home Depot. Thirty-seven back pats and eighty-one handshakes later, he had secured the phone number of the riveted waitress and was drinking a glass of wine an admirer had handed him.

"We did it, stud," Julian said proudly as he approached Annie, Mike, and Daniel, wrapping an arm around his speechwriter. "You see the feedback I'm getting?"

"Mike, we're good to go now, right?" Julian asked, turning to Martin. "We'll be able to handle that section of my district?"

"Julian, if just one of those sound bites makes local news, we can take most of your signs down and start hiring office staff," Martin exaggerated. "This is ours to lose now. No screw-ups … from anyone."

"From anyone" had the validity of a counterfeit hundred-dollar bill. "No screw-ups" meant Julian. The candidate nodded in agreement.

Daniel was blissful, proud, and wide-eyed at his new future. It had been a good few weeks for him and things were looking even brighter. He knew he had to find a way to earn more money right now but his long-term prospects of working as a writer in politics had rapidly improved. The home run speech today and Martin's business card supported that notion.

Martin sought to buffer his warning to Julian with an overture toward fraternity, looking at Daniel, Julian, and Annie before him. "Why don't we go throw a couple back at that little English pub off Maryland? I'm buying." Daniel was delighted. Getting to know Martin seemed just as important as knowing Julian, and Annie's declaration of his good guy status added to the appeal.

"I'll take a pass but give my pint to Daniel-son," Annie answered. "I've got to help clean this mess up."

"I'm in," Julian said. "But I can't stay long."

"Why's that?" Martin asked.

"First, I gotta get back over there and talk to that beautiful little cocktail waitress, and then I've got some fundraising to do late tonight."

Martin just shook his head, mindful that Julian's definition of fundraising meant that he had already disregarded the "no screw-ups" admonition and that Mike would be cleaning up messes too. Martin would soon discover, as Annie had with a wine stain on the Working Women's cloth banner, that not everything can be completely cleaned.

CHAPTER 4

Few watering holes in the Las Vegas Valley offered patrons the atmo-
spheric character of the Crown & Anchor Pub near the university.
Were it not for the bartop poker machines, a photo taken inside the
venerable establishment could have been mistaken for a shot of most
any dive in downtown London.

The walls did their best to convey English style. Nautical themes,
Guinness posters, and more than a few TVs blaring Premiership football all mimicked a British original. The battered wood tables, broad
ceiling beams, and massive center bar collectively served to separate
Crown from the stucco competition. But above all it was the beer that
offered the literal taste of England. Bass, Harp, McEwen's, and every
other classic libation from anywhere in the Queen's first dominion gave
the popular watering hole liquid culture.

Most any night the pub was a mosaic of Vegas citizenry. Businessmen
and politicos meandered draught in hand with their sleeves rolled up,
ties loosened, and jackets left back in the Lexus. In counterbalance,
tattooed and pierced ne'er-do-wells shot pool upstairs in a cloud of
clove-smoke or pounded a Black and Tan in a dimly lighted corner.

At the bar, cantankerous limey bartenders with one eye on the patrons and the other on the Chelsea vs. Manchester United broadcast
gave intermittent service to those who troubled them with a request. It
was here that many of the better lines of the evening might be offered
at the sonic edges of a garage band given five square feet in which to
play covers. Crown was as local a place as you find in Las Vegas, ironic
as that may be for a British pub surrounded by sagebrush.

Daniel entered the pub first, eager to get the night started. He'd
tried to plan what he'd say to Martin and Correa tonight, wanting
not to sound too eager, yet enthusiastic about their individual needs.
Would they be paying customers, he wondered, or would this be gratis

like every other political job he'd heard of with candidates using their campaign platforms as catch-all bait for free labor under the guise of volunteerism?

Martin arrived soon after and his stride conveyed to Daniel a can-do attitude that was devoid of the bravado he'd normally expect a player of Martin's import to exude. Mike Martin was the roof of confidence and the floor of arrogance. Daniel waved to Martin as he surveyed the bar. Martin headed to the corner table Daniel occupied, slapping him on the back, grasping his hand warmly, and saying, "Good to see you, brother."

It was oddly genuine, Daniel thought, still surprised that Martin had wanted to meet him after the brief exchange earlier. "Good to be here, Mike. I've heard great things about you," Daniel replied.

"And I've heard good things about you and your family, Danny," Martin said. "Your name is associated with a certain work ethic that I value. I hear you're an East Coast guy—a fella who can be counted on. And Annie says you can write like the dickens ... or was it that you write like Dickens? No matter, I need fellas like you around."

It was strange to hear all this from Martin, Daniel thought. Mike had clearly spoken to someone about him after he left the Working Women event. Daniel wondered what else this background check had revealed. Did they know he was waiting tables? Did that matter? What else did they know about his family?

"I'm happy to help, Mike. I want to get involved." He paused, but Martin said nothing. "It sounds like you did a little homework on me. I guess I shouldn't ask to whom you spoke."

"That doesn't matter," Martin replied. "Your dad's known to be a stand-up guy—someone who values his friends and can be relied upon. Like I said, that's a commodity out here. Your pop's the school teacher out of Pittsburgh, right?"

"Yes, he is," Daniel answered.

"See, East Coast guy," Mike stated.

"I gotcha," Daniel agreed, not really grasping the entirety of the remark, but not wanting to burden a compliment or to look clueless in front of Martin.

Glancing toward the door, Daniel recognized Correa, who located them instantly. Julian was freshly shaven and had a nice-fitting V-neck shirt on that showcased his physique and skin tone. He looked to be about six foot three and had the gait and posture of an athlete. As Julian made his way toward the table, he paused to kiss the cheek of a wait-ress who had crossed the room to greet him, handing him a whiskey from an order of four destined for other customers. Julian took a quick drink, smiled, then leaned over a dining couple to grasp the hand of a gray-haired gentleman enjoying a cigar with his single malt.

Julian finally arrived at their table, making an exaggerated sigh as if fatigued. "This campaigning shit is hard," he said, ineffectively masking his sheer love of the attention. "I can't walk past anybody can I, Mike?"

"That's the way it works, Julian," Mike agreed. "You gotta touch 'em all."

Another waitress walked by and Martin let out a light cry for help. "Madame, we're dry here!"

"Well, let's fix that straight away," she said in a hearty British accent, setting a bowl of pretzels on the table. "Whaddya havin', lads?"

"May I order for us, Daniel?" Martin inquired.

"Sure," Daniel agreed. "There are no wrong answers when ordering beer."

Daniel wanted to be one of the guys, but wasn't quite sure whether professional types like Martin valued fraternity or decorum foremost. He wanted to be cool with Martin, not a lush.

"My good man and I will have a Boddington's Ale, miss," Martin an-nounced. "And Correa seems to be ahead of us both. We'll catch you soon, Julie."

"You blokes are splitting a pint?" the waitress asked seriously.

"No, we're just friends. Two beers, please," Daniel clarified sarcasti-cally, followed by laughter from both Correa and Martin.

"Aaaah, it's good to be here with you boys," Martin offered, becoming more brother than father with each passing moment. "I don't do enough of this anymore. I swear, when I worked on the Hill we spent every night in a pub like this near the Capitol. We'd play darts until we were counting points for it sticking in the wall. I've never slept so little in my life."

"Were you working for the senator then, Mike?" Julian asked.

"Yes, I was, though he probably didn't know it," Martin responded. "I had just graduated from law school and thought that the world would be at my doorstep. I finished near the top of my class, but I couldn't see myself working at any of the firms that were interested. Either it was in the wrong state or it was the wrong gig. I didn't go to school that damn long to be miserable working for Big Tobacco. You know what I mean?"

"I think I do," Daniel replied, understating the daily torment that was his identical plight.

"So I took a gig for your senator out here because I liked his stance on a few issues that mattered to me and because I thought Nevada would grow and I could get in early. I helped write some pretty good pieces of legislation, but the pay was for shit," said Martin, pausing to take a drink from the pint glass the waitress had just delivered. "Can't have it all, I guess.

"Next thing I know, I'm running his office out here, making good contacts, and then I start in the private sector ... lobbying, sitting on some charitable boards and trying to build a good name. It's gone all right," he said with a little smile. "Momma's proud of me. I got her picture taken with Ted Kennedy last time I was home. That goes a long way with most of the gals her age back in Boston. *Now* she thinks I'm important."

He took a few pretzels in hand and politely raised the wooden bowl to Daniel and Julian. Daniel took a few, but Julian waved it off.

"Low-carb diet?" Martin asked teasingly.

"Nah, I've got a gluten intolerance," Julian answered seriously, seemingly uncomfortable revealing his dietary issues. "Can't handle wheat products … beer, bread, stuff like that."

"What about you, Julian?" Daniel said. "What brought you here?"

"Her," Julian replied, his eyes following a slender blonde who shimmied past them in the now-crowded bar. "I came here for her."

Mike and Daniel laughed as they watched Julian pretend to salivate. Daniel thought that despite their polish, both Julian and Martin seemed to be regular guys.

"Actually, I came out here to play football," Julian explained. "I wanted to be out West and I thought I could get more playing time at a smaller program like this one. They gave me a scholarship and I've been here ever since. So I started taking poli-sci classes and liked them. I interned at the governor's office and helped on his re-election campaign where my Spanish came in handy. Afterward, the governor told me that with my Latin background and some local support I could be a candidate for that vacant commission seat. What did I have to lose? Either way I raise my profile and everybody at least knows the governor's got my back, right?"

"I understand," Daniel said. It always amazed him how breaks came ever so simply and unpredictably, like falling stars. All it took was one little opening, though it appeared guys like Correa got multiple openings. Daniel did the math and realized it was his turn for show-and-tell, but he worried that his Horatio Alger story didn't have the triumph part yet as Martin's and Correa's did. *Best to keep this brief and idyllic.*

"You know, I'm a writer by trade and I want to write stuff I care about and believe in," Daniel said honestly. "I can't see myself extolling floor plans for home builders or trying to make Steve and Edie sound hip in the *Show Guide*. Maybe I'll have to do that eventually to pay the rent but right now I'm just trying to find something to be passionate about."

"Here, here," said Martin, raising his glass in what would be the first in a parade of toasts that night. "To passion and to loving what you do. It is indeed a noble path."

The men finished their drinks and ordered another round. Three rounds later, all formality had been dismissed and the language became more direct. Correa continued to check his gleaming watch often, and Martin put a big arm around him asking, "Late for your hot date?"

Correa paused, considering his response. "I am late for *a* date," he replied. "Let's just say a mature woman and I will be spending some quality time in her limousine a little later on."

Daniel began to hum "Mrs. Robinson" and Martin let out a belly laugh. "A limousine?" Martin inquired.

"A *Hummer* limousine," Correa replied.

"So you're going to get a Hummer hummer?" Martin asked, pleased with his pun, the alcohol postponing his concern for Julian's risky behavior.

"Yes, I am," Correa confirmed. "She's one of my strongest supporters."

"Do I know her?" Martin asked.

"Nah, probably not," Correa quickly answered.

"So what's next for you, Mike?" Julian asked, effectively changing the subject.

"Getting your ass elected," Martin responded. "Both the mayor and the senator want your butt on the commission. You've got friends in the right places, Julie. And I don't mean Hayes."

Martin preferred to work in the familiar, using colloquial form and nicknames as a code that he liked you. Daniel thought that Martin smacked of a guy who wanted the guys he grew up with around still— to keep him grounded in the whirlwind of politics and Las Vegas.

"Yeah, I know," Julian concurred. "They've been great to me. I'll be there for them too, if I can help. Same goes for you, Mike. You've done a lot for me too. I won't forget that."

Martin turned and looked at Daniel, who was finishing another Boddington's. "How we gonna get this kid on the team, Julian? Can you break off a little of that new money coming in?"

"Sure," Julian agreed. "After that speech tonight I'd be a fool not to use him."

Martin ran his fingers through his hair, perhaps attempting to tousle it a bit to match the wrinkled shirt he was wearing. "I was telling you earlier that I've got a couple other small races where I can use your help, Danny. The candidates won't be as smooth as Correa here, but they're good men. They'd be good for the city. I can get you some money from their funds."

"I'd love to," Daniel replied, guessing that the pay wouldn't be enough for him to throw away those classifieds on the Mustang's passenger seat. "If you say they're good people, then I'm happy to do it. You tell me how to start."

"Get with me at my office Monday and we'll make the calls together," Martin told him. Correa looked down at his watch again, tapping it as if to imply the time to leave drew closer.

Martin put a fatherly hand on each of their shoulders, drawing them closer like a quarterback in a football huddle. "You know, boys, we're all pretty young in this biz and we all do different things," Martin said with an unusually serious look on his face. "If we stick together, *really* stick together ... watch each other's backs, do what we can to help whenever we can, form a team here ... we can do great things for a long, long, time."

Daniel couldn't take his eyes off Martin and even through the pub brew he knew the importance of this discussion. He'd finally found his opening. Annie must have really sung his praises for Martin to be so trusting.

"And we can do great things *here*," Martin added, pointing down at the ground. "We can really make Vegas and Nevada better. As we rise through the ranks we can make sure that our kids grow up in a good place to live." He leaned back and looked at Julian and Daniel as they sat in front of him, like students in class. "Do you want to be a part of something like that ... where loyalty matters?"

"Definitely," Daniel said, incapable of masking his enthusiasm.

"Sure," said Julian. "That's what I'm in this for, to make a difference, right?"

"Then let's make a pact right now," Martin declared, extending his hand. "We stick together, no matter what."

Daniel reached quickly for Martin's hand and took it. He and Martin looked up at Julian who followed in kind, placing both his hands over Daniel's and Mike's.

"Now get to your Hummer hummer, Julie," Martin said, breaking the seriousness of a moment that had just raised the stakes for all of them.

CHAPTER 5

The alarm's morning report roused Daniel from an uncomfortable slumber, his rest aggrieved by the dehydration from a long night of drinking with Julian and Mike Martin. He and Mike had called it a night when it was really a morning and Daniel gulped a bottled water while he scanned the classifieds. He was intent on finding a way to get out of the rib racket, mindful that speechwriting was bonus, not sustenance, for now. Most ads seemed oddly cryptic, and he feared that nefarious telemarketing and/or canvassing sales opportunities loomed behind the *"PR Rep Needed. No Education Required"* contradiction. But with his new political relationships burgeoning, Daniel felt comfortable answering an ad for a *"Governmental Affairs Representative"* at an unfamiliar agency on the north side of town. He could drop two potent names and knew some of the landscape of Las Vegas's political terrain. Perhaps the timing was right.

The next morning Daniel took a seat in the human resource director's small office, his résumé and a few writing samples in hand. Ms. Van Eman was a tidy, middle-aged woman with a smart business suit and a clean desk. She offered Daniel a coffee and reached for his résumé.

"Well, let me tell you a little about the position, Mr. Madison," Ms. Van Eman offered, skimming through his papers. "We're in the public relations business for small public companies ... companies that are traded on the stock market. It's our objective to help them broaden their corporate exposure by enlarging and diversifying their shareholder base. Since most are too small to gain institutional investment ... you know, big brokerages and funds, they have to target individual investors. That's where we come in. We have a huge database of investors who rely on us for financial content and recommendations. Our founder, Mr. Staglione, is a genius at marketing to small investors and building paternity."

Daniel knew very little about investing other than what he'd seen in movies or overheard. His schoolteacher father didn't have the discretionary income to play the markets and neither Daniel nor the elder Madison was much of a gambler at heart. "Interesting," Daniel said, wanting to say something. The walls in Van Eman's office were decorated with framed prints of European cities, just like the office's lobby. On every wall the large golden letters "V.S.E." peered down like the Hollywood sign.

"So, how does he do this ... why is he so effective?" Daniel asked.

"Well, that's where you come in, Daniel. You might just be perfect for us," Van Eman said, looking squarely at Daniel. "Can I ask you a question?"

"Of course, it's an interview, right?" Daniel replied, half-laughing.

"Have you ever dreamed of being a millionaire?" she asked seriously.

Daniel resisted the urge to head for the door, wondering if any good could come after a sticky get-rich-quick line like that. But he sensed that Van Eman believed what she was saying and wanted to discover why she did.

"Sure," he replied at minimum.

"Well, let's talk a little about that. I can see from the few clips here and your references, Mr. Martin and Mr. Correa, that you have a handle on politics. What we need is someone who can help us create headlines for our client companies. That's how we attract new investors to our deals. If you can help us interpret the political landscape and maybe even get some of your political buddies to look at some of the stocks we're handling, we can all make a lot of money,"

That doesn't sound so bad, Daniel thought. *It's just PR for public companies—same as any other big account.* "Okay, how does that get me to be a millionaire?"

"Well, Mr. Staglione is brilliant at choosing the right deals and marketing them," said Van Eman. "He's perfected a fail-proof method. When we take on a client, V.S.E. gets a huge block of their stock along with a retainer of cash to keep the lights on. If you work here, you get some of that stock. If we do our job—and with your help—the stock can double, triple, no telling … we all get rich when we sell it. Mr. Staglione has done it over and over again. Look around. We just need more firepower to take it to the next level, Daniel."

Van Eman seemed intent on hiring him, as if she had been waiting for a man with his exact skill set to apply.

Indeed, she had. "We can start you at three thousand dollars per month, Daniel. And of course you'd get a piece of any stock we bring in. What do you say?"

Daniel considered the opportunity to make sustaining cash with some long-term upside. It hadn't occurred to him that he'd be offered a position on the spot, and he tried to think of any reason not to give this a shot. It wasn't a contract. Should Martin or Correa deliver a full-time position, he could abandon ship at V.S.E. without complications. At worst he figured he was just losing a little time with the prospect of some real money and a governmental affairs entry on his thin résumé.

"That sounds great," Daniel agreed, shaking Van Eman's small hand. "When do I start?"

"I need you here first thing tomorrow," she said. "We've got a new gun safety company and it's right up your alley. See you here at seven-thirty."

Daniel left Van Eman's office and headed toward the marble-floored lobby. A saltwater tank full of brightly colored angelfish divided the lobby from an office where ten men in headsets tapped phone keys like miners digging for coal. The receptionist uttered, "V.S.E., can you hold?" like a well-endowed parrot, perched behind a black lacquer desk.

As he collected the personnel forms from Van Eman, a hulking figure entered the lobby through the front door. "Mr. Staglione, how was your lunch?" the receptionist asked, fixing her hair.

"Good, good, good," Vincent Staglione replied. "Da sushi was perfect."

Staglione stood about six-foot-four and looked as if he worked out twice a day. His gold shirt was fresh from the Versace fall collection and nightclub ready, fitting snugly and accentuating his broad chest and narrow waist. Tailored shorts yielded to thin bronze legs with the look of constant tanning bed exposure and ending in a pair of sock-less soft leather loafers. He had to be around forty, but was in a physical condition that many eighteen-year-olds would envy.

"Mr. Staglione, meet Daniel Madison, our new governmental affairs director," Van Eman announced. "He's perfect for us."

"Where'd ya go to school, kid?" Staglione asked, grabbing his hand and squeezing it commandingly.

"I went to UNLV, graduated with a communications and journalism degree. My interest has always been politics and—"

"It don't matter really," Staglione interrupted, looking at the angel-fish. "Back East it's 'Where'd ya go to school?' Out West, it's 'Didya go to school?'"

"Where did you go to school, Mr. Staglione?" Daniel inquired.

"I decided not to go. Started my own business right away. Made millions," he replied as he winked at the receptionist. "Rebecca, call my masseuse and tell her to meet me at my house at seven, not six. I gotta get my hair cut before I go home."

Daniel stood in the lobby wondering if he should leave or wait for further dialogue with Van Eman or Staglione, who was now picking his teeth with a V.S.E. business card and looking at his reflection in the fish tank glass.

"I'll be in my office, Rebecca," Staglione said, heading down the hallway.

Van Eman turned to Daniel and extended her warm hand again. "Good to have you on board, Mr. Madison. See you in the morning."

"I'll be here," Daniel said, unaware that both he and the angelfish were now in water well above their heads.

CHAPTER 6

It was nearing five o'clock when Daniel called Julian from his car. The first full week at V.S.E. had gone well, and the men decided to meet at a local microbrewery for a drink. Julian couldn't stop talking about how well fundraising had been going since the speech at the Working Women's event, and Daniel felt as if Julian truly valued their burgeoning friendship.

They met in the brewery's parking lot, each wearing a dress shirt and loose tie. As he walked alongside Julian, emboldened by his new vocation, Daniel felt more equal to the candidate who had seemed closer to Martin in status until now.

Daniel went to the bar and ordered for the pair, returning to hand a rum and Coke to Julian, who quietly noted Daniel's new confidence. At a table next to them an attractive blonde with stylish streaks in her hair flicked cigarette ashes into a black glass tray as she chatted with a middle-aged woman whose brown eighties-style hair feathered past her ears. The younger woman reached into a black Gucci purse to retrieve another cigarette, placed it in her mouth and glanced leftward to their table like a silent movie star. A book of matches lay still next to her Cosmopolitan.

Daniel stretched to take the matches in hand, but Correa's height advantage provided the benefit of a longer reach as well. Julian cradled a lit match after he struck it, as if wind would end the flame at any moment. She leaned forward and lit the cigarette, her hands grasping Correa's from the outside and guiding them gently toward her face.

"I'm Julian Correa," he announced, same as he had on a thousand porches in his district. "It's nice to see you, Judge Nielson," he added, turning toward the older woman.

Julian had a way of diving in and out, of aggressively pursuing women and then pulling back, ignoring them almost, like the deep sea fish with tongues that look like worms, until they came forward to take the bait.

"Hello, Julian," Judge Nielson replied. "The young lady you're igniting is my friend Sydney Banks. She's working for me now."

"Indeed a pleasure," Julian said, grasping Sydney's hand. "Have we met?"

Daniel knew immediately that "Have we met?" was the instrument of Julian's interrogation. After that he could query the girl for the details of her employment, hometown, high school, etc., under the guise of seeking the connection. He was building a profile.

"I don't think so. You don't look familiar," Sydney answered matter-of-factly, turning back toward the judge.

Daniel had the impression that Sydney knew exactly who Julian was—most did—but didn't want to give him the benefit of that celebrity. It was hard to imagine she worked for a respected District Court judge but didn't know the commission candidates, especially one her own age. She turned from Judge Nielson, breezing past Julian, and looked toward Daniel. "Are you a politician too?" she asked in a way that made Julian wonder whether "politician" was pejorative.

"Nope," Daniel replied instantly. "I work at Applebee's."

Julian, Sydney, and Judge Nielson laughed. Daniel wasn't quite sure why he had said that. "And I'm a writer," he quickly added, extending his hand.

"Daniel Madison, miss," he said politely as she gripped his hand.

"A pleasure to meet you, Daniel," Sydney replied politely. "This is Judge Nielson … or Susan when she's not on the bench."

"Good to meet you both," Daniel answered, looking at Sydney all the while. She had the lightest green eyes he'd ever seen. He thought they must be baby green eyes if there was such a thing.

"So what do you write, Daniel … when you're not at Applebee's?" Sydney kidded, unaware that Daniel was only briefly removed from the restaurant. With his boy-next-door looks and a good physique, women found Daniel attractive, but he imagined they saw him as too safe or boring and rarely approached them or reciprocated an initial flirtation. He often thought he lacked the panache or bad-boy swagger that guys like Julian exuded. More often than his friends knew, Daniel had taken girls home who'd had too much to drink and then slept on their couch until morning.

"A little fiction here and there ... nothing published yet ... and I'm dabbling in the political space," he answered.

"Don't do that," Judge Nielson teased. "They'll ruin you."

"Come on now, Judge," Julian kidded, wresting back control of the conversation. "It takes people like you and me to make a difference here."

Sydney took two fingers and aimed them toward her tonsils as if to induce vomiting. "Make a difference, huh?" Sydney asked, deflating Julian again. "Didn't I see that on the bumper of a Volkswagen bus on the way to a Grateful Dead concert?"

Julian retreated, not used to opposition so vocal ... or attractive. As he sat back in his chair, feigning great insult, a waitress arrived to see if the men needed refills. Daniel and the candidate both paused to examine the waitress, a young brunette with brilliant blue eyes. Her name tag read "Amber," and Julian ordered another round as he flirted with her.

"You're the guy running for something, right?" Amber asked. "You put a pamphlet-thingy on my apartment door."

"Yes, I am," Julian answered, stealing a glance to see if Sydney was watching the exchange. "But I didn't leave it on your porch, one of my campaign team did."

"I understand," Amber answered. "You look better in person ... younger."

"That's nice of you to say," Julian replied. "How long have you been in Vegas?"

"A couple of months or so," she answered, moving closer to him and putting her tray on the table. "I moved out here from Indiana with my girlfriend but she met some guy and moved in with him. I'm thinking of going home. I don't know if this place is for me."

"Sure it is," Julian answered. "A girl with your looks should have a thousand choices here. The way this city is growing, you'll own a place like this before you're thirty."

"You think?" she said, tilting her head to the side, enjoying the compliment from a man whose picture had once been hung around her door knob.

"Another Cosmo, please," Sydney interrupted. "With Grey Goose. Tell Andy it's for Sydney."

"Uh, okay," Amber replied. "I'll be right back," she said, smiling at Julian as she turned with the grace of a figure skater.

Julian winked at Daniel, turning his attention back to Sydney who was discussing something with Judge Nielson. "So, Sydney, how do you like the law?" Julian queried.

"It's all right," she answered in the minimum.

"So, Daniel, who inspires you?" she said, turning her entire body toward Daniel.

Caught off guard and watching Correa grow momentarily red, Daniel stammered a response, "I'm a Dickens fan."

"You're a *what* fan?" Julian teased.

"It doesn't get better than *Tale of Two Cities*, does it?" Sydney agreed.

"It is a far, far better thing that I do, than I have ever done; it is a far, far better rest that I go to than I have ever known," Sydney began the quote from the character of the same first name as Daniel joined her in the recitation by the fifth word. They ended laughing together and clinking their glasses in an untitled toast. Julian sat quietly with his back to the chair, visibly unnerved.

Amber returned with their drinks and turned her focus to Julian. "So, you gotta be pretty smart to run for commissioner, right?"

"Well, I suppose," Julian responded.

"You seem reallllly smart from that brochure I got," she answered.

"You grew up in Cuba, right?"

Sydney rolled her eyes at Judge Nielson.

"No, not really," Julian corrected. "My mother fled Cuba when she was pregnant with me. I was born here."

"Awwww-awww," said Amber. "That is soooo neat." Recovering from a moment's reverie, she added, "I gotta get to my other tables. It's really nice meeting you, Julian."

Daniel couldn't make up his mind whether Amber or Sydney was more attractive, with their appearances so different. He knew he had never been out with a girl as beautiful as either of them.

"Where's your office, Daniel?" Judge Nielson asked, perhaps on behalf of Sydney.

"Actually, I recently changed offices," Daniel said, half-lying. "I just took a position with a PR company last week, and I'm doing some consulting for this fine candidate next to me." Julian had already gone through half of the most recent drink delivered by Amber and was cutting the end of a cigar, preparing it to be lit.

"What firm is that?" Sydney inquired.

"Small specialty outfit called V.S.E.," Daniel said. "They mainly handle public companies."

"Well, congrats on the new gig," she offered, smiling through the sentence.

Julian stood up, as if to leave. "If you'll excuse me, I need to visit the men's room."

"Take your best shot," Sydney quipped as Julian walked away without acknowledging her remark.

"So, tell me, Daniel," Sydney said. "Would you be willing to help me on a little writing project I've got?"

Oh, now I get it, Daniel thought. *This is why the hot chick is giving me the time of day. She wants me to do her homework.*

"I suppose I could," he said, wishing he could think of a way to say no. "What's it for?"

"Just a little presentation for a pet project," she explained briefly.

"That'll be fine," he said. "Shoot me an e-mail with the details."

"Why don't we get together to hash it out?" she asked, making him wonder if perhaps her interest was genuine.

"That would be fine … when?"

"How's tomorrow for you?"

"Works for me," he replied. "I'm open tomorrow."

"We oughta get going, Sid," Judge Nielson announced. "It's been a long day and I'm tired. It was nice meeting you, Daniel. Please tell Julian good night for me."

"Give me a call tomorrow morning to firm things up, Daniel," Sydney urged, handing him a business card with her name on Judge Nielson's letterhead. "It was very nice speaking with you." She leaned in to kiss him gently on the cheek very near his mouth. He thought how she didn't smell like smoke.

Daniel watched her leave the table and walk around the brass divider that separated the bar from the restaurant as he held her card in his hand. He hoped she wouldn't notice that he was staring at all of her as she exited. At the door she turned and gave a small wave.

"She's a bitch," Julian said in Daniel's ear way too loudly as he returned from the restroom. "I hate chicks like that."

"Like what?" Daniel asked.

"Little rich bitches," Correa fumed. "Think they're all that."

"She's hot, dude," Daniel said.

"She's okay," Julian argued. "I'd hit it, but it's not gonna be a long-term thing for me."

"Since when do you do long term?" Daniel kidded. Both men laughed and Julian let his cigar ashes fall to the floor. Amber returned with two more drinks and two chilled shots of Don Julio tequila.

"A little present from me," she said in a light, sweet voice, setting the drinks down in front of both men, but clearly making the offering for Julian's benefit. "It's an, er-uh, campaign donation."

"It's a great donation," Julian announced. "And I don't have to disclose this one either." Daniel and Julian downed the shots and set their glasses on Amber's tray.

"Thank you very much," Daniel told Amber.

"Amy, sit down with us," Julian asked.

"It's Amber," she corrected. "I guess I can for a minute or two. I only have one other table." Julian took a brochure from his suit's interior pocket and laid it on the table top.

"Hey, that's the one that was left on my door," Amber said.

"This one is different," Julian said, taking a pen from her tray and scribbling his cell phone number just below his picture on the brochure. "This one has my personal number on it."

Julian pushed the brochure toward her and she took it quickly, smiling.

"What are you doing next Wednesday night, Amber?" Julian asked.

"I'm working here," Amber said. "I'm taking all the shifts I can to make up for my roommate leaving me with the rent."

"That's too bad," Julian said. "I wanted to take you to an event where I'm speaking. It's a pretty big deal."

"Ohhhh," she groaned. "Maybe I can get someone to cover for me? Can I call you tomorrow?"

"You have my number now," Julian answered, his confidence restored.

"Danny, let's get out of here," he said.

Julian and Daniel paid their tab and walked toward the door, the dark night a stark contrast to the five o'clock sun under which they'd entered. "She's not the sharpest knife in the drawer," Julian declared. "But she's hot."

"That she is, my friend," Daniel agreed, deciding not to mention his success with Sydney this evening.

As Daniel exited through the double doors, Julian's phone rang. He glanced at it and immediately complained, "Fucking Hayes." Daniel looked back at Julian, waiting for explanation or instruction. "I gotta take this, Danny, or this asshole will never stop. I'll talk to you tomorrow."

Daniel wondered again about Frank Hayes, a name he'd heard uttered dubiously by Mike Martin and Julian. Frank Hayes was wondering who Daniel was too.

CHAPTER 7

Daniel headed to the Mustang in the brewery's parking lot and took his keys from his pocket. As he approached his vehicle he could see two young men sitting on and against the vintage vehicle.

"Can I help you?" Daniel asked insincerely, irritated that one of the young Hispanic men had his ass on the hood and his feet on the front bumper. Both wore white muscle-shirts, long khaki shorts, and had their hair shaved to short stubble. A variety of homemade tattoos littered their arms and the first man had a golden boxing glove charm on a chain around his neck. These weren't valets.

"Nope, we're just waiting for somebody," one answered without looking at Daniel as if the car was public furniture.

"Can you wait for somebody somewhere else, bro?" Daniel asked. "And get the hell off of my car?"

"You could ask me nice and I'll consider it," the man replied, looking at Daniel directly before turning to his associate. "Don't you think he should ask nice, Carlos?"

Carlos's face bloomed into amusement, pleased with his cousin Mario's haranguing of Daniel. "I'm not ready to go even if he asks nice," Carlos replied. "I like this old car. I could fix this bitch up, holmes."

Daniel was neither amused nor patient, and their gang costumes had him uneasy. He put his keys back in his pocket and looked at both men before moving toward the driver's door that Carlos was leaning against. As he reached for the handle of the unlocked door and began to open it, the movement displaced Carlos slightly from his perch. Daniel used the narrow opening to toss his cell phone on the passenger seat. As he stepped inward, Carlos's first punch caught him across the cheek. Before he could turn and face his attacker, another punch had landed near his eye, forcing him to the parking lot's blackened asphalt.

Daniel put his hands on the ground, palms down, trying to gain some sense of balance. The blast had him off-kilter and he knew that Carlos loomed behind him. As Daniel rose to his feet, Carlos put his dirty shoe on his shoulder, pushing him back. "White boys don't get to tell me what to do."

Daniel crawled two steps and stood up, using the car's rear bumper as a barrier behind which he could safely pull himself to his feet. He turned to face Carlos, whose head peaked just below Daniel's nose. "You gonna do something, white boy?" Carlos said, his hands tightened into fists.

Daniel approached Carlos, his own hand curled and drawn back. As he did so he felt the searing pain of blunt contact in his right ear. Mario had circled around and hit him from behind. Daniel knew this was bad. Both men were much smaller, but there were two of them and he wasn't at all recovered from Carlos's opening attack. As he turned to locate Mario, Carlos hit him squarely under the eye and he felt yet another release of blood develop.

"Hold that motherfucker, Carlos," Mario ordered, preparing to blast Daniel again. Mario walked carefully toward him, loading up for a massive punch like a boxer with an opponent who'd been down twice in the round. As he approached, Carlos let out a loud wail. Julian had appeared, grabbing Carlos by the neck and spinning him around to face him. Carlos looked stunned, not anticipating the two-on-one would turn into a two-on-two with men significantly larger than he and his cousin.

"This ain't your problem, Mayor," Carlos stammered, somewhat recognizing the public figure tightly holding his neck. Julian hit Carlos on the bridge of his nose and it went flat and broken. Blood ran out quickly, and Carlos stood there as if waiting to fall. Julian's grasp of Carlos had given a recovering Daniel an opportunity to turn and confront Mario, who was right in front of him in a boxer's stance. Daniel hit Mario squarely in the mouth with a jab and followed with an uppercut that dropped the author of his cheap shot. Mario fell to the dirty lot in a heap, lying on his stomach with his face on his forearm. The gold

43

boxing gloves charm lay in the black dust between Daniel's Mustang and a new Mercedes.

"He must just like boxing," Julian chided with a hand-collar on Carlos. "Because that bitch can't fight."

Daniel looked up at Julian, his own body sore and bleeding from multiple wounds. His newly purchased gray slacks wore the lot's black dust coupled with blood from scrapes inside his clothing and his dripping left eye. Carlos stood in front of Julian nearly motionless, somehow still maintaining his wavering stance.

"You like that dirty shit, eh?" Julian asked Carlos. "Hit somebody from behind, jump somebody ... all that ghetto shit, huh? Dirty fucking Mexicans." Carlos started to speak, but as he did, Correa hit him with a brutal forearm that knocked him from his feet. Daniel watched as Carlos fell near his cousin, who had made no new attempt to stand up.

"Let's go," Daniel ordered, remembering the rough lessons of his neighborhood growing up. "Somebody's gonna call their boys and there'll be ten of 'em up here in a few minutes ... and they'll be packing."

"Fuck them," Correa shouted as he peered down at the vanquished. "They'll get knocked out too." Daniel grabbed his arm, attempting to drag him off. Julian shook off Daniel's grasp and walked to the sprawled men on the pavement. Mario turned his head to look up as Julian delivered a thunderous kick to his face. A few customers were gathering at the entrance, watching the fray from afar.

"HEY!" Daniel shouted, afraid to call Julian by name with witnesses on hand. "Man, this is gonna be in the papers tomorrow unless we get the hell out of here now."

Julian turned as if awakened and nodded affirmatively.

"I got dropped off. Give me a ride, all right?" Julian said, panting from the adrenaline and jumping into the Mustang's passenger side.

"Sure, Jule. After that, I probably owe you a free speech or two," Daniel joked through the growing discomfort. He looked over at Julian who now wore a wide smile on his face.

44

"How's that for loyalty and sticking together, Danny?" Julian said, laughing and speaking at the same time. "Think that's what Martin was talking about?"

CHAPTER 8

August 2000

Daniel wasn't quite sure what to wear to dinner with Sydney, wondering if it even mattered given the remains of his black eye from the parking lot fracas a week before. He'd explained to Sydney what happened, though she continued to be unimpressed by Julian despite his rescue of Daniel. They'd met twice over the past week under the guise of a project that Sydney never mentioned once they were together. Chemistry was increasing, and Daniel was flattered when she invited him to dinner at her home where she still lived with her parents.

Daniel parked more than a few feet from available spaces closer to the Banks' driveway, not wanting the predictable oil droppings from his car to offend his hosts any more than his lack of a pedigree might. He'd stopped at a liquor store along the way and purchased a ten-dollar bottle of wine, choosing as obscure a brand as he could find, hoping the bottle's anonymity might mask its price. Daniel toted the bottle in one hand and nearly fell down as his toe caught in a massive crack in the property's long driveway. He wondered if anyone had heard the Mustang's unsubtle approach and come to the window, only to witness his dubious entry.

As he reached to knock on the oak front door, Sydney pulled it open. She was wearing a plaid skirt and thin cotton top, barefoot, and with her hair down. Daniel completed an obligatory once-over without speaking until Sydney interrupted.

"You done?" she said sarcastically, recognizing Daniel's full-body review.

"Uh … yes … sorry," Daniel stammered. He started to tell her she looked "breathtaking" but declined the Harlequin cliché an instant before utterance. "It's really nice to see you."

"Good! Because I've told everyone about you," she exuded. "They can't wait to meet you." Sydney took Daniel by the hand quickly and he had to shut the door with his right foot as he held the wine bottle. She led him through a living room and down a hallway so long that a white rabbit should have been present. At the end of it they came upon a turn-of-the-century-style Victorian parlor complete with Tiffany lamps, wood-paneled walls, and Sydney's parents lying in wait.

Sydney's father, William Banks, was much older than Daniel anticipated, appearing to be in his late sixties. Mr. Banks was mostly bald with a golf junkie's tan and he wore a set of huge tinted eyeglasses that had been stylish in the disco era. Holding a lemonade, her mother Wanda sat demurely on a supple leather chair with big brass rivets, like a muse in the old Coca-Cola ads.

"Well, look what the kitty-cat brought in!" Mr. Banks effused. "Get over here!" Daniel prayed that Mr. Banks was speaking to his daughter, completely unsure if the beckoning was directed at him. The worry ended when Mr. Banks looked at Daniel and said, "Nice shiner, Petey."

Sydney bounded over to her father and jumped in his lap, wrapping her arms around his neck. "I've got the most amazing daddy in the whole wide world," she baby-talked. "Best businessman Vegas has ever known." Her skirt caught oddly beneath her weight and bare skin to her inner thigh was revealed to Daniel.

Don't look, don't look, Daniel instructed himself.

"Daddy ... Mother ... this is Daniel Madison, the boy I've been telling you about," Sydney said. "And these are my parents, Mr. and Mrs. Banks."

Daniel nodded toward Sydney's mother and leaned forward to shake a pinned-down Mr. Banks' hand. Sydney had shifted one tan leg leftward and was even more exposed. *Can't she feel that?* Daniel thought. *Doesn't she know?*

"So you're the politician that's dating my daughter, eh?" Mr. Banks asked, taking off his Harry Caray glasses and setting them on an end table.

47

Sydney responded before Daniel could reply, "No, Daddy, he's a writer. He does stuff for candidates and with the stock market."

"That's right, sir," Daniel affirmed. "I'm not a politician."

"Well, that's good," Mr. Banks said. "I've never met an honest one. I went to school with a few of the fellows who are supposed to be leaders of this state. Christ, they're useless."

"William!" Sydney's mother scolded, speaking for the first time, a hint of the Texas accent of her youth persisting. "Your language."

"I do apologize, my lady," Mr. Banks replied.

"I understand, Mr. Banks," Daniel agreed. "My father says about the same thing. And I'm trying to be careful who I work with."

"With whom you work," the older man corrected.

"Daniel wrote a speech for Julian Correa and everyone said it was fantastic," Sydney announced, still with a little-girl affect to her tone. Daniel realized that Sydney, like Martin before, had done some homework. Perhaps Judge Nielson had been at the Working Women event.

"Well, son, my daughter is very impressed with you," Mr. Banks said as he nudged Sydney from his lap. "And I like to see her happy."

"Let's have some supper, shall we?" Mr. Banks instructed as they left the study and returned to the long hallway. The four of them entered the kitchen, which looked like the set to film a commercial for an all-purpose cleanser. Bright walls and white cabinets with porcelain knobs shouted their cleanliness. A heavy-set black woman stirred a simmering pot on the range top. A bouquet of food aroma offered a Thanksgiving-like ambience.

"We're gonna need a few more minutes, Missus Banks," the cook informed in a gravelly voice that sounded like a fairy tale ogre.

"That's fine, Louise," Mrs. Banks replied.

A younger girl in her early twenties entered the room in sweatpants and a Nike T-shirt, plucking an asparagus tip from the pot with her fingers. "Those ain't done yet, Teena," Louise informed her as she spit the bite into the kitchen sink.

48

"Daniel, this is my youngest daughter, Teena," Mrs. Banks said. "And this is Sydney's friend Daniel Madison." Teena had the look and swagger of a tomboy and looked more like her father than Sydney, who favored her mother.

"Aaah, a new victim," Teena chided without looking at Daniel, searching the countertop for food on which to graze. "What's the over/under on this guy lasting the month, Pops?"

"Teena!" Sydney injected as her father laughed softly. "Don't start."

"So how long you been seeing, Syd?" Teena asked, gesturing for Daniel to follow her to the adjacent patio. Sydney watched them exit as her mother handed her a few glasses to put on the dining room table.

"I don't know if we can even call it 'seeing' yet, Teena," Daniel replied as he settled into a soft patio chair. "It's just been a week or so."

"She's a pain in the ass. But she's my sister, so I guess I'm supposed to say something like 'be good to her.' Hey, you want a beer?" Teena said, moving along.

Teena tilted her head upward and hollered, "Sydney, bring us a couple beers!" Daniel laughed again, amused by the lack of courtesy between the sisters. He and his sister could be this way too. "Anyone's better than that little jackass she was dating last year. I thought I was going to have to kill that guy." Teena's energy was definitely masculine, Daniel noted, and she seemed serious about her remark. He'd wagered she'd fought a boy before.

"Why's that?" Daniel asked, eager to know. Before Teena could answer, Sydney emerged, beers in hand. Behind her came Mrs. Banks, who had donned an apron sometime since they'd left the kitchen. "Dinner's ready, kids."

The family and Daniel took their seats as Louise began to serve. A pot roast, asparagus, and cheesecake later, dinner had concluded without much more than light discourse among those seated. Mrs. Banks really didn't say much, and Mr. Banks seemed to have lost interest in the conversation. An awkward silence fell over the group until Daniel rose from his seat. "That was a wonderful meal, Mrs. Banks," he said, placing his cloth napkin on the table. "Thank you for letting me dine with you."

"You're certainly welcome, Daniel," Mrs. Banks replied. "Thank you for bringing that bottle of wine. We'll have to open it on another occasion."

"Or to cook with," Mr. Banks added with a nod toward a smiling Teena.

"Sydney, would you give me a hand clearing a few of the plates?" Daniel asked with a quick wink.

"Oh, Louise will get those, Daniel," Mrs. Banks said.

"I'm sure she's got plenty to clean up in the kitchen after a meal like this," Daniel said. "Let me earn my keep." Sydney seemed startled and pleased as she joined Daniel in gathering dishes and cutlery. Daniel noted how she grabbed silverware first and carried it en masse to the kitchen, not using a plate to collect more efficiently. It took them a few minutes to finish and then Sydney and Daniel were out on the patio alone. Las Vegas nights could be sublime with the day's heat dissipated and no humidity or biting insects. They each pulled up a second chair, elevating their feet.

"Seems like a nice family you got here, Sydney," Daniel said. "I'm glad you had me over."

"And I'm glad you came, Daniel," Sydney agreed. "Now, we can spend a little time together." She pushed back from the table and promised to return promptly. An old dog had wandered from somewhere in the backyard and placed his reddish muzzle on Daniel's leg. "Hey, old boy," Daniel said, petting the Irish setter. Sydney returned with two small glasses and an amber-colored bottle in hand. She set the container on the table, rotating it so Daniel could read the label.

"You ever had Louis XIII before, Danny?" Sydney asked proudly. "My father gets a bottle every year from his business partner but he never drinks it. Last year Teena ruined half a bottle trying to soak cigars with it."

"Can't say that I have, Sydney," he said, wondering if she seriously thought he might have tried a $1,500 cognac before. "We're more the beer type."

She removed the blown glass stopper from the bottle, pouring two shot-sized deposits into each of their crystal glasses. Pushing one gently across the table, Sydney raised her glass, signaling Daniel to do the same. Daniel noticed that she had returned to being the confident woman he'd met at the brewery, shedding the doting daughter bit from before dinner. Daniel lifted the glass and let the cognac's vapors dance above the rim, breathing the light aroma as his father had shown him with the far lesser brandy he kept in the cupboard of his boyhood home. He drew the glass to his mouth, allowing the smallest portion to enter. It did taste fantastic—just not $150-a-glass fantastic. Maybe he just lacked the acumen to fully appreciate the liquor. Sydney tilted her glass to her lips. Daniel thought how everything this girl did was elegant and sexy ... except for maybe how she sat on her father's lap. That was just sexy.

He wasn't sure if she was showing off or if this was who she truly was. He figured either way it was good. The old dog had lain down at his feet and was snoring. A deep rippling snore caused them both to laugh and lean forward simultaneously to pet the animal. With their heads just inches apart, Sydney kissed Daniel on the lips. He leaned forward as far as the chair would allow him, tasting the cognac on her mouth. A moment later she was in his chair with no distance between them. Daniel was lost in the affection and the consequences, replaying the night's events as the two entangled. *Did Teena really think I wouldn't last the week? Does Sydney do this all the time?*

Sydney paused, as if conscious of something inappropriate. Daniel figured she'd suggest they terminate the high school make-out session before someone came upon them. She stood up quickly, leaving the bottle of Louis XIII on the table and took Daniel's hand.

"I should go," Daniel offered, wanting to control when he left and work on that cool shtick that Julian was always advocating and enacting.

Sydney led him toward the front door, passing the kitchen and the dining room in the process. As the entryway to the massive house came closer, she turned and went down the long hallway in a new direction, heading somewhere he'd not yet been.

At the end of the hallway she pushed open the door, leading him inside. He felt her skirt hit the floor as he took a step into the darkness. Moments later his shirt had done the same and Daniel knew their union was moments away.

"You'd better lock that door," Daniel said, pulling back, concerned about the parents and their half-open door mere feet away. He had no idea where the brash Teena was at this point.

"They never come in here," she said. "The door doesn't even have a lock on it." Sydney was completely naked at this point, gently pulling at Daniel's clothes and leading him to the highest bed on which he'd ever been.

When the act was finished Daniel laid on his back, her face nestled against his chest. He kissed her forehead in the darkness, wishing he could see her and better commit the night to memory. The moment had been labored by his distracted analysis of its impact, the unlikely side effect causing her to be impressed by his stamina. "When we gonna work on your project, Syd?" Daniel asked, wanting to see her again as soon as possible. "I've got time tomorrow."

"What project?" Sydney responded, seemingly sleepy. She moved her body and face closer to Daniel, pulling a blanket up to her chin.

"There never was a project, was there?"

"*You* were the project, Danny," Sydney explained, moving her right hand affectionately against his cheek.

"So we started this thing off with a lie, eh?" he kidded.

"A good lie," she said in the soft, persuasive way that would someday guide him to his most desperate hour.

CHAPTER 9

September 2000

Daniel had settled into a groove at V.S.E. and was growing to like some elements of the job. He enjoyed seeing his press releases hit the galaxy of online financial sites and wondered as to the extent of their reach, imagining stock tycoons and fervent day traders reading his copy with impassioned interest. Nonetheless, he was keeping a close eye on Julian's promising commission race, hoping to get back to politics and speechwriting as soon as possible. Meanwhile, his father implored him to learn what he could about the stock market while he worked at V.S.E., feeling that the financial knowledge would serve Daniel well at better-income stages of his life.

Staglione had Daniel writing press releases for a gun safety company V.S.E. was representing, hoping to generate investor enthusiasm for the equity. The company's device prevented the discharge of a firearm with a simple and clever blocking of the gun's hammer. It seemed that every school shooting or accidental gun fatality was grist for a press release, which, in turn, attracted new investors. "We make 'em understand that StopShot is the solution to dat problem," Staglione would blare in his Brooklyn accent every time he issued Daniel a dictate to craft a blood-red press release. "And make sure you get da stock symbol in dere … up real high."

By the second release Daniel had submitted for Staglione's approval, Vince was smitten with profitable possibilities. Daniel wasn't sure if Staglione had ever read any book front to back, but he did seem able to discern which news and subsequent press releases would be beneficial to the stock. On days when they had news out that created trading volume and price appreciation for StopShot, Daniel could hear Staglione in his office on the speakerphone with the company's management, laughing and congratulating each other like relatives in a maternity ward. On these occasions, Staglione would be affable, effusive—and it was safe to go into his office. Other afternoons, when StopShot shares were down or the market was taking a bath, Staglione was best left alone.

The guys in the phone room, who always seemed to be coming and going, warned each other about Staglione's market-related and ever-mercurial mood swings. His office door had been repaired numerous times from vicious slams, and none of the tacky Motel 6-grade paintings were affixed to walls near Staglione's lair. Even the golden V.S.E. displays nearby were double-nailed like the framed photos at a Chili's restaurant. Today, Staglione had entered ebulliently, beaming at the prospects of turning a triple homicide at a North Carolina middle school into a StopShot buying frenzy. "Danny, I got great news! We're gonna be rich," Staglione said, plopping into a seat in Daniel's office, a wave of cologne filling the small space in an invisible olfactory cloud.

"Look at dis shit, kid," Staglione said, offering a newspaper and tearing a corner from his Power Bar like a lion on an antelope carcass. "Another one of dem school shootings." Staglione once had bragged to Daniel about finishing at the top of his class, but his misuse of language betrayed the potential veracity of that remark. Perhaps he'd been home-schooled, Daniel wondered.

Daniel took the morning paper from Staglione and looked at it briefly, having already seen the morbid headlines on an Internet news site hours before. Staglione normally didn't make it to the office until ten or eleven a.m., saying he was managing the company's portfolio from home where he could concentrate. Because of this, V.S.E. was really two companies: one with Vince on deck and the other with him out of the office. When he was gone, the only real work that happened was at the reception desk where investor and client calls were appropriately received. In the bullpen where the guys were supposed to make phone calls to brokers and penny stock players, fantasy football leagues and social discussion prevailed. More than once Daniel had seen the guys congregated around a computer monitor, marveling at a porn site's feminine contents.

But when Staglione hit the front door everyone was on point, not wanting to be caught playing and receive an on-the-spot dismissal or a Stallone-in-*Rocky* tirade. Those were the worst with Staglione, already a physically intimidating figure, going off into a high school football coach rant about loyalty, and dedication … and, of course, money. "We can all get rich here, people," Staglione would announce in what he felt was a motivational speech. "But we gotta do our jobs." Staglione spoke about money in the "we" sense at a rate that would have made Karl Marx proud. Everyone was driven to perform for the team, working at minimal rates with the glittering promise of a stock windfall in which they'd all share. Some bought into this promise, pinning pictures of sports cars and trips abroad to their bulletin boards. Others openly chided it, though never in front of Staglione. That level of dissent would not be tolerated.

Daniel handed the paper back to Staglione, who was pulling a chest hair through his rayon shirt. "Look at how dat thing just popped through der," Staglione said, child-like and amused. "We gotta use this news, Danny. Get something ready quick. We gotta capitalize now." Staglione's Sicilian-blue eyes widened at the prospects of the release, oblivious to the morbidity of the subject matter. Vincent Staglione would always accept the monkey's paw.

"All right, I'm on it," Daniel said. "Give me thirty minutes and I'll have something."

"I need it as fast as you can," Staglione ordered. Every minute's money I'm—we're— losing. The market closes at one, kid."

Daniel turned to the Internet, reading the details of the gory incident and looking at the yearbook pictures of the victims and shooter. From looking at the four kids, it wasn't immediately clear which of them had been the killer. They all had that fresh-faced awkwardness that junior high school kids often emit. He finished the release quickly and printed a copy to take to Staglione in his corner office. Walking down the hall, a balled-up piece of paper whizzed past his head from the bullpen where the phone jockeys were already pushing StopShot to a list of platinum credit card holders, promising a hot news release any minute. Daniel turned to see who the pitcher was, his eyes finding another employee his age staring conspicuously into a book amid a flurry of frenetic activity all around him. "Al, you jackass," Daniel called, causing Al to smile a confession while staring into the book. "You throw like a girl."

"What's up, college boy?" Al asked Daniel as he greeted him with a powerful handshake. "Stag says you got some more sausage for the grill."

"I'm working on a release right now," Daniel answered. "Taking it to Vince's office for approval."

"Approval?" Al asked, acting confused. "You must be going to read it out loud to him. I think he's borderline illiterate." Daniel laughed, half-agreeing by not defending Staglione.

"You want to go look for women tonight?" Al asked.

"I'm kinda seeing this girl now ... but I'll go out with you guys," Daniel replied.

"How nice," Al said sarcastically, preparing another paper snowball for his next office ambush. "Call and get permission and let me know."

"I don't need to do that," Daniel answered. "When and where?"

"I'll let you know," Al replied. "Holler at me before you leave."

"Sure thing," Daniel answered. Al Morris and Daniel had become friends over the past few weeks beginning with Al inviting him to join some of the phone guys for lunch. The others saw him mostly as a suit, or worse yet, Staglione's proxy and messenger, confusing his and Staglione's frequent conversations for allegiance. But after the first lunch and the shared concoction of a lie to cover their late return, Al and Daniel realized they had similar upbringings and personalities, albeit with a few stark differences. Al was market savvy and seemed to know everything about stocks and Staglione's motives. He was also a beast of a man, larger even than Staglione, yet he led the phone group with his big personality and intellect. Daniel also noticed Al's carefree style when it came to V.S.E., as if he could take or leave the job. Al was the only African-American at V.S.E. and, unlike Staglione, he favored loose clothing that hid the muscular build of a guy who doubled as a personal trainer.

Once, when Staglione was going off on another young dialer at the top of his lungs for straying from the script, Al had made a point to stand up quickly as to confront Vince and his invective. Staglione paused mid-vulgarity and turned cautiously toward Al. "Go on," Al beckoned, completely nonplussed and seizing Staglione's control momentarily. "I'm just throwing my drink in the trash by the door."

Staglione, clearly humbled by what he had at first interpreted as a physical threat, offered only a weak summation, "It better get better, fellas," he muttered before making a quick exit. Al hadn't threatened Staglione overtly enough to get fired, but he had made a point that Vince needed to be mindful of at least a few boundaries. This had further galvanized Al's leadership among the men around him.

Daniel passed Staglione's personal secretary, Dottie, who served Vince as best she could, wearing multiple hats, including cook, appointment setter, and psychologist. Daniel had seen the older woman in the break room often, preparing celery and tuna salads for the always dieting Staglione. Other times she guarded the door when Vince was on one of his top-secret conference calls, most of which were loud enough to be easily heard by V.S.E. crew in nearby offices. Dottie had tried to tell Vince unsuccessfully once that discretion and speakerphones were rarely companions.

As Daniel entered, he courtesy-knocked the door, looking for Staglione. Vince's desk was covered with thick prospectuses from various small-cap companies, towering piles that resembled a strange game of corporate Jenga. Reaching the desk, he discovered Staglione, who was doing push-ups on the other side.

"Vince?" Daniel called.

"Ninety-eight, ninety-nine, one hundred," Staglione counted aloud. Daniel had not heard him counting until he called his name.

"Gotta take care of yourself, kid," Staglione said, rising from the floor. "You work out?" Staglione wiped his brow with a towel hanging over the back of a chair.

"I lift a few times a week and stay pretty active," Daniel answered.

"If you ever want some pointers, let me know," Staglione offered, putting a gold watch back on. "How old you think I am?"

"Aaah, Vince, I hadn't really thought about it," Daniel answered, declining to patronize Staglione. "Hey, I've got this release ready and ..."

"Forty-one, Danny," Staglione reported through his panting. "And I'm still bangin' honeys younger than you."

"That's great, Vince. Didn't you want to get this release out ASAP?" Daniel asked, redirecting Staglione, who was sweating in more than one area.

"Yeah, let me see dat," Vince said, taking the release and skimming it. "Put a little more color in the top part, Danny. Pump up da violence."

"Doddie!! Get my salad ready!" he yelled through the doorway. Daniel looked to see Dottie bounding from her chair and down the hall, two yellow pencils extending from behind her ears like antennas on a radio-controlled dune buggy.

"You sure we want to do that, Vince?" Daniel inquired. "You don't think it's going to be a little over the top?"

"Nah, you gotta keep things exciting for people," Staglione explained. "People like things colorful. That's why action movies sell so good. These Internet investors ain't stock brokers, Danny. You gotta draw dem a picture."

"Yeah, but don't you lose some credibility when you exaggerate stuff, Vince?" Daniel offered, trying to be as non-accusatory as possible with his employer.

"Dan, I gotta have a home run on dis StopShot deal," Vince said seriously, still breathing heavily and near-collapsing into his black leather chair. He kicked off his alligator loafers and crossed a moist bare foot across his leg. Daniel instinctively took a step backward. "I've got a ton of dis company's money locked up in it. Dat's your money too. But I also gotta bunch of investors from New York in dis deal. I've gotta make them money or it won't be good. Dey're not forgiving people."

"Okay, I'll punch it up," Daniel obliged. "I just want to be careful."

"You're doin' a good job, Danny. You're a big part of dis place," Vince said. "Hey, whadya doin' for dinner? Maybe we could talk about ways to help StopShot?"

"I'm supposed to be going out with Al and the boys," Daniel answered.

"Meet up with dem later," Vince overrode. "We've got business to discuss."

"Okay," Daniel consented. "I'll make it work."

Dottie entered the office with a deep bowl filled with Staglione's rabbit-friendly fare. "Here's your lunch, Mr. Staglione," she said, setting the bowl on top of the desk calendar in front of him. "And here's today's mail." Staglione flipped through the usual ads and solicitations, stopping at an ivory-colored envelope with raised gold lettering. He opened the letter and began reading, slightly aloud as he muttered some phrases for Daniel's benefit.

"Hmmmn—investment—uh huh—positive influence—support—uh hmmn," Staglione semi-read. He paused and looked up, considering deeply some aspect of the letter with his brow furrowed. "Danny, you know dis word?" he asked, handing Daniel the note.

"They seem like dey want to hire us, but dey say dey want to use our pragency? What the hell's a 'pragency?'" he asked humbly. "Do they mean 'prodigy' or somethin'?"

"A pragency?" Daniel said, taking the note. "I'm not sure that's even a word." Daniel read the note until he got to the vexing phrase.

"Vince, they're not asking us to provide a 'pragency,'" Daniel explained, trying to remain solemn. "They're saying they want to use our PR agency."

"I'll get those changes to you right away," Daniel said, biting his lip as he exited quickly.

CHAPTER 10

Staglione loved Italian food, often saying it was his one vice and the reason he worked out so often. When Daniel arrived at the posh Italian restaurant in the Rio hotel-casino, Staglione was chewing warm breadsticks like a beaver making a dam. "Danny!" Staglione beckoned as Daniel entered, small pieces of breadstick hitting the air with the annunciation of the "D" in Daniel's name. "I'm starvin', kid. I couldn't wait much longer. You're killin' me here."

"I don't think I'm late, am I?" Daniel inquired rhetorically, knowing he was on time.

"I don't know, kid, but you gotta order fast. It takes a lotta dem calories to keep this body runnin'," Staglione explained, leaning back so that Daniel could review his physique. "Waiter! We're ready ovah heres."

"The osso bucco's fuckin' amazing here," Staglione informed Danny as a startled waiter arrived. "It's da best I've had outside of Little Italy back home."

Daniel took a menu from the waiter and looked it over quickly. He wasn't sure what he wanted, but it wasn't osso bucco. "I'll have the veal parm, sir," Daniel requested as Staglione raised his eyebrows in a look of surprise.

"I'll have the osso bucco, Gary," Vince ordered. "Dan, I thought you were gonna have da osso bucco?"

"Nah, I don't really care for it," Daniel lied, having never eaten the dish but wanting to avoid the Staglione dictatorial two-step.

"All right, kid, but you're missin' out. Dat's what I'm havin'," Staglione further emphasized. The waiter gathered the menus and accepted Staglione's suggestion to expedite the cook's preparation for a good tipping customer. Five minutes later, a couple of house salads arrived and Staglione had moved from culinary recommendations to business matters.

"I like you, kid," Staglione said through a mouthful of half-chewed romaine lettuce and an obliterated crouton. "You're smart, real smart, not like dose friggin' idiots in da bullpen."

"I appreciate that, Vince," Daniel said. "But there're some smart guys in there too."

"Dey're all morons," Vince objected as he stabbed his cherry tomato. "You gotta babysit dem to get anything done. All dey can do is call investors and run dere mouths."

"Isn't that their job, Vince?" Daniel asked gently.

"Dere job is to make me money," Staglione corrected. "And they rarely do dat. But you get in on time and do a good job, Danny. I appreciate dat and you're gonna make a lotta money with me."

"That's good to hear, Vince," Daniel offered, knowing that if a victorious Julian offered him a position on his commission staff, he'd be gone post-haste.

"Listen, kid, I know you don't know much about da stock market, but you got dis gift for making things sound good ... the way people wanna hear things. I'm getting real good feedback from our big investors about da releases you and me write," Staglione said, adding a writing credit of his own. "They know that's what makes da wheels go 'round in dis business."

"Well, let's keep doing that if it makes them happy," Daniel concurred. "That's easy enough." The waiter arrived with each of their meals and Staglione eye-raped the osso bucco as if he'd not eaten for a week. Using only a fork, he tore a three-inch piece of meat from the bone and thrust it into his wide mouth, his jaws masticating rapidly. Daniel began to eat when Staglione produced a series of unintelligible syllables through a wall of meat bouncing through the interior of his open mouth like a pair of jeans in a dryer.

"I can't hear you, Vince," Daniel said, not sure how to tell Staglione that he didn't speak fluent carnivore. "Can you repeat that ... in ten seconds or so?" Daniel was speaking slowly to Vince, as if he were impaired, hoping the oral delay would give Staglione enough time to absorb the massive meat load. Staglione grasped his water, dumping a half glass of lubricant into the mine shaft that was his throat. At first, Daniel thought Staglione might be choking, but his calm demeanor and attempt at conversation suggested this was more manner than anomaly.

Vince set the water glass down and continued his oration, this time unencumbered by the dinner fare. "Danny, I'm like you. I come from regular folk—not rich people," he said, leading Daniel to believe he was guessing about his parents' net worth. "And I needed some help to get dis company started. So, I took on some not-so-silent partners, people who trusted me and put a lotta money in dis company and da ones we represent."

His face grew serious and he leaned back in his chair, withdrawing from his previous looming posture over his dish. "Our last deal back-fired and the company got shut down," Vince said, looking humble for the first time since Daniel had known him. "My guys lost a couple mil and it got a little scary for me." Daniel wondered what "scary" meant to a guy who revered hyperbole.

"So, I waited a long time before I took another company on. Den I found dis one. Dis StopShot thing's gonna be yuge with all dem school killins goin' on."

"Yuge?" Daniel asked, unfamiliar with the word.

"Yuge," Staglione affirmed. "Bigger den anything I ever done."

"Okay," Daniel agreed, not so much with Staglione's assertion, but more so to himself as he figured out what "yuge" meant.

"So, I've got everything riding on dis deal," Staglione said, leaning in again as if telling a secret. "And I've got all my boys' money in it. It's gotta work. Dey're friends of my fadder's, but dat don't matter. If I don't get dat two mil back in der pocket, it's gonna get ugly. Real ugly. And dat's where you come in." Staglione pointed a steak knife at Daniel for emphasis. "I got biiiiiig plans for you."

"Well, I'm happy to help, Vince," Daniel said. "Just let me know what you want done."

"What I want is to ask you a question, Danny," Vince said, setting his fork down flat on the table.

"Shoot," Daniel replied curiously.

"Can I trust you?" Vince asked, his eyes riveted on Daniel's, a new mood present at the table.

"I think so, Vince," Daniel said. "I've got nothing to hide."

"Dat's not what I mean, kid. I want to know if you're loyal, because if you are,we can make a lotta money togedder."

"I'd like to think I'm loyal," Daniel responded, not sure what else to say or where this was going. He didn't want to verbally sign a blank contract and have the terms added later.

"Well, den you're gonna have some new responsibilities, some leadership at V.S.E.," Staglione said. "But you're gonna have to just trust me on some of dese things and not ask a bunch of questions, okay?"

"Okay," Daniel agreed, not sure to what he really was agreeing. Staglione had ingested several more massive bites, as if the meal were meant to be consumed in quarters. He sipped a glass of Chianti gracefully, a kinetic contradiction to his carnivorous voracity. Vince appeared satisfied, both by the meal and the contents of their conversation.

"I know I can trust you, kid," Staglione said. "But don't ever fuck me over and I'll make you a millionaire. You got a trip around da world comin' if you keep doin' what you're doin'. And I don't care about da speeches you're writing in your office as long as my shit gets done first, all right?"

Daniel was wondering how Staglione knew he had edited a couple of speeches for Mike Martin in his office on his lunch hour. "Speeches?" Daniel asked.

"Yeah, I had Ivan, da tech guy, look over your hard drive a few weeks ago. It's standard V.S.E. procedure. We deal with a lotta sensitive documents. But like I said, I don't care as long as da work I'm payin' you for gets done good and first. Compared to what dose freakin' morons download and look at, you're a fucking choir boy. And your political pals might come in handy later. Dose guys always got stroke at da SEC. Dat's da Securities and Exchange Commission and dey can be a real problem for guys like us. Fuckin' feds."

"Uh, okay," Daniel replied meekly, feeling a little invaded and fortunate at the same time. He wondered if the tech guy had seen the gushy letter he was writing to Sydney. Staglione hadn't mentioned it. *Note to self,* Daniel thought, *everything to be done on a disk that can be removed.*

"So, what time are you meeting da morons?" Staglione asked.

"Al's meeting me here in an hour and then I suppose we'll get a drink somewhere. I don't know who or if anyone else is coming. How 'bout you?"

"I'm gonna head over to da nightclub," Staglione said. "Dey got dat seventies band in dere and dere's more easy girls than a whorehouse. Hey, if it's just Al, why don't you twose join me? I gotta fantastic table in da VIP. We'll have young honeys hangin' all over us."

"I'll see if that's cool with Al," Daniel answered. "I'm not sure what he's got planned."

"He'll wanna come. Who wouldn't? Let's go play a little craps to kill da time," Staglione suggested, beginning to ask a little more than in his usual directives.

"All right, but I'm just watching," Daniel agreed. "You don't pay me enough to blow it on a craps table."

"Dat's all about ta change," Staglione said seriously. "Now dat I know I can count on you."

Staglione headed directly to a craps table at the end of the bustling casino pit, as if it were his favorite. He tossed ten hundreds in front of the boxperson's seat as he drew a long cigar from an ostrich-leather carrying case. Staglione's swagger and manner reminded Daniel a lot of an older version of Julian, sans the charm and guile. An hour later, Staglione was up two grand and Daniel was bored, scanning the casino's eclectic horizon for Al's large torso. He wasn't sure if he could stand another high five from Vince as he made the point. Gambling had never held much appeal for Daniel as he couldn't grasp the notion of sitting down willfully where the odds were stacked against the player. "It's like fighting a guy bigger than you," he once told a friend who wanted to spend their small paychecks on hands of twenty-one. "You might win, but the odds say you're probably going to get your ass kicked."

Staglione colored out, taking his chips toward the casino cage, happily humming parts of an indiscernible song. Daniel turned to follow when Al spun him around. "Still workin' for da man," Al teased, simultaneously mocking Staglione's speech patterns and Daniel's perceived obedience.

"Dude, we just had dinner and talked basic biz," Daniel explained, wanting to appear as anything but Staglione's house pet. "I need this gig for a while longer, Al."

"Well, let's get going," Al said. "Tell Captain Growth Hormone your shift is over."

"Growth hormone?"

"Yeah, growth hormone," Al said. "I worked out with him at his place a couple times when I first started at V.S.E. He wanted tips on training. One time I went into his kitchen to get a water glass and opened the wrong cupboard. Your buddy Staglione's a pharmaceutical test pilot, bro. One whole cupboard was shit that ain't regulated by the FDA, if you know what I mean. Ain't nothin' about that guy real, Danny."

Staglione returned from the casino cage, waiting until he was on top of Al and Daniel to shove a thick wad of hundreds into his Louis Vuitton wallet. He looked up to see if Daniel and Al were paying attention, only to find both men staring away as if at a group urinal. "Al, buddy," Staglione said affectionately, hugging Al in the warmest of greetings. Al peered over his shoulder, rolling his eyes and gesturing "Let's go" toward the door with his eyebrows.

"Glad you could make it out with us," Staglione said. "It's good for company morals."

"You mean 'morale'?" Al corrected.

"Dose too," Staglione agreed.

"I've got plans, Vince," Al said.

"I've got a table for us in the VIP at da club," Vince offered triumphantly. "Why don't you and Danny come in for a few, see if you like it, and then go do your own thing if you're not havin' a good time."

"What do YOU wanna do, Danny?" Staglione asked, sending a needy gaze to an uncomfortable Daniel. It was clear Staglione did not want to be the lonely old guy in the club.

"I don't care," Daniel said, maintaining neutrality. "You wanna just stick our heads in for a minute, Al?"

Al turned to Staglione. "You have a table IN the VIP, right?"

"Dat's right," Staglione said. "Girls everywhere."

"All right, we can go for a little while," Al conceded. Staglione turned on the utterance of his compliance and Daniel fell in behind him. Al leaned over Daniel's shoulder whispering his frustration. "I ain't paying for shit in there," Al whisper-yelled. "And watch how much shit I order off the top shelf."

"He won't care," Daniel replied. "He just won a couple grand at craps and likes to flex his wallet anyway."

Staglione was entering the club rapidly, cruising past lines and cashiers. Like Julian, Vince knew where the rubber met the road and past beneficiaries of his tipping moved forward to greet him like a visiting dignitary at the White House. The nightclub doubled as a showroom and a dance hall, with large booths defining the VIP section. Staglione led Al and Daniel to a booth where there was a bottle of champagne already on ice. A bouncer at the front door had radioed ahead to tell the VIP host that Staglione was en route. They took their seats, and Staglione popped the cork on the bottle like it was 1999. He filled their glasses and set them in front of each. Daniel nodded appreciatively as Al moved his glass a few inches away from his setting.

"How 'bout dis!" Staglione declared.

"It's nice, Vince," Daniel replied. Al acted as if he hadn't heard him.

"Hey, Vince," Al began, turning to Staglione. "When we going to get our cut of that little biotech deal? It's been five months now."

"Al, let's talk about dat some udder time," Vince said. "Drink your champagne."

"I don't drink champagne," Al replied dismissively. "I thought we'd have that money in by now. You said that—"

"Al, you know that it takes da lawyers weeks to get dat opinion letter done and den I've gotta pick da right time to sell it," Vince explained, visibly irked by Al's doggedness on the issue. Daniel leaned in to hear better and Staglione looked as if he could kill Al for bringing it up in front of him. "You don't want me to just blow outta all dat paper in a hurry and neither does the company."

"Been a long time, Vince," Al responded, less aggressively, but also irritated. "And we gotta eat too."

"You'll eat fine, Al," Vince said. "Drink some champagne. That's good shit."

"Waitress, bring me a Scotch and soda, please," Al ordered, ignoring Staglione. "Something aged." Al turned to Staglione, as if to show his independence and measure the result of his provocation. Vince, however, was unaware of any dubious order, instead whispering in the ear of the VIP man and pointing to a cluster of girls dancing together below. With an affirmative nod, the VIP man disappeared.

"Now it gets fun," Staglione promised. "Honey time." As they looked up, Al and Daniel saw the VIP man returning with two young girls dressed in black cocktail dresses and spiked heels. Both girls looked fresh from the cover of *Seventeen Magazine* in their nightclub outfits. The VIP man withdrew the velvet rope from its mooring and waved the girls through. Daniel wondered if they had used fake IDs. Staglione stepped out of the booth, awaiting his introduction from the host. "Ladies, this is Vincent Staglione, one of the most important businessmen in this town. He's 'The Man' here."

"It's nice to meet you girls," Vince said. "Would you care to join me and a couple of my guys here?" Al rolled his eyes again at the notion of him being one of Vince's guys.

"Hey, bro, can I get another Scotch over here?" Al ordered from the VIP man as he dumped the contents of his first drink under the table near Staglione's feet.

"So, whad're yer names, girls?" Staglione inquired as one girl slid into the booth first, resting between Al and Vince. Staglione entered next, with the second lass to follow, leaving Stag with a "honey" on each side.

"I'm Jasmine and she's Marnie," said the man-locked girl in the booth's interior.

"Dose are greeeeaaaat names," Staglione announced like a cereal box tiger. "I've never seen a fat girl named Jasmine or Marnie. You girls like champagne?"

"I do!" Marnie giggled. Daniel thought that there was no way she was twenty-one.

"I like anything with alcohol in it," Jasmine cooed.

"I'll get you some hair spray then," Al said mockingly.

"You're a big guy, aren't ya?" Jasmine said, not realizing that Al had made fun of her. She squeezed Al's large bicep and cooed again. Staglione grabbed Jasmine by the wrist, turning her toward him as he poured the girls each a flute-full of champagne.

"You're gonna love dis," Staglione said. "It's great French champagne. Da best!"

"All champagne is French," Al corrected. Staglione crossed his arms like an invisible straitjacket restrained him, using the awkward motion to more gracefully raise two full champagne glasses to each of the girls' mouths. Jasmine leaned in to guide the drink toward her and Marnie simply stuck her tongue in the glass like a kitten with a saucer of milk. Daniel watched from afar, mildly amused at the awkward seduction and that Al had again thrown a full glass of aged Scotch away, this time into the rose vase on the table while Staglione showed the girls his muscles. He hadn't consumed a drop of liquor yet, but had to be racking up a nice punitive tab for Vince.

"Don't you drink?" Daniel whispered.

"Like a fish," Al said. "But I'm not drinking his stuff. I can waste far more of his coin throwing it away. It's much more efficient. This is how I keep from killing him."

"Okey-doke," Daniel agreed, assuming the pair had more history that justified Al's sentiment.

Jasmine leaned in and put her head on Al's shoulder as if intent on sleeping there. "You're so big and strong. I bet you make a little girl feel safe." Al looked at Daniel with a semi-surprised look on his face. Jasmine was a pretty kid, but just that, and Daniel was beginning to wonder if she'd even reached the age of consent, let alone legal entry to the nightclub.

"I guess Vince is right every once in a while," Al conceded. Daniel wondered if Al could tell how young the girl was given how close she was to him. Daniel had the benefit of staring at her that Al didn't.

"You are a pretty little thing," Al said to the girl with her eyes closed and cheek pressed against an arm nearly the size of her head. "You come here often?"

"You did not just ask a girl if she comes here often?" Daniel teased, just as Al would have done if the situation were reversed.

"Yes, I did," Al said, mildly embarrassed. "And you don't mind at all. Do you?"

"Not a bit," said Jasmine. "I just want to hold your big old arm for a while. Usually, big guys like you are rough in the face. You're kinda pretty."

Staglione, who had his arm draped around Marnie's lean neck, turned to watch the exchange curiously. "Oh, he's pretty!" Daniel said, seizing the opportunity to chide Al once again. "Pretty Boy Al. What year were you prom queen at your high school, Nancy?"

Al smiled good-naturedly, enjoying Daniel's camaraderie and the pretty girl clutching his arm. He let the waitress come and go without ordering yet another disposable Scotch. Staglione had turned back to Marnie, whom he had been feeding champagne, and stroked her hair away from her face with the back of his hand, a diamond pinky ring glistening in the intermittent dazzle of a radiant disco ball.

Al was engaging in conversation with Jasmine who answered his cliché query with a confession that she and Marnie had just graduated and driven out from Amarillo to become go-go dancers. She and Marnie were staying in a weekly hotel and looking to find work at a club by showing their stuff on the dance floor, hoping to turn management's eye. Daniel remembered that he was pretty unaware at eighteen too, a fact he couldn't deny given the pencil-thin moustache on his freshman university ID and choice of a baseball cap for all occasions.

Jasmine seemed buzzed but Marnie was blasted, her thin frame not large enough to absorb Staglione's fountain-like dispensation of that fine French champagne. Daniel watched as Staglione rubbed her bare arm with his hand, seemingly affectionate, but every so often his fingers grazing her breast. Al and Jasmine had begun debating Texas high school football, playfully engaging each other in the banter. Daniel could tell that Al was getting more interested in Jasmine, who also seemed to be smarter than she initially appeared, albeit completely unsophisticated. It didn't hurt that she was from Texas where Al had grown up.

Marnie was kissing Staglione now, her eyes conveying her alcohol intake with the half-open look of the cartoon cat Garfield. Daniel sat back like a judge at a prize fight, thinking about Sydney and how he wasn't the least bit jealous as resident fifth wheel. Staglione didn't bother him nearly as much as he bothered Al, and he liked Al a lot. Even still, he wasn't wild about Staglione's advances toward a girl twenty years his junior and not in complete control of her faculties. He was hoping Al would get a phone number from Jasmine and that the girls would leave alone.

But as the next hour passed, Marnie was increasingly woven into

Staglione's attire, with Jasmine and Al hitting it off like old friends. Jasmine got up to use the restroom, taking with her a struggling Marnie. "You girls gonna be right back, right?" Staglione asked as they departed the booth.

"I'm comin' right back to you, Vinnee!" Marnie sang, spilling the contents of her purse. Daniel kneeled to the floor, helping Marnie gather her belongings as Vince tended to his cigar. The bubble gum, birth control, tampon, and Tweety Bird keychain revealed more about Marnie's youth and personality than bones to the oracle.

"Thank you, David," Marnie said.

"No problem," Daniel replied, realizing the uselessness of a correction. The pair departed like partners in a three-legged race, Jasmine steadying the duo.

"Whud I tell ya," Staglione said proudly. "Too easy!" Staglione started to slap Al on the shoulder for emphasis, but a stern look from Al halted that motion and Vince converted it to a high-five attempt, which was also unrequited. Though the tension made him uneasy, Daniel admired Al's strength of character and that Staglione's employment of him didn't give him a pass or warrant patronization. It made Daniel consider if he was maintaining enough autonomy with Staglione around.

The men sat quietly other than for Staglione to order another bottle of champagne and Al another Scotch. "You like dose things," Staglione said, looking for an ice-breaker with Al.

"Love 'em," Al replied.

The girls came back to the table and Jasmine slithered back into the booth next to Al. His mood changed instantly when she set her hand on top of his. Marnie sat next to Staglione in no better condition than before. Staglione whispered in her ear and then made a baby-faced pout as she looked back at him shaking her head. "Come on, Marnie," Vince protested. "It'll be fun."

"It's late and I'm tired," she argued weakly. Staglione whispered again and her expression visibly changed. "That sounds fun!" she exclaimed.

"But Jasmine has to come too."

"No problem," Staglione said quickly.

"Fellas, we're gonna take off," Staglione announced to the rest of the party. "Gonna hit the jacuzzi at my place."

"Come on, Jasmine. It'll be a blast," Marnie said. "We're gonna take Vinnie's Porsche."

"That might be fun," Jasmine agreed. "Let's go, Al, I gotta see what you look like with that shirt off. You coming too, Danny?"

"Nah, dey both gotta go home," Staglione interrupted. "Dey got a big day at da office tomorrow."

"We do?" Daniel said, not loudly enough that Staglione could hear him. Al was riveted on Staglione, instantly angrier than Daniel had ever seen him.

"Here's my number, Al," Jasmine said, kissing red lips on the table napkin above her number. "I want to see you again."

She leaned in to whisper in Al's ear and the big man held her arm firmly. "Al, I'm sorry, but I can't let her go to this guy's house by herself. Please call me tomorrow. Please." Al released his grasp as Staglione began his exit, holding Marnie's hand as she held Jasmine's.

"Son-of-a-bitch," Al grumbled. "I fucking hate that guy. Waiter, bring us two more bottles of that champagne and another Scotch for each of us."

Al turned to Daniel, "That jackass forgot to close out his tab. Let's get out of here before he brings the drinks back."

CHAPTER 11

October 2000

Across town, Julian was entering the offices of Frank Hayes, his stomach in knots wondering why his unsettling benefactor had summoned him. The brief voice mail had been as vague as it was commanding, ordering Julian to Summit Communications.

Summit Communications had been the only real advertising agency in Las Vegas when the town was small and it was active in political races in addition to traditional advertising and PR efforts. Its owner, Frank Hayes, had established himself as a force in local politics for a multitude of reasons. First, he understood the city's persona and appetite better than anyone. He'd grown up just outside Las Vegas and watched it expand from a vantage point few possessed. In addition, his successes with candidates over the decades gave him friends in important places, which led to anchor tenant accounts such as the Convention Center. This, in turn, provided Summit with a massive budget and prospecting tool for other large contracts.

The city's recent population explosion had attracted heavyweight firms from Los Angeles and New York, all clamoring for the juicy casino accounts and massive media-buy commissions. But Hayes realized what the new guys didn't, that the thin margin political races were where the rubber hit the road and that guiding elected officials' campaigns was what led to the fat casino and strip club deals. In a campaign he'd learn their dirty laundry as he prepared them for damage control should those facts be revealed by an opponent. It was part of his "critical path" when representing a client. Polish their image, set platforms to meet the demographic and to prepare for any last-minute bombs from the other side. But those bombs could come from Hayes too if a client "didn't remember his roots," as Hayes liked to say. Frank Hayes had a long memory and a short temper.

He'd beckoned Julian on short notice just a half hour before. Julian tried to get out of it by saying he was in basketball clothes and underdressed for Hayes's opulent smoked-glass office. But here he was, sitting in gym shorts and a Heineken T-shirt in front of the city's biggest power broker without a name on a gaming license.

"How's it goin', kid?" Hayes asked from a broad oak desk garnished with intricate carvings. Hayes' window offered a tight gaze of the Strip, like a spy cam shot from the waist of the Stratosphere. "What's the latest?"

"Everything's going good, Mr. Hayes," Julian said. "Money's good, signs are everywhere and they say I'm polling very well."

"That's good, that's good," Hayes said, his suntan evidencing a recent visit to the family retreat in St. Croix and complementing his gray hair. Hayes was fit and dapper in the George Hamilton mold, minus the mole. "You get over to the teachers' union and sit down with Jerry Limmer yet?"

"No, no yet," Julian admitted.

"But you got over to The Palisades Casino to pick up their donation, though?" Hayes asked, moving his hands above the desk and pushing closer. His pinstripe suit was a stark contrast to Julian's gray T-shirt and green beer logo. Julian said nothing, knowing that Hayes knew the answers to both questions before he'd asked them.

"I asked you a question, Julian," Hayes said, his voice intensifying.

"Look, Frank, I just haven't had the opportunity to yet," Julian tried to explain.

"You had the time to take some little whore in the back room at The Unicorn," Hayes said. "I brought you to those guys because they matter to me and because they should matter to you. That means making friends with them and earning their confidence. It doesn't mean banging the help in the manager's office and taking bottles of Cristal out the back."

"I didn't order the Cristal, my friend did, and I didn't bang anyone," Julian responded, his voice rising but still mindful of his subservient position with his campaign's chief sponsor.

"I don't want to hear that Bill Clinton bullshit, Julian," Hayes said. "Whether you got head or ass in that office, I've got to pay for it because you can't do shit for them yet. And if you don't get elected, you can't do shit for them ever. You understand me, amigo?"

"Yes," Julian said.

"But that's not even the point, Julian. I told you to go over to the teachers' union and sit down with Jerry," Hayes said in a more fatherly tone.

"He's a schmuck," Julian countered, mustering a moment of courage.

"He's a schmuck who means a lot to your goddamn race, moron," Hayes said. "I'll tell you again: You're not here unless the senator asks me to help you. The senator must win Southern Nevada to keep his job. This is done by controlling the council and commission races and mobilizing voters to get to the polls for those races in their neighborhoods. The teachers' union rep—schmuck or not—brings you their dollars and their endorsement, which we then use to make those smaller-class-size brochures you're handing out seem realistic. So when you blow off that schmuck over there, everything starts to go to shit.

"And do I have to remind you again what a big fucking deal it is to be a commissioner in Clark County, where you get to control all those multimillion-dollar casinos on the Strip? This ain't the county commission in some podunk part of the world whose biggest decision is what day to hold the harvest festival. You immediately become one of the lords of Las Vegas."

"I understand, Frank, I'll get over there soon," Julian said.

"Here's his home phone number," Hayes said, wadding up a Post-it with the union rep's name and number and tossing it in front of Julian. "Because if you don't win this race, your greasy ass will be back in Miami scraping pelican shit off the deck of some rich white guy's yacht. We understand each other?"

"We understand each other, Frank," Julian said, boiling inside and placing the balled-up Post-it in his shorts pocket.

As he left Frank's office, his temper hidden and ablaze, Julian thought how very good it would feel to plunge a dagger into the space inside Frank Hayes where a heart normally resided.

CHAPTER 12

Daniel put on his basketball shoes and a polo shirt, knowing he had to make one stop before he and Julian headed for a pick-up game at Sunset Park. With his eldest niece's birthday coming Saturday he needed to find a gift. Renee would soon be ten years old and Daniel thought he'd get her tiny diamond earrings.

Casa de Oro Jewelry wasn't far from Sunset Park and Daniel figured he'd swing by after picking up Julian. Daniel's family had patronized Oro for as long as he could remember, and his father and the operators seemed to know ninety percent of the same people. His father taught their youngest son in high school, and the owner's wife was the daughter of a well-known poker player. Daniel's father had always moonlighted as a poker dealer to make ends meet for the four-kid Madison family.

His father often lauded the honesty of Oro's proprietors, Angela and Antonio Rosales, liking to say that it was one of the few places where you didn't have to check the price. When Daniel told his father he wanted to get Renee some jewelry, he said to just call and tell Antonio what he could spend and it would work out. This was unusual for Mr. Madison, who had once measured gasoline from a pump into a ten-gallon container to see if the meter was accurate.

The store was a snapshot of Old Vegas with customers looking as if they had jumped off a velvet painting of 1970s-era Sin City. White-haired paisans with onyx cufflinks and pinky rings tried on gold nugget bracelets sold from an estate. Twentysomething men surveyed loose diamonds of all sizes and handed Angela tear-outs from bridal magazines with designer settings to replicate.

Angela noticed Daniel and bellowed out a raucous "Hell-O, Danny!" as a boy she'd seen grow up entered. Antonio walked over to where Angela was bear-hugging Daniel and put an arm on his shoulder.

"You're gonna love them, Danny," Antonio said of the diamonds he'd picked out. "They'll look great on her. You don't smoke no more of those Cuban cigars, did you?"

Daniel turned right to where Julian now stood a pace or two behind. Antonio hadn't realized they were together given the assembled crowd in the small store. Without answering the cigar query, Daniel guided Julian to the counter, preparing to introduce him. Antonio and Julian's eyes met, and Antonio extended his hand awkwardly, reaching forward long before Julian was close enough to grasp it. Julian took his hand and shook it firmly as Antonio's memory wandered over Julian's face.

"This is my friend Julian Correa," Daniel said. "And this is Antonio and Angela. They own this store. They're good friends of my family."

"It's a pleasure to meet you, Julian," Angela said.

"*Estas Cubano?*" Antonio inquired, still holding Julian's hand.

"*Si,*" Julian agreed. "My mother and father are both Cuban." Antonio released Julian's hand and told Daniel he'd be right back. Julian shifted impatiently from foot to foot.

"What are you fellas up to today?" Angela asked.

"Just a little basketball tonight," Daniel answered. "Gotta keep Commissioner Correa interacting with the public."

"Oh, I knew I recognized you from somewhere," Angela said. "Antonio had black hair just like you when I met him. And more of it. Of course, he didn't speak good English like you do."

"I was born here," Julian said.

"I tell you something, if I'd spoken English then, I wouldn't be with you now," Antonio chided his wife good-naturedly as he returned. "I was telling you that I didn't like you in Spanish when you were chasing me."

"You sure got over that fast," Angela countered.

"Never mind her," Antonio said. "Take a look at these." Antonio opened a small black box to reveal two sparkling diamond earrings. They were larger than Daniel had expected.

"Thank you," Daniel said sincerely, appreciative of the gift that were these earrings.

"Looking for any jewelry, Julian?" Angela asked.

"Not right now," Julian said. "I just wear a little necklace my father gave me, and I've never had much use for rings. They feel funny on my hands." Antonio and Angela peered at Julian's large, ring-free hands and the rope chain with the little gold bird on the end.

"Well, if you meet a nice girl, remember our little store," she said. "Any friend of Danny's ... you know. And good luck with the election."

"That's very nice of you," Julian replied, looking at his watch as if to signal to Daniel his desire to leave. Daniel hugged Angela as Julian exited hastily through the front doors. Antonio reached to give Daniel a hug as well and then braced his shoulders with both hands, like a father sending his son off to college.

"How long you know that kid?" Antonio asked, nodding to where Julian had been.

"Just a little while. I'm doing some speeches for him."

"That kid's no good. You keep your distance, Danny," Antonio warned with the type of serious instruction he gave Daniel from time to time. "You're a good boy. You don't need his kind of trouble."

Antonio laid his rugged palm affectionately on the edge of Daniel's face as a puzzled Angela looked on. Daniel always appreciated Antonio's concern for him; it was warm and sincere. But he wondered if this was just another of Antonio's Cuban sore spots ... *or had Antonio met Julian somewhere before?*

CHAPTER 13

Around 1960

As Daniel and Julian left the jewelry store, Angela scolded Antonio for scolding Daniel, telling him that to deride his friend was rude and inappropriate. But Antonio's mind had already left Las Vegas, traveling to Cuba some forty years before when his father was still alive and he stood in the family jewelry store where he learned his craft.

Antonio could still feel the balmy air that unforgettable morning of his youth, full of the humidity that would make the day unbearable by three o'clock. Palm fronds hung motionless, no breeze to buoy their tropical dance. The day was still and muggy, prohibitive to effort of any kind. Women would tie their hair in tight buns today, unmanageable for any other purpose in the moist air.

The Rosales Jewelry Store opened at exactly ten a.m. every day though Antonio's father was in each day at eight, preparing the store and perfecting repairs before the rich mujeres sauntered in demanding his service and attention to their needs. These were the real daughters of the revolution, he thought, the true beneficiaries of Castro's overthrow of Batista a few years before and the new holders of wealth. For a group whose promise was to feed everyone, to improve life for all Cubanos, they sure spent a lot of money on jewelry in his store. It was too bad their husbands took much of the money back for the government's programs or so they said when they'd visit him in their uniforms. "For the people," they'd explain as the bills slid into their trouser pockets.

Behind his store a tattered mattress tilted at an angle to the external wall, a pile of brown coconut husks next to it—some bowls, some food. Under the shade of the bedding sat two thin teenage girls who guarded their home from others dwelling in the back alley while their mother and father used the daylight to look for anything to eat. The advertised benefits of Castro's revolution had not yet extended to the denizens of the back alley, unless you counted the profits earned from the predators who found their way to the alley at night to poach the young boys and girls from their papas for a half-hour at a time. It was the days after these visits that the family would eat beans and meat atop their dirty mattress instead of the coconuts, mangos, or bananas they ate most days. This was also why their papa could not look at them.

Back inside, Antonio's father, Diego, told him to watch as he filled a mold with gold melted to a malleable consistency. As the charm took shape Antonio could see the form of the little bird, the Tocororo, come to life—two shallow sockets empty where its eyes should be.

"This is for your cousin Eva," Diego said. "I've been keeping a little gold left from each piece I make so I could make her this pendant."

Eva's mother, Lita—Antonio's aunt and Diego's sister—had died last month at thirty from influenza. She had taken ill on a ride to the south, contracting the illness on a crowded bus. Her husband had been killed two years before in an automobile accident, and Eva and Lita were inseparable. At thirteen, Eva was a blossoming Cuban beauty and Lita looked closer to twenty-one than thirty, her black hair and dark, deep-set eyes a remnant of the Spanish conquistadores who colonized the island. It was Lita who kept the church in the family, devotedly maintaining the family Bible and sharing the stories of Christ with the children.

Antonio watched as his father pulled a small floor board beneath the chair leg of his sturdy workbench, exposing a shallow pocket containing a weathered canvas bag. He'd seen his father use the space before, placing documents mostly in the hiding place. From the bag Diego withdrew a small ring, gold with two diamonds centered in the filigree.

Antonio recognized it immediately. It was Lita's ring, and he had never seen her without it, except for when they buried her. "My father made this ring for Lita when she got married," Diego told his boy. "No one is as good as your grandfather was with gold. He could do anything.

But the diamonds—they are not so good."

Diego grabbed a small tool and gently worked the edges of the stone as he heated the ring over a blue flame on his desktop. The warm gold released its grip on the white gems and Diego collected them as they fell onto the black velvet on his workbench. "I'll put these in the pendant," Diego told Antonio. "The bird will have her mother's diamonds. They are not the best diamonds, but they are her mother's diamonds." He paused. "Her mother's ring we save for when a man asks me to have her hand."

Diego let Antonio set the stones in the golden bird's eyes, wanting him to be part of the gift as well. The boy adored Eva as his father did and saw in her the qualities of his lost aunt. When his mother scolded him, it was Eva who came to his defense, sneaking him candies when she could, just as Tia Lita had before. The piece bloomed with the insertion of the diamonds, their internal flaws unnoticeable to the naked eye and surrounded by the brilliance of the burnished yellow gold. "She will love it," Antonio declared. "When can I give it to her?"

"*WE* will give it to her tonight," Diego said. "It has been one month today since we lost Tia Lita. She will be on Eva's mind more than usual." Diego looked out the back window of the store at the trees standing still on the sides of the alley. He thought of his beautiful sister as he polished the pendant in his hand over and over beyond necessity.

"Papa, we must open now," Antonio said. "The customers are at the door."

Diego walked to the front of the store, setting the golden bird in a corner of the display case as he hurried. He yelled over his shoulder for Antonio to place it back beneath his work table as he searched for the key in his always-full pockets. Antonio instead was headed to the back door where he gave a piece of his buttered bread to the girls in the alley.

At eleven a.m. the store was a flurry of rich women embroiled in their daily ritual, shopping for the necessities of Cuban Communist aristocracy—glittering jewelry, Italian clothing, and French perfume, a vibrant silk scarf like the American movie stars were wearing. Later they'd meet at a café to discuss the virtues of The Revolution and how handsome El Comandante looked at the last gala.

He was like an irresistible father, Señora Rodriguez liked to say. A partisan like Castro was beautiful even in the dark Havana nights, a man whose fervent patriotism cloaked him in resonant appeal, albeit amid the harsh brutishness required of a master general. She never said those things at home, only to the other wealthy wives. A woman of Cuban aristocracy knew her role in 1960.

Señora Cristina Gutierrez was especially obtuse this morning, pressing Diego as to why the necklace she had left for repair late yesterday was not yet done. Diego suffered her scorn and told her it was only because he wanted to give her treasures the care they deserved. He would hand polish it too, he promised, so it would look better than before.

"That will be fine," said Señora Gutierrez as she surveyed the display cases. "But I will expect it first thing tomorrow and I will assume a discount for the delay." Diego nodded without saying a word. This was nothing new and he had begun to add a little extra to the cost of repairs and items sold to Señora Gutierrez and her friends, knowing they felt they must work him for a better price. He winked at Antonio as he lifted a tray of rings out for Señora Gutierrez's friend, Señora Elena Monterrey, another scion of society and equally demanding.

The women pored over the offerings of the Rosales Jewelry Store, offering succinct criticisms and tacit approvals to Diego. Señora Monterrey informed Diego that she would consider the purchase of a bracelet set in rubies if he could replace them with her favorite emeralds. Diego looked at the twenty-seven stones set expertly in the piece and told Señora Monterrey he would see what he could do.

As the women ran Diego from one end of the store to the other, a man in uniform and his son entered. The boy was exactly Antonio's age of seven and he had met him on the street once a year or so before where he mocked his work clothes and asked if his family lived in the back alley with the rats. "No, you bastard," Antonio had responded angrily, preparing to fight the tall, slender boy until Señor Calderon, who owned the market next to the jewelry store, grabbed his collar and pulled him quickly behind a stand of fresh fruit.

"This is not a boy you fight right now, Antonio," Señor Calderon instructed, his bushy white mustache riding his words. "If you win this fight, you lose and your family loses. His father is a powerful and vindictive man."

"But he insulted me, called my family garbage," Antonio cried to his neighbor.

"Suffer the insult today and remember his face," Calderon advised, touching the boy's chest for emphasis as he did his own young son. "This is not the best fight for you today. Wait until you have the higher ground."

Antonio made eye contact with the boy as he came through the door, a step behind his lumbering father. *He doesn't recognize me*, Antonio thought. He noted how vividly he remembered the terse exchange last year while figuring that the boy had so many squabbles like it that it didn't stand out to him now, even here in his father's store and with Antonio right in front of him.

As his father moved through the store in his officer's uniform, the women greeted him with compliments and deferent nods of greeting. "Capitan Del Rey, so nice to see you this morning," offered Señora Gutierrez. "Ramon is getting very tall … and handsome like his father."

"Yes, he is," Capitan Del Rey agreed. "He'll start at the academy next month. For a young boy he shows uncommon brilliance. He will be a great partisan."

Antonio put his hands in his pockets to hide the fists he had made. He would not go to the academy. In fact, he didn't even want to stay in Cuba. Like his father, he wanted to join his family in Miami, where everything was different. The stories he heard of clean, peaceful streets where everyone could be rich excited him. He wanted that for his papa.

His mother and father would quarrel about when they could attempt to brave the unpredictable sea, to leave their family here forever. And now they had Eva under their care.

Capitan Del Rey's booming voice interrupted Antonio's quiet contemplation. A man of short stature with twenty pounds of girth warming his belt, his voice evoked images of a much larger figure, one like Antonio's father who had been a boxer in his youth.

"Rosales!" Del Rey called. "I need your attention immediately."

Del Rey walked to the display cases ahead of the women who happily relinquished their space at the counter like heifers as a bull neared the trough. "Tomorrow is my anniversary and I have been so consumed with my duties that I have not had time to obtain a proper gift for my wife, Mireya," he said. "She will understand as she knows how very much is expected of me by my people, but I desire to please her."

Diego moved to the center of the store where Del Rey and Ramon waited and began to show them items from his cases. Antonio noted how father and son's eyes were identical, their odd shape and camel-like eyelashes passing from generation to generation. "No, that will not do," Capitan Del Rey said when Diego pointed to a resplendent necklace of bourbon-colored amber and milk-white ivory.

"Show me something nice, man. I am looking for something exquisite for Mireya," he said loudly, speaking more to the women in the room than to Diego.

Diego moved to his left where the more elaborate pieces were displayed. "How about this, Capitan?" said Diego, pointing to the gold and ruby bracelet at the end of his display cases.

"That is beneath her, Rosales," Del Rey answered snidely after a second's inspection. "Why would you show me that garbage?" The word garbage made Antonio's stomach turn.

"I don't like that one either," echoed Señora Monterrey. "I just finished telling him that the piece wasn't of a quality sufficient to be sold."

"You are right, Señora," the Capitan concurred, turning his attention further left. "What is this piece, Rosales, the golden bird? This is something I haven't seen."

"That *is* new," noted Señora Gutierrez. "I like the diamonds in the eyes. Very nice work and detail. Fine quality stones. Where did this come from, Rosales?"

"It is a piece I am making for my little niece, Señora," said a now nervous Diego. "My boy forgot to put it away when we opened this morning. I have to put it away now. Antonio, come here, please!"

Antonio hurried to his father's side, a piece of soft cloth in his hand to receive the Tocororo charm he hadn't heard his father say to put aside. As his father reached to place the bird in the young boy's cloth, Capitan Del Rey grabbed Diego's wrist, his short, thick fingers like a fat brown spider on his father's muscular forearms. "Not so fast, Rosales. I'm looking for something exactly like that," he said, his hand now on top of Diego's. "Let me see that for a moment."

"But, Capitan, it is not for sale. It is a gift for my niece," Diego said. "Her mother died and ... "

"Nonsense!" Del Rey interrupted. "You had it in a display case, did you not? Is that not where you place the items you have for sale? Aren't these items all for sale? Are you just trying to get me to pay more?" Ramon watched his father intently, his eyes fixed on the increasingly unstable exchange.

"No, no, Capitan," Diego said. "I would not do that. The item has no price, it is not for sale. My boy forgot to place it in the back. We were working on it this morning and—"

"It is exquisite, Capitan," chimed Señora Monterrey. "Almost as beautiful as Mireya. I can hardly believe it was made by Diego."

"How much, Rosales?" Capitan Del Rey asked tersely. "I will take it today."

"It is not for sale, dear Capitan," Diego said softly. "It is for my niece—her mother died a month ago and the diamonds are from her—."

"Wrap it for me now," he ordered. "We will discuss the price when you are less emotional. You are a jeweler, Rosales. You can make or give your niece anything you want. I know these things cost you nothing." Diego wore only a small gold wedding band.

"But Capitan ... " Diego begged. "She has lost her mother."

"Enough of this!" the Capitan declared, reaching upward and slapping Diego across the right side of his face. Antonio stood motionless, a deep swell of guilt permeating his body. He hadn't felt like this since they lost Tia Lita.

Next to his father, Ramon smiled broadly as the elder Del Rey spoke. "I provide you the good life of a Cuban citizen, a comrade, and you treat me like this when I want simply to spend good money in your little store?"

"Papa!" Antonio shouted to his father who stood silently in front of the Capitan, who had taken the golden pendant from his hand.

"Go to the back, son," Diego said to his boy, never taking his eyes off the Capitan, who was admiring the glimmering Tocororo in his hands. Diego's face was red on both sides.

"No need to wrap the piece, Rosales," Del Rey said. "I will give it to her just like this. She will be most pleased."

With that, Capitan Del Rey turned and left the Rosales Jewelry Store with Eva's bird and Lita's diamonds in his shirt pocket.

"What a powerful man," Señora Monterrey said to Señora Gutierrez so that the Capitan could hear as he exited. As father and son reached the jewelry store's front door, Ramon turned and looked toward the back of the shop where Antonio peered cautiously, his cheeks wet with embarrassment and pity for his father. Ramon returned the eye contact that Antonio had made when they entered the store, smiling widely and nodding tauntingly toward Diego's son.

He does recognize me, Antonio was certain as he recalled Señor Calderon's lesson a year before. *And I will always remember that face.*

As Angela drew him from his memory with a grasp of his hand, Antonio knew that in Julian Correa he'd just seen that face again.

CHAPTER 14

October 2000

Daniel and Mike Martin had agreed to meet to catch up on the latest events in each of their lives. Martin loved the scenery of Las Vegas and the periphery, the desert colors a stark contrast to the blue-green hues of Massachusetts' flora and coastlines. Mike had been encouraging Daniel to go for a hike in Red Rock Canyon where they could spend time alone beyond the range of the incessant interruption of their cell phones. Martin's phone seemed to ring but once a day—the first call of the day—and from there it was an incessant sequence of call-waiting beeps and new conversations. Daniel's communication was less prolific, but he too fielded a constant stream of calls from Sydney and Staglione, the latter often sharing panting "brainstorms" as he served his treadmill.

The morning sun lit the dew on the rocks and shrubs, illuminating and removing it simultaneously. Ambitious hikers were beginning to fill the roadsides, stretching and bending as they embarked on the scenic novelty of the rust-red geology just outside Las Vegas. A gang of ornery burros bayed nearby, releasing a complaint or request discernible only to other burros. Small turquoise-speckled lizards moved slowly in the early morning cool as grasshoppers leapt from rock to bush to rock in their a.m. scamper.

"I never get over this place," Martin said, his fingers locked behind his head as he stretched and looked upward at the iron-colored columns of rocks. "I hope they never build all the way up here. This place needs to stay just the way it is—just the way God intended. It's bad enough they put a road through here."

"It's beautiful," Daniel said. "My father had some friends visit from Italy once and this was the first place they wanted to see. One of them told me they grew up seeing pictures of the rock formations in their textbooks."

"You ready?" Daniel asked.

"Yep, let's get a move on," Martin said. The men walked a light trail, traveling slowly enough that the surrounding aesthetic was not lost. The morning sky offered intermittent clouds that varied the backdrop for Red Rock Canyon's scarlet-banded formations. The combination was often breathtaking, like a bold statue on a pedestal in front of an Impressionist painting, and the increasing morning light revealed new colors and hues like a curtain on a stage. Five minutes of walking with their heads tilted toward the clouds passed before either spoke.

"Sooooo, how's that new job going, Danny?"

"It's all right," Daniel replied. "It's not what I want to be doing, but I've been able to put away some money and my cousin found a little house for me that I think I can afford now. I closed Monday."

"Aaah, that's great," Martin said. "It doesn't pay to be a renter in a place growing like this. Your house will be worth a million bucks in twenty years."

"What exactly they got you doing? It's a PR firm, right?" Martin asked as he stepped over a dead yucca branch that had fallen in the path. The green shrubs dotting the terrain all had lavender flowers on them this time of year.

"Pretty much just press releases. They've got this gun safety device, and the CEO just wants to make sure that every time there's a school shooting we get the product out there," Daniel said. "Because they say it's a solution to the problem." Daniel had to stop himself from using an intonation and tenor that sounded like Staglione.

"Yeah, that's a hot issue," Martin agreed. "The politicians are mining it too."

"I just take what they give me and make it sound good," Daniel said, distancing himself a little.

"Good for you, Danny, but I wouldn't get too comfortable there," Martin said as he tightened the laces on his Timberlands. "Julian's race looks like a lock given the poll numbers and the way he breezed through his primary. If he doesn't do anything else stupid, he's in and we're going to get you on staff. I've made it clear to him that I want that and he's amenable."

Daniel said nothing, allowing Martin to continue. "That speech you wrote for the Working Women's event came at a very critical time for Julian. He owes you."

"He doesn't owe me," Daniel said, kicking a loose rock as he traversed the path. "That's what we agreed to do for each other, right? We share our skills among the group."

"You're right," Martin said. "But that was one helluva speech. At the very least it showed what you can do for him."

"When you say 'doesn't do anything else stupid,' what exactly do you mean?" Daniel asked, fairly certain he knew the essence of the answer.

"Same problem he's had since day one," Martin grumbled as he climbed. "He's screwing everything that moves. And he's got no discretion. I can't tell you the fires I've put out for him already. I'm not accustomed to lying to people or to telling men to relax when I'd kill him myself if he did it to me."

"He's built some powerful enemies, Daniel," Martin continued, pausing to get his breath. "And they won't forgive him—not these guys. Trust me on that."

"I hadn't realized it was *that* bad, Mike," Daniel said. "Will it affect the election?"

"I don't think so. Not at this point," Martin said. "It's not the sort of thing that gets run on the front page, and it's not like some old casino owner's going to hold a press conference to announce that Julian's been banging his pretty young wife. Normally, they will throw money to your opponent, but Julian's so far ahead that that would be a complete waste. It's more likely they'll just wait and pick their spot down the road. But they'll get even. These Old Vegas guys always get even."

"Do you want me to talk to him about taking it easy for a while?"

"If I thought he'd listen to you, I would, but I'm afraid that's just who he is. At least he's a bachelor," Martin said. "I think he thinks it's cool, like he's JFK or something. He'll be a commissioner soon and that will provide some insulation. Julian will have considerable power, and the casino guys who hate him won't be able to come straight at him. He can affect their businesses too easily."

"He's been seeing this girl Amber for a little while—apparently in addition to his other extracurricular pursuits. Maybe I can get them to double date with me and Sydney sometime. It might cut down on his free time."

"That might be a good idea, but he'll probably just cram more sex and adultery into his remaining free time," Martin lamented as the men looked down into Red Rock. "I don't even know how anyone can piss this many people off, let alone have sex that often. He's like a bull ... in an adulterous china shop," he said, grinning, before changing the subject. "How're things going with that Sydney girl anyway? You guys getting to be a thing I take it?"

"Yeah, it looks that way," Daniel said, thrilled to be calling Sydney his girlfriend to Martin. "She's just amazing. We talk together like my buddies and I talk, you know. And I can't stop thinking about her."

"That's great, man," Martin said. "But take things slow. She's got her share of baggage."

"Baggage? What, does she have a kid I don't know about?" Daniel kidded, but still taken aback.

"She used to date one of the local rich kids and got a rep as a bit of a gold digger," Martin warned as politely as he could. "I was at a breakfast at the Country Club one morning and she was working the group a little, giving little kisses and schmoozing like *she* was running for office. As soon as she left, a couple of the old money broads in the room were knocking her pretty hard for chasing all the rich boys around and hustling their parents."

"But her family has a pretty nice place. They seem plenty well-off, Mike," Daniel said, defending her as best he could.

"Not the kind of money she's into, Danny," Martin said. "There's rich people and there's the truly wealthy."

"I wonder what she's doing with me?" Daniel asked. "It's not like I'm the cash cow you're describing."

"Not sure ... maybe she just sees your bright future, Danny boy," Martin said. "Because you are a very ugly man." Martin laughed and slapped Daniel in his familiar way. Daniel laughed too as they surveyed Las Vegas from the west, the Strip's eclectic edges defining the city's hub.

"What's next for you, Mike?" Daniel asked as the men stared outward like scouts in an old Western.

"I think I'd like to run for governor," Martin answered quickly, his eyes fixed on some landmark of the city. "I think I can get the most done from the governor's mansion, and in a year or so I'll be in a financial position where I don't have to sell myself to be a candidate. I won't be beholden to anyone ... for the most part."

Martin turned toward Daniel. "The governor's seat will be up in the air in two years," he said. "No significant candidate has thrown his name out there yet. I think this may be my time. If half the guys I've helped give me their support, I've got a real shot."

"Wouldn't that be awesome?" Daniel said. "Governor Martin. I can hear myself saying that."

"You'd best not be saying that to me, Danny," Martin corrected gently. "If I'm lucky enough to ever be governor, our friendship will be the same. Nothing changes. That's one of the reasons why I need you working in Julian's soon-to-be office. You need some public service work on your record. That way I can get you a nice position up north with me in Carson City. And I don't mean a juice job for one of my boys—I don't do that—I mean putting you someplace where a man of talent and character can make a difference. I need East Coast guys."

They returned to the beginning of the trail as the sun traveled to its apex. Non-hiking tourists were furiously clicking cameras at mugging children on massive rocks, and two burros were raiding a chip bag from the backpack of a non-attentive hiker as small birds and a ground squirrel battled for the crumbs. Martin and Daniel mutually pledged to do this more often, both knowing the unlikelihood of their schedules allowing such a recess. With the general election drawing near, Daniel wagered that Martin would be a phantom until election night.

The Mustang's creaky driver door commemorated his re-entry and he dropped his water bottle onto the seat where his cell phone lay. A half-mile down the road toward town, the signal bars relit to confirm the phone was useable. It rang immediately, and as Daniel reached for it the screen announced, "Call Ended."

Signal must be weak up here too, Daniel thought.

It rang again and Daniel quickly answered. "Hello." Silence followed and Daniel stared at it briefly before hanging up, shifting the Mustang's gears as the road required. The caller ID read "Private Caller."

Daniel reached to turn on the radio and the phone rang once more. "Private Caller" again crossed the cell phone's screen and Daniel answered an irritated "Hello?" No response came through the phone but Daniel could hear a television in the background. "Hello? Hello? Helllooooo!" he repeated, growing frustrated. A light laugh found his ear, and before Daniel could speak, the caller hung up.

None of his friends had "Private Caller" ID displays and most had given up playing crank call games in junior high. It also seemed like the caller had been trying to reach him for a while, given the phone's instant ringing upon re-entering the sphere of signal. Daniel laid the phone in his lap and drew closer to the edge of town. He turned the radio to a classic rock station and let the early fall breeze rush through the vents of the Mustang. Tonight he and Sydney would be going to dinner and a movie and he hoped she would stay the night instead of creeping out in the morning's early hours. This was the first time Daniel had lived absolutely alone, and having Sydney in the house made the place seem like his home. Awakening to her in the morning would be bliss.

An Eagles tune ended and in the brief expanse of quiet preceding the next radio offering Daniel realized his phone was ringing yet again. Bright sunlight blazed through the car's rear window, making his caller ID impossible to read. Expecting the silent treatment yet again, Daniel answered the caller with an abrupt, "What?"

"Huh?" came the caller's response, which Daniel quickly identified as Julian.

"Julian? Hey, man, what's up?" Daniel said, toning his rancorous greeting down to congenial levels.

"Havin' a bad day, Danny?" Julian asked sincerely.

"Nah, man. It's been a good day. Somebody's just been calling me and hanging up over and over again."

"That sucks. Who's doing it?" Julian asked.

"No idea," Daniel replied. "It just started."

"Probably just a kid or a wrong number. It'll stop," Julian consoled. "Hey, you got a minute?"

"Sure, I'm just driving back from Red Rock. Wussup?" Daniel answered.

"Well, I need another speech. Something to give to trial lawyers, so I guess it needs to say bad things about limits on the size of judgments," Julian explained.

"Didn't we already put out a brochure saying you were for some tort reform to make it easier on doctors and limiting skyrocketing malpractice insurance?" Daniel asked.

"Yeah, but none of these guys saw that piece," Julian said, laughing. "Can you get something done quickly?"

"Are you sure you want to play both sides?" Daniel asked, needing to confirm.

"Yeah, the doctors and lawyers are great donors and I'm building my war chest for the next campaign. Just throw it together, man," he requested.

"All right," Daniel obliged. "But I think it's risky, bro."

"Don't worry, I've got it all under control," Julian said. "Also, I wanted to talk to you about after the election, Danny. You've been a good friend to me. Reliable, loyal, and you do a good job. I went to Martin the other day and told him I had to have you on my staff. I know the party likes to stack the offices with their own guys, but I made sure he knew I needed you on board."

"Jule, you know I want to work in your office. That's great," Daniel affirmed, wondering who between Martin and Julian was bullshitting him. "We just got to get through the end of this campaign nice and clean, right?"

"Yeah, whatever," Julian said dismissively. "I ain't losing, bro. You can bet on that."

Daniel decided not to go at Julian directly, sensing he would be defensive, and not wanting to change the tone of a conversation in which he'd been offered a job he deeply wanted. He'd bring up a positive to steer the conversation back. "So, what's the buzz on your candidacy among the donors?" Daniel asked.

"Donors have been strong," Julian said. "But I've become Mr. Popularity with the developers, strip club owners, etc. You oughta see the ass-kissing they're doing with this poor Cuban boy. I'm gonna be rich!"

"Last I checked the commission gig doesn't pay all that great, Julian. You'll be a civil servant," Daniel teased.

"Yeah, but when I'm done they'll want me as a consultant," Julian explained. "When I get elected I'm good forever. Correa Consulting will kill it."

"How's Amber doing?" Daniel asked, changing the subject from Julian's braggadocio. "She called me the other day to ask what size shirt you wore, like we were the Odd Couple. I just guessed you were an extra large."

"Everything on me is extra large," Julian boasted. "Amber knows that better than anyone. She bought me this five-hundred-dollar sweater from some Italian place in the Forum Shops. She must've worked a week to pay for it. Man, is she dumb."

"I never thought she was going to recite Tennyson but I didn't think she was all that dumb, Julian. And she really does seem to care about you. Might not be bad to try the monogamous thing for a while."

"Can't do it, Dan," Julian stated matter-of-factly. "I'm bored out of my mind when I'm alone with her … unless we're having sex."

"Really? It's that bad?"

"Absolutely. Worse yet, she had me over to the house the other day for dinner and I saw a picture of her mother on a table. She looks just like Amber."

"So? Amber's hotter than hell. What's the problem with that?" Daniel wondered.

"She looks just like Amber with about fifty pounds of woman strapped on her," Julian said, starting to laugh again. "She's huge. If she cuts herself shaving her legs, gravy will come out."

"What's that got to do with Amber?" Daniel inquired again.

"You always gotta look at the mamas," Julian instructed. "That's how you know what you're getting into. Amber's gonna be two-bills by the time she's forty. I can't do that, partner."

"You're deep, man," Daniel scolded sarcastically as he neared his neighborhood.

"Call it what you want, Danny, but I know what I can live with and what I can't," Julian said. "Because I admit I'm shallow about that stuff doesn't make me any worse than a guy who won't admit it."

"You have a point there," Daniel said. "So what're you going to do? She's in love with you."

"Yeah, I know," Julian said. "What I'm doing is trying to stay with her as long as I can. So, I'm messing with a couple different women so I don't get too bored with Amber."

"Oh, you're doing that for her?" Daniel asked incredulously. "How kind of you. Julian. You think you might want to just take it easy with the ladies until the election's in the bag?" Daniel asked. "You want some woman-scorned fiasco at a public event somewhere—some chick with running mascara and one of your shirts cut to shreds yelling at you on the podium?"

"Not gonna happen, Daniel," Julian assured him. "I own them. They do what I tell 'em."

Daniel pulled into his new driveway and shut off the car's engine, looking at the home's exterior for a few minutes as he had every day since he had moved there. He still couldn't quite grasp that this was his.

"Okay, Julian. Just be careful," Daniel said. "You've got a lot to lose."

"I appreciate the concern, Danny, but don't sweat it. Everything is beautiful," Julian said before turning sincere. "Hey, man, I really appreciate you doing this new speech for me. I love you, brother. You're the only real friend I got out here."

"I appreciate that, Julian. I'll talk to you soon," Daniel said, closing the phone and walking to the front door.

Five seconds later, the phone rang again with "Private Caller" on the display. "Yes?" Daniel answered harshly. A soft laugh was audible, the same television playing in the background. "Who is this? Who's there?" Daniel asked sharply. The light laughter continued for a moment longer before the caller hung up.

CHAPTER 15

V.S.E. had become increasingly intense of late, and the stress of the darkening situation was evident on Staglione's suntanned face. StopShot shares had not appreciated in value much despite V.S.E.'s best efforts. Vince was constantly cursing the "shorts" for holding the share price back. Short sellers, as Staglione was oft to explain, "were da scum of da Earf" who preyed on small, up-and-coming equities. They also were attracted to companies they believed to be over-hyped.

These investors would gamble that a touted stock was going down, selling shares they didn't own to willing buyers and pocketing the money. Then, if the stock depreciated as expected, they would buy it at the reduced value to cover their "short" position. Their only risk would be if the stock did go up above their short entry price and they had to make up the difference out of their own pockets.

Since the shorts didn't have to invest real money on the front end, they could release an unending stream of stock into any potential interest and increase in volume. In essence, there was no way the stock could go up in value with shorts sitting on the bid price, feeding seemingly unlimited shares into the market. This virtual supply would almost always meet demand.

Staglione knew there was but one way out of this abyss—create enough hype that the shorts were afraid even they couldn't supply enough stock to keep the price down. If Staglione could generate monster buying volume that the shorts couldn't meet day after day, then StopShot's price would rise. Vince's wet dream scenario would have this happen with the shorts getting scared and being forced to buy the fast-appreciating shares on the open market to cover and negate their exposure.

This "short squeeze" would create a slingshot effect and a "gap-up" in the prices of StopShot's shares. His New York investors would be tapping diamond rings gleefully on the steering wheels of their Mercedes, and Staglione wouldn't have to be considering a one-way ticket to Belize anymore.

To do all this Staglione knew he had to get something out there telling Wall Street that StopShot was real, not just a fleeting widget crafted opportunistically to feed on the spate of school shootings. StopShot needed traction, and sales, and revenue. And he needed Daniel.

Vince called Daniel into his office, forcing Dottie to retrieve Daniel and escort him rather than using the office intercom. Daniel walked with Dottie along the hallway and past the bullpen where the men were playing a game of Nerf war ball while one sentry stood look-out for Staglione. Al had wheeled his chair into a corner, watching but not participating.

Daniel walked into Staglione's office and sat down in the chair opposite the desk. Vince had his back to Daniel, staring into a computer monitor and eating a stick of celery. He sat quietly, not wanting to interrupt Vince if he were tabulating a number. After three minutes had passed Daniel wondered if Staglione had forgotten he was there. "Vince?" Daniel asked. "You wanted to see me?"

"Just a minute, kid," Vince replied. "I'm concentratin' on somethin'." Vince wheeled the black leather chair around, placing his feet atop his desk and his hands above his head. Dark sweat marks were visible under his arms, and Staglione had a look of purpose and determination.

"I got some good news, Danny," Staglione announced. "For me, for dis company, for StopShot. And for you."

"What's that?" Daniel asked, curious what could be good for all of them.

"Well, our little company had a very big day," Staglione said, unwittingly parroting Jerry Maguire. "StopShot closed an enormous sale. Dose little things are gonna be everywheres."

"Great," Daniel said. "We could use some big news. It would be nice to stop chasing ambulances."

"Hey, dose stories are what keeps dis place's doors open, Daniel," Staglione scolded. "Remember dat. People here depend on you."

"I understand, Vince," Daniel said.

"Anyways, StopShot got a contract to sell a million units through a big new distributor," Staglione said. "Dis is yuge."

"That's awesome," Daniel said. "I'll get to work on a release right away. What's the name of the distributor? Where are they based?"

"The distributor is B.A. Marketing and dey're in Brooklyn," Staglione said. "Brooklyn, New York."

"Gotcha," Daniel said, writing the info on a Post-it. "Are we announcing the price per unit or the terms of the agreement?"

"Nah, not yet," Staglione replied. "I don't want dose friggin' shorts pickin' the details apart trying to stir up shit until we start the manufacturing."

"Okey-doke," Daniel said, starting to rise from his seat. "I'll get the release going. Give me a half hour if the phone doesn't ring."

"Sit down, kid," Staglione ordered. "I want to talk to you."

Vince stood up and walked to a black iron safe poorly hidden by an artificial palm tree. He rotated the dial to the appropriate combination and opened the thick door. Daniel watched out of the corner of his eye, not wanting to focus on any aspect of Staglione's effort but curious as to Vince's purpose.

"Here we go!" Staglione crowed. "Dis is da one."

Staglione folded the paper in his hand longways, gripping it like the seal on a love note. He sat down at his chair and pushed closer to the desk, his proximity indicating some profundity was on its way. "Kid, I told ya before, you do a good job here. Dere's only two people I can count on in dis place and da other one prepares my salads for me, if dat tells you anything. I'm gonna make a commitment to you because of dat, because of da little talk we had."

Staglione took the sheet of paper and unfolded it, placing it face down on the desktop. He pushed it with two fingers across the surface

100

toward Daniel, who only stared down at the offering. "Go ahead, take a look. I think you'll be pleased."

Daniel did so without speaking, taking the heavy bond paper and turning it over. The borders were like a grade school award, with laurels and raised ink expressing value. Across the top was the StopShot logo that Daniel often saw in his sleep.

In the middle it read, "This certifies that Daniel Madison is the owner of 500,000 shares of StopShot Inc." Daniel was stunned. He knew the math immediately; the certificate was worth a quarter of a million dollars. StopShot's share price of fifty cents was a more known number than nine or five in the office.

"Vince, you're kidding me? This is mine?" Daniel asked, not fully believing.

"Dose are yours, kid," Staglione said, his voice effecting the pride of a father handing down a grandfather's watch to a grandson. "You've earned dem."

"That's a lot of money, Vince," Daniel asked, still looking at the certificate.

"Daniel, I want you motivated," Staglione explained. "Dat stock dere is restricted stock. You can't sell it for a year. You've done enough to earn it already but I want you to fall in love with your job around here. I need you to do whatever it takes to make things work."

"Vince, I'm on the team, man," Daniel assured, already mulling what he could do with the proceeds from this stock and forgetting for the moment all about joining Julian at the commission office.

"You can figger it out yourself, Danny," Staglione said. "If we can get StopShot up to two bucks, you'll be a millionaire. How's dat sound?"

"Sounds good to me, Vince," Daniel agreed. "Wow."

"It's yours to keep, kid. Now get in your office and make that announcement about the new deal smokin' hot."

"You got it!" Daniel said, bounding out of the office and down to his desk, the certificate in his hands.

"Whatcha got there, college boy?" Al asked loudly as Daniel passed briskly.

"Nothing much," Daniel lied as he began to jog to his office, knowing the treatment he got from Staglione could be a wedge between him and Al.

In his office Staglione had commanded Dottie to get StopShot's CEO, Allan Baxter, on the phone. "Mr. Baxter is ready on line one," Dottie reported.

"Put 'em through, Doddie," Staglione shouted at full volume. "And close my door."

"Allan, you dere?" Staglione asked as he picked up the handset on the phone.

"I'm here, Vince. How's it going out in Sin City today?" Baxter asked congenially.

"Everything's good. Real good," Staglione replied. "We're gonna get da distribution news out on da open tomorrow and my guys are already workin' da phones. You're gonna see volume pick up riduhway. I think this is gonna scare da shit out of da shorts. This is exactly what they fear da most. Real news. If they think we're gonna have a deal like dis, then they'll assume that revenues are sure ta follow."

"It's pure genius, Vince," Baxter said. "I love it. You know, none of us here makes a nickel in salary. We have to sell our shares to get by. And fifty cents ain't cuttin' it, my ginny friend."

"Everybody's gotta eat, Allan, and we're gonna be eating better," Staglione professed. "I got da kid on board. Getting him dat certificate will be werf its weight in gold with him, and it won't cost us a nickel."

"He understands he can't sell it for a year?" Baxter asked.

"Yeah, I explained it to him," Staglione said. "He doesn't know shit about da markets but he makes all this stuff sound real good, like it's straight off of Wall Street. And *his name* is gonna be on all dese press releases from now on. Not mine or yours."

"That's the real value, Vince," Baxter agreed. "We need to have plausible deniability. That kid's our buffer, and the way he writes, no one will think he's a rookie. He's the perfect fall guy if we need it. With his political buddies he might just get a slap on the wrist."

"Best part is, by the time that restriction comes off in a year, we'll be so far down the road that it won't matter that the stock is worth a penny," Baxter laughed. "It'll be worthless … and I'll still own the patents. I never did put those in the company. We can do this all over again in another shell."

"I'd call you a smart man if I thought dose StopShots actually worked," Staglione said, laughing too.

"I guess you're right about that," Baxter said. "But I just bought a place in St. Bart's with my most recent sale of StopShot. I guess it's good for something … just not keeping kids from shooting each other."

"You know, Allan, I was thinking about that distribution agreement we're announcing with my brudder-in-law's toy company," Staglione said. "Where the hell we gonna put all da StopShots we're gonna have to make that ain't never gonna get sold?"

"Get the stock up to a buck and I'll buy an island and name it Isle of Staglione," Baxter said. "We'll put them all on it."

"Sounds good to me," Staglione agreed. "I just gotta keep da Brooklyn boys happy. Gettin' this pig to a buck will do dat."

CHAPTER 16

Daniel sat at his desk with the blue-ink stock certificate in his lap. He navigated his Internet browser to the Yahoo! Finance page and typed in StopShot's stock symbol. Daniel knew full well the offer price for StopShot was fifty cents but he needed to look at it, to see that real integer and calculate the five hundred thousand shares times that number over and over again. *I can pay off my house*, he thought. *What a relief it would be to not have to feed that monster each month.*

As he began to shape the announcement Daniel felt a swell of mixed emotion. Staglione had said the shares were for work he'd already performed, but he knew he hadn't done a quarter of a million dollars' worth of work. He realized the phone should ring soon from Julian, once he was formally elected. Did these shares tie him to Staglione for much longer than he'd planned? Regardless, Daniel wanted the release to be top notch and queried search engines to see how Fortune 500 companies announced similar distribution deals. After surveying releases of this kind and thirty minutes of writing, the press release had taken shape and Daniel was satisfied enough to take it to Staglione.

I wonder what impact this will have on the stock? Daniel pondered, reading his own words and pre-calculating the difference in the value of his new stock if it rose a nickel, a dime, or a quarter per share. Daniel had only thought of V.S.E. and its many warts as a stepping stone, but this new opportunity changed the landscape dramatically, making him a partner. Daniel blew past the bullpen and cruised into Vince's office. Dottie didn't stop him anymore. Daniel coughed lightly to announce his entry as Staglione flipped through a Porsche brochure.

"Whatcha got for me, buddy boy?" Staglione said feverishly, sporting a look of unbridled anticipation.

"Take a look, Vince," Daniel said, handing him the draft. "News like this doesn't need much help and I re-did the 'About StopShot' section to punch it up a little."

Staglione sat back in his chair, his mouth moving rapidly as he muttered the words to himself. "It's not good enough, Dan."

"Okay, what can I do to make it better?" Daniel asked.

"It doesn't have no excitement, no drama," Staglione explained. "Dis is like a comin' out party for StopShot. We can only do dis once. It has to be perfect."

"What kind of drama, Vince?" Daniel genuinely inquired. "We've covered just about every school shooting that's happened the last few months. We're all over that."

"You need to say somethin' 'bout how many lives dese things are gonna save," Staglione said, becoming more animated. Daniel saw Dottie walk past the open door and down the hallway. "Make up a number like sixty school kids are killed a year, and if dese things were on all da guns, dat wouldn't happen."

"Make up a number?" Daniel said incredulously. "I wouldn't know where to start."

"Just make one up!" Staglione said, his voice growing louder. He furrowed his brow, pondering something deeply as if he were reading the information from the inside of his forehead. "I got it. I know what dis needs. Here's what you're gonna do. Make up a number and say dat da StopShots will save dat many kids if dey're on all da guns in America. I want you to name names. Go get some of dose kid victims from Columbine and say dat kid would still be around today if people used StopShot. Investors will go crazy. We'll even offer to donate some StopShots to da parents at dat school. It's beautiful."

Daniel sat silently, waiting for Vince to finish and thinking how he could best articulate his objection. "Vince, man, we can't just make up a number based on nothing at all," Daniel said, speaking softly. "And we can't use some poor murdered kid's name just to get a little hype. What will their parents think?"

"Who gives a shit?" Staglione roared, standing up. "Da kid's dead … from some friggin' unsafe gun dat dese StopShots would have stopped.

Don't we have a right to say dat?"

"But there's got to be a better way to do that, Vince. We'll be seen as bloodsucking opportunists if we put those dead kids' names in there with made-up numbers. I'm not going to do that." Daniel braced himself for Staglione's explosion. He knew it was coming but he couldn't put his name on a press release that said what Staglione was requesting. Kids had been shot in drive-bys at Daniel's high school, guys he played football with, and he couldn't imagine their parents seeing their murdered children's names used so avariciously and blithely.

"YOU'RE GONNA DO WHAT THE FUCK I TELL YOU, KID!" Staglione screamed across the desk so that Dan was sure he felt Vince's breath. Staglione's crooked bottom teeth were openly displayed as he exploded, and spit shot from his mouth on the hard consonants. "I just gave you a quarter of a million dollars and you've gotta new house, son. You're not in a position to be Mr. Integrity."

"I'm not writing that, Vince," Daniel replied as calmly as he could despite the adrenaline coursing through his being. "I can't be a part of that." Vince twisted his face into an expression of pure ferocity, like a prize fighter during the referee's pre-fight instructions.

"I'M NOT DOING IT!" Daniel shouted and headed for the door. Staglione stood up and moved aggressively to the door as well, reaching outward, intent on blocking Daniel's exit. As he reached to do so, Staglione's hand found a softer substance than the door frame he had expected. Al was standing in the doorway and had wrapped his huge brown hand around Staglione's fist, consuming it like a boa constrictor swallowing a rat.

"What the fuck are you doin' here?" Staglione hollered as he tried unsuccessfully to remove his hand from Al's grasp.

"You raise your voice at me again and I'm gonna put this hand of yours down your fucking throat," Al said sternly. "I've had it with you trying to intimidate people."

"LET ME GO! YOU'RE FIRED!" Staglione screamed. "DODDIE, CALL

SECURITY!"

Daniel was paralyzed, not sure what to do to quell the situation ... or if he even wanted to end the fracas right away. He was still reeling from Staglione's bombast and illicit request.

"I might be fired but you're getting an ass whippin'," Al informed Staglione as he released his hand. Staglione instantly ran to the opposite side of his desk, past Daniel who had been motionless since Staglione's first eruption.

"GET OUTTA HERE!" Staglione ordered. "DODDIE!" It was impossible that Dottie was out of earshot given the volume of the discourse. Instead, she had been corralled into the bullpen by one of Al's boys for her "own protection"—and to prevent her from dialing security.

"This is long overdue," Al said enthusiastically, taking his watch off and putting it in his pocket. Most of the bullpen guys had gathered in the hall, and no one was making an attempt to prevent the pending beating. "You've bullied people around here with your money and your old man muscles, and you're about to get a taste of your own medicine."

Staglione didn't know what to do. Al was the only man in the office who could take a physical stand with him and he was bigger and younger. He also seemed to be well-motivated in his desire to pummel Staglione. As Al rounded the desk Staglione quivered, literally hiding behind Daniel.

"Al, don't do it, man," Daniel said.

"Two minutes ago this jackass is screaming at the top of his lungs at you and you're gonna defend him?" Al asked incredulously. "Why don't you stop selling out, Dan?"

Daniel knew that Al was right, at least in regard to the selling out part. But Daniel had new responsibilities that Al didn't. Staglione hadn't actually put his hands on Daniel, which even Daniel knew would be unbearable, but a tirade might have to be suffered to make the note. "You're right, man. You're right," Daniel agreed as the trio circled the desk in an odd orbit. Staglione was eyeing the door to make a break away.

"I was just telling him that I wouldn't do something when you came in here. That's why he was yelling, bro," Daniel explained. Al's opinion mattered to him, even more so given Al's coming to his aid just now.

"It ain't worth it, Dan," Al said, his pause causing Staglione to stand still as well, maintaining the desk as a barrier. "No money's worth working for this washed-up, morally bankrupt idiot. I'd rather pick fruit."

Staglione started to speak, finding it impossible to not respond to the undressing Al was giving him. "You son-of-a—"

"Vince!" Daniel interrupted. "Shut up or he's gonna kill you." Staglione abided the warning.

Al had pursed his lips, clenching his teeth in a cosmetic expression of his frustration. "You're lucky he's here, Vinny," Al informed his former boss. "Because if he wasn't, I'd throw you out the window and let the road crews clean the grease spot."

With that, Al turned and headed for the door. The bullpen guys parted quickly, providing the enormous man with a wide berth in which to take his leave. As he reached the door, Daniel called out to him without regard to Staglione's presence in his own office. "Thanks, man," Daniel said sincerely. "I appreciate it."

Al turned and stared first at Staglione and then Daniel. "Get out of this shithole as soon as you can, Danny," Al said. "This isn't what you're meant to do." He turned back to Staglione and locked his eyes on Vince's shaking frame. "If I hear you raised your voice to anyone in this office ever again, I'm going to wait for you in the parking lot," he said. "There won't be any warning."

Al walked down the hall and got his jacket from his desk. He grabbed his coffee mug, threw a couple of pieces of paper in the trash, and walked silently out of V.S.E.'s office. Staglione sank back into his chair, the sweat circles under his arms having grown so large that they nearly connected. His face was expressionless and his body flaccid.

"I'm going to put the first release out that I wrote, Vince. It's the right thing to do. And then I'm going to take the rest of the afternoon off,"

Daniel informed Staglione, who stared blankly out the window.

Daniel returned to his office, gathered his keys and cell phone, and walked out of the offices as Al had just moments before. Dottie re-emerged from the bullpen and knocked on Vince's closed and locked door. "Mr. Staglione? Are you all right?"

As Daniel waited for the elevator, tears gathered in his eyes. He wasn't sure if it was because of what Staglione had said and done to him today, or because of what the last ten minutes had revealed about his character.

CHAPTER 17

The rough combustion of the Mustang's engine resonated through the interior of the vehicle as Daniel drove with the radio off. His thoughts refused to abandon the altercation and the guilt he felt because Al had lost his job and he still had one. It didn't make sense to go home to his empty house with options limited to the talk shows exploiting wayward teens, fatherless babies, or people living with deformities. He couldn't handle that today.

Instead, he steered the car to the Wendell Street Lounge, a pub in a lower middle-class neighborhood that had been around as long as Daniel could remember. When he was a boy, his father would take him there for a hamburger and a Coke, and the old men regulars in their turquoise bolo ties would make the football-crazy kid name the coaches of all the teams in the league or recite stats he'd memorized from the backs of trading cards. Over the years, the pub had aged with the neighborhood around it and would often be populated by a peculiar blend of construction workers, schoolteachers, and the occasional shady inhabitant. Its tourist-free environment kept the place local and "Old Vegas."

That was what Daniel felt he needed, something old and familiar. He parked his Mustang around back as he had a hundred times and walked in the rear entrance. A rush of secondhand smoke and the odor of cooking French fries welcomed Daniel to the venue as always and he took a seat at a corner of the bar where there were no gaming machines. A neon sign flickered irregularly above, signaling its imminent demise. An older woman with enormous reading glasses deftly poked the illuminated buttons of a bartop poker machine like Liberace, processing the hand's value with speed and efficiency. A cue ball and an eight ball sat alone on the green felt of the pool table where two Las Vegas police officers ate complimentary Philly cheesesteaks at a nearby high-top.

Rudy, the day shift bartender, was washing bourbon glasses in the sink and chatting with a silver-haired gentleman at the center of the bar, nodding in agreement. Daniel looked up at the television to see a Cubs-Pirates game at Wrigley Field and wondered if his dad was watching it at home. Rudy turned and greeted Daniel with a warm handshake, catching up with him in just a few questions, an art form perfected by bartenders. Daniel didn't have the stomach to eat but settled for a draft beer and some peanuts, figuring he'd catch enough of the game to be conversational with his dad later that night.

Daniel's dad followed the Pirates as if each game was for the pennant despite the fact that the small-market team was generally out of the race by the end of May, unable to compete with the likes of the New York Mets and their enormous payroll. The Pirates were much like the Wendell Street Lounge for Daniel, a portal to a different, easier time. Rudy slid a draft to Daniel, who took a deep drink. Three chairs down, the silver-haired man had ordered another and Rudy was again nodding his assent.

"You a lawyer, kid?" the man near shouted to Daniel over the ringing of the older gal's four-of-a-kind.

"Me?" Daniel asked, startled by the query. "Far from it."

"Whaddya do, son?" the man asked, sliding over one chair and lowering his voice proportionately. His voice had the erudite lilt of the old newsreel narrators.

"I'm a writer," Daniel begrudgingly told the man, who appeared to be in his seventies, as he stared at the TV screen.

"Well, whaddya write?" the man asked.

"Do we know each other, sir?" Daniel said coldly, attempting to signal his desire for solitude.

"I doubt it," the man answered. "I've never been here before."

Daniel studied the man briefly. He was well-groomed and his suit was pressed and clean. Only the loosened tie around his neck prevented him from passing military inspection. Daniel wondered if he were a lounge singer or high-roller casino host. He certainly wasn't shy.

"Name's Randolph Hart, but you can call me Randy," he said, extending his hand. "So, whaddya write?"

"My name's Daniel Madison," Daniel consented as they shook. "And I write PR mostly … for politicians, companies, whoever's paying, I guess." The last admonition seemed to come from somewhere under Daniel's conscious mind, a confession he was making to the man and himself.

"I'll bet you're good," Randy surmised with a friendly tenor.

"I'm all right," Daniel said, thinking this wasn't what he came here for, to pass the time with an overdressed old man who'd soon segue to "in my day" diatribes. He tried to act as if he were truly interested in the ball game. Daniel had finished his beer now, downing it much more quickly than he usually did.

"Rudy, send my friend Daniel another beer on me," Randy instructed the bartender. Rudy pulled the tap and carried the full beer to Daniel.

"From the gentleman," Rudy said like a maître d' at a fancy restaurant.

Daniel held the beer up in token gratitude and nodded his insincere appreciation. A four-dollar draft wasn't going to make Daniel become an engaging conversationalist—not on a day like today.

"So, I see you like the Cubs," Randy guessed.

"Actually, I'm more of a Pirates fan," Daniel replied, wondering where Al was right now. He considered how Al was the kind of guy he wanted to be in a lot of ways … sincere, loyal, a man of conviction. But that only worked in comic books and Greek tragedies. Daniel worried about how Al would get by until he found another job.

"About the only thing less fortunate than being a Pirates fan is being a Cubs fan," Randy said. "Then again, I used to watch Roberto Clemente play right field for the Pirates. Saw him play my Cubbies at Wrigley. Nothing like him in the world. He could do it all. You kids talk about this Air Jordan, but you never saw Clemente. The things he could do. And I'm from Chicago. I love Michael Jordan. But Clemente was something else."

Here we go, Daniel thought. *Now I gotta suffer through the generational gap shit.* Randy was looking at him, awaiting his reply to the Clemente remark.

"He was great, I'm sure," Daniel replied reluctantly. "My dad talks about him."

Daniel turned the chair toward Randy, and looked at him seriously. "Randy, it's nice to meet you and I appreciate the beer, but I've had a heck of a day. My boss screamed at me, my friend got fired, and I'm not sure I like who I am right now. I just want to have a beer in peace and watch a little bit of this game."

Randy put his palms up like a twenty-one dealer changing tables. "No problem, kid. No problem." Randy withdrew a long wallet from his suit jacket's interior pocket and threw a crisp hundred on the bar. "Rudy, it was nice speaking with you this afternoon. And if you don't mind, buy this young writer another beer whenever he's ready."

"Young man, it was nice speaking with you too," Randy said as he stood up. "I hope your day gets better."

"Thanks, Randy," Daniel said, feeling a little guilty now that Randy was leaving. "I'm sorry that I'm a little out of sorts." Rudy brought another draft over as Randall Hart exited the Wendell Street Lounge.

"Seems like a nice guy, Rudy," Daniel said, attempting to explain his curt behavior with the affable older man. "I'm just not in the mood for chit-chat."

"I'm not mad atcha," Rudy said in his usual warm and congenial manner. If Rudy hadn't become a bartender, he'd have been perfect as a doorman in a New York apartment building, amiably greeting strangers and friends alike. "I think he just wanted to talk and take his mind off things," Rudy explained, getting Daniel a fresh bowl of peanuts. "He was on the way back from a funeral."

"Aah, that's what the suit was for," Daniel said. "I thought he might have been a lounge act or something."

"Nah, he told me he's retired Air Force," Rudy said. "He said his wife died Monday and they buried her this morning at the cemetery by your old high school. He stopped here on his way home."

"You're kidding me," Daniel said, his heart sinking deep into his stomach. "That guy just buried his wife this morning?"

"Yeah," Rudy confirmed. "He had one of those little programs from the funeral in his hand. He kept looking at it until you got here. Looked like a yearbook picture on it from waaaayyyy back. Pretty girl with that big foo-foo hair from the forties, you know."

"Awwwh shit, Rudy," Daniel lamented. "I ran that poor guy off and he just put his wife in the ground?"

"He said they were married fifty years," Rudy said. "You don't see that too often these days."

Rudy turned to get another vodka for the woman playing the slots and Daniel was gone, a twenty-dollar bill on the bar top where he'd been seated. He was angry at himself for his rudeness. The fact that he didn't know the man's situation was of little consolation. He had hardly expected his day would get worse by stopping at the bar, but it had, and he wasn't sure what could change the vibe.

Fifty years, Daniel kept thinking. *What's he going to do now? How do you find something to replace fifty years?*

Daniel pulled into his driveway and tried to open the garage door, which was non-responsive. "Figures," Daniel muttered as he half-slammed the Mustang's driver door and walked up the pathway to his house. He turned the key to the lock and walked in, setting his keys in an old cigar ashtray by the door. The answering machine blinked rapidly and Daniel wondered if it was broken too. He pushed play and the only audible tone was the sound of someone hanging up. *Why don't people leave messages anymore?* Daniel thought. His parents were notorious for calling and not hanging up completely, allowing his answering machine to capture an argument about how best to cook meatloaf or a discussion of how Daniel wasn't ever home anymore.

But it was not his mother or father this time. The caller ID read

"Private Caller," just as it had in the car at Red Rock the other day. Eleven non-verbal hang-up calls had been left. *Who the hell is doing this?* Daniel wondered, trying to think whom he might have pissed off. Behind him he heard a noise inside his house and he turned quickly. Daniel noticed the television was on with "MUTE" on the display. He was positive it hadn't been so when he left that morning.

Daniel grabbed a steak knife from a drawer in the adjacent kitchen and began to search the house, heading for the bedroom first. The only things of value to him were in there. The bathroom light lit his bedroom dimly and he reached for the wall switch.

"Why don't you put that down before you get into trouble with it?" came a familiar voice from the darkness.

Daniel recognized Sydney's voice instantly, and his intruder fears were instantly abated. As he drew closer to the bed he could see her there in one of his old fraternity rush shirts and only that. He pushed open the cracked bathroom door to allow more light to illuminate the room and Sydney.

"I was going to surprise you at work but they told me you left early," Sydney said. "I asked them if you were sick and the girl told me that wasn't the reason. Is everything all right?"

"No, not really," Daniel replied, using her nudity to wash the bitter morning away if but momentarily. "I'll tell you all about it later." Daniel kicked off his shoes and lay down next to her, his right leg crossing over both her slim thighs. She buried her head, chin, and mouth into his neck.

"You know, Syd, when I'm with you, I really just don't have any problems," Daniel said out loud, revealing more than he did normally.

"That's what I want to hear," Sydney said, extricating herself and climbing on top of him. "Because even when I'm not with you, Daniel Madison, I don't have any problems. Just knowing I'm going to see you is enough." Sydney held Daniel's wrists and controlled the intercourse from above, not allowing him to reach for the condom in the top drawer of the nightstand.

"Syd, be careful," Daniel warned half-heartedly as she enveloped him. "We don't need any surprises right now."

"Don't worry, Dan," she countered. "I started taking the pill a few days ago. We'll be fine." With that she stopped speaking until they both were ready to rest. She had fallen asleep against him and though his arm was numb he couldn't believe how good it felt to have her there. Sydney was the antidote for Staglione, the old man at the bar, and the way he felt about himself. An hour later the phone rang in the bedroom, awakening them both. Daniel gently pried Sydney from him and reached for the phone.

"Hello?" Daniel greeted. Again there was nothing on the other end save the static of an open line. Daniel repeated his hello once more and then set the phone handset down next to the base.

"Who was that?" Sydney asked.

"Somebody keeps calling me and hanging up ... or laughing," Daniel said. "It's the weirdest thing."

"Do they ever say anything?" Sydney asked, growing concerned.

"No, they just call and sit there ... or they hang up on my answering machine."

"How long has it been going on?" Sydney inquired, her questions becoming more pointed.

"About a week or so," Daniel said. "It doesn't happen every day, but when it does, it goes on for a while. That's why I took my phone off the hook. I'll get my numbers changed tomorrow. That'll stop it."

"No, it won't," Sydney said seriously. "He'll just get it again."

"Who will?" Daniel asked, disturbed immediately. "Who will get my number?"

"My ex-boyfriend, Danny," Sydney said apologetically. "I'm so sorry you got dragged into it."

"What are you talking about?"

"I used to date a guy named Clint Zigler, of the Zigler Ziglers," Sydney explained, pulling her hair up with a tortoise-shell clip. "You know, the family that owns The Unicorn and a bunch of other stuff in Vegas. Anyway, he went back to college after we had a little summer romance and we just sort of grew apart. So I ended it and started dating a little here and there.

"Well, he graduates and comes back to town to start working in the family business and he starts calling me over and over again, trying to get back together and I wasn't interested anymore. Everything with him was about money and sex and it was fun to be courted like that and eat at the nicest places ... but when he came back I saw him for what he was, a spoiled little man with a sense of entitlement and a bad temper."

"I know who he is," Daniel said. "We're about the same age and I had friends that went to private school with him. He's a dick."

"Yes, he is," Sydney agreed. "But he's a rich dick and he's not used to being told no. If it wasn't for Teena threatening to kill him if she sees him, he'd be at my house every night. It's been over a year since we split and he won't let go."

"So you think it's him calling me?" Daniel asked, growing angry that Zigler was targeting him for nothing.

"I know it's him," Sydney said. "He told me that he was going to deal with you."

"Why didn't you tell me this, Syd?" Daniel asked, standing up, growing angry at the lie of omission.

"I was going to, Daniel," she said, taking his hand and guiding him back to the bed. "But I didn't want to say anything until you liked me more. I didn't want him to run you off, and if I told you right after we met, you might have thought I wasn't worth it. It's happened before."

She put her head down, bit her lip, and looked back at him, "I wanted to be worth it."

"Sydney," Daniel said in a half-scold, half-affectionate way. "You shoulda told me."

"I think he's harmless for the most part, Daniel," Sydney consoled. "He usually just does the hang-up thing to get under your skin. But it works. That's how he ran off my last boyfriend."

"How does he even know we're dating?"

"He told me he saw your car at my house," Sydney answered reluctantly. "He said he ran the plates through a cop buddy. He knows your name, where you live, everything."

"Fantastic," Daniel said. "Give me his number, Sydney. I'll call and get this out in the open."

"Don't do that, Daniel," Sydney pleaded. "That's exactly what he wants. Please, can we just ignore him? Just for now?" Sydney squeezed his hand and wrapped her bare leg across his thighs.

"We'll see," Daniel answered, pondering how best to deal with yet another problem.

"Honey, don't let this ruin your day," Sydney said, not knowing yet what his day had entailed. "Think about how good we are together … how good we feel together." She was in full charm mode and it melted Daniel instantly.

"Let's go have some dinner, Danny," Sydney suggested.

"I don't feel like going anywhere, Syd," Daniel replied.

"Good," she said smartly. "Because I have a pot roast almost done in your oven."

Daniel smiled and located the smell of a cooking pot roast from the air. "How'd you get in here anyway?" he said, realizing she didn't have a key.

"Your daddy loaned me his key," Sydney said proudly. "He loves me."

"I'll bet he does," Daniel agreed, knowing his father would indeed love for his son to be dating the daughter of a respected businessman. "Where's your car?"

"In the garage," Sydney said. "I wanted to surprise you."

"That you did, Sydney," Daniel confirmed, referring to more than just her unexpected entry.

CHAPTER 18

November 2000

The phone rang incessantly at the Madison residence, and Daniel finally took his home phone off the hook just to prevent the disturbance. His cell phone also had become useless as Zigler left dead air messages over and over again. Daniel created a work-around for the short term, having Sydney and some of his other friends Instant Message him on the computer, requesting his call. In this manner he could still be reached by most, but it created a problem with his parents, who weren't exactly Internet aficionados. In Daniel's last attempt to teach his father how to e-mail, the elder Madison continued to refer to the computer as "the TV." Because of this Daniel made a point of calling his parents proactively and in doing so was forced to reveal the source of the problem. His father had become infuriated once he knew, telling Daniel that the Zigler kid came from "bad stock" and that "he'd kick his father's ass if it continued."

Daniel calmed his cantankerous father, who didn't need any extra agitation as he headed into his seventies, telling him he would talk to Mike Martin about the harassment. Martin generally knew or could make a call to the more important business leaders in the area. In reality, Daniel had no intentions of doing so yet, fearing Martin would use the episode to embolden his "Sydney's a gold digger" warning.

Other than the telephonic intrusion, life had been a lot easier the past few days. Staglione seemed to have been humbled by the blow-out and the stock was up precipitously, approaching a glittering dollar per share. The atmosphere was the most pleasant it had ever been at V.S.E., and Daniel was marking X's on the calendar like a kid in December, imagining what he would do with all the money when the one-year restriction on the sale of his StopShot stock was over. He hadn't told

Sydney about it, fearing at least a little that the new money might change things between them given Martin's previous remarks.

Most importantly, today was Election Day, and every indication and poll suggested that Julian Correa would become the city's youngest-ever county commissioner. Daniel expected today's triumph to be a watershed for them all; Julian would be a commissioner, Martin a proven maker of men, and Daniel an election-winning speechwriter. He and Sydney would meet everyone this evening at the election night gala at the Tropicana Hotel, where supporters, candidates, and dignitaries would meet to hopefully celebrate the party's collective victories.

The early November air was resplendent with the fall smell of wood-burning fireplaces and a gentle chill enough to beckon sweaters from the dresser. Leaves began their deathly descent from the mulberry trees, and yards traded their green luster for the brittle yellows of the coming winter. Daniel picked Sydney up around seven p.m. at her home, her one-off Italian-made powder blue gown a socioeconomic contradiction to his venerable Mustang and borrowed sport coat. Sydney regularly made a point of calling his car "a classic" or "muscle car" in a disarming attempt to spin its considerable age and deteriorating condition but the fact that she did so reminded him that it was also always on her mind. He just needed the old car to last until the restriction came off the StopShot shares and he could purchase a newer ride, maybe even keeping and restoring the Mustang that had served him for so long.

Sydney took a seat as Daniel shut her door, smiling her appreciation for the chivalrous gesture. As Daniel walked behind the vehicle he noticed a shimmering silver Ferrari with darkly tinted windows ease slowly a few doors down her street.

"Gonna be a big night," Daniel said enthusiastically as he fired up the engine. "Should be a lot of fun."

"I'm so happy for you, Daniel," Sydney said sweetly. "How long until you can quit V.S.E.?"

"Not sure, Syd," Daniel answered as they navigated toward the

Tropicana. "I need to get the job with Julian first. I can't afford to quit until that job is in the bag."

"He'd better give you a job considering all you've done for him," Sydney said.

"It was mutually beneficial, Sydney," Daniel responded. "I've already gotten a lot out of knowing Julian."

"He's so busy thinking of himself, Daniel, I don't know if he has any idea how good you are."

"He knows we work well together. He's appreciative," Daniel said. "Why can't you ease up on the guy?"

"How much time do you have?" she answered sarcastically. "I've got more than a couple reasons, not the least of which is that I know two different girls whose hearts he's broken."

"You never mentioned that before," Daniel said, surprised by her selective revelations yet again. "Who'd he do that to?"

Daniel knew that what Sydney said was probably true. It fit Julian's womanizing modus operandi, and it explained Sydney's attitude toward Julian the night they all first met.

"Just a couple girls I know," Sydney said. "Same story with both of them: He charms them, makes them fall in love, and then dumps them when he gets bored. I wouldn't have such a big problem with it if he didn't spend so much time telling them how they were meant to be together. He's just a letch."

"Well, try and get along with the letch tonight, please," Daniel said. "It's a big night for all of us."

"Of course," Sydney agreed. "Isn't that what a politician's wife does?"

"I'm not a politician," he corrected with a smile, loving that she had referred to herself as his wife.

They parked the Mustang around the back of the hotel and walked through the casino. As they neared the banquet room, they heard a chorus of cheers coming through the double doors. The walls were full of campaign posters and the red, white, and blue ribbons used for the Fourth of July and election nights.

"And with eighty-two percent of precincts reporting, Julian Correa leads his opponent with sixty-six percent of the vote!" an amplified voice boomed through the banquet room. A reciprocal roar came from the crowd. The room looked like Mardi Gras sans the bare breasts as champagne, plates of food, and exuberant revelers raucously approved of the reported results. Everyone Daniel knew with any relationship to politics was on hand, looking to celebrate successful candidacies. These nights were always bittersweet, though, with losses suffered inevitably. The magnums of champagne would serve both causes.

Daniel and Sydney spotted Mike Martin, and Martin gave a welcoming wave as they drew near. "We're looking good, Daniel," Martin proclaimed. "The tough precincts are in and he's looking strong. It's just a matter of time."

"That's fantastic, Mike," Daniel said, grasping his hand. "Congratulations. I know what you put into this race."

"I just wish he did," Martin lamented. "If he knew about half of the shrapnel I've taken to protect him, I'd be satisfied. But he's such a hotheaded prick I don't even tell him most of what I've got to do to get him elected."

"I'm sure he has an idea," Daniel said. "We probably don't know half the stuff he does either." Sydney turned and stared at Daniel, not accustomed to hearing him out of character as Julian's protector and apologist. "Where is he?" Daniel inquired. "Shouldn't he be here?"

"I guess he's planning on making an entrance," Martin sighed with eyebrows raised. "He's probably in a room upstairs ... working on his speech."

Julian was riding the Tropicana's elevators down, having descended from a suite that he'd been given. From there he could watch the election returns until he knew he was safely ahead, with no risk of suffering in public. He had done so alone.

As Julian entered the hotel's lobby a woman in front of him dropped a folder full of papers, scattering them everywhere. She bent to retrieve them, careful to not expose herself in her form-fitting burgundy evening gown. Brown curls fell against her cheeks as she leaned over the mess.

"Let me help you there," Julian offered, collecting the loose paper alongside her.

"Thank you," she said. "That's very kind of you."

"Not a problem," Julian said. "A woman in a dress like that shouldn't be anywhere near a dirty floor."

"Too late for that," she said, laughing. "I guess you didn't notice the tire track on my skirt."

"Not with legs like you've got."

She paused to acknowledge Julian's forward remark with a grin, seemingly surprised and a little embarrassed.

"I'm Julian Correa," he said proudly.

"Meredith Jensen," she said, shaking his hand with two free fingers as she gathered the paperwork. "You're the commissioner, right?"

"Almost," Julian said with a smile.

"I'm on my way to the election party. I'm guessing that's where you're going as well," Meredith said.

"That's right," Julian said. "So, how'd you get the tire track? You ride a hawg?"

"Not exactly," she said. "I'm a doctor, and on the way over here a little boy got hit in the crosswalk by the car in front of me. He's fine but I had to stop and check him out. Wound up being a few bumps and bruises … and a flat tire which he inadvertently rubbed against my gown. *Que sera.*"

"Well, that was very kind of you," Julian said. "Not enough people in the world like you."

She smiled warmly as she stood up, papers back in her folder. "Well, thank you for your help, Mr. Correa," Meredith said. "I hope you win tonight."

"Me too," Julian replied as he tried to think of a way to capitalize. "Maybe I'll come see you if I get sick."

"Well, I'm a pediatrician," she said. "So, I'm not sure how that will work."

"Hmmmn," Julian stalled. "I'm pretty immature. Maybe we can make it happen."

"Maybe we can," she agreed congenially, handing him a business card with her name and office number, surrounded by multicolored children's hand prints.

When they approached the front door, Dr. Jensen paused to place her name on a *Hello, My Name Is* tag laying on a table near the entrance. Julian declined the label and surveyed the front part of the room for Amber, who had been waiting for almost an hour, shifting awkwardly from foot to foot. She'd been wondering where he was, picturing carnal activities in her increasingly suspicious mind. As always, when he arrived and kissed her cheek she forgave him and assuaged her lingering doubts with the splendor of his presence.

"Where the hell is Julian?" Mike wondered out loud as he searched the room.

"Keep your pants on, Mike," Julian said, coming up behind the group. "I'm right here. I just had to pick up a victory cigar from the gift shop." Amber trailed Julian only slightly and he let go of her hand as he entered the assemblage. "I tried to call you to tell you I was running behind, Danny, but your phone was turned off."

"Long story," Daniel said. "You're here now. That's all that matters." At the main entrance, Daniel saw a red-faced Annie coming through the door in labored fashion, carrying something in a large plastic case. Her twelve-year-old son, Joshua, was also carting a plastic container of some sort, though he seemed to be doing so with greater ease than his sweating mother. Daniel excused himself from the circle and strode toward Annie, intent on helping her with her load.

"Howdy, Annie," Daniel said as he took the case by the handle. "You working for U-Haul today?"

"Just some voter registration stuff that Working Women needed me to bring from the office," she said, panting. "Jack is at a conference in D.C., so Josh and I get to be the mules. Of course, nobody said it was sixty pounds."

"It's every bit of that," Daniel agreed. "Hey, Josh. How are you, buddy?"

"I'm good," Josh replied demurely. He had his mother's complexion, but lacked her outgoing nature. His glasses and round face gave him the appearance of a blond Harry Potter. Annie had tried to get him to play sports, even asking Daniel to take him out for a little one-on-one once while her husband was up north at the legislative session in Carson City. But it clearly wasn't for Josh, and he and Daniel had instead gone to a movie. Annie said soon after how much Josh appreciated not being forced to do anything and that he liked Daniel.

"I gotta sit down," Annie informed Daniel and he quickly retrieved a folding chair. "I got caught in traffic in the Spaghetti Bowl and had to literally run to make it here," Annie said. "Have they done the final precincts?"

"Should be any time now according to Martin," Daniel answered.

"Annie, I need to get back to my date ... and Julian," Daniel explained. "I'll see you in a little bit. Take a break for a minute, would ya?"

"Josh, pal. Can you get your mom a bottled water?" Daniel suggested.

"Sure, Daniel," Josh said.

Daniel walked briskly back to Sydney, Julian, and Amber. Mike Martin had been called away, presumably to prepare for the announcement of confirmed winners on stage. Julian was brimming, eager to take the stage and read his acceptance speech.

"Almost there, my brother," Julian beamed, hugging Daniel lightly.

"It's in the bank, Julian," Daniel said. "You deserve it. Drink it in, man."

Sydney seemed focused on other people in the room and hadn't said much, greeting Julian and Amber with a weak nod when they arrived. Daniel wondered if it was the mention of his phone being turned off that had soured her mood.

A waiter came by and everyone took a champagne flute from the tray.

Near the stage, Mike Martin was being handed cards with the night's results on them. "Ladies and gentlemen, may I have your attention!" Martin effused into the microphone. "I believe I have some results you may be interested in." The crowd fell silent in anticipation, as if someone had paused the once-percolating group.

"Tonight, the Sacramento Kings defeated the Los Angeles Lakers by a score of 101 to 96. That is all," he said straight-faced and feigned leaving the stage. The crowd growled a collective groan, which bloomed into a laugh. Most were not accustomed to seeing Martin playful. Julian was licking his lips and nervously putting his hands in his pockets and taking them out as he awaited the formal declaration of his victory ... and the attention that would surely follow.

"Just kidding!" Martin said, laughing just a little and holding a sheet of paper up above his head. "I do in fact have the *election* results you all desire."

"With one hundred percent of the precincts now reporting, I am most proud to announce that Clark County has a new leader. Ladies and gentlemen, please welcome Commissioner-elect JULIAN CORREA!"

Julian turned and shook Daniel's hand and then hugged him so ferociously that Daniel's feet came off the floor for a moment. Amber stepped forward to embrace her date as well, but Correa never acknowledged her, shaking hands with all those nearby. Daniel had never seen Julian this jubilant and wondered what a feeling it must be to reach this public zenith, to come from the poverty he had endured and to survive the perils of a campaign ... and himself.

Julian seemed a foot taller than those around him as he walked through the middle of the crowd, purposely taking the most difficult and populated path. Julian lived for this attention, the approval and affirmation. He'd envisioned this day for a long, long time, thinking about it on the boiling-hot walks through constituent neighborhoods or the time he spent glad-handing the deep-pocket crowd for donations. It also got him through the reamings he'd taken from men like Frank Hayes over and over again.

It was all worth it, Julian thought. *They can never take this away from me.*

Julian joined Martin onstage eventually, sharing a warm hug as Martin whispered in Julian's ear. Daniel wondered what Martin might be saying, but he felt confident as to the subject matter.

"I will," Correa mouthed in affirmation as he turned to walk to the microphone above his celebrating supporters.

"Wow!" Julian exclaimed, breaking the ongoing applause from the group. "Man, this feels good! Thank you all so much!"

"I've got a lot I want to say to all of you," Julian said, seeming genuinely appreciative of the crowd's adulation. Sydney and Daniel were holding each other closely. Sydney was pleased for Daniel despite her trepidation regarding Julian. She knew this was good for him ... and maybe for her too. As they moved closer to the stage, Daniel reached out for Amber's hand. She had been riveted to Julian's form—as usual—and Daniel didn't want to leave her there in the back alone. Amber put her hand in his and followed them, thankful to be included.

They circled around the back of the crowd to get near the stage, avoiding Julian's populist route. As they passed the front entrance, Daniel saw Annie, still shiny from glistening sweat and blank-faced. He knew immediately something wasn't right as she appeared to be hyperventilating. Josh was holding her hand, unsure what to do. As Daniel released both Sydney and Amber's hands he saw Annie fall to her right, landing awkwardly on her side. He could hear the tiny breaths coming from her mouth like little hisses as he knelt next to her.

"SOMEBODY GET SOME HELP!" Daniel screamed, loud enough to turn nearly every head in the room. "CALL 911!"

Daniel rolled Annie to her back as her eyes rotated toward the top of their orbit. She had lost consciousness now and her breaths were almost inaudible. One leg bent awkwardly under her, twisted in the fall from the chair. Joshua was frozen and standing with both hands in his hair, as if squeezing his own head.

Julian had stopped speaking as most of those who had been listening were now watching the woman in the back fighting for her life. Dr. Jensen had joined Daniel and was checking her dwindling respiration and heart rate. Daniel looked up and shouted again for someone to call 911 as the young doctor began CPR, violently pressing Annie's chest as her skin color grew whiter and whiter.

"Come on, Mom," Joshua said solemnly, neither yelling nor crying the words. He smacked one hand into his other nervously, watching the battle for his mother's life five feet in front of him.

Daniel noticed Joshua and called for Sydney. She knelt at Daniel's side as he held Annie's hand. "Take Josh outside," he instructed. "He doesn't need to see this."

Sydney walked around Annie and took Josh by the arm. He resisted at first, calmly repeating "Come on, Mom," as he watched a stranger give her air.

On stage, Julian remained as if he expected the life-and-death situation to be quickly cleaned and removed like a streaker at a football game. By the time the ambulance arrived twenty minutes later, Daniel was terrified that any successful effort to resuscitate his friend and mentor would result in the awakening of a woman who had suffered massive brain damage from the time she had been without oxygen. Dr. Jensen had given her CPR and breathed air into her lungs, but she couldn't get Annie breathing on her own.

Sydney peeked around the doorway from the hall where Josh sat with his head in his hands. When the paramedics sprinted past him with his mother on the gurney, tears began to flow. Daniel ran behind Annie and the paramedics, instructing Sydney to have Martin call Annie's husband to tell him what had happened and that he was taking Josh to the hospital.

Julian sat down on the stage, his moment lost. A tray of champagne flutes sat next to him where a waiter had left them when Annie fell. Julian picked one up and drank its contents. Most of the crowd had milled out into the hall, trailing Annie from a distance and chatting about how terrible it was to have this happen in front of her son. Within fifteen minutes of her departure in the ambulance, the room was nearly empty, the evening finished.

Sydney found Martin, who followed Daniel's instructions and called Annie's husband in D.C., awakening the man on Eastern Standard Time. Mike went to the stage and consoled Julian, who seemed genuinely disturbed by the event.

"Are you close to Annie?" Martin asked, preparing to console Julian, who he knew had gone to college where Annie taught.

"Not particularly, Mike," Correa replied. "I really don't know her that well."

"Well, congratulations, Julian," Martin said awkwardly. "You are now a county commissioner."

"Yeah, that's true," Julian agreed, his somber tone more indicative of a personal defeat than an event he'd anticipated so greatly that he hadn't slept last night. Sydney returned from the hallway where she had gone to take a call. When she re-entered the hall, only Julian and Martin remained.

"Mike, Julian," Sydney said somberly. "That was Daniel. Annie didn't make it."

Martin lowered his head, looking despondent and distressed. "I've got to go," he said. "I need to get down to the hospital. You know, she was the first person out here to befriend me. And you both know how much she means to Daniel."

Neither Sydney nor Julian said a word. She sat a few feet from Correa, who was staring at the confetti and torn streamers on the floor. She looked at him and saw for the first time a man devoid of bravado, ironically, on his most triumphant day. "I'm sorry," she said, recognizing his loss too. Without acknowledging the remark he handed her one of the flutes of champagne from the silver tray and loosened his tie. Where Amber had gone neither of them knew, especially since Julian had completely forgotten she was there.

CHAPTER 19

"**S**hit," Julian bemoaned, altogether too loudly considering that Sydney was but the length of a drink tray from him. "I cannot believe that happened tonight of all frickin' nights."

"It's really unfortunate," Sydney said. "That poor little boy. Did you see him? He was just sitting there, pleading for his mom to pull through. I'll never get that image out of my mind. Never."

"This isn't how I pictured it all," Julian said, holding a champagne flute and gesturing toward the empty hall. "I thought this would be the night I never wanted to end—a giant party, the whole election stress behind me … everyone would be here celebrating. It was supposed to be *my* night.

"And instead, a lady who eats too much has a heart attack in the middle of my speech," Julian continued in a tone that barely contained the disgust inside him. "I am just about to give my victory speech and this woman is on the floor in the back, making a scene."

"Annie died, Julian," Sydney said. "She didn't plan it. Her heart stopped."

"You're right," Julian agreed, sitting up straight and gathering another flute. "You know, I get in trouble for my honesty. But I never really liked her. And I know she didn't like me."

"Really?" Sydney asked, surprised by Julian's revelation. "I kinda felt the same way. Well, I guess neither one of us better say this to Daniel. He had her on a pedestal."

"He has *you* on a pedestal," Julian corrected with a wry grin, tapping her champagne glass with his own. "So how come you don't like me?" Julian asked, relaxing a little.

"Who said I don't like you?" Sydney deflected.

"Someone has to say it?" Julian chided. "I know when a woman doesn't like me. That is in the rare event it ever happens."

Sydney made a "whatever" face, rolling her eyes in an exaggerated manner.

"Let's just say your reputation preceded you," Sydney explained. "I know a few nice girls you turned into train wrecks."

"Who?" Julian asked curiously.

"Do you remember anyone named Elaine or Wendy?"

"No, not off the top of my head," Julian said honestly.

"I think that's part of the problem," Sydney said. "You don't even remember their names, but they say you broke their hearts."

"Come on," Julian protested, his somber mood ameliorated by discourse that certified his studly self-image. "That's a pretty one-sided view, Sydney. I mean, can you really break a woman's heart … if she doesn't want to have her heart broken?"

"That makes no sense," Sydney said. "What woman wants her heart broken?"

"Women want to feel things," Julian said. "They want passion, love, danger, sadness … they want the roller coaster. You know this."

Sydney said nothing, pondering the veracity of Julian's assertion through her own life experiences.

"You know I'm right," Julian insisted. "If there were no heartbreak, love would have no context." Sydney noticed that Julian looked different up close. His skin was imperfect and his teeth a little crooked. Even though he was defending his philandering, he was also more approachable than she had ever seen him. Perhaps he'd been humbled by the night's debacle.

"You're trying to romanticize the using of women?" Sydney challenged.

"I'm not romanticizing anything," Julian said. "I'm just saying that everyone is in it for what's best for them."

"But you mislead them," she countered. "You tell them that you like them so much and that you can see yourself with them forever."

"Yeah, I do do that," Julian admitted with a guilty smile. "Wow, you really did talk to someone I've been with."

"I wasn't making that up, Julian. I know girls you've hurt."

"I didn't hurt them," Julian said. "They hurt themselves."

"Oh, do go on. How do they hurt themselves?"

"Look, women use *me*," Julian declared. "These women date me, sleep with me, because I fill some fantasy. Do you think they ever consider if they're any good for me? If they are what I really want? Or do they just want some 'Latin love' from a good-looking Cuban boy, or to be able to tell their daddies that they're dating some big-shot politician? So, because I play the part of the fantasy I'm a bad guy? Because it doesn't work out for them forever? Nothing works out forever."

Sydney seemed both troubled and comforted by Julian's revelations, bothered that they might be true and yet pleased that he had come clean to her. "Well, we can agree on that," she said, tapping Julian's glass with a full champagne flute the same way he struck hers previously.

"And that neither one of us much cared for Annie Halpern," Julian said, locking in another connection with Sydney. "Does that make us bad people?"

"Nope," she answered quickly. "That just makes us honest, right?"

"That it does," he agreed, smiling at her.

They chatted for another hour, clearing the plate of champagne flutes and swapping stories from college, politics, and past loves. It seemed the discourse had added dimensions to the flat perceptions each had of the other heading into the night. By the time the custodial crew brought in the industrial vacuums, both were feeling better about the bittersweet evening ... and each other.

"You know, I'm glad we had a chance to talk. Maybe you don't hate me anymore," Julian suggested.

"I never did hate you, Julian," Sydney clarified. "But whatever it was I felt, there's less of it now ... so let's just say I understand you better. Maybe we're not so different."

"I was thinking the same thing," he said. "So when's Danny picking you up?"

"I had forgotten entirely about it," Sydney said. "I was supposed to call him an hour ago. I wonder where he's at. I don't want to bother him. He's probably with Josh. That's best left alone this late at night. I'll call a cab."

"I have a limousine outside," Julian offered. "I had it booked for my big celebration tonight. It's a shame to waste it."

"Are you sure it's not out of your way?" Sydney asked politely.

"It can't be out of my way when I don't know where I'm going," Julian said. "Let's get going before the cleaning crew runs us off. Grab one of those champagne bottles and let's roll."

Sydney did and the two headed for the hotel's main entrance where Julian's limousine was waiting. They looked like the Homecoming Court in their formal wear.

"Commissioner Correa," said the driver as he opened the glossy black door, having heard the election returns while waiting outside. "Congratulations, sir." The title reminded Julian of what he had accomplished, of the journey that had culminated in the night's rewards. It felt like graduation night, Julian thought, a plateau that had been reached, never to be taken away. He was the youngest commissioner ever in this city of opportunity and his choices now were many. People would have to respect him now, whether they liked him or not. This had been a good day.

Sydney slid to the left side of the limo's rear seat, turning the sound system on as she fumbled with the champagne bottle's cork.

"Give me that," Julian said, taking the bottle commandingly.

"Where to, sir?" the limo driver inquired, looking over his right shoulder through the portal between the two compartments.

"Where to?" Julian asked Sydney.

"Let's just cruise the Strip until I've had enough champagne to forget what I saw tonight," Sydney declared, already well ahead of her usual consumption pace. Sydney kicked off a pair of Jimmy Choos and crossed her legs casually on the back seat, seemingly intent on a delayed return to the Banks' property.

"Sounds good to me," Julian said. "Oh shit, where the hell is my date?" They both laughed, realizing that hours had passed and that Julian was just now realizing Amber had been absent for most of the night. "I wonder where she went? That's okay. I was just telling Danny that I'd had it with her."

"Let's not talk about Danny right now," Sydney instructed, changing the air for Julian immediately. "Hand me the bottle, please."

Julian knew the two sentences assembled together formed a dubious invitation. Sure, Sydney was his friend's girl, *but this is who I am*, Julian thought through the champagne. You can tame the lions at the zoo, but if a gazelle is in the cage, it will be eaten. From the African savanna to San Diego, lions always eat gazelles.

As Julian approached with the champagne bottle their lips met, more in a grip than a kiss. In moments their clothing cluttered the narrow floor of the stretch limousine. Both Julian and Sydney realized the window between the driver's cab and the luxury compartment was open … and both wanted it that way, a shared perversion and desire to be seen.

The recklessness would not end there, and the exchange would never have been dubbed romantic. Sydney scratched Julian's back in ways she'd seen in bad eighties movies, and Julian was intent on being better than Daniel, needing to hear he was more powerful, more attractive, and more fulfilling. Why, he wasn't sure.

In the end, it may well have been all those things, and the two slumped into the seat after climax like passengers having survived a plane crash. There was no soft kiss to ease the withdrawal of their union, no wanton gaze to seal the joining of souls or other cinematic themes. Instead, there was the shared pragmatism of two people in a willful act to be excused as the byproduct of the free-flowing champagne in future revisionist history.

"He can never know," Sydney said, pulling herself together. "This is just a tonight thing."

"That's fine, Sydney," Julian said, sitting comfortably nude on the seat.

"I don't want to break your heart," he added with a grin.

Sydney rolled her eyes again and yelled to the driver to take her home, giving the address. The driver nodded, not sure if he should acknowledge anything he'd heard or been forced to see. Ten minutes later, the limo pulled onto Sydney's street and she looked at Julian. "We're never telling him, right?" she asked/ordered.

"Who would that benefit?" Julian answered.

"I'll see you around," Sydney said.

Julian nodded and scooted forward in the limousine. "Take me to The Unicorn, please."

"Right away," the driver complied as he turned the lengthy car around. As he did, a silver Ferrari parked in front of a neighbor's house screeched its tires so furiously that the sound made Sydney's mom turn on the light in her bedroom. Sydney looked out her own window too late, just missing the car's departure.

Now Clint Zigler knew about Julian too.

CHAPTER 20

The white pews of the church were a stark contrast to the vibrant array of color and jubilance at the election night gala but the people were nearly the same. It was as if everyone had simply changed clothes and moods, shedding campaign pins and carbonated beverages for the drab garb and black umbrellas of the rainy day funeral.

A considerable crowd milled outside the church's massive doors with students, peers, and politicos exchanging hugs and stories from their time with Annie. Joshua and his father stood solemnly by the doorway, the elder Halpern shaking hands and receiving condolences while his son stood with his face free of expression.

Jack Halpern had asked Daniel to speak at the funeral, representing the legion of former students in attendance. Jack knew Daniel was one of Annie's favorites, but Daniel agreed only reluctantly, having never spoken to a group this large before.

Daniel's father accompanied him to the church though he had never met Professor Halpern. "I want to pay my respects, son," his father said. "I know she meant a lot to you."

Sydney met them in front of the church, and she greeted both Madisons with kisses to the cheek. Daniel squeezed her hand tightly, telling her he needed her close by with the press of his palm in hers. She leaned inward, wrapping her arm around his and drawing him close. Daniel turned her to square their bodies for a hug as his father waved to a friend from the high school where he used to teach. As Daniel looked up from Sydney's shoulder, he saw Julian speaking nearby with a small circle of mourners, some of whom he recognized as Working Women members.

"We've lost a legend," Julian reported with a shake of his head. "She was a mentor to me. When I came to this town she was the first one to befriend me.

"She'll never know how much that meant," Julian gushed on. "When she told me that I had something special, I knew I could do more … maybe even great things."

"Well, she was right, Commissioner," said one smitten woman. "You have done great things."

"Not compared to Annie," Julian said. "There just wasn't anyone like her. She will be missed."

Daniel was aghast at the bizarre rhetoric and intensified his embrace of Sydney to a point where his father wondered if he was all right. Julian had never said a positive thing about Annie, let alone agree with praise uttered by Daniel.

"Son, are you okay?" Mr. Madison asked, turning Daniel's attention.

"What?" a startled Daniel answered. "Yeah, I'm fine."

Daniel watched Julian receive hugs from each of the women to whom he was speaking. One woman laid an affectionate hand against Julian's face as she spoke. "I know she's proud of you, Mr. Correa." Julian grabbed her hand and squeezed, much in the same manner as Daniel had grasped Sydney's warm hand a moment before. Daniel was seething inside, a toxic blend of grief and contempt. His despair over Annie's death coursed through him, transforming into anger searching for a place to breach, like ice forcing a crack in a sidewalk.

Sydney knew something was wrong but Julian's presence nearby negated her focus on Daniel. In her mind she was mulling what would happen with Daniel should her tryst with Julian become public knowledge. She hadn't told anyone and wouldn't, but Julian was another matter. The same dangerous unpredictability that had made him so attractive also gave her great cause for concern.

"Let's get inside," Daniel suggested. "I need to be close to the front." The trio began to head for the door when Julian approached, looking stately in a new black suit and shimmering violet satin tie.

"Hi, guys," Julian said cheerfully, his bright mood aggravating Daniel further. "Nice turnout."

Daniel said nothing as Julian shook Sydney's hand and reached for his father's. "I'm Julian Correa, sir," he said as Mr. Madison received his grasp. "You've raised a fine man."

"Thank you, Julian," Mr. Madison responded. "It's good to finally meet you. Daniel speaks of you often." Daniel was looking away, delaying the inevitable greeting with Julian, who was unaware of his boiling rancor.

"Danny, buddy, you gonna be all right?" Julian asked. "I know how hard this must be for you."

"Yeah," Daniel said, stifling the barrage inside him. "I'm just barely holding it together."

"I'm here for you, man," Julian said. "If you need anything." With that Julian retreated into the crowd, looking to mingle beneficially among the mourners. Daniel watched him slip into the black-garbed gatherers like chimney smoke into a star-free night.

"I need to go inside," Daniel repeated solemnly.

Sydney led the way until they reached the steps into the church and Daniel had to pause to assist his father over them. As he reached the top step he saw Julian yet again in a loving embrace with another attendee. Julian brought the heel of his palm to his eyes as if wiping a heartfelt tear from the corner.

You've got to be kidding me, Daniel raged to himself, his heartbeat escalating at a rate normally reserved for physical confrontation.

"Where do you want to sit?" Sydney asked, interrupting the inferno.

"I don't care," Daniel said brusquely. "I just need to get inside." They took a seat near the front where Daniel could easily reach the pulpit when it was his turn to speak. He couldn't bring himself to pass her body yet, which was lying in an ornate coffin near the pulpit. From his seat, he could see a tuft of Annie's red hair above the coffin's frame.

An organ playing a hymn muted the conversations from outside as most took their seats silently. As the last of them sat down, a priest emerged and began his oration. Daniel could see Jack and Joshua in the front row, the latter fidgeting with the large buttons on his suit jacket, refusing to look anywhere near the direction of his embalmed mother. Mr. Halpern wept openly, wiping his face with a handkerchief as the priest spoke of heaven and Annie's place in God's arms. Daniel grasped and re-grasped the folded notes stashed in his breast pocket, nervously checking and re-checking to make sure they were there. There were many things he could say about his lost friend, but he wanted most of all to convey her value to him, understanding that it would resonate with others who had been aided by the dynamic woman.

Mr. Halpern walked to the pulpit, thanked the priest, and addressed the crowd. He spoke of the pretty young girl he'd met as a rookie reporter when he delivered sandwiches to the newsroom his final year of college. She teased him relentlessly the whole first year, and he couldn't muster the courage to ask her out, fearing she'd undress him with her biting wit every time he returned with a delivery if she said no or things didn't go well. Finally, when his degree was close at hand and his delivery days soon to be over, he ventured the invitation to a movie and dinner.

"I thought you'd never ask," Annie answered. "As long as we go out for something besides sandwiches."

Jack told of their inseparability in marriage and how their love had bloomed through the losses of each of their parents. When Joshua was born, Jack said it was the only time he'd ever loved anyone more than Annie. "I may have been wrong then," Jack said to the gatherers as he looked downward at Josh, who was now staring at his mother. "I love that women completely, the same as I love you, son. Thank God I have you, this piece of her even still."

Josh didn't react but Sydney did, weeping at Jack's remarks. Most in attendance were, as Mr. Halpern left for his seat, appearing to be unable to finish. As he sat in the front pew he pulled his boy close to him, their heads resting against each other as Jack wept and the young boy picked at a loose string on his coat. The priest nodded toward Daniel, who was battling his own release of tears. It was difficult for him to hear of Annie in the past tense and to see the impact of her demise. Until now he'd thought of her in relation to his own loss of friend and mentor, not grasping the full severity of a life-love and mother departed.

Daniel arrived at the pulpit and exhaled too closely to the microphone, the deep breath making an awkward sound throughout the church. "G-g-g-ood afternoon," he stammered as he pressed his notes flat across the pulpit. "My name is Daniel Madison, and Annie Halpern has been an important person in my life for some time now. I imagine from seeing so many of you touched as I am by Regent Halpern's moving story that she meant a great deal to you as well. I think I know why.

"Annie Halpern was a woman unlike any I have known, a giving spirit in an ornery package. This was a woman of rare dedication who chose to help young people at great personal expense, who invested her heart and soul into those whom others often dismiss as obligations—or just a job—and made this community a much, much better place. I know there are many of you like myself for whom Annie was the difference between success and something less than that as she used her good name to get us in the door, or to find us a way to make the rent, or to grab us by the ear when we were too full of ourselves.

"This was a person who did not need to work with kids for pay, which makes all the more clear that she was a woman paid in a different kind of currency, who measured her success in the employment of her students, in graduations of forty-year-old single moms, and in the hope she nurtured in a young writer in whom she saw some flicker of talent.

"Annie Halpern's tireless and humble effort to help those she encountered is a model of benevolence and dedication. I've never said this before, but my first year in Annie's class I was lost. I couldn't find my way in college, hadn't met any friends, and didn't think I could ever make a living. The thought of taking my life in this desperate hour was becoming more attractive in my mind.

"One Wednesday I received notice from an instructor that I couldn't pass my algebra class and that I should probably drop the course. I couldn't imagine how I would tell my father, who had given me part of his small retirement income to pay for the semester. During a break before Annie's journalism class, I visited the computer lab and researched on the Internet how to slash my wrists. I decided to finish the school day and to end my life in my car so my parents wouldn't have to find me.

"I sat in Annie's class that day, oblivious to the lesson she was teaching. I grew more committed to my decision and wrote the suicide note during the class. I wanted Mom and Dad to know it wasn't because of them. I just felt I was a failure."

Mr. Madison's face displayed the expression of a man hearing of the near loss of his only son for the first time. He pursed his lips and tilted his head forward, overwhelmed by Daniel's account of his troubled past. Sydney took Mr. Madison's hand like a daughter and smiled at the shaken older man.

"After class," Daniel continued, "I walked to the door and Annie called me back. She pulled up a chair next to her desk and asked me to sit down. I obliged, wanting only to be polite and to get on with my grim task. But then something happened. Annie told me of a program she was in charge of for young writers, a grant and special training. She and I had not spoken privately before and this came as a great shock.

"She told me she thought I had a gift and that it needed to be fostered. At first I declined, reluctant to abandon my difficult resolve. She insisted, pleading with me to nourish what she saw in me. I broke down right there and told this woman what I was planning. I even showed her the suicide note I had just written. She read it and told me that it was more proof that I was meant to be a writer, that I used words in a way that was important.

"Well, I never made it to my last class that day. Annie took me directly to her house for dinner and to play Trivial Pursuit with Jack and Josh. By the way, Annie won. I slept on her couch while she called my mother to tell her we were working on a project and not to worry."

Daniel paused and stepped backward for just a moment, aware that he had just shared his most private moment with his father, Sydney, Julian, and a room of mostly strangers. The revelation had not been included in his notes and he hadn't intended to discuss the event. But when he saw Annie from his vantage at the lectern, he felt he owed her the truth—that everyone should know.

"Someday, I hope they name a school for my friend Annie so that I can share with the students there her model of public service wherein a life is measured not by annual income, public office, or how far one has risen up the corporate ladder, but rather by the impact we have on those who need our help the most. In the end, our society will be defined not just by the best of us, but by our humanity to those in their darkest hours. That perhaps is Annie's greatest lesson and certainly her legacy."

As Daniel left the lectern he offered a labored smile at his friend asleep in her coffin and headed toward the pew where Sydney and his father waited. Passing the Halperns, Jack mouthed the words "Thank You." Daniel nodded in understanding and Joshua rose to his feet and embraced his mother's pupil, crying for the first time since her passing.

Daniel held the boy for a moment as a church full of watchers watered the mourning. "There's a lot of her left inside you, Josh," Daniel told the weeping boy. "I can't wait to see how you use it."

The young man nodded and returned to his seat next to Jack. As Daniel watched him nestle protectively under his father's arms, he wished he could do the same.

CHAPTER 21

Daniel decided to avoid Julian for a while in an effort not to say anything detrimental to their friendship and his job opportunities. Julian's performance at Annie's funeral wasn't something Daniel would be able to quickly forgive or forget, but he knew confronting him about it wouldn't have positive results. Mike Martin had told Daniel repeatedly that attempts to reason with Julian about his womanizing had sparked bellicose responses.

Julian would take office shortly and the promised job would follow. Even though Staglione's castigations had been purged by the threat of Al in the parking lot, Daniel was having his doubts about V.S.E. the longer he was there. Something didn't add up, and he was beginning to realize that StopShot's stock volume was comprised of the hopeful investments of real people. Across cyberspace, people were reading the salacious releases Staglione was paying him to author and they were spending money on shares of StopShot.

When he first graduated, Daniel had turned down a sales job at a friend's car lot, not feeling entirely comfortable pitching vehicles to strangers. Now he was doing it from the comfortable anonymity of the Internet, his only tangible attachment a contact name in the release and the V.S.E. phone number. Something wasn't right and he knew it, further increasing his desire to work in Julian's office. He never fully recovered from Staglione's outburst either or how he'd sat there meekly as Al displayed the rectitude of a man of honor.

Meanwhile, in another venue, Julian was also feeling impuissant, sitting like a misbehaving child in the principal's office as Hayes laid out how Julian would begin his career as a commissioner.

"Now it's time to take the bull by the horns, Julian," Frank Hayes said firmly, sitting on the edge of his desk and looking down at a weary Julian. "We're gonna make you a star."

"How're we going to do that, Frank?" Julian asked, always uncomfortable that he appeared to be the last to know the plans for his own future.

"Well, the first thing you do is pay your friends back," Hayes said. "That starts with being someone who remembers the favors you've been given. It also means that you continue to improve your position so that you can help your friends. Think long term."

"What do you want me to do, Frank?" Julian asked, his voice mired in reluctance.

"Well, some of our good Mormon commissioners want to change the way the strip clubs operate. They've got some no-touch laws in mind for Sin City," Hayes explained. "And if anyone knows how that will sound a death knell to those places of businesses, it's you."

Julian nodded, remembering the undressing Hayes had given him previously for his dalliances at The Unicorn.

"So, we have to make sure that none of these rules get passed," Hayes said. "Here's how it works: We know we can't change the two Mormon votes in support of the restrictions. That comes directly from the church and they can't buck that. But I know both these guys have seen the inside of a strip club more than once, so they're not personally passionate about the issue. They just can't go against the church. This means they're not going to lobby the other commissioners. You with me so far?"

"I'm with you so far," he said. Julian tolerated Hayes in a way he wouldn't allow others. Perhaps it was that Hayes had been instrumental in his success ... or that he truly feared him.

"What you have to do is secure three other votes so that you can swing the decision," Hayes said. "Forget talking to Sampson. He's an ordained minister for some hole-in-the-wall black church in Northtown. You're not getting him on board. But that leaves the other three, and each one of them has a pet project they care about. Get to each one of them and trade your vote on their issue for their vote on this issue. Got it?" Hayes loosened his tie as he spoke down to Julian.

"Simple enough," Julian said. "We done?"

"Not yet. But don't come across like Mr. Titty Bar either," Hayes instructed. "Explain to them that the topless clubs are the only real traffic in these areas, how many people they employ, etc. You don't want to look like the topless club's lap dog this early in your term or we'll never get you to be chairman of the commission. And we're going to need that later on when we've got zoning issues."

"Do I need to disclose the donations I got from some of the clubs already?" Julian asked.

"You gonna disclose a hand-job, Correa?" Hayes snapped back.

"I mean some of the cash they've given me for signs and stuff," Julian replied.

"If you didn't disclose it during the campaign, you're sure as hell not going to now," Hayes ordered. "And they won't either. If they gave you cash, that money was completely off their books."

"Who else knows about this, Frank?" Julian asked, tempering his concern with deference. "Does Martin know?"

"Martin doesn't know shit," Frank said. "He'd never go along with this. He'd probably report us and hold a press conference. But he's just about done," Hayes said, lighting a cigar inside the office. "His turn is coming. We've grown tired of him."

"What's that supposed to mean?" Julian asked.

"He's not a realist, and he's cost me money for the last time. There's always one goody-two-shoes who screws it up. And now he's got to go."

Julian looked puzzled, calculating in his mind whether Hayes and his legion had enough clout to take Martin head on. Mike Martin wasn't exactly a pushover and had strong relationships in the senator's office and throughout the political world. But Frank Hayes played by different rules.

"He's got to go?" Julian said incredulously, his fingers curling around the burnished edge of the chair in which he sat. "You're going to kill him?"

"Don't be ridiculous, Julian," Martin chided. "I know you grew up in Little Havana with a *Scarface* poster on your wall, but we do things different out here. He'll be taken care of *our way*. Your best bet is to distance yourself from the train wreck he's about to become. You don't want to get any on you, sport."

"It's going to be that bad?" Julian asked, pondering briefly the friendship that Martin had extended him. "This has to be done?" Julian's response reflected more a minimal abiding of the pact with Martin and Daniel than an expression of his genuine concern. He wanted to be able to say to Daniel that he'd argued for Martin, however impotently, after Mike was eventually handled.

"I don't want anything to do with it," Julian warned, his voice rising in potency for the first time in the meeting. "This can't have my fingerprints anywhere."

"Why would it, Julian? You're not going to do anything but call your friend Martin and tell him you're going to meet him where I tell you," Hayes explained calmly as if this were common practice. "You're going to set up a little meeting in a restaurant presumably to discuss some commission bullshit, life at large, how you're growing genital warts— whatever—and you're not going to make that meeting.

"Our friend the killjoy enters and should be sitting by himself at a table with an empty seat that's waiting for you. From there, we're gonna send in our girl." Hayes had a Cheshire-smile washing over his broad face from silver sideburn to silver sideburn.

"Who's your girl?" Julian asked, curious and concerned as to how vendetta jobs like this were executed. He knew it was important to learn this process too. Mike Martin had fewer enemies than he did.

"Just a little sweetheart on the payroll," Frank said. "She's a known porn star and escort whose career could use a little jumpstart."

"She'll sit down in your seat with Mike, strike up a conversation, and see how long she can keep him there," Hayes said, returning to his chair behind the desk. "If we're lucky, he'll take the bait and they'll leave together. But I doubt that he will. Saint Martin is probably 'above' that,"

Frank said mockingly. "But it won't matter. That will just be the cherry if he does leave with her. The damage will have been done already."

"How's that?" Julian asked, realizing that what was unfolding in front of him was the revelation of a Sword of Damacles above his own head to be lowered whenever Hayes wanted.

"Well, we're going to tip off the local gossip columnist that two high-powered politicos are meeting for an intense discussion. He's smart enough to get somebody at the table next to you who can hear it all … and who can take a surreptitious picture or two. When you don't show, it will be The Trixie and Mike Martin Show," Hayes explained. "And the next day, Mike Martin, man of honor, will be the star of the gossip page with his new paramour. She'll quickly hold a press conference detailing her relationship with the sexually depraved Mike Martin, conveniently coinciding with the release of her new adult video. You see where this is going, kid?" Hayes said proudly, staring ominously at Julian, eyebrows raised.

"I see it," Julian said. "Pretty dirty, Frank."

"Is it dirtier than fucking your best friend's girl while he's at the hospital with his dying friend?" Frank asked.

"How the hell … ?" Julian said, immediately incensed. "What the fuck, Frank?"

"Come on, Julian. Be an adult here, would ya?" Hayes said paternally. "You think we're going to put all that money into you, all that work into getting you from no-name to commissioner, and not see it through? Of course the limo driver was our guy."

"You didn't need to have someone watching me in the back of a limousine, Frank," Julian protested. "That's my business."

"Christ, Julian. You left the goddamn window down for the driver to see. Now you want privacy?"

"It had better not happen again, Frank," Julian said as he stood up quickly. "I'm in now and you're not my father. I know I owe you, but if something like that happens again, we're done."

"Sit down. You're done when I say you're done, Julian," Hayes reported, nonplussed by Julian's newfound backbone. "If you behave and do what we ask—what you should do—then we'll make a ton of money together and you'll climb the ladder. Soon you'll be chairman of the commission and then we can pick a big office ... mayor, governor, congressman, senator." Each uttered word progressed in intensity like a New Year's countdown as Hayes outlined Julian's possibilities. "But if you fuck us ... well, let's just say that what's about to happen to Father Mike will appear to have been kind. You'd be far easier to get."

"I'm not going to be anybody's boy, Frank," Julian proclaimed.

"But you already are, Julian," Hayes said. "Embrace that."

Hayes rolled his chair closer to the desk as if preparing to utter some wisdom to the young buck. "Look, Correa, every guy like you has a guy like me. Harry Truman had Pendergast, LBJ had Bobby Baker, and Kennedy had his daddy and that bootleg money. If guys like you could make it on your own, you wouldn't need a Frank Hayes calling the shots. Without someone pulling the strings, lining things up, you're just a good-looking kid with a two-color brochure and sore feet. What good does that do anyone?

"It's a system, kid. A flawed system. We didn't create it. Shit, we didn't even ask for it," Hayes defended. "But if we didn't stack the deck, we'd get dealt off the bottom. Somebody else would hold the best hand and we'd be the ones fighting for scraps. Would you prefer that? Because the State Assembly's full of guys like that who just want to hold office and go to the parties. But they're not going to make any real money without a guy like me. It's not gonna happen.

"And if you do someday decide you want to do something good for the community, you can do a whole lot more as governor than you can heading up the transportation committee in the Assembly."

What Frank was saying made sense to Julian but he wasn't sure if he could stomach the subservience in perpetuity. The scheme to disrobe Martin politically sat ill with him and he knew it was both an instrument of Mike's demise and a warning of what could be his own.

"I gotta go," Julian said without agreeing.

Frank Hayes stood up, as if permitting Julian to leave. "It's good working with you, kid."

"Right," Julian replied abruptly, the emasculating discourse too severe to offer anything more obsequious. Julian pulled the pewter-tone handle of the door and tossed his jacket over his shoulder. Frank let him get one foot on the other side of the threshold before he ventured a final query.

"So how was she? That little Banks girl?" Hayes asked. "I never much liked her father."

"Outstanding!" Julian said, returning to character and allowing Hayes to have the soothing locker-room moment he sought. "Best I ever had."

Julian walked down the hallway leading from Frank's office. *There's no way I can be his bitch forever. Maybe he needs to go. Maybe I need to make that happen.*

CHAPTER 22

December 2000

Daniel tossed on washed-out jeans and an old football jersey and headed for the door. He and Julian were supposed to meet Mike Martin for bar food and a college football game, giving them a chance to survey the new landscape with Julian taking office in a few weeks. He expected this would be the point when they could discuss his employment in detail; the title he'd hold, pay, etc. Staglione had been coming into Daniel's office once a day to give him the latest calculation on the rising value of his stock, somehow sensing he might be growing disenchanted. As he pulled into the parking lot of Three Angry Wives Irish pub, Martin phoned to say he was running behind. Entering the bar, Daniel saw Julian sitting alone in front of a widescreen television, two empty shot glasses nearby.

"Hey, brother," Daniel said. "How long you been here?"

"I had a friend of mine drop me off an hour ago," Julian answered.

"Who's that, Amber?" Daniel asked.

"Nah. I haven't heard from her since election night," Julian said. "Saved me the trouble of the break-up conversation."

"So, how you been?"

Julian seemed preoccupied and was drinking at nocturnal rates at 4:30 p.m.

"I'm all right, man. Under a lot of pressure," Julian said with a labored tenor. "We need to talk."

"Okay, Julian. What's shakin'?"

"Look, you and Martin have done a lot for me. I really appreciate everything," Julian began. "You're a big part of my success. But there's a complication now."

Daniel's stomach sank. *Here comes the "I can't hire you" speech.* He knew he couldn't continue to work for Staglione whether he got a

150

position with Julian or not.

"What's that?" Daniel asked because he had to, not because he wanted to hear the answer.

"Mike's dead, Danny," Julian said like a doctor in the waiting room of a hospital. "He's through. Nothing can be done about it, and we've got to cut our ties immediately. You're on my team now. You represent me," Julian explained, affirming to Daniel's momentary relief that the job was still in place. "And the shit storm that's about to hit Mike Martin can't get on us."

"Wait, back up, Julian," Daniel said, focused now on his friend Mike's concern. "What shit storm? What did Mike do? What's going on?"

"He's got enemies, dude," Julian said. "His political career is over. We can't do anything about it." A party of Notre Dame fans screamed over a fumbled kickoff, and Julian's utterances became inaudible. The pause gave Daniel enough time to suffer the second sinking feeling in his stomach in the past two minutes.

"What's going to happen to him?" Daniel inquired fearfully.

"He's getting set up, Dan," Julian said. "They're gonna put him in a room with a whore and then she's gonna tell everyone they're an item. It'll be all over everything. He'll have no credibility in Vegas. He'll probably have to go back to Boston with his tail between his legs."

"No, no," Daniel said, shaking his head. "That can't happen. You've got to put a stop to it, Julian. If you know about this, then you know who's pulling the strings. Make them stop. He's a good man. He's been good to us. This can't happen."

"I tried, Daniel. I really did," Julian said as sincerely as he could. "I tried to make every deal I could. I offered my vote on things and I told them I'd hire people from their group in the office. None of it mattered.

"Danny, you gotta believe me. I did everything I could. These guys aren't negotiators. I can't stop it. And obviously you can't say anything. I'm only telling you so that you steer clear. You don't want to be with him when this all goes down, and you don't want to be doing any damage control after it does. That will put you in the line of fire. Lose his number."

"Julian, he's gonna be here in ten minutes … to hang out with his so-called friends," Daniel reminded him.

"Put on a show. Everything's fine," Julian said. "Buy him a beer, talk about the game. You know, business as usual."

"Julian, we made a pact to protect and help each other," Daniel recalled. "Does that mean nothing?"

Julian turned closer to Daniel, emphasizing his point. "Look, bro, this can't be stopped or I would have stopped it already. All we can do is make sure we don't get dragged down with him. Yeah, it fucking sucks. Yeah, he's a good guy. But this is politics. People get screwed all the time. I knew this going in, and so did Mike."

As Julian spoke to Daniel he realized how much he sounded like Hayes.

"That's not good enough for me," Daniel objected. "I didn't sign up for that."

"But that's the way it is," Julian shot back as he raised a hand to catch the barmaid's eye. "Waitress, get my boy a Patron."

"You want a lime in your tequila, sir?" the waitress asked Daniel.

"I couldn't care less," Daniel said dismissively, sending the waitress on an abrupt exodus. Daniel sat quietly aggrieved as Julian ate peanuts and watched the game. A few minutes later, a gentle squeeze from behind on his and Julian's shoulders signaled Martin's arrival.

"What's goin' on, Mike?" Julian greeted, rising to give Martin a friendly hug and becoming the thespian he had been at Annie's funeral. Daniel sat still, acting engrossed in the game and offering his hand to Mike.

"It's so good to be here with my boys," Martin announced warmly. "Hey, Danny, that was amazing what you said at Annie's funeral. People were talking about it for days and days afterward. By the way, I've got a nice little scholarship fund started for Joshua too. By the time he's eighteen, he'll be able to go anywhere he wants."

"That's really nice," Daniel said, Martin's benevolence fueling his own guilt. "I'm going to take him to a movie this week."

"And you, Mr. Commissioner, I've got good news for you too," Martin said, exhibiting an especially blissful mood today. The release of the weight of the elections appeared to have freed Martin in many ways. Daniel noted Martin's ragged Red Sox hat and washed-out jeans. He'd never seen him so loose.

"Really? What's that, Mike?" Julian asked.

"Well, I recommended you to the senator, and you're going on a little diplomatic mission to China next summer," Martin said, pleased to offer his friend Julian the prestigious opportunity and résumé builder. "You'll be on an economic tour of China and Hong Kong as the senator's emissary, joining other big shots sent from across the country. You're going to be meeting the kind of guys who could help you win a major election someday."

"Man, that's great, Mike," Julian said eagerly. "What will it all entail?"

Daniel wrinkled his brow and looked in Julian's direction, signaling his difficulty in seeing Julian mine Mike for this favor, yet resigned to accepting the treachery that lay in wait for him. Julian looked through Daniel as if he were a neon bar sign and part of Wives' décor.

"I'll get you everything on that later," Martin said. "Trystyn Wilcox from the senator's office will get you going. And call your doctor about getting the vaccinations you'll need for that trip. Some of that stuff needs sixty days in advance time."

"I will, I will," Julian said. "Man, that's gonna be fun." Daniel's blood felt cold and still, the lie of omission in the room growing unbearable. Julian was sagging backward in his seat, infinitely comfortable and picturing himself in the Far East among ambassadors and chief executive officers. Daniel leaned back too as Martin watched a replay of a Notre Dame touchdown during the halftime show. He thought about Staglione and his dubious press releases, Sydney, and Zigler's unrelenting phone calls. He pictured his father at Annie's funeral and the glossy way her face looked in the casket. He pondered the things he'd been a part of, even if indirectly, since he'd left college. Friends now seemed to be filtered through the portal of need first and virtue second, as if they were rated in dollar signs next to their names in some value Rolodex. In high school and college he'd sought out the fellows who would hang tough in a fight or pick you up in the middle of the night when the Mustang blew a tire. Today it was about who could do the most to move you forward. Those would be your friends.

As the waitress brought another round to the trio, Daniel grasped his pint and leaned forward. "Gentlemen, we agreed some time ago to stick together and to protect each other," Daniel said. "And so far we've seen this fine young man elected to office as a testament to what we can all do. Today I believe our relationship takes another step forward," Daniel continued as Julian began to grow unsettled. "Today, it's time to really stick together."

Julian tried to shake his head in a narrow parameter, indicating as profusely as he could without Martin seeing that Daniel needed to keep his mouth shut. But Daniel's intentions were set and he stared through Julian's protest just as Julian had done a few moments before.

"Mike, Julian has learned of what appears to be a significant threat to you," Daniel revealed. "I know he's uncomfortable bringing this bad news to you, but it's for your own good that you know now before it's put in action."

"A threat to me?" Martin said. "From whom?"

Daniel washed his face of expression, knowing he'd forced Julian's hand. Julian was erupting inside but realized that any outward reticence to tell all to Martin would make him look collusive with Mike's enemies. His only choice was to tell Martin what he knew or Daniel would do so at Julian's expense.

"They're going to come after you with some slutty chick in a restaurant, Mike," Julian said somberly, his mood a reflection of the hot water he was soon to be in with Hayes, courtesy of Daniel. "They're going to make it look like you're with her, and she's a hooker, the Dick Morris thing. They're setting it up so that somebody from the media will watch the whole bit, and she's been instructed to say you two are an item."

"Son of a bitch," Martin said, his light mood replaced by a man now bracing for battle. "How long have you known about this?"

"We just found out," Daniel answered, sparing Julian the opportunity to lie once more.

"I already know who's behind this, that rotten bastard," Martin declared. "This is Frank Hayes' handiwork. He's threatened me before when I wouldn't play along with his bullshit hustles."

Julian nodded.

"What are you gonna do?" Daniel asked.

"Well, I'm not going to let any hookers stand with me anywhere I go," Martin replied with a hint of levity. "And I'm going to go to a reporter I trust at the paper now and tell her in confidence what I think Hayes may be up to. That way, if they try this anywhere, I've got the antidote in the bank. But that just means that I've deflected this first salvo," Martin said, knowing Hayes might come after him from another angle.

Martin shook his head in disgust. "You know what all this is over? They wanted to rezone some land near downtown for high-density residential development and I told him that some of us thought it was better as an art district. He made some arrogant remark about him knowing what was best because I wasn't from here.

"And he got told to go fuck himself. When he left my office he added how my opinion wouldn't be worth much in the future anyway. I just blew it off knowing what a hot-head he is. Guess I was wrong."

Martin paused and looked at Julian, extending his hand toward him. Julian placed his hand in Mike's and the men shook slowly. "This means a lot to me, Julian," Martin said. "I won't forget this."

"Listen, I'm going to get out of here. My mind is racing with what I've got to do now," Martin explained feverishly. "I'll call you both soon."

"Thank you again, Julian," Martin said. "I know what you must have gone through in deciding to tell me this."

"No problem," Julian replied. "It was the right thing to do."

Martin patted Daniel on the back affectionately and left briskly through the bar's doors. Julian turned immediately to Daniel and shot daggers from his eyes. "What am I going to do now, Dan?" he boiled. "Do you know what Hayes will do to me once he finds out I warned Martin? This will make *ME* his enemy. You've thrown me into the lion's den."

Daniel knew he had, but he also knew he had no choice, regardless of an expected future with Julian. They made a pact, and letting Martin perish didn't honor that covenant. "I couldn't let him swing," Daniel explained. "Like you said, we had to do the right thing."

"Do you know how much trouble 'the right thing' has put me in? You ambushed me, Danny. That's not what friends do. I don't know how you think it honors some bar agreement to protect each other by putting my neck in the noose."

"Let's deal with that together ... with Mike ... you and me ... " Daniel said, trying to assuage Julian's anger.

"Oh, we're going to deal with it together, all right," Julian said. "When Hayes finds out that Martin knows, your name's gonna be in that story too. It's not going to be just my problem."

"Fair enough," Daniel said matter-of-factly.

"Now he's your problem too," Julian said, wanting to unsettle Daniel.

"I heard you," Daniel said, growing angry at Julian's retaliatory threat to him.

"I'm leaving too," he said to Julian, wanting to remove himself from the noxious air of their discussion and throwing a twenty on the table.

"Have a good one," Julian said sarcastically, looking back at the game.

"You need a ride?" Daniel asked.

"Danny, finding a ride right now is pretty far down my list of current problems. I'm going to—I'm not sure what I'm going to do." He stared blankly at the TV above the bar. "Go home, Daniel," he said. "Don't worry about me. Why start now?"

Daniel left without responding to Julian's sarcasm. Julian had a right to be pissed, but he'd also forced Daniel's hand by refusing to warn Mike Martin.

He got into the car and noticed two things right away—his cell phone sitting on the driver seat where it had fallen out of his pocket and a plate of what appeared to be dog excrement on the passenger seat. The odor, even in the colder air of late fall, was overwhelming. He threw the feces into the parking lot and picked up his phone. Thirteen "Private Caller" calls all but assured Daniel the shit bomb had come from Zigler. Daniel looked around at the dusty lots that surrounded the newly constructed sports bar.

That guy carried a bag of shit from God knows where just to leave it in my car, Daniel thought before deciding that the fact he'd been following him was of equal concern. His phone rang again and he grabbed it, intent on answering Zigler's latest harassment. "This is Dan," he said boldly.

"Danny, you still in the bar?" Mike Martin asked.

"No, Mike, I'm in the parking lot trying to get the smell of dog shit out of my car," Daniel replied bluntly.

"Yeah, I feel the same way after I leave Julian," Martin agreed, assuming Daniel was being metaphorical. "Look, I know what you just did, Danny. I know he wasn't going to tell me."

"How'd you know?" Daniel asked.

"Because you brought it up," Martin said. "If he really wanted to share info like that, he'd be rushing to tell me, to get the full value of it. He wouldn't let you get the credit. And just so you know, I've been bracing for something from Hayes for a while. I'm not the first guy to ever piss him off ... and he has enemies too."

"So what do you do, retaliate?" Daniel asked. "Do you threaten him now?"

"Nah, Danny. The only thing that happens for sure in a pissing match is that everyone gets piss on them. What I need to do is just let him know I know and then he'll be so worried waiting for *ME* to do something that he won't be on the offensive," Martin said. "That'll give me time to figure out the long-term play."

"Sounds like you know just what to do, Mike," Daniel said, as he opened and shut his door like a flapping bird's wing, trying to chase the fecal stench from the vehicle.

"Daniel, what I also know is that you are truly my friend, that you can be counted on," Martin said. "It took guts to do what you did today, to risk pissing off Julian."

"Well, as Julian said, it's the right thing to do," Daniel said. "We made a pact to look out for each other. I assumed that didn't just mean when it was convenient."

"A man of honor does the right thing without regard to consequence," Martin said. "A man of intellect figures out how to make that work."

"Well, hopefully I can figure out how to do that," Daniel said, not sure if he truly could marry the two. "I'll just start with trying to do the right thing."

Daniel and Martin hung up and Daniel headed homeward. Sitting at a red light his phone rang again. The odor in the car hadn't improved much. The caller ID read "Private Caller."

"Hi, Clint," Daniel said sarcastically. "Thanks for the present." No response came from the other end of the line as usual.

"What's the matter, tough guy? You're man enough to sneak into my car and leave a load of shit but you're afraid to talk on the phone? What kind of pussy are you?" Daniel asked, eager to provoke his attacker. "What I don't understand is how fucked in the head must you be to carry a bag of shit around in your own car just so you can put it in mine. You're willing to stink up your own car just do the same thing to me."

"But I didn't have a bag of shit in my car," Zigler said ominously, speaking for the first time and sounding like a kidnapper on the line with the abducted child's family. "I had your present inside me."

The line went dead before Daniel could respond.

CHAPTER 23

Daniel was furious over Zigler's odious invasion and arrogance on the phone. He knew that he now had to confront Zigler directly. *It's time to meet in person*, he thought. Turning the tables and entering Zigler's world would definitely change the playing field, but whether it served as water or gasoline on the fire remained to be seen. Additionally, getting Sydney to tell him how to find Zigler might not be so easy.

As he pulled into his driveway, Daniel was pleased to see Sydney's car parked outside, allowing him an opportunity to request Zigler's information right away without having to dwell on a possible confrontation with his girlfriend. Daniel entered his home expecting Sydney to come running like she normally did, bestowing affection as if he were returning from overseas. But as he shut the door, Sydney was nowhere in sight.

Across from the front door Daniel could see the small bathroom near the kitchen was occupied with what appeared to be Sydney's feet milling near the door. He approached, and as he began to tap the door to announce his arrival home, he could hear her voice raised in a pitch that indicated the intensity of the dialogue.

"It's not funny, Clint," she said sternly. "It's disgusting. You're disgusting."

Daniel stopped short of knocking, listening curiously once he'd heard her say Zigler's first name. Sydney had given every indication she didn't speak with Zigler, whom she knew was tormenting Daniel.

"If you think this is the way to win me back, you're wrong," Sydney declared through audible sobs. "It just tells me how crazy you are. You think I want to live my life like that?"

"I know you do, Clint," she said after his reply, her voice reducing to normal tones that made it hard for Daniel to hear without pressing his ear against the bathroom door. "But I don't anymore. We had our time and it didn't work."

"I know that too," she said. "But that's not enough to keep us together. That's just one part of a relationship."

"Look, Clint. I appreciate how you feel," Sydney said empathetically, apparently having sat down in the bathroom as her voice softened. "But you've got to stop. I love this man. He's a good man and you're not going to run him off like you did the other guys. This guy's different.

"I'm sorry, Clint, baby," Sydney said gently, resuming the flow of tears and labored voice. "But things have changed. This used to be cute, having you scare them off and us getting back together. But it's over. I'm going to marry this guy."

Sydney let out a long, heavy sigh as Zigler protested her announcement. "No, no, no," she objected. "It's over. Don't do anything anymore.

"If you do, I'm going to call your dad and tell him, Clint," she threatened. "You know how he'll react to anything you do that brings shame to the family. The crap-in-the-car episode will kill him." Sydney pushed at a tiny piece of paper that had fallen to the floor as Zigler raged. She pursed her lips.

"Don't threaten him again, Clint," Sydney ordered. "I've taped this call and tomorrow I'll put the tape in my safety deposit box. If something happens to him, I'll give it to the authorities.

"Oh, yes I will," she asserted. "I told you, it's not cute anymore. It's not a turn-on and it doesn't make you look powerful. It makes you look pathetic."

Daniel was catching most of Sydney's side of the dialogue and was both warmed and dismayed by the repartee. She was saying all the right things, but she was also having a long conversation with a man who seemed to know his every move, who had just defecated in his car, and to whom she said she no longer spoke.

"I've gotta go, Clint," Sydney said. "Go try to be happy."

Daniel heard the cell phone close with a loud snap as if Sydney was punctuating the call's finality. He backed up and sat down at the kitchen table, waiting for her to leave the bathroom. He could hear the water run as Sydney washed the tears from her face. Soon after, she emerged, and as their eyes met she knew Daniel had been listening to her conversation with Zigler.

"Hi," she said meekly, her hair pulled back as if she had been readying to put on makeup.

"Hi," he said in a voice not much above a whisper. "Do we need to talk?"

"I think so," she said in a continuance of her weak voice. Sydney took Daniel's hand and led him to the couch. "I don't know how much you heard, Danny," Sydney said, her wet eyes puffy and pink. "But I'll tell you whatever you want to know."

Sydney slid closer to Daniel, looking to lay her head on his shoulder. He stopped her, firmly taking her arm and making her look upward. "I don't know what to make of that call," he said. "I heard you tell him that you two were done, but clearly you've been keeping things from me for a long time. Do you know what that sociopath did to me today?"

"Yes, I know. He called to tell me," Sydney admitted. "He thought that would impress me."

"Why would he think that, Syd? Who outside of a gorilla uses their excrement as a weapon?"

"I agree. It's disgusting and appalling. I told him that. Danny, honey, I haven't been totally forthcoming about my relationship with Clint."

Daniel withdrew from her embrace.

"Yeah, I gathered that when you called him 'baby' on the phone ... the same guy that shit in my car today," Daniel said, annoyed and offended. The "baby" utterance had rekindled thoughts of Sydney and Zigler's so-called summer romance, of the time Sydney had said it was just about sex and other anecdotes that conjured lurid images in his mind.

"That doesn't mean anything, Daniel," Sydney explained. "I was just trying to make him go away. If you were listening, you heard me tell him that over and over again."

"I want to know where he lives, where he hangs out, and I want HIS cell phone number," Daniel commanded, gesturing with his finger.

"Leave it alone, Danny," Sydney pleaded, reaching for his hand and taking it into her own. "I threatened to go to his dad today. He doesn't want that. He's obsessed with pleasing his father and taking over the business. He won't want me telling his dad what he's been doing … or what he did today. Please, Daniel. Trust me on this?"

"Sydney, I don't know what to think," Daniel said, unsure how to process Sydney's telephone conversation with Clint or this one now. "I want all that information, Syd, but I won't do anything as long as it stays quiet. If I hear from him again, I'm going to pay him a visit.

"And I want the information to be accurate," Daniel said firmly. "No more lies or deceptions."

"I promise," Sydney said. "No more secrets between us."

Daniel took her hand, thinking how he'd heard her say she was going to marry him. It hadn't been that long since they'd begun dating, but the intensity of life around them had forged a deeper relationship that was difficult to accurately measure in linear time. They had been thrust together like a couple on a reality show, replete with challenges that expedited their commitment and defied standard timelines.

"Okay, Syd," Daniel relented as she lay her head in his lap. "Let's put that chapter behind us, and hopefully today is the end of it all."

Sydney rose from his lap, her eyes wet again. "Danny, I've got one more secret I need to share with you."

Daniel grimaced and exhaled a worried sigh. *What now?* he thought, wondering what further frustrations he'd have to endure on a day like today. Sydney's face had become more colored and bright, devoid of the pale discomfort of the Zigler discourse.

"Daniel, I'm pregnant," she announced proudly, as if the pair had been trying for ages.

"You're pregnant?" Despite the blooming fear, the chaos of the day, and every other loose end that the pregnancy exacerbated, he knew he was happy. This confirmed their relationship, built a wall against Zigler, and gave him a child with a woman he wholeheartedly adored.

Sydney nodded an affirmative "Yes" and kissed him with a closed mouth that nearly pushed him backward on the couch. "I'm so happy!" Sydney gushed. "Will you marry me?"

"I'm not sure if that's how it's supposed to be done," Daniel laughed at Sydney's proposal as his body vibrated with the themes of fatherhood and marriage. "But if it means spending the rest of my life with you, I'll say yes to anything." She looked at him with feigned irritation, beckoning Daniel for the actual verbal agreement.

"Yes, I'll marry you, sweetheart," Daniel said, the moment purging the day's troubles from his consciousness. "I can't wait to have a baby with you."

CHAPTER 24

It had been a week since Daniel and Julian parted inauspiciously, and Daniel hadn't heard from him since. He wanted to call and tell him about the baby, but he wasn't sure how Julian would receive him after the blow-up. It was strange not sharing the news of the pregnancy with Julian as he had with Mike Martin and his other friends. Everyone knew now except for Julian … and Sydney's parents. Daniel was hoping Julian had come to understand why he'd forced his hand and at least respected his reasons. With the baby seven months away, Daniel needed the job on Julian's staff more than ever.

Throughout the week Daniel and Mike Martin had spoken daily, the way Julian and he used to do. Mike was now confiding greatly in Daniel, welcoming the friendship galvanized by the trust earned last weekend. Martin needed someone in whom he could confide, venting and strategizing about his own battles on a higher plane. In turn, Daniel shared some of the details of his episodes with Clint Zigler. Martin pledged to help vigorously upon Daniel's request, which gave him some degree of solace.

Martin was also furious with Julian, and Daniel couldn't help but recognize the irony in the fact that his honoring of the commitment to loyalty among the trio had in essence been the instrument of its demise. Mike knew all the details of the scheme to discredit him and saw Julian's acceptance of it as a choosing of sides and de facto enemy status. And while he was through protecting Julian, as he often had, he also wasn't ready to let Julian know of his contempt for him or to declare a formal war.

"There's never an advantage in telling your enemy that he's your enemy," Martin explained over the phone as Daniel paced around the parking garage at V.S.E., dodging smoke breakers in his search for privacy. "It's always better to be a sniper than a foot soldier. I'll pick my spot.

"But he's got a little juice now with the favors he can do as a commissioner," Martin said, considering any action he might take against Correa. "Heck, I can probably hurt him most by not doing anything, and by that I mean I'm done looking out for him. He can put out his own fires."

It was difficult for Daniel to be caught in a cold war between his two most valued political allies, and he was again hearing tacit threats from one about the other. He wasn't sure how he could maintain neutrality and honor the now-impossible agreement among them. But it wouldn't matter for long.

Daniel hung up with Martin and caught Julian on his cell phone as he headed into the gym, telling Daniel coldly that he only had a minute to talk. He could tell from Julian's gruff tone that he wasn't over their blow-up yet.

"No problem, Julian," Daniel said, wondering whether Julian's tone suggested it might be wise to inquire about the job later. "I just wanted to catch up with you. It's been a little while."

"Yeah, I've been busy," Julian said matter-of-factly. "I've got a ton of things to do. I'm buying a house on the golf course, and I've been seeing this girl almost every day."

Here we go, Daniel thought as Julian reverted to previous form, announcing material acquisitions and female conquests as usual.

"Excellent," Daniel said audibly. "Congrats on the house. Who's the new girl?"

"She's a doctor," Julian said. "Nice girl. Perfect for me right now. It sends the right message."

"Now you're talking," Daniel agreed. "Stability registers well with everyone who matters to you."

"I'm not unstable, Daniel," Julian said defensively.

"No, that's not what I meant, Julian," Daniel said, trying to repair his remark. "What I was saying was that an elected official as young as you are inherently looks less stable than a family man with a little gray in his hair. Being with a doctor won't hurt.

"Where'd you meet her?" Daniel asked, trying to bumper his explanation with a quick segue, hoping Julian wouldn't challenge him.

"I met her on election night," Julian answered to Daniel's relief. "She's the girl that was trying to save Halpern."

Daniel knew immediately who Julian was referring to, the moment etched indelibly into his memory. He couldn't recall her face, but he remembered clearly the unsuccessful compressions on Annie's chest and breaths into her mouth. The images swirled through his mind like tiny pin pricks as he wondered if Julian had picked up the doctor before or after the CPR session.

"Really nice girl, Danny," Julian continued. "You'd like her. She's smart, pretty savvy about the world, and she's not a pushover. We haven't even had sex yet. Anyway, I gotta get going, Dan. I'm standing outside the gym, man."

"Okay, bud, I just wanted to touch base and make sure everything was cool with us," Daniel said, having to rush his game plan a little. "I wasn't crazy about the way we left things last weekend."

"We're good," Julian said. "Everything's all right between us. You did what you thought you had to do."

"I really appreciate that, man," Daniel said, relieved. "I was hoping you would understand. I just had to make sure that Mike was—"

"Forget about it," Julian interrupted. "What's done is done."

"Fair enough," Daniel agreed, happy to have dismissed the incident and repaired the rift. "So, when are we gonna start putting together your office?"

"I started this week," Julian said as Daniel hung on each word. "I've got a lot of work to do."

"Well, put me in, coach," Daniel said jovially. "Say when."

"Yeah, I've been meaning to talk to you about that," Julian said. "We might not be able to get you in on the timetable I want, Danny." Daniel knew instantly that Julian was lying. There was no timetable and there was no job for him. Never would be. But he wanted to make Julian say it all, to force him to construct and act out the lies while the elephant in the room ate peanuts.

"What changed, Julian?" Daniel asked tempestuously, his disappointment only partly masking a primer of anger. "I thought me coming on board was a done deal."

"Yeah, me too," Julian said with less than his usual attempt at believability. He wanted Daniel to know this was the price for last week's betrayal, but he didn't want to say it, to be quoted later to Martin or anyone else. "But the senator's got a guy he's grooming, and he wants his feet wet in local politics. I can't say 'no' to a United States senator, Daniel."

"Of course not," Daniel said, returning to the dance. "But why all of a sudden?"

"Look, man, I have to get going," Julian said. "I've only got an hour to lift before Meredith picks me up." Daniel fumed as he thought of the dismissive remark Julian offered, giving his workout greater weight than the retraction of the job offer promised and earned.

"Hey, do what you gotta do," Daniel superficially agreed, remembering Martin's remarks on not tipping your hand to your adversaries. "I understand. You had no choice."

"Exactly," Julian said expeditiously. "But as soon as something opens … well, you know."

"Sure," Daniel said. "I'll look forward to that."

"All right, man, cool," Julian said, searching for an exit. "I'm gonna run. Let's play some basketball soon, okay?" Julian's conscience authored the friendly remark, coating the melancholy discourse with an affable ending.

"That'd be great," Daniel said insincerely, wanting nothing more to do with Julian at the moment. "Let's do that soon."

"All right, bro, you take care," Julian closed, realizing after he hung up that his final remark implied incongruently that they wouldn't be speaking anytime soon.

It didn't matter. Daniel already knew they wouldn't.

CHAPTER 25

The disappointment resonated eerily throughout Daniel, sparking myriad emotions. He couldn't help but play his contempt for Julian on the taut heartstrings of his pending fatherhood, escalating his loathing to something more pronounced. Julian didn't know yet that Sydney was pregnant, but Daniel doubted if that would have mattered at all. Julian had betrayed him now, used him retroactively in doing so, and robbed his child of something promised, planned, and earned. But despite the bitter flavor of the lost job, Daniel recognized that a part of him welcomed the defeat, knowing it closed the door on what he'd become party to of late. With the commission job gone, so too was a river of guilt flowing from the acts he didn't challenge or question as he sat placidly like Congress for McCarthy while the rope of the moral gallows swung over and over again.

As Daniel rode the elevator back up to his office at V.S.E. he scolded himself for not seeing Julian's rebuke ahead of time, for allowing the indignity of the rejection. This was a man who disposed of people indiscriminately, excising them and their needs when their service to him was no longer of use. Martin had him right, he thought, and now as victim instead of witness, it was his turn to feel the sharp blade of Julian's character issues.

Two floors higher, a woman and a little boy and girl joined him on the upward-bound elevator. She thanked him with a smile as he held the door while they entered. The little boy's baseball cap had the San Diego Padres baseball team logo from a decade before and the hat had white sweat marks around the edges that looked like salt-colored stalagmites. His sister, who appeared a year older, had on cheap plastic shoes from a strip mall discounter and her pink T-shirt was too small for her by at least a summer.

Both children stood obediently at their mother's side, clean-faced and demure. The woman's hands bore rough fingernails that indicated she was a laborer of some variety, and her eyes displayed the crow's feet of a woman who rested sparingly and didn't have the makeup to hide her fatigue. As they rode silently, Daniel found himself staring at the boy, who held a thick stack of tattered baseball cards in his right hand, bound by a light brown rubber band.

They departed at the fifth floor, and Daniel noted the "Occupational Training Office" sign positioned directly across from the elevator with an arrow pointing down the hall. Daniel watched the children trail faithfully behind their mother as the doors began to close. With six inches left until the doors met, the little boy turned and waved goodbye to Daniel. He quickly mustered a wave through the fleeting space as the little boy stood smiling.

It was midday, and Sydney had said she would drop by so they could go to lunch together. As he returned to V.S.E., the receptionist pointed down the hall toward his office with a ballpoint pen, indicating that Sydney had arrived. Daniel looked at his watch and realized it was nearly 12:15 and that Sydney had been waiting at least fifteen minutes. Crafting an apology in his mind before realizing the Julian story would suffice, Daniel walked briskly to his office only to find both chairs empty and a note on his desk from the receptionist that read, "Amber called to say goodbye." He picked up the note, confused that the receptionist had indicated Sydney's arrival and that his normally early girlfriend hadn't called to say she would be late.

Daniel headed back toward the receptionist to ask what she had been pointing to but as he did so, he noticed two of the bullpen guys acting out a lewd charade through their room's glass wall. One guy lumbered about as if he were a caveman morphed with a gorilla, pounding his puffed-up chest and gesturing wildly, as if enraged. Next to him, the smaller of the dialers leaned over the desk and batted his eyes at Daniel like a porn star. The caveman promptly positioned himself behind his fellow player, thrusting his hips in an unmistakably carnal sequence.

Daniel laughed at the performance, amused as usual by the phone room antics. He wasn't quite sure what had prompted the display until he saw the giver of the pair pick up an imaginary handful of food and chew wildly with his mouth wide open while continuing his lurid endeavor.

Okay, the savage is Staglione, Daniel determined as the faux lass uttered wild and silent wails of hedonistic passion. *But who is he nailing?*

The male end of the tandem stepped backward as if frustrated, making sure to feign his awesome length by taking multiple steps to remove himself completely. Breaking the third wall, he turned to the glass where Daniel stood befuddled.

"Hey, jackass, Staglione's been in his office with your bitch for twenty minutes," he yelled loud enough to overpower the acoustical restraints of the glass wall.

Daniel looked back at the receiver, who was still in full character, mouthing the words, "I love him more, Danny. He's *yuge.*"

Daniel turned and walked as slowly as possible back toward Staglione's office, not wanting the duo to think they'd rattled him. As he drew closer, he heard Staglione's voice boldly declaring something followed by Sydney's audible laugh. He loved that laugh. Sydney was sitting in Staglione's own desk chair, apparently having been seated there by Staglione himself. He was leaning over her shoulder, pointing out things on a wide computer monitor displaying stocks in play.

"And dis one right dere bought me dat purple Porsche you prolly saw sittin' out front, Sydney," Staglione said. "Dere's only like forty of 'em ever made in dat color."

"What do they do at that company?" Sydney asked as Daniel stood outside the office door bringing his finger to his lips, instructing Dottie not to announce his presence. Daniel knew he was going to hear things he wouldn't like, sensing the inevitable like moviegoers at a horror flick. But he wanted to hear it, expected it, readied for it.

"I think dey make software or somethin'," Staglione answered. "I never really looked at it. Some of my boys back home are makin' it run. When I got in it was two cents. Now it's almost a dollah.

"So, Sydney, a girl like youse has gotta have some preddy hot friends, right?" Staglione transitioned as he maintained close proximity to Daniel's fiancée.

"Oh, I don't know," Sydney deferred. "Daniel and I pretty much just stay at home anymore. I've lost touch with most of my old party girls."

"Aaaah, come on now, Sydney," Staglione pleaded as he rubbed her back. "You gotta know a pretty girl who would like to meet a guy with a lotta money who wants to spoil her."

Sydney leaned back in the chair, forcing Staglione's hand from her back. "I really don't, Vince," she said.

"All right den," Staglione said. "I guess you think I'm too old. But I can go all night." Sydney didn't know what to say, having just met Staglione, but predisposed to dislike him from Daniel's daily reports of Staglione's oft-inappropriate behavior. The remark hung like ocean jellyfish until Staglione expelled it with small talk. "So, you got a little baby in dere?" he cooed in an awkward high pitch that Sydney surmised was his take on baby talk.

"Just a little one," Sydney said, glad the subject had changed from sexual endurance to infants.

Staglione kneeled at Sydney's side and reached for her stomach like Little Red Riding Hood's wolf. "Can I feel it?" he asked as Sydney looked toward the doorway where Daniel now stood. "Can I feel it kicking?"

Daniel entered the room without knocking, disregarding any sovereignty with his wife-to-be sitting inside. "Come on, Sydney, let's go," Daniel said in a tone he quickly regretted, misdirecting his frustration to Sydney.

"I'm coming," Sydney agreed eagerly.

"Where youse twose goin'?" Staglione questioned.

"To lunch, Vince," Daniel said dismissively. "I'm taking my fiancée to lunch."

"All right, but be back by one," Staglione said, commanding Daniel in front of Sydney like a dog urinating on front yard bushes. "I got a project for you."

Daniel took two steps outside the door, holding Sydney's hand and looking down the long hallway that led to the front door. He paused for a second, as if multiplying three-figure sums in his mind. "I can't do it," he said, so lightly that Sydney couldn't make it out. "I just can't do it anymore."

Daniel told Sydney to stay where she was, and turned to reenter Staglione's office. "Whatcha need?" Staglione said without looking at him, back in the cockpit in front of his trading screen.

"I'm done, Vince," Daniel announced.

"You didn't even eat yet," Vince said, looking now at Daniel. "Good. I need anudder release done right away. Some deadbeat dad killed his wife and kid at a daycare in Iowa."

"I quit, Vince," Daniel said in the same somber tone. "I can't work here anymore."

"What're you talkin' about?" Staglione protested loudly. "You can't quit here with no notice. You got people who rely on you!"

"That's not my problem, Vince. There are lots of other writers out there," Daniel responded, never moving from his stance just inside the door.

"Sit down. What is it, you want more money? Fine, I'll give you more money ... and stock."

"That's not it, Vince," Daniel explained. "It doesn't even matter now. I just can't keep doing this. Take care."

Daniel turned and walked down the hall, grasping Sydney's hand as he rejoined her. Staglione stood in the doorway, his mouth open wide.

"You're never gonna make the kinda money you can make here, kid!" he yelled, torn between chiding Daniel for quitting and hoping to persuade him from leaving. Daniel ignored it all as he and Sydney walked hand in hand toward the front door. As he rounded the corner into the lobby, he could see all the bullpen fellas golf-clapping their approval.

He turned and walked back past them into his office, going directly to his file cabinet. Staglione had come down the hall and was staring at Daniel as he sifted through the folders.

"All dose files are da property of V.S.E.," he proclaimed loudly. "You can't take none of 'em."

"I don't want your files, Vince," Daniel said boldly as he pulled a stock certificate from a folder labeled "personal." "But this is mine." Staglione began to block the door but quickly reconsidered, presumably under a swift remembrance of Al's promise. Daniel skirted past him as Staglione sorted through his limited vocabulary for something to say.

Daniel returned to Sydney and headed out V.S.E.'s doors for the last time. As he and Sydney descended the elevator, it stopped again at the fifth floor and the small family rejoined them, the mother's face illuminated with what Daniel gathered was the promise of something better found in the training office. The kids were more animated now, emboldened by their mother's optimism and her translation to them of what the new job meant. Sydney looked down at the little boy and Daniel could see for the first time that she wanted a son.

In the parking lot, he opened Sydney's car door for her. Alone for the first time, she asked Daniel through the driver's window, "Why today?"

"It was time," Daniel said and then told her of Julian's treachery just a few moments before he'd found her in Staglione's office.

"Honey, I don't care if I have to go back to Applebee's or work two shifts to make the note and support this kid," Daniel explained under the warmth of the midday sun. "But I need to be somebody our child can be proud of, somebody you can be proud of. I can't do that here."

"I am always proud of you, Danny," Sydney said as they hugged in the middle of the parking lot. "You know what's right."

"Maybe I do now," Daniel said, having no idea what his next move would be, but knowing that shedding Julian and Staglione today meant that tomorrow he would awaken without the angst of a man mired in guilt and doubt. That would have to be enough.

Daniel thrust his hands in his pants pockets and felt the message from Amber. He dialed her number as Sydney left the parking lot with a supportive wave.

"I'm leaving tonight," Amber said confidently, as if asserting something more. "I'm going home. Vegas isn't for me."

"I'm sorry to hear that, Amber," Daniel replied. "I'm glad we got a chance to know each other."

"Yeah, you're about the only decent guy I ever met out here," she reported, thankful for Daniel's patience when she was in search of a wayward Julian. "And you've got a girlfriend."

"I've got a fiancée now," Daniel corrected softly. "And I've got a baby on the way."

"Really?" Amber said, genuinely pleased for Daniel. "You guys are going to have a beautiful child."

"Thanks … so why the sudden move, Amber?" Daniel asked. "Why go home now?"

"I needed to make a change," Amber explained. "I always felt out of place out here, you know. Like I was at Disneyland or something. Nothing's really real.

"But actually, it was Julian more than anything," Amber added. "I just found myself tolerating things I never would have before, letting him get away with treating me that way."

"I completely understand," Daniel said. "I know that had to be rough."

"Look, he is what he is," Amber said. "He didn't trick me. I let him do what he did. And I tolerated it over and over again because I thought being with a guy like Julian made me feel better about myself. Like I was doing something good out here.

"But every time he used me, every time he lied to me, I just felt dirty, you know, like I was some rented whore," she continued, speaking more clearly than Daniel had ever heard her. "And I probably would have stayed out here and let him play me whenever he wanted if I hadn't gotten pregnant."

"You're pregnant, Amber?" Daniel said, surprised. "I don't know what to say to that."

"Well, don't say anything," she answered with a newfound confidence. "Especially not to Julian. He's never going to know about this baby. You're the only one in Vegas who knows. I don't want his money and I don't want him. I'm going to stay at my mom's until I can get a job doing something. But this baby isn't going to call Julian daddy. I can't let that happen."

"I'm so sorry," Daniel consoled, disregarding his fading instinct to defend Julian. "I won't say a word to him."

"Don't be sorry, Danny," Amber said, more upbeat than Daniel. "I'm going home to have a healthy baby with my family around me. Everything gets better from here."

"That's true," Daniel said. "I'm sad to see you go but I can appreciate your decision. Believe me, I can appreciate it."

"Yeah?" Amber asked, "I can only imagine what he's done to you. I guess Julian just uses everyone he can, eh?"

"Not anymore, Amber," Daniel responded. "He's lost me as a friend and he's lost you too."

"And he's lost a child he's never going to know about," Amber added. "Stay in touch, will ya?"

"Absolutely, Amber," Daniel said. "Get home safe."

CHAPTER 26

February 2001

Daniel knew that he and Sydney needed to get married in a hurry. She was just three months along, but an uncomfortable conversation with her parents the previous night left no other impression than to make Sydney an honest woman as soon as possible. Sydney's father was a pragmatist, and though he made it clear he completely disapproved of what he called their "teenage recklessness," he insisted they marry before the baby was born, enhancing the blooming disappointment of a mother who had dreamed of her only daughter's well-planned and grandiose wedding day. But all agreed it was necessary to keep the old man from losing his sanity and acting as if Daniel wasn't at the dinner table on future Sundays.

The only quick solution besides an elopement that Sydney didn't want and that Daniel couldn't afford would be a chapel wedding at one of the cracker boxes on the Strip. Gauche as the prospect seemed, Sydney was thrilled that she could still wear her mother's dress and be married in front of her friends and family. They simply had to choose between the place where Joan Collins tied the knot and where a drunken Dennis Rodman had wed Carmen Electra.

After declining some agency job offers that Mike Martin put together, Daniel started his own public relations firm, taking on mostly small real estate clients from the valley's raging building boom and enjoying an ample distance from the stock market and politics. He opened a small office downtown, borrowing two thousand dollars from his father as a cushion against his rent and mortgage. Mr. Madison had been thrilled to provide the money, taxing as it was, for a son he mistakenly felt needed him less each day.

Against the yardstick of the glittering commission job and the whirlwind that often was V.S.E., the pedestrian copy and regurgitation of new home editorial copy for the local real estate section of the Sunday paper were delightfully mundane. Daniel likened them to an oft-uttered saying of his father's about how there were few things as satisfying as painting your back fence. Daniel had never appreciated the remark until he took on his real estate clients and the alacrity of their writing needs, which were rendered without much risk of failure or disaster—just like his father's proverbial and literal fence. It wasn't the stirring work of a tear-jerking speech or the ambulance-chasing headlines of a market-moving press release, but it was satisfying his clients and paying his bills. That had value.

As Daniel's efforts waned to less-complicated endeavors, Julian's prospects appeared to be headed in the opposite direction. It seemed each night that Commissioner Correa was speaking to reporters about the commission's stance, becoming the handsome face of the governing body. Frank Hayes smiled from his velvet office as Julian claimed the television spotlight, charming reporters like a hundred girls before, delivering sound bites and ratings as a bouquet of microphones reached out to him.

Every time Julian attended a charitable event or party fundraiser, his picture made the news, most often with Meredith by his side. Daniel wondered if he was at all faithful to the young doctor or if he sought the sheets of others, as he had with Amber.

Daniel and Martin rarely spoke of Julian now, with Martin only occasionally mentioning that Correa was becoming an even hotter commodity among the city's elite businessmen. Martin would punctuate any remark uttered in regard to Julian's ascent with a supplemental forecast that his dishonesty and treachery would soon catch up with him. Martin theorized that Julian could only control himself in any situation for so long before he either consumed or destroyed it entirely. Julian's charm and intelligence afforded him the ability to penetrate and succeed, but his avarice and moral turpitude made his stance on any such lofty precipice shaky.

"Just waiting for the fireworks," Martin cajoled. "It should be fun to watch."

Daniel agreed, though he didn't think of Julian that much anymore, despite his ubiquity on the local news broadcasts. As his wedding date drew near and Sydney continued to plan out loud for both the nuptials and the baby's arrival, thoughts of Julian were a luxury of emotion.

Zigler had been calling Sydney every day, and he was testing the limits of Daniel's restraint. His deal with Sydney involved Clint calling *his* phone, so technically Zigler wasn't breaching Sydney's agreement. But that deal had been struck before Daniel knew she was pregnant and Zigler's calls always upset Sydney, who was carrying a baby now. Still, Sydney had pleaded with Daniel not to seek out Zigler, selling Daniel on her suggestion that the wedding would be the line of demarcation that Zigler needed to forfeit the contest. Daniel wasn't so sure, but had yet to force Sydney to provide Clint's contact information.

Daniel asked his high school friend Fred and Mike Martin to stand with him on the tiny stage where the wedding would be performed, marrying his past, present, and future with the invitation of his better friends. Fred and Mike were socioeconomic opposites, but the night before the wedding at the pub near Daniel's house they were brothers of shared virtue and honor. Daniel knew he could count on either man for most anything.

Sydney's preparation for the wedding had been furious as her mother and a girlfriend micromanaged the details like nanotech scientists, arranging and perfecting each nuance. As the women droned on in person and on the phone about colors, and flowers, and hairdos, and invitations, and the likely weather, Daniel came to appreciate the blessings of a smaller wedding service.

Sydney slept at her mother's house the night before the wedding, maintaining the façade as her father wished. It hadn't been said, but Daniel knew Mr. and Mrs. Banks were hoping that six months from now people's memories would fade. Perhaps the incriminating math might not be known and this child might look like a honeymoon baby. At the very least they figured Sydney wouldn't be walking around visibly pregnant wearing just her maiden name.

On the wedding day, Daniel rode with his father to the church, enduring instructive speeches of an unparalleled display. Daniel smiled as his father gave advice on handling your wife, being faithful and then, painfully, how to please a woman. The car grew small and warm as Daniel tried desperately to halt his father's amorous instruction, wanting to hold up a sign that screamed, *"You're married to my mother!"*

Eventually they arrived and Daniel leapt from the car as if it were a rodeo bull, craving the outside air and the comparatively pleasing sounds of the Strip's car horns, traffic, and a random Mariachi band nearby. Fred and Mike Martin stood at the door of the chapel, poorly concealing their passing of a flask of booze, seemingly wanting to be caught like kids spiking the punch at a high school dance, seeking credit for the mischievous effort. It pleased Daniel to see Fred and Martin hitting it off, his friendship their only outward commonality. It galvanized in him the appreciation of the mettle he saw in each and, in turn, himself. Character wore both blue jeans and tailored suit pants.

Daniel knew that Sydney and her entourage were in a waiting room at the rear of the chapel, applying and reapplying eye makeup to Sydney's face as her mother ruined her own. Her father was nowhere to be seen, though Daniel suspected he was in the family car with a wine bottle treading the line between coerced tolerance of the imperfect ceremony and the ability to walk the aisle with his daughter.

The blue sky provided a window of sunlight in the February afternoon, and their rented tuxedos offered just enough warmth to stand outside in comfort. The green needles of the chapel's desert pines betrayed any scenic expression of cold. Colorful annuals dotted whiskey-barrel containers around the building's edge. The venue's wedding planner gave the men warnings in five-minute increments, his voice lilting in a high and feminine tone that Fred was physically incapable of not mocking in imitation, much to the delight of Mike Martin, who normally would abstain from such political incorrectness.

Daniel's father joined the men, quizzing Mike Martin about the senator's activities at a rate to which a mildly inebriated Mike Martin wasn't effectively responding. The jovial tone gave Daniel supplemental comfort as he prepared for a formal declaration of a lifelong union.

Daniel finally relented, taking his first swig of the Kentucky Bourbon in Martin's sterling flask when he thought he saw a Ferrari entering the chapel's lot. Daniel had been on the lookout for the car Sydney said was Zigler's favorite, though he soon dismissed it as just another in the parade of high-end sports cars that cruised Las Vegas Boulevard day and night. If ever there were a place to see a car like that, it would be here.

The handful of guests from both the Banks and Madison invitations milled outside, with only Sydney, her mother, and her maid of honor, Debra, somewhere else. Mr. Banks was standing near the door, arguing in whispered vehemence to a rarely embarrassed Teena. Daniel noticed Mr. Banks' left shoulder against the wall, his suit rubbing against the rough stucco in a manner a sober man would not allow.

Not my problem, Daniel thought. *I like him better this way.*

The wedding coordinator had just poked his head out of the chapel's main entrance like a clock cuckoo when Daniel spotted Clint Zigler standing in the floral-lined walkway staring directly at him. The last time Daniel had seen him in person was when they were all in high school and some kids from his school had partied at a bonfire in the desert with the private school kids from across town. He never knew what had drawn the two groups together and it never happened again as a brutal fight broke out among the clans, life imitating the art of *The Outsiders* film.

Daniel remembered Clint, who had brought a massive stash of beer in the back of a jacked-up pickup, doling it out like a Red Cross worker at a disaster. When Daniel had gone to grab a beer, Clint refused him for an unknown reason as loyal beer beneficiaries stood sentry. Daniel let the spurn go, but had asked who he was, hearing only that he was a "rich asshole" from his high school friends and two kids who went to Clint's school.

This evening Zigler didn't look like he was attending a wedding. He looked like he was coming to break one up. Clint was staring ominously, as if his mere presence were supposed to send Daniel fleeing. Daniel noticed that he hadn't grown since their high school meeting and that he was much heavier than in high school. His hair was thinning at the edges and his black T-shirt was tucked into his pants in a way that accentuated his loathing of situps.

"Well, look who's here," Daniel said acrimoniously to his groomsmen. "I'm pretty sure that little fat-ass isn't on the guest list."

"Who's that, son?" Daniel's father asked, hearing in his son's voice an uncommon tension.

"That's Clint Zigler, Dad," Daniel said. Zigler was now smiling, enthralled by the anxiety he was generating with his presence.

"He looks just like his father. Same dumb look.," Mr. Madison said. "What's he doing here?"

"That's the guy that took a shit in your car?" Fred asked as he tried to readjust the ill-fitting tuxedo pants around a beer drinker's midsection. "I thought you were making him up."

"I'm sure he's here to harass me or to bother Sydney," Daniel said, his heartbeat escalating. "What else is new?"

"Dude, I'll rip his throat out," Fred declared, his speech proportionate to a reasonable consumption from the flask.

"Take it easy," Martin beckoned as he held Fred's wrist, ever the diplomat.

"Why don't you get out of here, son?" Martin yelled to Zigler, who had drawn closer.

"Why don't you worry about your own life, Mikey," Zigler said. "My dad says you've got plenty to be worried about."

"What's that supposed to mean?" Martin inquired.

"It doesn't mean anything," Daniel said. "The fat kid just likes to talk shit."

"Careful, Daniel," Zigler said, stepping closer yet again. "You've seen what I can do. You sure you want me as an enemy?"

Daniel took another step toward Zigler when his father grabbed his arm. "Not now, son," he said firmly. "There's a pretty girl inside waiting for you. Don't give in to this."

The reference to Sydney made Zigler wince, creating an internal tumult that he was hoping to provoke, not experience. The gathered guests encircled the five men, like a planned after-school fight in the parking lot.

"Yeah, I guess he's right," Daniel said reluctantly as he pondered the merits of striking the man who had tormented him for so long. "I need to go get married TO SYDNEY, right?"

"That's right, son," Daniel's father said as Zigler grew more angry at their indifference. "Go get your bride."

Mr. Madison had said the latter in the provocative possessive, effectively infuriating his Napoleonic target. Zigler fumed, seeming to grasp the finality as Sydney suggested. As the four men turned to walk into the church, Zigler's anger forced a courage that he hadn't mustered in previous months of stalking Daniel from a distance. He grabbed at Daniel's black jacket from behind. Zigler stood in front of Daniel, defiant, mustering whatever ferocity his round face could convey.

"Come on, you white trash low-life," Zigler antagonized with what he thought was his biggest gun.

"What'd he call him?" Fred said, wondering if the insult were meant for him. Martin and Fred were still holding each other's arms in their dark suits, like dual grooms on a same-sex wedding cake.

"Take my coat, Fred," Daniel said as he began to shed his black tuxedo jacket, careful not to let the pinned carnation fall from the lapel. "This won't take long."

As Daniel turned, freeing one arm from the jacket Clint Zigler drew back and lunged, throwing a haymaker intent on hitting Daniel's head from behind. But Daniel had turned to his left as Zigler's wild punch went over the top, narrowly missing its mark.

As Zigler's body lurched from the miss, his head turned upward in an awkward effort to regain his balance. Daniel hadn't fully extricated himself from the suit when the next punch came.

Mr. Madison blasted Zigler directly on the chin, sending the younger man sprawling like Mike Tyson in Tokyo. Zigler took four wobbling steps to his right before landing perfectly in a whiskey-barrel of blooming annuals.

"Dammmmmmmmmmn!" Fred exclaimed as Martin stood with eyes wide open. "Your dad just knocked the shit out of that guy." The assembled guests were as speechless as Martin, not knowing the back story nor accustomed to pugilistic opening acts before their nuptials. Daniel looked at his father, who was opening and closing his injurious hand like a black-and-white-era prize fighter, staring down at his opponent, waiting for the ten-count. Imaginary flash bulbs were bursting around him. The episode reminded Daniel of the time his father had charged out of the family home with an old Smith & Wesson, chasing off five teenage thugs prying an eleven-year-old Daniel's fingers off his new bicycle.

The cuckoo-clock wedding coordinator reappeared at the door, deliriously waving to Daniel to hurry along and oblivious to the half-conscious Zigler splayed in a planter.

"Mr. Madison, that was a helluva punch," Fred said admiringly. "He's gonna feel that tomorrow."

"His daddy's gonna feel that today," Mr. Madison said confidently. "I wonder who the kid will say did it? He's not going to want to tell people that an old man popped him."

"Who cares?" Daniel said, laughing a little that his aging father had been his savior. "At least we know I can get married in peace. Come on, boys."

As the men opened the door and began to walk in, Daniel turned back to mock his fallen foe. "Nighty-night, Clint. We'll miss you at the reception."

CHAPTER 27

August 2001

"**D**ANIEL, I NEED YOU!" Sydney wailed from the bedroom. Daniel was pulling on a pair of dress shoes in front of the television in the living room, watching the morning news as he downed a coffee and Pop-tart before work. He sprang to the bedroom quickly, knowing the distress call from a woman four days past her due date required no squandering of time.

"My water broke," Sydney said in a voice that fused anxiety, enthusiasm, and fear. "And I'm having contractions."

"Wow, are we going to have to get new sheets," Daniel instinctively teased to Sydney's complete lack of amusement.

"WHO FREAKING CARES!" Sydney shouted, her voice indicating a contraction to complement the puddle.

"I was kidding, Syd," Daniel said, realizing his attempt at levity would find no purchase now. "Should I get your bag?"

"YES! GET MY DAMN BAG!" Sydney said unpleasantly as her pulse quickened. The Lamaze class hadn't really addressed the level of abuse that could be expected as the contractions intensified.

The urgency of the moment required an obedience that had Daniel running bags to the car, grabbing Sydney's robe and slippers, and taking a verbal pounding throughout. Her breaths became labored and her contractions more acute as they drove to the hospital. Daniel worried that Sydney's car might wind up being the baby's first nursery.

He managed to reach Sydney's mother from his cell phone as they drove and Sydney's shouting and exclamations caused Mrs. Banks to ask seriously if they were having a domestic dispute. He corrected her quickly and she ensured him the Banks family would soon join them at the maternity ward. Daniel dialed his father and mother too, keeping the call brief and asking his dad to call his friends on his behalf.

The hospital admitted Sydney quickly, ascertaining from her dilation that the baby would be arriving soon. Sydney had arrived too late for an epidural and was vacillating between praising Daniel lovingly and cursing him for not getting her to the hospital quickly enough to receive the pain-killer.

Sydney's contraction-related exclamations had become comedic, with Sydney even laughing at them between the waves of pain. Still, the baby's pending arrival had Daniel as nervous as he'd ever been, trepidatious about every aspect of the process. Sydney gripped Daniel's hand tightly, looking up appreciatively at her husband. Their first six months of marriage had gone mostly smoothly, with only the occasional argument about money breaking the harmony of the newlyweds. Sydney's previous state of affluence was making the modest trappings of their home life difficult, and her withdrawal from regular fine dining, travel, and shopping often manifested into some direct or indirect criticism of Daniel. He knew she was struggling with the loss of her figure to the pregnancy and the domestic life of her maternity, but her occasional complaints about their fiscal state made him wonder if he could ever satisfy her completely.

"I wonder if our baby will have your green eyes or my blue eyes, Sydney?" Daniel asked, hoping to distract her from the pain. "I guess it's a safe bet that its hair will be blond like both of ours though, eh?"

"Our baby will be beautiful, Danny," Sydney said warmly. "How could it not be?"

"Mr. Madison?" the nurse's voice interrupted. "You've got some friends waiting in the hall and I believe it's your father who keeps trying to sneak down here. We've threatened to call security twice already."

"I'll speak to him," Daniel answered, laughing, as Sydney smiled widely.

"Please do, and advise him that being a biology teacher does not qualify him to be in the delivery room," the husky nurse added as she began to examine Sydney.

"I'll tell him that too," Daniel replied as he looked back at Sydney. "He's gonna be a heckuva grandpa, isn't he?"

"Hurry back, Danny," Sydney said sweetly, a few minutes short of her *Sybil*-generating contractions. Daniel entered the white hallway, looking for his father. Seated twenty feet farther down, Mike Martin and his father sat alongside a massive Al Morris.

"Hey, fellas," Daniel said.

"How's she doing, Danny?" an invigorated Mr. Madison asked. "Is my grandchild here?"

"Not yet, pops," Daniel answered. "And you've got to let those nurses work. We don't need them pissed at us."

"Awwwww," Mr. Madison replied with a dismissive wave of his hand, using an unintelligible sound to convey his displeasure.

"We'll wait it out down here, Danny," Mike Martin said helpfully as he put his arm around Daniel's father. "Mr. Madison still hasn't told me how he first met the senator."

"It was 1963, and I was at the Golden Nugget ..." Mr. Madison started on cue. Daniel restrained a smile and winked at Martin, knowing he'd handled Daniel's currently choleric father perfectly. He turned to Al whom he hadn't seen since the dubious day at Staglione's office.

"Morris ... what are you doing here?" Daniel inquired.

"My buddy's having a baby," Al explained. "Aren't I welcome?"

"Of course you are," Daniel said, realizing his question, borne of surprise, might have come out wrong. "I just have no idea how you knew we were here. My dad called you?"

"Nah, you did," Al said. "I was on my way to the gym and I pick up my cell phone to hear a woman screaming and calling you a son-of-a-bitch. I thought you were having rough sex. I think you accidentally dialed me."

Daniel reached down and realized his car keys and mobile phone were in the same front pants pocket, a mixture that had generated inadvertent calls from his phone in the past. "I'm glad you're here, big man," Daniel said. "It was meant to be."

As the men shook hands, a nurse came down the hall, calling Daniel in impassioned form. "Mr. Madison, you'd better get in there if you want to see your baby born."

"Hey, Dan, piece of advice—be the first base coach, not the umpire," Martin advised. "Trust me, I've got plenty of friends with kids. You want to be up around her head holding her hand, not over the doctor's shoulder looking at the crime scene."

"Ohhhhhhh," Daniel replied as he grasped the concept. "It's that bad?"

"I'm told it can be," Martin said, laughing a little. "One of my pals said it took him six months to shake the image."

Daniel turned and sprinted down the hall. As he entered the room he found a half-dozen medical professionals at battle stations and Sydney staring at the doorway.

"Baby, get over here," Sydney called, her voice encumbered by the fatigue of the delivery. Beads of sweat dotted her forehead and her perspiration-drenched hair clung to the side of her face like a wet paintbrush. "The baby's almost out." Daniel remembered Mike Martin's advice and went to Sydney's side, stroking her flaxen hair with his fingertips. Sydney was pushing as best she could and soon a cry pierced the air. A look of relief washed over Sydney's face, and Daniel knew it was a welcome blend of healthy baby and abatement of the pain of labor. A nurse quickly cleansed the baby's nose and mouth and presented the little girl to Sydney.

"Congratulations, Mr. and Mrs. Madison," said the formerly intense nurse who had now transitioned to a more congenial posture. "She's beautiful. Pretty long too. Must've been cooking inside you nicely those extra four days."

"Look at her, Sydney," Daniel beamed, oblivious to anything the nurse had said. The baby girl's red face made Daniel think of a prize fighter, thanking God and his trainer after a victory, their faces battered and flushed. Sydney pressed her lips against the baby's head, their lipstick-free color nearly the same as the infant's skin tone. Sydney's hair was mussed in a way that she had never allowed Daniel to see and her face was a palate of natural colors. With the little girl in her arms, Daniel had never seen her more beautiful.

"Her face is shaped just like yours, Sydney," Daniel reported. "And her little lips make that cute little *M* just like yours do." Sydney turned her head to survey Daniel's description, eager to see the shared traits with her daughter.

"Mr. Madison," the nurse called from the doorway. "Is that your father trying to hide behind the pillar at the nurse's station?" Daniel looked past the nurse to see his father peering from behind a column like Inspector Clouseau, trying to peer into the delivery room.

"Tell him it's all right to come in now," the nurse relented. "As long as your wife is up for it."

"I'm up for it," Sydney said as she looked up from the peaceful child nestled against her bosom. "Let him meet his granddaughter."

"Come on in, Dad," Daniel waved and mouthed to his clandestine father. "Come see this beautiful little girl." Daniel gently cupped his hand behind her tiny head just as he'd been shown in the Lamaze classes. As his father hurried into the now-placid delivery room, Daniel walked over to a window where the building's fourth floor offered a broad view of the city.

"Sweetheart," Daniel whispered to the little girl looking up at him. "I'm gonna give you everything. I will always be there for you. Daddy loves you."

"She's a beaut, son," Daniel's father said as the first parental tear ran down Daniel's cheek. Mr. Madison turned and walked over to Sydney, kissing her forehead as she looked nearly asleep. "You did good, kid ... real good.

"I'm going to get out of your way so that your mother can come down here," Mr. Madison told Sydney. "I've seen what I needed to see."

"Thank you, Grandpa," Sydney said pleasantly through a weak voice, the title buoying a jubilant Mr. Madison further. "Send my mom and dad in and then let's get Daniel's mom too. Then I'm going to take a little nap."

"That's fine, honey," Daniel agreed. "I just want to look at this little girl as long as they'll let me."

CHAPTER 28

September 2001

"**B**etter watch your head, kid," Frank Hayes warned as Julian lined up behind his golf ball in the desert pine-lined fairway. "That foursome behind us might hit onto us if you don't hurry."

"If they hit onto us, I'm gonna wrap my nine iron around somebody's neck," Julian said reactively.

"See, that's the kind of thing you can't do anymore, Julian," Frank said as Julian sized up his shot. "You're a big deal now, out in the public eye, crafting important rules to govern our fair city." Hayes' lecture had the insincere tone of a game show host describing a prize.

"But I can say that sort of thing, Julian," Hayes continued as he gestured to himself, his voice taking on a more gritty tenor. "I'm not a public servant, and the only thing that matters to me is how much money I've got, who owes me a favor, or who knows that I can bury them. So, take as much time as you want, kid. If anyone hits onto us, I'm gonna personally shove a golf ball up their ass."

Julian tried to concentrate on the dimpled white ball in front of him, his mind divided between the physical task and deciphering Hayes's double-meanings. Frank was always flexing in front of Julian, directly and indirectly reminding Julian who was boss. Correa had done everything he'd been asked as a commissioner, securing every vote for Frank's guys and killing any ordinance that might be less than beneficial. Unfortunately, none of it mattered to Frank, and Julian knew the ledger would never be even. Frank refused to quantify the favors he had done for him and by refusing to do so prohibited Julian from ever paying the bill in full.

That was exactly how Hayes wanted it, using the bottomless debt to control the young commissioner, who had now become chairman of Southern Nevada's most important governing body. Julian's star was rising and with it Frank's demands. Each prickly insult or testosterone-fueled diatribe fostered a contempt that Julian knew he couldn't bear much longer.

Today's golf outing was the prototypical Frank Hayes double-edged sword. Hayes would undoubtedly emasculate Julian throughout the day, but he was also developing a relationship for Julian with two considerable sources of power in Las Vegas: a wealthy Mormon bishop and a strip club owner.

Julian's ball sailed to the right of the green without the arrival of any projectile from the other foursome. "Nice shot, Julian," Hayes faux complimented him. "You're only twenty yards farther from the pin than I am."

"Maybe when I'm as old as you are I'll be as good," Julian shot back. "Of course, you'll be dead then."

"That's funny," Frank responded without laughing.

"Hey, maybe you can have your head frozen like Ted Williams and I can bring you out here on nice days," Julian taunted, enjoying a verbal attack on Frank in the safe covenant of golf shit-talking.

"Oh, Julian," Frank answered icily. "What makes you think you'll live longer than me?"

Julian didn't answer, and Frank left it at that, putting his ball in easily as Julian three-putted. Frank parked the cart next to the restroom after the turn at the ninth hole as did the remainder of their diverse foursome.

"How you hittin' it, kid?" asked Bruce Zigler as he patted Julian on the back.

"I stopped keeping score around the fifth hole if that tells you anything, Mr. Zigler," Julian replied. "We didn't play much golf where I come from."

"I thought you were from Florida," Zigler said, his ivory-white golf shirt and pants more appropriate for strawberries and cream at Wimbledon. "That's one of the top golf locales in the country. My kid brother's got a club outside of Tampa. He plays five days a week."

"I guess what I meant to say was that kids in my neighborhood didn't play much golf," Julian said. "Golf isn't real big among the Cubans."

"Oh, I see," the elder man acknowledged as the breeze freed a long strand of white hair from a combover. "Really never knew too many Cubans. We've got mostly Mexicans out here, you know." Julian noted how Zigler referred to Mexicans as pestilence, simultaneously equating them to locusts and Cubans as Frank grinned at their dialogue.

"How we doin', boys?" said the last member of the foursome as he handed each of them a beer in a plastic cup. "Sure is nice out here today.

"To hittin' 'em better, eh?" said Bobby Henson as he raised his own beer toward the heavens. "Hey, Frank, you want to get a little something to eat after we're done? You know I can't go straight home after we've been drinkin'." Henson's voice had the beginnings of a Southern accent that was really the last remnant of one, having been diluted each year after his rural Oklahoma youth gave way to a Las Vegas adolescence when his parents moved the family.

"She'll have my hide if I miss church and I come home from drinking," Henson explained as he wiped his neck with a handkerchief he kept in his pocket.

"Don't they have a back-up bishop when the starter can't make it?" Hayes kidded as he returned to the group, beer in hand.

"Somethin' like that, Frank," Henson agreed. "As long we keep our tithing in, everyone's happy."

"Your tithing's gotta be pretty significant, Bobby," Hayes said. "I think your little company's tacking up the drywall in every new home in the city."

"We'll do every one you bring us, that's for sure," Bobby agreed, his round face holding a smile between deep, boyish dimples. His neat haircut gave him the white-collar look of a doctor, but his small eyes reminded Julian of something else. "They ain't never happy and I'm a bishop. Hell, I had to stop using a Mormon tax guy 'cause I was afraid he was gonna tell 'em what my real gross income is. I'm using that little Jewish fella you got, Frank," he reported as he sipped the remainder of his beer like aged wine. "He does a fine job."

"Well, you're welcome … for the contracts and the Jew," Hayes replied. "Happy to help a friend."

"We've got a sweet little reciprocity network going now," Hayes began his sermon, taking his place at the head of the table like a father at Thanksgiving. "That's why I've got you all here. There's some work to be done."

"That's for sure," Zigler confirmed in animated form, looking straight at Henson.

"Easy there, Bruce," Hayes said to Zigler. "Bobby's one of the good guys. He's on the team."

"I'm sorry, Frank," Bruce said, looking flustered as he wiped his brow with a silk handkerchief. "But if we don't stop this thing, I'm through. I'll turn the place into a damn Starbucks and sell the son-of-a-bitch." His jewelry danced as he spoke, a mixture of gold, platinum, and white gold apropos only in a place where the Statue of Liberty looked down on King Arthur's Court and an Egyptian pyramid.

"Bobby, we gotta get your people to back off on this ordinance to ban alcohol in all the strip clubs," Frank said. "If it passes, it's real bad for Bruce. The Unicorn needs all the business it can get right now with the corporate competition cutting into his market."

"It wasn't my idea, Frank," Bobby explained. "And I don't think anyone really gives a hoot if it passes or doesn't pass. It's just a vehicle, you know … to have our guys look more family oriented."

"I understand exactly what it is," Frank said as Julian looked on, waiting nervously to discover his own part in the play. "You pick a conservative issue, use that as a rallying cry that you've got to get people who care about 'our issues' in office, and then run your own candidates into the bolstered turnout. That's nothing new. They'll do it with gay marriages next."

"But it can't pass, Bobby. You've got to get them to ease up on that. Spread the word to the bishops to get their members to stop pressuring the other commissioners, and Julian will bring them over our way. Without any constituent pressure they'll be easier to flip. I'll deliver your candidates the two races you guys need to even things out. And I'll keep feeding you construction business, my friend."

Once again, Julian was the last to know what he would have to do, with Frank showing him how the man moved the marionettes.

"So, we've got that settled for now," Hayes said. "Bruce, we'll straw poll the commission about a week before the election to make sure that it won't pass. That'll give Bobby enough time between now and then to kill the Mormon support from the inside. And Bobby, we'll run a poll on the two races you care about so your people know your two Mormon candidates are a lock.

"Everybody happy?" Hayes asked, punctuating his plan with a request for assent.

"I think I can sell that," Bobby said as he extended his hand to Bruce Zigler.

"I appreciate it, Mr. Henson," Zigler said genuinely. "I'll enjoy the back nine a lot more with this out of the way."

"Well, should we get back out there before anyone else passes us?" Bobby asked Hayes, acknowledging the food chain with the simple request.

"One other thing before we do, Bobby," Hayes said. "I wanted to see if you could help Julian here with something."

"Why sure," Bobby said amiably. "Whaddaya need, Commissioner?"

"I have no idea," Julian said blank-faced, looking toward Hayes. "What do I need?"

Dismissing the sarcasm, Hayes began his next strategy session with the men. "Well, I think our man Correa here is showing the mettle and, more importantly, the demographic appeal to run for governor next year. If we can add one more layer to his candidacy, he's a shoo-in."

"Frank, there's already a strong candidate in the field," Julian said, interested and puzzled. "And the election is just a little more than a year away."

"I wouldn't worry about him. He's going to drop out, he just doesn't know it yet," Hayes said with trademark confidence. "He hasn't had enough time to spend any party money yet. That's all that matters. You'll have a war chest waiting for you, Julian. With voter registration just about dead even statewide, it's always a crap shoot. And we can get you even better looking.

"Julian, that little doctor gal of yours is Mormon, isn't she?" Hayes asked, the answer already known to him.

"She grew up Mormon, but I've been with her almost a year now and she's never been to church," Julian explained, uncomfortable as to where this might be going. "I think she's more or less an agnostic. She had a change of heart in med school."

"Was she baptized?" Bobby asked.

"I think so," Julian answered. "We talked about this a little when we first started dating. Neither one of us is real passionate about organized religion. No offense, Mr. Henson."

"None taken, son," Henson replied. "It's not always for me either."

"Well, that's going to change, Julian," Frank said with the supreme arrogance that made Julian bristle. "We've got to add that extra layer."

"I see where you're going, Frank," Bobby said. "That sure won't hurt."

"We're gonna put you on the squad, Commissioner," Bobby said, wrapping a burly arm around an uneasy Correa. "Get your bathin' suit ready, brother."

"Oh, no. I'm not converting to anything, Frank," Julian said. "The Mormon religion sounds like a beautiful faith with the strong family values and all. I've read a little about the theology and it seems real nice, but you don't want me. I can't see myself being Mormon."

"Can you see yourself as governor, Julian?" Frank asked.

"Well, yeah, you and I have talked about this. That's always been my goal," Julian answered, afraid what that confirmation meant to this discussion.

"Well, sport, your Latin-ass and party-boy ways won't go over north of Las Vegas in those cow counties unless you've got some conservative credentials," Hayes said, moving his verbal pawn forward. "With Meredith already Mormon it looks natural and genuine. And Bobby here will fast-track the process for you."

"Frank, man, I don't know about doing something so drastic," Julian resisted, partly because it was Frank's idea and that he'd sprung it on him by surprise, as if his opinion didn't matter. "My mother's a devout Catholic."

"I'm pretty sure that's the first time you've ever mentioned your mother, Julian," Hayes said. "How close can you be? She wasn't even here on election night." Julian sat silently, hating Hayes more with each denouncement and dictate.

"Well, give it some serious consideration," Frank said, easing off strangely. "It would wash any gigolo reputation you have away, especially when you get married and settle down."

"Not too settled down to come to my joint once in a while, though," Zigler teased as older men liked to with the youngest in the group.

"I'll think about it, Frank," Julian said, still irritated that Hayes had ambushed him. "We'll have to see. I'll talk to Meredith and see what she's comfortable with. We haven't even set a date to get married yet."

"See if she's comfortable with being the first lady of Nevada," Frank retorted. "Meredith's a smart girl. This is the right move for your family. Maybe you'll start a family while you're up in Carson City. There's nothing else to do up there."

"It'll be like that TV show *Benson*," Henson offered jovially.

"Fan-*tastic*," Julian said sarcastically, eager to return to the links and away from the discussion of his spiritual free agency.

"Wish my boy would meet a nice girl," Zigler offered to no one in particular. "The kid needs to settle down and focus on his business. I got twenty Russian models a night in the club and this kid's chasing some married broad. I'll never understand it."

"That reminds me, Bobby," Zigler said. "Candy's in from Seattle this week. She'll want to see you."

"She is, is she?" Bobby noted with a smile borne of pleasant memories. "Well, I may have to drop by and give you another estimate on the renovation, Bruce."

"Aaaaah, this is what I like to hear," Hayes said pleasantly. "All my friends working together so nicely. It just warms my black heart."

Julian feigned a smile as they got back into the golf cart. Hayes was right about friends working together, and after this conversation Julian knew that someday a powerful friend of the father he had never met might have to help him with Frank Hayes.

CHAPTER 29

December 2001

"Look at those big brown eyes," Mike Martin said as he awkwardly held the little girl in his thick arms. "I've got to get me one of these."

"You need to find someone who'll let you lay on top of her first," Daniel kidded as Sydney warmed up baby food in the kitchen. "But we'll let you rent Sofia so we can go out on Friday nights."

"Hold on there," Mike said. "If I don't go out on Fridays, how will I find someone to lie on?"

"I guess you have a point there," Daniel conceded. "But she sure loves her Uncle Mike. She never cries when you hold her. Even my dad doesn't have that effect and he's here twice a day." The baby's dark eyes danced as the men spoke, as if their kidding were infant theater. Her thin light brown hair held two pink bows that Sydney insisted she wear each day since someone had called Sofia a "handsome little man" in the grocery store.

"So, what's the latest at work?" Martin asked as Sydney returned to collect Sofia.

"Well, it isn't that we've got nowhere to store all the money we're making," Sydney interrupted, setting a bottle of Belgian beer down in front of each of them. Daniel shot Sydney a hostile glance as Martin tried to keep his face still amid the acrimony.

"Things have been a little slow lately, Mike," Daniel explained. "Two of our main accounts brought somebody on in-house and we haven't replaced the business yet. We're keeping our head above water, and I've been going in a couple hours early to prospect for new business."

"Dan, if you need anything—" Martin began.

"No, Mike, it's nothing like that," Daniel said. "We're just not getting rich, you know? The bills are paid, food's on the table, we just aren't making the big money. And some of us are used to big money," Daniel said as Sydney returned the hostile glance.

Martin looked like the defendant at a felony sentencing, doing his best to remain expressionless amid the newlyweds' bickering.

"But this house is full of love!" Martin exclaimed, erupting humorously and loudly, his big voice startling the four-month-old baby in Sydney's arms. Daniel and Sydney both laughed, desirous of a departure from the squabble. Sydney soothed the child with soft shhhhhhh's that turned the beginnings of a sputtering cry into a placid coo. As the baby calmed, she returned to the kitchen for the evening feeding.

"You know, Mike, everything's been pretty good here since the wedding," Daniel said in a voice that could only be heard by Martin. "I absolutely love that little girl. When I got married I kind of felt like it fulfilled me, like my heart was full. But when Sofia was born … I've never felt anything like it. If marriage fills your heart, being a parent makes your heart bigger.

"There's nothing I wouldn't do for Sofia," he continued. "If she's got a diaper rash or her stomach is upset, I totally blow it out of proportion I love her so much. A friend of my mother's used to say having a child was like wearing your heart outside your body. Man, is that ever true."

"You realize that's two heart metaphors in about three minutes," Martin said, needling Daniel.

"Pretty sappy, eh?" Daniel asked, aware that his exposition might not make sense to a bachelor like Martin. A year ago, it wouldn't have made sense to him either.

"It's hard though," Daniel confessed as Martin listened attentively. "Syd's not used to being a housewife, and she's not used to a budget." He lowered his voice further and leaned in as if telling Martin a government secret. "She's great most of the time, Mike, but she's really having a tough time with the money issue. The other night I stopped at Walmart on the way home and bought Sofia a little sleeper. I thought it was cute, but when I brought it in and she saw it she started to cry, telling me that I wouldn't understand.

"I understand that she thinks something from Walmart isn't good enough for our baby. But man, it's a freakin' sleeper, not a prom dress. Chances are she's going to puke on it every time she wears it. Must we purchase designer sleepers?"

"She'll be all right after awhile," Martin said. "You know, a lot of women get postpartum depression. My sister had to be treated for it after my nephew was born. She was miserable."

"She's not miserable," Daniel said. "She's happy most of the time. I don't think it's postpartum depression, I think it's *past purchase* depression.

"Sydney's just not getting what she's accustomed to, and the baby's made her more sensitive to the issue, kind of like the way I tend to overreact to anything with Sofia's health or safety. But my stock from V.S.E. is ready to be sold. It's been a year and it's not worth what it used to be, but the proceeds will definitely give us a big shot in the arm. That'll be a real Band-Aid for Sydney."

Martin looked like he understood and sipped from a bottle of beer he'd had sitting in front of him for a few minutes. "So, have you heard from the little guy lately?"

"Zigler?" Daniel asked. "Yeah, I think he still calls and hangs up here once in a while. Right before he hangs up I say into the phone, 'I'm telling my dad!'

"He hasn't said a word for a long time. I think he just does it to tell Sydney that she's still on his mind. I can live with that. I know where she's sleeping at night and I completely trust her."

"Probably best to just ignore it entirely, Danny," Martin advised. "It's hard to predict what crazy people will do. He's not all there, as you know." Martin looked at the red digital numbers of the clock on the cable box and leaned forward. " Danny, I've got a red-eye flight back to D.C. tomorrow morning, so I'm gonna hit the road … that is, unless you want me to give you two some family therapy?"

"Let me get your coat for you," Daniel said, dismissing Martin's little tease. "What are you going to D.C. for?"

"I'm going to ask the senator for his blessing on a gubernatorial campaign," Martin said calmly, as if that wasn't a bombshell announcement. "Rumor has it that McCallister is out of the race because of some personal issues. They'll have to find someone fast."

"Really? You're kidding? Man, why didn't you tell me earlier?" Daniel asked incredulously.

"Didn't want to jinx it," Mike explained. "I wanted to come back and hopefully tell you the good news. You know, I don't want to pull a 'Julian,' but if I'm elected, your money troubles are over. You're the first guy I'd have on my staff. I can hire you to do all my speeches and press releases, Danny. That should get Sydney off your back a little."

"So now I've got to be sitting here like a kid on Christmas Eve waiting for you to tell me if you're going to run, eh?" Daniel said. "Thanks a lot.

"Hey, man, have a good trip and best of luck with that," Daniel said as he shook Martin's hand affectionately. "Forget about what that does for us ... I really want that for you."

"Thanks, buddy," Martin said. "You'll be my second call after I let my mom in Boston know what he says. She's been going to church twice a day to pray for me since I told her."

Sydney carried Sofia to the door to say goodbye, and Mike made her laugh yet again with a series of silly faces. "She is a cutie," Martin said to Daniel. "I'm so glad she looks nothing like you."

"Take care, Mike," Daniel said, laughing as he closed the door.

Neither Sydney nor Daniel mentioned the money quarrel again that night, and other than the usual fuss with Sofia at her last feeding, the night was uneventful. Daniel didn't mention Martin's potential candidacy to Sydney, not wanting to exacerbate the growing financial sore spot with an uncertain golden parachute. Still, he pondered the possibility in detail, asking himself if he wanted to re-enter a political race after the disappointment of the past. But Martin was a far cry from

Julian and his absence of character. Mike was a man Sofia would soon call "Uncle Mike."

The next morning Daniel made a point of telling Sydney to get her mother to watch Sofia this weekend and to schedule dinner anywhere she wanted. Sydney leapt at the opportunity, pondering out loud which of her previous gourmet haunts would be best to revisit. Daniel cringed as she named a litany of luxurious places he had never been to, telling himself that his meeting with Staglione this morning had to go well.

As he entered through the doors of V.S.E., Daniel noticed immediately that there was no receptionist. The office seemed cold, and the aquarium was full of green algae, the colorful saltwater fish nowhere in sight. He stood there for a few minutes, awaiting another human appearance. When none arrived, Daniel headed down the hallway toward his old office and Staglione's master suite. One by one he passed empty offices, including the abandoned bullpen, with phone after black phone sitting stationary on faux wood desktops. At the end of the hall sat Dottie, same as before, but wearing a headset that confirmed she now doubled as a receptionist for whomever was still calling the ghost town of an office.

"Hi, Dottie," Daniel said pleasantly. "I'm here to see Vince."

"Hello, Mr. Madison," Dottie responded professionally, as if the sparse offices housed a Fortune 500 firm. "Mr. Staglione is expecting you. Go right in."

"Okay," Daniel agreed, not sure what to make of the overt formality. Staglione's door was partially open and his office dimly lit.

"Come on in, kid," Staglione said as Daniel's hand grasped the door knob. Staglione rotated his leather chair to greet Daniel, following him like a skeet shooter. "How ya been, Danny? Been awhile, eh?"

"Yeah, about a year," Daniel said, not sure what the passage of time had done to soften the blow of the way things had ended. Daniel looked back toward the door and thought of how Al had entered the office to rescue him, sacrificing his job in the process. "Looks like there have been some changes here."

"Yeah, we're on ta phase two," Staglione said nonchalantly, as if all the changes were volitional. "We don't need da staff we used to have. It's just bad overhead and half of dem were morons, as youse well know. Da stock has enough support from da right market makers dat doin' what we used to do don't really madder all dat much. Da company just has to continue to execute da business plan and sell more of dem StopShots. Dey're really crankin' 'em out at da factory."

"Oh, that's great," Daniel said. "I see that the stock's pulled back quite a bit, so any good news might help."

"Yeah, we couldn't sustain dat price forever," Staglione explained. "We had some early investors who had to move dere stock and it took a hit. But dey're out now and dey're happy, so overall it was good for da company."

"That's great, Vince," Daniel said, beginning the segue to his rehearsed speech. "That's why I came to see you."

"I know why you're here, kid," Vince said confidently. "Maybe I can help."

"That would be great, Vince."

"So, I can probably bring you back on here part time, Danny. But you'd havda do things my way. No more backtalk like before. Hopefully now dat you've hadda taste of da real world you realize how good you had it here, no?" Vince said, waiting for Daniel to agree.

"Wow, Vince," Daniel said. "I don't know what to say."

"You don't gotta say nuttin," Vince continued. "Let's just let bygones be gones." The malapropism made Daniel pause for a second, delaying his response.

"That's very kind of you to offer me the job that I quit, Vince," Daniel said matter-of-factly. "But I've opened my own firm and we're doing all right. What I wanted to see you about was the StopShot shares. It's been a year and they can be sold now."

"Oh, is da first year up already?" Vince said insincerely. "Man, how da time flies."

Daniel knew Vince was aware that it had been a year because Vince and the company had declined his request to lift the restriction and allow the sale. But he knew now that by law Vince and StopShot didn't have to permit the sale at the one-year mark, and that he might have to wait another year before he would be allowed to sell without the company's—or Vince's—permission. That wouldn't help with his current Sydney-related money issues.

"Yeah, the first year's up, Vince," Daniel said, trying not to infect the superficially affable tone with any of his suppressed frustration. "I had my lawyer put in the paperwork and he said it got rejected."

"Oh, was dat yours, Daniel?" Vince said with the genuineness of a starlet victim in a B-movie. "Sorry about dat."

"Yeah, that was mine, Vince, and I've got a baby now," Daniel said. "We could really use that money you promised us from the stock."

"Yeah, well I can't do dat," Vince said coldly. "It's nodda good time."

"Not a good time?" Daniel said incredulously. "You promised me that I would be able to sell in a year when you gave me the stock for all my hard work. It's bad enough that the stock's a fraction of the former value."

"I hear ya," Staglione responded dismissively. "We just can't afford your volume now. If your shares hit da market, da stock will tank even worse. We're going to do a financing soon and we can't have da stock fall any lower. Come back in a year."

"Come back in a year?" Daniel said, his voice rising in tone and tenor. "Vince, I need out of the stock now."

"I really can't help you with dat, Daniel," Vince said as he began to clip his fingernails. "But I can keep you busy with some writing if you want."

"So you won't sign off on the stock?" Daniel said, knowing the answer but wanting to clarify.

"Nah, can't do it," Staglione said as he clipped a nail loudly. "It wouldn't be good for anyone."

"You planned this all along didn't you, Vince?" Daniel asked, finally beginning to see the full spectrum of the hustle. "No one sells their stock, do they? There are birdcages across the country lined with worthless StopShot paper."

"Welcome to da stock market, kid," Staglione said paternally. "You've learned a good lesson here. Never get paid on da come."

"Oh, thanks for the lesson, Vince," Daniel effused sarcastically as his hands glistened with sweat. "You've been a fine teacher."

"Sorry, kid," Vince said. "Besta luck to ya."

Daniel stood up without saying a word as Vince assembled his nail clippings into a neat pile, like a waiter gathering crumbs from the table between courses. As he reached the doorway his anger got the best of him and he turned back to Vince, who was still focused on his manicure. "Maybe I'll just drop a dime to the Securities and Exchange Commission and see if they're interested in anything I have to say," Daniel said.

"You sure you wanna do dat with your name all over dose press releases?" Staglione asked without ever looking at Daniel. "I never signed off on anything, as you might recall. And with your political background, good luck playin' da babe in da woods, Danny. You're gonna look like da freakin' mastermind.

"Hey, but congrats on dat baby," Staglione said as he looked up at Daniel at last. "I'm sure you'll be a great dad with your morals and all."

A dejected Daniel turned and hastily exited the office, knowing he'd been had. Daniel felt like a carjacking victim who had to watch the perpetrator circle the block repeatedly in his vehicle.

Staglione waited to hear the front door slam shut and then dispatched Dottie on an errand to the first floor, getting her out of earshot. He picked up his office phone and dialed a number. "Da kid just left," Staglione reported. "It was about what we expected. He made a few threats which I did my best to discourage.

"I know that," Staglione answered. "That's why we're having this conversation.

"All right, put it in motion," Staglione agreed. "It has to be done. We can't let him cause a problem right now. Take care of it."

Staglione hung up the phone as Daniel was slamming his car door in frustration. He rested his head on the Mustang's steering wheel and recalled how he'd felt this same way in this very place the day Julian betrayed him and he had quit V.S.E. A little over a year had passed and he was still just getting by financially. And now there were two insatiable mouths to feed. He left the key in the ignition unturned and reached into his pocket for his mobile phone. Maybe Martin had some good news.

"Daniel, my brother ..." Martin began to sing the Elton John song before pausing to allow Daniel to speak. "How's my niece?"

"She's fine, Mike," Daniel answered. "It's always a war to get her to eat and she can't hold cereal down, but we find other stuff."

"She sure looks healthy," Martin said. "She's very aware for a baby, really observant."

"Yeah, she's great," Daniel agreed, wanting to move on. "So, where are you right now?"

"Daniel, I am sitting on a bench in Boston Harbor, staring at the sea like an old man," Martin confessed.

"You're in Boston? I thought you were taking a red eye to D.C.?"

"I was in Washington first thing this morning to meet with the senator, who summarily rejected my request. Then I hopped a plane to Boston," Martin explained.

"Man, I'm sorry," Daniel said to a clearly humbled Martin. "What happened?"

"Well, I made my best argument, explained to him how the time was right, politely reminding him of my efforts on his behalf and for a score of other candidates and he agreed that I should be the guy to run for governor. So, I sit there like a jackass, thinking that I'm in and that we're going to just start talking strategy—and then comes the 'but.'"

"The 'but'?" Daniel asked.

"Yeah, the part where the senator said, 'But we've already got some-one else in mind, Mike.' I'll give you one guess who that might be."

"No, man ... you're not gonna tell me that useless bastard is going to run for governor?" Daniel said, knowing already that he was.

"Governor Correa," Martin said somberly, his disgust seeping through his usual professionalism and polish. "How's that make you feel?"

"You know how it makes me feel, Mike," Daniel answered quickly. "It's hard to believe that a guy who does the things he does can continue to climb the ladder."

"Daniel, I console myself knowing that he pays a price for what he's doing, and it's probably one that I wouldn't be willing to pay," Martin said. "The senator seemed as if his hands were tied, like the decision wasn't his. I'm guessing Julian has rallied some considerable support. He does have that dirtbag Hayes on his side."

"Mike, I'm really sorry," Daniel said. "When are you coming home?"

"I don't know," Martin said. "When I left the senator's office I hopped the first plane to Boston. Figured I'd take my mom out for dinner and break the news gently. But when I got off the plane I had a cab bring me down here. My dad used to sit here with me for hours on the week-ends. We'd just talk and talk and talk.

"So, I'm sitting here, staring at the sea, talking to my friend Daniel back in Vegas," he said with the clarity of a man who knew he hadn't lost on merit. "I think I'm trying to figure out what I want to do next. Maybe politics isn't for me."

"Mike, there's a lot of things you can do," Daniel said, not accustomed to authoring pep talks to men of Martin's stature. "Remember, this opportunity didn't even exist two weeks ago. It wasn't a part of your master plan. Just go back to that."

"Yeah, you're right," Martin agreed. "But there's something to be learned here. I'm not sure if the political process rewards loyalty, or honesty, or integrity, Dan. In fact, I'm pretty confident it discourages it."

"You'll get no argument from me," Daniel said. "That's why I'm spending my days writing about oversized lots and granite countertops." Both men laughed a little as each sat near still, surveying their scenery while pondering their path.

"Daniel, I'll give you a shout when I get back into town," Martin said, preparing to end the call. "We'll head over to Crown and throw a couple back. I'd really like that."

"That sounds great, big guy," Daniel affirmed. "Call me when you get home."

Daniel hung up the phone and instantly wondered where Sydney might have made reservations. He figured he was going to have to feign a stomach illness and sneak a meal at home when Sydney wasn't watching. That way, he could order a small appetizer and keep the price down. If he didn't, he'd be into his father's two thousand-dollar cushion by the end of the month.

As he drove homeward, he thought of seeing Sofia and of playing with her on the couch in the living room. She loved to lay on his chest and look up at him as he played peek-a-boo and made her ears flap like Dumbo. Nearing the house, his phone rang again with "Private Caller" displayed. Since no one he knew used a Private Caller setting, Daniel could always recognize the anonymous-intended label as Zigler. "Do I have to call my dad?" Daniel began, teasing his tormentor as usual.

"I know something you don't know," Zigler said in a voice he hoped sounded deranged and antagonistic.

"Oh yeah, what's that?" Daniel asked reflexively, not particularly interested in whatever lunacy Zigler was serving today. "Is it that old men hit hard?"

"I know something you don't know," Clint Zigler sang into the phone yet again.

"That's nice, Clint," Daniel said. "But I've got to go home to my pretty wife and my pretty little girl. Don't you have to go spray Purell on the strippers' poles right now?"

"I know something you don't know," Zigler said a third time. Then he hung up with a satisfaction he hadn't had in a long, long time.

CHAPTER 30

"This is just wonderful, Daniel," Sydney said as she sliced a thin piece of foie gras served with brioche toast and apricots. "It's absolutely divine."

"I'm glad you're enjoying it, sweetheart," Daniel replied in character as he surveyed the room's patrons against the salmon-colored walls and black tablecloths. Everyone was dressed resplendently, with those over fifty in gowns and European suits while most diners under the half-century mark sported the latest in casual chic, ready for a night of clubbing and after-hours joints.

Sydney was in her element, among the city's upper crust and where she saw herself. Her pre-maternity figure had completely returned and she purchased a sleek black dress for the evening, ignoring or refusing to acknowledge that the dinner itself was a financial stretch for the Madisons. As the sommelier returned with a bottle of Italian wine Daniel had never heard of, a microwave burrito continued its digestion in his stomach.

"Honey, you've got to order something," Sydney insisted, replete in sophistication. "Otherwise we're going to waste a half-bottle of Brunello di Montalcino. You know you can't drink wine on an empty stomach, and I'm only going to drink a glass or two."

"I'll order a little something," Daniel agreed, picking up the lead-heavy menu once more. "Maybe just a little spinach salad."

"I'm sorry you're not feeling well, darling," Sydney said, the terms of endearment to dollar ratio on par with phone sex. "It's a travesty not to take advantage of this wonderful cuisine. It's going to be a special evening."

A groundswell of frustration was slowly forming within Daniel's scapegoat stomach as he weighed Sydney's improving disposition while the bill mounted. She hadn't been this nice since before Sofia was born, and he couldn't help but be offended by the relationship between her kindness and his currency. It was also disconcerting that she had already ordered the most expensive appetizer on the menu and a $400 bottle of wine he had no chance of fully appreciating. Daniel was pretty sure wine pairings didn't usually include burritos.

"It's good to be out together," he lied, wanting it to be so. "It's nice to see you pleased." Daniel hoped to have a sublime evening with his wife, but the expensive fare tore at his contempt for Staglione and the disappointment he shared with Mike Martin. But he'd promised this to Sydney in good faith and he knew that to retract it now because of events she never knew about wouldn't be right.

Sydney was surveying the menu, holding it like a pirate reading a treasure map. Daniel wondered if she were reading the food descriptions or simply the prices to the right, searching for the most expensive items.

"What are you settling on?" Daniel asked, wanting to end the expense suspense.

"I believe I'll have the butter-basted Maine lobster with sweet pea coulis," she replied, confirming Daniel's accurate suspicion that she would choose the most expensive entrée offered. "What are you having, love?"

"I'm gonna stick with that spinach salad," Daniel said, fuming internally. "But I think I'm going to have a little of that red wine now."

Daniel poured his own painkiller as the waiter arrived to take her order. "Ms. Banks, have you made your selection?" he asked, resting his hand curiously on Sydney's shoulder.

Ms. Banks? Daniel thought, wondering why the waiter called her by her maiden name. He had heard her make the reservation under the name Madison.

Sydney repeated her order to Daniel's dismay, and Daniel offered his pithy selection without looking at the waiter. "Thank you, Damon," Sydney said as the waiter departed for the kitchen.

"How do you know his name is Damon?" Daniel asked as he filled his wine glass nearly to the brim. Sydney followed the rising purple fluid with consternation, not accustomed to Daniel's unrefined display.

"I've known him for some time."

"How's that?" Daniel followed, wondering why she was forcing him to play twenty questions.

"Oh, I used to come here quite a bit," she said, cutting the buttery goose liver with the precision of a surgeon. Sydney nodded toward Damon, who was standing nearby. She placed her fingers around the base of her wine glass and he gracefully poured the remainder for her. Daniel wondered if she was afraid she wouldn't get any more if she didn't claim it now.

"Seems like a nice place," Daniel began innocuously. "Did you just sort of fall in love with the food or have a friend who worked here?"

"Let's change the subject, shall we," Sydney said with a commanding sweetness. "It was a long time ago, a beautiful baby girl ago."

Daniel smiled at the reference to Sofia, just as she had hoped. Soothed, he still wanted to make Sydney say what he suspected. "You used to come here with Zigler, right?"

"Yes, I did," she said without hesitation, knowing Daniel wasn't giving up. She paused for a moment, pondering a response to Daniel's next question and deciding to head it off on her own terms. "I have always loved the wine, the food, the ambience. And when you said we could have a nice evening out, I thought what better than to bring my favorite man to my favorite restaurant." She reached across the table and placed her hand on his.

Daniel wasn't sure if it was entirely bullshit, but it didn't matter. He would rather be a fool in Sydney's glow than a more learned man somewhere beyond the warmth. He smiled an "It's all right" smile as they shared a peaceful moment.

He considered what to talk about next, wanting to parlay the tender exchange into a tender evening, when his phone began to shake inside his pants pocket. "That's my phone," Daniel explained as he withdrew his hand from Sydney's. "Probably your mom asking where something is for the baby."

He didn't recognize the area code and mouthed "I wonder who this is?" to Sydney as he answered the phone from an unknown number at seven p.m. on a Friday in Las Vegas.

"Hello?"

"May I speak with Daniel J. Madison?" the caller requested.

"This is Daniel. Who's calling?" he replied, pleased it wasn't Zigler, who was fresh on Daniel's mind.

"Hello, Mr. Madison. My name is John Gillespie, attorney at law. I have some good news for you."

"Rarely does good news begin with an attorney calling," Daniel said succinctly, the wine sinking in.

"That's true," Gillespie conceded. "But I believe we may have a common interest and I think I can help you."

"How's that?" Daniel answered, cutting to the chase and unwilling to endure any more formality this evening.

"Well, have you been doing business with a Vincent 'The Stag' Staglione and representing a 'StopShot Inc.,' currently being publicly traded on the Over the Counter Bulletin Board of the stock market?"

Daniel's face made an expression of surprise as Sydney tuned in. She mouthed, "What is it?" as Daniel considered what to tell her of the call now and later.

"You've got my attention, John," Daniel told the caller. "I *have* had the misfortune of dealing with Vincent Staglione."

"Great, then I do have the right Daniel Madison. Is it true that you worked in some capacity for Mr. Staglione and StopShot?" Gillespie inquired. Daniel remembered Staglione's assertion that he would be a fall guy for any enforcement actions regarding StopShot and though he'd dismissed them mostly as saber rattling, the possibility hovered during the call like a storm cloud. But if Gillespie had the ability to reach him on his cell phone, he already knew exactly who he was and where he had worked.

"Yes, I was among the many employees-slash-victims there," Daniel said. "Can we start a support group?"

"Maybe so," the caller said without showing any indications that he knew Daniel was joking. "But would it make you feel better if I told you I think we can help you recover most of the value of that stock you own?" If Sydney thought Daniel expressed surprise previously, she might have wondered if he were sitting on a wet spot now.

"How're you going to do that?" Daniel asked, eager to hear a solution to what he thought was a lost cause.

"Well, Mr. Staglione might be good at manipulating stocks, but he's not very good at covering his tracks," Gillespie said. "Our forensic accountants have identified the location of most of the proceeds of the sale of the StopShot stock he's been moving over the last year and a half. On Monday, we're going to get an injunction in federal court to seize the funds, which are held in a different name. From there we just need to have the various plaintiffs substantiate their losses to the court once we've secured a judgment. Mr. Madison, you could be looking at a fairly attractive payday."

Damon returned with a different bottle of wine and presented it to Sydney, who looked uncomfortable. She winced an assent and he uncorked the bottle. "Mr. Gillespie, this is music to my ears," Daniel said. "I was just wondering what to do next about this and it's most opportune of you to call … even at dinner with my wife. Do you really think we can get some of the value I had coming to me?"

"Mr. Madison, I think we can get all of it and maybe even treble damages if we can show he did this maliciously," Gillespie said, painting a lucrative picture. "That means we might be able to secure you three times the peak value of the equity, minus our thirty-five percent, of course."

"Of course," Daniel agreed, not sure how attorneys in this capacity were compensated. "And that would be amazing to get anywhere near that much money." Sydney looked up from the gentle pouring of the new bottle, her interest piqued anew. Her face still wore the mixed expression of discomfort and satisfaction as her eyes trained forward.

"Well, I apologize for calling you this late in the day but I just learned of your presence from our team here this afternoon," Gillespie said. "I wanted to let you know right away what we're going to do and see if you wanted us to include you in our class of plaintiffs. We'll do right by you, Mr. Madison."

"Yeah, that sounds great," Daniel affirmed, not in a position to scrutinize the offer when his own attorney had told him that he couldn't do any more to help. "What do I need to do to get started?"

"Well, quite literally nothing, Mr. Madison," the attorney said. "Right now, we just want to lay in the weeds until we control and confine his assets. That's the first step. So, I ask you kindly not to mention this conversation or our intent to Mr. Staglione or anyone who might take similar action. If we warn him, that money will be so far off-shore it'll take Jacques Cousteau to find it again."

"I won't do anything, Mr. Gillespie," Daniel said, his night's fortunes changing like an ocean's tide. "I'll just wait for your instruction."

"Perfect, Mr. Madison. That's what I wanted to hear. I think with your knowledge of Mr. Staglione's modus operandi you're going to be of great assistance in establishing his fraudulent intent."

"Can I reach you at this number, Mr. Gillespie?" Daniel asked.

"Absolutely. Just dial me directly. You don't need to go through the secretary. I'll take your calls personally."

"This is great news," Daniel said. "I'm thrilled to have your help, John."

"I'll be in touch, Daniel," Gillespie concluded. "You have a good night, sir. Enjoy your meal."

Daniel closed the phone as Sydney's eyes begged for explanation. "It's a long story, Syd, but that was fantastic news," Daniel said, wondering what to tell and what not to tell. "I think I'm going to order a steak."

"But your stomach?"

"Nothing could bother me right now," Daniel beamed. "That was a very good call."

"Not even if I told you that Clint Zigler is in the corner booth over there and just sent over this bottle of wine?" Sydney asked meekly, sincerely not wanting to spoil Daniel's elation. Daniel looked over Sydney's shoulder and saw Clint in the corner booth, his eyes already fixed on them. He set his napkin on his plate and immediately rose to his feet, heading for Zigler's table.

"Danny, don't," Sydney pleaded as Daniel continued on his path.

Zigler's smile vanished as Daniel came within striking distance, and he tried to cover his discomfort with a look of confidence. His date appeared to be one of his father's employees, clad in only slightly more than her work uniform.

"Clint, thank you for the bottle," Daniel said without sarcasm or rancor, somehow motivated to not allow the night and its recent rewards to be tainted.

"Uh ... yeah," Zigler answered meekly.

Daniel stepped into the silence, taking a chance that a resolution might be possible. "Look, man, we're about the same age and we've both got bright futures in front of us."

"Well, one of us does," Zigler shot back in a voice that wasn't much above a mumble. Daniel knew that since his father had laid Zigler out, he held the ultimate trump card, and Zigler's softened voice negated the efficacy of his barbed reply.

"I'd like to think there's no gain in us continuing this stupid feud," Daniel said. "So, I'm going to take your bottle as a token of what I want to believe is your recognition that we can co-exist in this town."

Clint looked perplexed, having expected his and Sydney's favorite bottle to draw a fiery response from Daniel. He had braced himself for the confrontation and knew that security nearby would detain Daniel before he could suffer a father-and-then-son ass-whipping.

"Maybe we can, Dan," Clint said. "Who knows, maybe we could someday be friends."

"Let's not go that far, Zigler," Daniel said, assuming Clint was being sarcastic. "But we don't have to torture each other either."

"Sounds fair," Clint said, extending his hand affably.

Daniel shook his hand, the same one that had been balled into a fist at his wedding, intent on sucker-punching him. "Have a nice dinner." Daniel turned and began his return to his table, thinking that no greater good could come beyond the impromptu accord.

"Hey, Daniel," Zigler said nicely as Daniel turned back toward him, some ten feet from the table. "I know something you don't know."

"I'll bet you do," Daniel said, shaking his head, feeling foolish for his benevolent attempt at peace. He walked briskly back toward Sydney, not giving Zigler any opportunity to craft new mind games. Sydney looked as if she were resting on broken glass, with any motion likely to cut deep wounds.

"How'd that go?" she asked uneasily, unsure if she wanted to hear his answer.

"It went all right," Daniel said, returning the selective answering technique Sydney had employed earlier in the meal. "I think I'll drink a little of his wine."

"It's a great wine," she said, careful not to let her response suggest any appreciation for Zigler. "We should drink it." Daniel refilled his empty glass with Zigler's offering and considered asking Sydney if she had any idea what Zigler's latest refrain meant. He decided just to drink the wine and let Zigler's remark fall impotently to the floor. Gillespie's call had made Sydney's night out manageable, enjoyable maybe, even if it meant he likely would be tapping into his father's loaner money before the lawyer could deliver his promised proceeds. With what he'd confirmed about keeping Sydney happy, that day couldn't come soon enough.

CHAPTER 31

June 2003

"I can't live like this," Sydney said through wet eyes as Daniel watched her shut the kitchen cabinet doors loudly. "I'm going to ask my father to help us out."

"I'd rather you didn't, Syd," Daniel said. "Especially since we don't need his money."

"Especially since YOU don't need his money," Sydney responded, her voice boiling over the Madisons' perpetual money problems. "There's sooooooo many things we need, Daniel."

"But there's nothing we have to have," Daniel replied, trying to give Sydney some perspective. "We have everything we really need. We just don't have everything we really want." Sydney came to Daniel's side and knelt next to him, laying her head on his shoulder. She looked up and took a moment before she spoke.

"Honey, it's just not enough," she began, the undefined "it's" making Daniel uneasy. "I want new clothes, new furniture. I want to go on vacation. I want to go somewhere besides a bar or a movie. And I want more for Sofia. She's almost two, and we're at the point where she's going to go from daycare to preschool. All the good places are expensive."

"Sydney, we still have time to prepare for that and I've got irons in the fire," Daniel said, thinking of the stock lawsuit that Gillespie continued to tell him was proceeding nicely.

"It's not just that, Daniel," Sydney continued, playing her hand through Sofia. "She needs other stuff too."

"What does Sofia need?" Daniel asked, growing angry. "She has everything she needs. That child wants for nothing. Nothing!"

Daniel's frustration formed into words he hadn't said before.

"What you want is to be spoiled like your daddy and your boyfriends used to do, Syd. Well, you didn't marry somebody like that. I am who I am and I've never promised you anything I couldn't deliver."

Daniel held both her hands and moved his body so he could make definitive eye contact. "I want to make more money too," he said. "But I also know that except for you continually making me feel like shit because I'm not haulin' it in, I'm pretty happy, you're pretty happy, and that little girl asleep in her bed is damn happy. Isn't that enough, Sydney?"

"It isn't," Sydney replied as tears flowed once more. "I want more out of life than to be June Cleaver."

"Sydney, give it time," he pleaded. "We'll get our chance, honey. It'll happen."

"All right, Danny," she relented for the moment, her voice softening from the weariness of an argument they had routinely. "What choice do I have? I could never leave you. I'd never find another man who's as good to me as you are … even if you are broke," she teased, causing him to throw a wadded-up napkin at her playfully. Daniel pulled her closer and they exchanged a reconciling kiss as Sofia walked into the room, dragging a baby doll by the arm.

"How was your nap, baby girl?" Daniel asked as he plucked Sofia from the floor, setting her on top of her mother, who was still seated on his lap.

"Brandy lick face. Wake up," she said, perturbed that the Madisons' pug had violated her sleep.

"She did, did she?" Daniel said, laughing gently at Sofia's face scrunched into a look of displeasure. "Well, it was time to get up anyway. You and I are going to the park this afternoon."

"I go swing," she said, enthused at the prospect of their day together. "And eat candy. And ice cream."

"Well, we'll see how the day goes," he answered for Sydney's benefit, knowing she wouldn't allow Sofia to have both treats in the same day. "Have I ever told you that you're the most beautiful little girl in the whole world?"

"Yes, Daddy," Sofia said plainly.

"I guess I did," he said and kissed her forehead. "And I'll probably tell you again this evening."

Across town, Julian was also holding a little girl in his arms as her mother ran through their schedule out loud. "Julian, are you listening?" Meredith asked as he fed his daughter the remainder of a formula bottle.

"Yes, I'm listening," Julian answered. "I can listen to you and give Risa her bottle. I'm an excellent multi-tasker."

"I'm sorry, Julian," Meredith apologized. "I don't mean to be short with you. It's just that we've only got two days down here before we're back in Carson City. We've got to get everything taken care of here at the house before we go and have dinner with your mother tonight. We've got to stay on the itinerary."

"Baby, every day of my life now I have to be on the governor's itinerary," Julian complained. "We get a couple days back in Vegas without any official business and you've got me moving on military time. I don't want to be Governor Correa today."

"I understand," she said. "Let's try to make the most of our day. We'll have a nice lunch and then we can go to the Fashion Show Mall and do some damage."

"But I confess I'm a little uptight about meeting your mother tonight," Meredith admitted. "It's just strange to not meet the person who raised you until three years into our relationship. If I were her, I'd be a little bitter."

"Hey, she's had every opportunity to come out here," Julian protested, beginning to count on each finger. "She was invited to my first election, our wedding, the inauguration, and Risa's birth. She never came to anything." Julian's speech was peppered with the staccato Cuban accent he had acquired from the very source of his anger. "The only reason she's here now is because I'm the governor and she wants to drop my name in restaurants and stores to see what it's worth. Too bad her name's not 'Correa' or she could really cash in."

"Why isn't her name Correa, Julian?" Meredith asked. "Did she get remarried when your father died?"

"She never divorced my father," Julian explained. "When she left Cuba she left him too. So, when we got here and I was born, she changed her name to Correa—her maiden name—so that he couldn't find her for a while. When my father was killed, she changed it back to Del Rey. She knew my father still had friends here and being the opportunist that she is, she figured *Del Rey* had more cachet than *Correa*. I was too old to change my name and I never saw the benefit. My dad never tried to be a father to me. He could've come here many times, but he was too busy being a fat cat back in Havana."

"Do you know what happened to your dad, Julian?" Meredith asked.

"Not really," Julian said. "My mom just said he got stabbed by a homeless man late at night in an alley."

"Didn't you ever talk to him when you were little?" Meredith asked, finding out more about a subject that Julian usually avoided. His frustration with his mother had opened a window on his contempt as he justified his rancor for her to his wife.

"He'd call once in a while, I think just to check on my mother," Julian said. "But he never called and asked for me. Most of the time when they were done arguing, she would just say 'Talk to your boy' and hand me the phone.

"It was pretty much just small talk … he wasn't mean or anything. It just wasn't anything real special. It was like talking to some uncle you never met. It felt obligatory. When he died no one even called to tell us. We just got a box with some pictures of his family and some of his personal stuff.

"I kept them. I don't have any hatred for him or anything. I just don't have a real strong feeling one way or another. Sometimes I look at his old pictures or wear his old watch or necklace, but it just doesn't feel like it should with your father … like the way you and your dad are, hugging each other when you meet." Julian looked down at Risa, who had now fallen asleep, juxtaposing her parenting against his lack thereof.

"Is that where you got that little gold bird you wear?" Meredith asked. "I thought it looked like some sort of antique."

"My mother told me it was my grandmother's," Julian explained as his fingers surveyed the perimeter of the small bird with the white-diamond eyes. "My father wore it after her, so I wear it. I'll give it to Risa someday. It's a little feminine, I guess."

"Thanks for telling me all this," Meredith said, having never pressed Julian to satisfy her curiosity. "I always wondered why you never spoke much about your father. I didn't realize he had never come over."

"From what I've heard, he was a big shot in Havana," Julian said. "My mother said when they first started dating he was the man, that they could go anywhere and doors swung wide. I guess my grandfather was a friend of Castro … pretty high up. My mom says my father became meaner than hell. I think he was most of the reason she left Cuba."

"I'm really sorry that you never had that, Julian," Meredith consoled. "But you're going to get to be the father you never had. And you're do-ing great so far. I think you're an excellent daddy."

"Thanks, Meredith," Julian said, pleased that she had acknowledged what he thought were intermittent efforts at best with his daughter. "That's the most important thing to me."

"Let's get going, shall we? I'm kind of eager to get the day rolling. I'm dreading the dinner with Mom. Don't forget I've got a meeting tonight," Julian reminded her. "Don't wait up."

"Who're you meeting so late?" she asked.

"Well, coincidently, I'm meeting with an old friend of my father's," Julian said, shaping his answer with the filter he used for public speech. "I think he might be able to help me with an ongoing problem I've got here in Southern Nevada."

"Really? An old friend of your dad's? That's a bizarre coincidence with your mother here in town," Meredith said.

"It's not that bizarre when you consider that when Castro opened up his prisons in the early eighties a ton of Cubans came here," Julian explained. "I guess they were attracted to all the gaming and the work available to people who don't speak English. Anyway, my father told me about a guy he grew up with who lives here named Felix that I should look up if I ever have a problem. I think he can help me with some issues I've been having."

"What kind of issues?" Meredith inquired as she measured powdered formula into a baby bottle.

"Just more trouble with Frank Hayes," Julian said.

"I can't stand that man," Meredith said boldly. "I've never been around anyone who makes me as uncomfortable. It's like there's a ghost in the room. Why do you continue to let him come around?"

"Let him?" Julian asked incredulously. "You think it's optional? He's been the guy behind both my campaigns. He thinks I owe him. But that's about to come to an end. I can't do his bidding anymore."

"So how does your dad's friend come into this?" Meredith asked. "He knows Frank?"

"Yeah, he knows Frank," Julian lied, wishing he hadn't revealed so much about his plans. "I think he can persuade Frank to ease off a little. My father gave me the impression once that he's a strong negotiator."

"Okay, Julian," she replied, satisfied in her naiveté. "I'll get Risa's bag, then I'm ready to go."

CHAPTER 32

The smoke-gray air of CJ's Crib spewed from the pub's front door like steam from a Manhattan street grate. Inside, two homecoming queens turned waitresses moved from table to table like honeybees, intoxicating patrons and deflecting spontaneous crushes. At the end of their shift they'd shed their aprons and take seats at the bar, playing away the night's compensation in a not-so-vicious cycle of commerce.

Behind the bar, a husky bartender named Hoss made change and mixed drinks with equal haste, becoming everybody's best friend as night and day revolved outside the windowless establishment. Bartenders were paid by the hour in Las Vegas—same as anywhere else— but the real money came from the players' tips after hitting a royal flush. Tell the player what machine was ripe for a jackpot and a barkeep might see a tenth of a several-thousand-dollar payout.

Despite the predictable gaming ambience of valley bars, most of them could be defined best by the stereotyping of their patrons. Some bars were full of bikers and their tattooed hangers-on. Others were after-softball joints with a dozen sports-emitting television screens and pitchers ready for hitters. CJ's Crib was a cop bar. Day or night the location was populated by Metro officers, rookie to veteran, off-duty and on-, eating, drinking, and making the place their own. Civilians patronizing the bar were warned to sober up before leaving more than any other place in town, with bartenders mindful that a DUI-hungry roller was always parked outside.

Tonight was like any other with a shift's worth of patrolmen playing darts, poker machines, and the jukebox. Some had just sat down while others' voices loudly affirmed their tenure at the bar with the bold as-sertions drinking men offer to each other.

"Another round, fellas?" the waitress asked two officers seated at a hi-top table as she collected two empty pint glasses and a shot glass over the blare of an AC/DC song.

"That's affirmative," answered a patron with close-cut hair and the look of a military man as he read the latest televised trivia question.

"Did you want another beer or a whiskey?" she inquired while the CJ's logo wavered across her breasts like a reflection in a funhouse mirror.

"Absolutely," Officer Jay Sheppard replied while his friend looked on. Stumped by a geography question, he turned his head from the trivia TV and looked at his partner.

"Man, that was a shitty day," he announced, spying a young blonde exposing a bounty of cleavage as she shot pool. "No wonder police officers eat a bullet at twice the regular rate, Craig."

"Not me, Jay," Officer Craig Peters said quickly. "I don't let it get to me. And when it starts to, I find a way to release it."

"How do you release seeing a kid who hasn't eaten for three days lying in his own excrement, Craig? I'm not sure there's an antidote for that."

"You'll get used to it, partner," Craig predicted. "My dad says everybody does. We haven't even been off probation a year yet, so they stick us in the worst places. That's why we see what we see. But it'll get better. Eventually we'll end up drinking Starbucks and cruising for ragheads at the airport. That's when it gets easy. But for right now, you gotta let go of the anger."

"I'm not going to see a shrink, if that's what you're suggesting," Jay replied as the waitress returned and placed their drinks on the table. "I'll just have to suck it up and rub some dirt on it. But that little boy today ... man, how does anyone let their kid live like that?"

"Those ghetto bastards don't think about their kids, bro. They're just looking for a fix. Hell, they'd sell that kid if they could," Craig contended, his voice full of contempt. "My rookie year I was riding with one of the older guys and we went on a domestic call at one of the projects down there off Main Street. The guy that was beating his old lady was missing an arm from a meth lab explosion and he was still pounding her with his good arm. He didn't even stop when we kicked the door in.

"I thought I'd seen everything. Then we heard a little girl crying down the hall. I go in there and she immediately hides under the sheet and puts her little butt and back to the wall, like she's trying to hide it. So I figure she's got some bruises and she doesn't want me to see them ... she's around eight, so she probably knows that Lefty will go to jail if I see the bruises. I go up to her as nicely as I can and I see that she's chained to the bed at the ankle. It's rubbed her raw and looks infected. Then I look around the room and see condom wrappers and these Polaroids. Each one of those pictures was some old fat fuck nailing her. These big, fat, dirty old men just going to town on that little girl.

"She told me that her father put the pictures on the Internet to buy her food. She made it sound like he was doing something noble. Meanwhile, the shitty little Section 8 apartment has top-of-the-line plasma TVs on the walls, leather couches, and a goddamn Sub-Zero refrigerator in the kitchen. Nicer stuff than I have."

Jay absorbed his partner's testimonial, measuring it against his own. If Craig had been intent on comforting him by offering a worse scenario, he'd been unsuccessful as it simply galvanized his own disdain for his new profession. "Craig, man, how do you get over seeing something like that?" Jay asked, in search of a remedy he could use.

"I'm not sure you can ever get past it, bro," he answered. "But you can do something about it. Something to keep it from eating at you like it's doing right now."

"Yeah? What's that?" Jay wondered.

"Well, for starters, I took the little girl out of the apartment and sent her down to Child Haven where she could get cleaned up. She screamed like we were killing her when we unhooked her and carried her out. Then I went back in and took every tooth I could out of her father's filthy head. That's what I had to do to get some peace of mind."

"What did the other officer say? Did he dime you out to IAD?" Jay asked, more than a little surprised by the violent confession. In three months of riding together, Jay had yet to see his high-strung partner erupt to that degree. Craig had been heavy-handed many a time, but the level of corporal punishment he just described hadn't been displayed.

"Nah, it was his idea … sort of," Craig said. "He saw that I was upset and asked if I wanted a little 'alone time' with the perp. I said yes and he escorted the tweaker mom outside so that Dad and I could have a talk. That's what I mean when I say you gotta find a way to release it. You can't survive if you don't let it go every now and then."

"Man, I don't know," Jay said, unsure of the proposed remedy. "I think it might create even more issues for me. It's bad enough going home after seeing stuff like we saw today. Adding in more violence … it would make things even more personal. I'm not sure I'd feel better. But I just can't shake the image of that baby today, laying there in that shit. Did you see how dehydrated he was? He'd pretty much given up. I think his bowel movement was two or three days old."

"That was pretty bad," Craig agreed. "But don't you ever wonder why we hear so many calls like that in these ghetto neighborhoods, Jay?"

"Not really. They get abuse cases in Green Valley too. The white neighborhoods have molesters and neglectors same as the hood."

"Not like this, bro," Craig countered. "I know the whole sociological argument … that poverty creates need and need creates crime … that's the drug-selling rationale. Whatever, let's just say that I accept that for argument's sake. But I can tell you this, I've worked most every area of Vegas, thanks to my dad, and you only see the really bad neglect and abuse in the hood. Shit like you saw today, Jay. You ever seen that kind of crime scene in Summerlin?"

"Well, no, not yet, but again I think there's an argument to be made that the poverty makes people more likely to make bad choices, that a mom who's selling drugs … or herself … starts to lose track of her value system. I guess that makes it easier to neglect or bring harm to your own kid."

"I don't buy it, man," Craig said, shaking his head for emphasis, eager to unveil his emotions on the subject. "I think life means less to these people. Most of them didn't even want the kids they have. Half of them don't even have dads. It's all fucked up.

"And we come down there when they're killing each other and right away we're the bad guys, Jay," Craig added, his hands against his chest in expressed offense. "They treat us like we're the ones doing something wrong. You know that."

"Yeah, you're right about that," Jay conceded. "No one's happy to see us in Naked City."

"Wouldn't it make you feel better to just pound some heads once in a while?" Craig asked, whispering vehemently to his partner as he checked the periphery. "Instead of having to go through all the paperwork and bullshit and court, wouldn't it be nice just to take a drug dealer that sells to little kids and put a fist full of his Ecstasy hits in his mouth? Would the world be better or worse, Jay?"

"I hear you," Jay acknowledged at minimum, hoping the answer would satisfy his partner. Jay pushed back from the bar top table, creating space between himself and the conversation. Craig exhaled a Marlboro upward, his blood warmed by the subject matter.

Craig Peters was never at rest—or at peace—and despite his assertions that his own take on therapy calmed him, Jay had never seen the fruits of the treatment. It seemed each day Craig was becoming more adversarial with the citizenry, perhaps even society, and Jay was one of the few relationships he had left. If it weren't for his father's status as a two-decade detective, Craig might not have survived his rookie probationary period or the continuing stream of complaints his sergeant indulged. His confrontational nature hadn't won him many friends among his fellow officers either. Despite it all, Craig was also the guy that Jay would most want with him heading into a convenience store hold-up with an armed intruder inside. Jay took a long drink of his beer as a familiar figure arrived at the table, pulling up a bar stool without asking.

"Good evening, ladies," Detective Brown said as he sat down uninvited. "I think I'll join you."

"Do we have a choice, Walt?" Craig kidded in a manner seasoned with some disdain.

"Not really," Walt answered unfazed as he beckoned for the waitress.

"What are you having, Walt?" she asked.

"Orange Juice … and bring me the breakfast special, please," the detective answered. "I'm working graveyard tonight."

"I heard you guys had a busy day in Naked City," he said. "I guess you had a nasty one."

"Same as any other day, Walt," Craig responded before Jay could. "It's the same bag of shit every time we go out. As long as they keep us down there it's going to be like that. At least the day goes fast with all the activity."

"Oh, I think your father's got you down there for a reason, Craig," Walt suggested. "But I suppose you know that."

"Yeah, I figured as much, though he denies it," Craig said. "I'm sure it's part of his 'make-Craig-a-better-cop' program. I turned thirty last year and I've still got him micromanaging my life."

"Your father's a good man, Craig. Cut him some slack," Detective Brown said. "He's been a friend to me throughout my career. You know, we were in the academy together and—"

"Yeah, yeah. You both have told me that a hundred times," Craig said obtusely. "What was the graduating class—like seven people?"

"What's that got to do with anything, kid?" the detective inquired through Craig's hostility.

"Never mind," Craig answered, ending the intensifying line of dialogue. "I'm always going to be Detective Hank Peters' little boy, right?"

"Lot worse things in this world, Craig," Walt replied as he turned and surveyed Officer Sheppard, who had been looking away from the table. "You could have the kind of father that little boy you guys found today had.

"Of course, that guy's going away for a homicide now," the detective added nonchalantly while he sipped his juice, as if reporting a stock quote.

"A homicide?" Craig asked as he looked over at Jay, whose face seemed more pale than a moment before. "What happened to the kid?"

"We got a call from UMC a little while ago, they said that he suffered cardiac arrest," Brown continued unfazed. "They can't tell the cause for sure yet, but it looks like dehydration was the primary factor. They'll upgrade the charges, of course."

Craig stared ahead at Jay, in search of any evidence that his previous dismay had evolved to something less restrained. As Jay remembered the skinny child's face and the blanket he'd wrapped him in, his superficial demeanor gave Craig no indication of his internal tumult. But instead of violent responses, Jay was thinking about the stuffed animal police dog he gave the doe-eyed child as they took him to the hospital.

"So, Jarhead, what've you been up to?" the detective asked, returning Jay to the present.

"Not a whole lot," Jay answered. "Just putting in the hours."

"Well, I've got to say I admire you, Jay," Brown said in what Jay knew was the prelude to a punch line.

"Why's that?"

"Well, you're probably the only guy in a hundred-mile radius wearing a teal T-shirt with a dolphin on it," Brown said, asserting himself once more.

"The Miami Dolphins are my favorite football team," Jay defended dispassionately, knowing that if he effectively won this verbal skirmish the unrelenting Brown would launch another.

"It's not the football team ... though they do stink ... it's the teal shirt with a fish on it," Brown explained.

"A dolphin is a mammal," Craig corrected. "But the shirt does make you look like a homo."

Jay rolled his eyes at the pair and then turned to review the pool tables, searching again for female shooters and their buxom displays as the little boy's image waned. The pub's brick walls were unusual for Las Vegas architecture, but the slots behind him at the bar confirmed the location. When Jay graduated from the academy he'd been brought here to celebrate, joining the fraternity of officers at their favorite watering hole. Most nights after he completed his shift Jay came to the bar to imbibe a segue to a gentler night, dismissing the day's unpleasant events and readying for an easy transfer into sleep. Jay tossed back the latest whiskey shot as the detective consumed his breakfast and Craig fidgeted with his keys.

"Hey, I'm gonna roll," Craig announced as Detective Brown sliced a piece of ham on the plate. "You okay to drive, Jay?"

"I don't believe that would be entirely accurate, partner," Jay said honestly, knowing he wouldn't pass his own field sobriety test. "Perhaps you could drop me off on your way home?"

"Sure, buddy," Craig agreed with a hint of frustration, apparently still worn thin from the exchange with Brown. "But let's get going. You can have someone else help you get your car tomorrow morning."

"Candy ass," Detective Brown teased without looking up from his hash browns.

Jay ignored the remark and followed Craig, who had left without a nod toward his father's friend. As he exited the bar, Craig was already opening the door to his white pickup truck, its wheels and fenders covered in thick brown mud. Jay lumbered in and immediately reached for the tuner on the radio. Craig smacked his hand like a perturbed parent and cautioned seriously, "My car, my radio. When we ride in *your* car we can listen to that 'Hee Haw' shit."

"No problem," Jay agreed, in no condition to effectively debate the issue as they pulled out of the parking lot. He began to pull the shoulder belt into place when it occurred to him that he'd left his police gear in his SUV parked back at the bar. "Craig, flip a bitch. All my stuff's in my car. I don't want that sitting in a parking lot overnight."

"It'll be fine, man," Craig said. "Let's go home. It's late and you're drunk."

"Dude, my gun is in there and so is my badge and uniform," Jay protested. "I don't want that jacked. Sarge would kill me if some crack-head starts pulling over young girls with my star on."

"Bro, fifty cops a night are at that bar on one side or the other of their shifts. You might as well have it parked at the station," Craig argued as they headed farther and farther from the bar. "Just get it first thing tomorrow, all right?"

"I guess," Jay said reluctantly.

Craig's disposition hadn't improved much since they left the pub, and a death-grip on the steering wheel indicated a tension unabated. Jay's head, which was leaning against the passenger window, flung to the left like an inverted pendulum as Officer Peters made a hard and spontaneous turn.

"Whaddya doin?" Jay asked through the gentle fog of his intoxication. "Where are we?"

"We're on the way to therapy," Craig answered like a tour guide at a European museum.

"I don't want to go to therapy," Jay said. "I want to go home and go to bed."

"Lighten up, Francis," Craig replied, quoting Jay's favorite movie, *Stripes*.

"Hey, I need to go get my bag out of my car," Jay asked again, forgetting that he and Craig had already discussed the issue.

"In the morning, I said," Craig reminded his partner as he withdrew his own gun from the glove box and set it between them.

"Why don't you roll down the window and get a little air on your face?" Craig suggested. "You're going to need to be on your game when we get down there."

"Down where?" Jay asked once more. "Where's my therapy at?"

"Same place where our day started, partner—back in Naked City," Craig explained. "I'm going to show you how to feel a little better."

CHAPTER 33

Julian steered a mid-sized rental car around the towering Stratosphere Hotel and into the urban bowels of Naked City, leaving the casino's neon aura and entering roadways lit only by the occasionally working streetlight. The neighborhood's reputation for violent crime had him uneasy, and the bleak appearance of the dilapidated residences only reinforced his trepidation. The uncomfortable subject matter of his meeting in a few minutes didn't help matters. Even still, with Frank Hayes continuing to pressure him in all directions, it was a meeting Julian knew he had to have.

Long-time residents and police officers knew this area of Las Vegas as Naked City, a name given to it decades before when showgirls living in the small residences close to the Strip sunbathed topless at the neighborhood pools. Over the years the neighborhood had spiraled from celebrity lounge to the worst ZIP code in Las Vegas, devolving into a place few outsiders would visit unless they were looking for a hit ... or a hit man. Even as real estate speculators and high-rise developers hovered like chicken hawks looking to acquire Naked City's real estate for sybaritic purposes, the dangerous daily lives of the current residents gave no indication of better tomorrows. Perhaps that's because they weren't likely to be welcome post-gentrification unless they filled out applications to be maids or gardeners.

When Daniel turned sixteen and began driving, his father warned him about two places: downtown Las Vegas and Naked City. Downtown was known for its heavy-handed security guards and high rate of suspicious suicides of card cheats from casino rooftops. Naked City was known for all things nefarious, including narcotics, prostitution, and murder.

The neighborhood reached its nadir in the early eighties when Fidel Castro dumped his prisons and mental hospitals onto crowded boats and sent them toward northern shores, freeing himself of the encumbrance and dishing it to the American infidels ninety miles away. And like any new immigrants, they sought work in places where it was easy to find. Many landed in burgeoning Las Vegas where family and friends had a foothold in the service industry and *Ingles* was *no necesario*. While some took jobs as waiters, mechanics, and landscapers, others reverted to criminal means, using Naked City's existing crime scene as an incubator and fortress. Two decades later, the area was still a cesspool of trouble, even if bulldozer-ready moguls salivated over the land's vertical prospects.

Julian hadn't seen poverty of Naked City's ilk since he was a boy in Miami, rushing home to lock the deadbolt behind him and call Mama to tell her he was safe. As soon as she made enough money to get out of the Cuban barrio, she did so, giving Julian white neighbors with whom to assimilate. It was there that Julian began to loathe his Hispanic past, shedding his Cuban roots when he could and comporting himself like a suburban teen from a middle-class family. And it was as he became a man in the new neighborhood that mother and son grew apart.

As a gubernatorial candidate, Julian hadn't been to any neighborhoods like Naked City, knowing that registered voters in the area probably were unlikely to answer the door when a man in a tie came knocking. Tonight, the intermittent bath of street lights made the scene look like an Escher painting of the set of a Jimmy Cagney film, exacerbating Julian's directional confusion. Most of the rundown apartments were missing all or part of the street number, and the square, multilevel shelters looked like a ghetto version of *Hollywood Squares* with heads popping out of windows like the game show's grid, each with a different purpose and intent. Julian fidgeted in his seat as he looked again at the directions he'd hastily scrawled on a piece of junk mail, hoping to find Felix Calderon's modest abode amid the Vegas *favelas*. He lowered his head to look up through the windshield again, searching for a street name that matched the one on his handwritten directions. Around him he felt the gaze of a dozen eyes peering outward like malevolent specters in a *Scooby Doo* episode. When a hand struck his window in what was intended to be an attention-earning knock, Julian's entire body quivered from the shock. As he turned his head like a teenager in a horror movie, he was relieved to see a female figure standing at his door.

"Roll down your window, bitch!" she mouthed through the glass as Julian pondered fight, flight, or obedience.

"What?" Julian said, having heard her perfectly, but entirely unsure of his next action. She had a bleach blond afro and her dark, weathered skin indicated both regular outdoor activity and a woman who was in her fifth decade. Her gray stonewashed jeans fit loosely enough to confirm she was not the original owner.

"You want a half-and-half?" she asked, offering today's prostitution special. Her teeth were aligned like ring posts at a boxing match with broad spaces between their four-corner configuration. As Julian considered how best to rebuff the offer, he wondered if her dental disaster was also an asset to her occupational efforts.

"No, thank you," Julian mouthed through the lightly tinted glass, more politely than was necessary. She turned summarily, yelling something in another direction to a man her own age sitting on a graffiti-covered power box. Ahead of Julian on the right, four young boys were taking turns dunking a basketball on a rim that hung lower than regulation, using an overturned shopping cart as a springboard to the hoop. Julian remembered when he and his elementary school friends had done the same, imagining themselves as Michael Jordan with sports photographers capturing their poster-ready efforts. Past the young athletes Julian spotted the house number 2320 that he was searching for and pulled his car to the roadside, parallel to three metal trashcans. As soon as he unbuckled his seat belt, two young Latino men were on both sides of his car, dubious bookends with one hand in their khaki pants pockets and the other swinging free.

"Whatcha need, holmes?" asked one loudly enough to penetrate the window. "Coca?"

Julian looked again at the house number and the street sign, wanting to make sure this was Calderon's place before he faced the natives. The numbers hadn't changed, so Julian opened the door.

"I asked you whatchoo need, homie," the man asserted, his voice beginning to border on menacing. "You need to stay in your car. I'll get whatever you want, ese."

Julian rose with the door between them, his head looming over the smaller man, whom he thought looked familiar. Governor Correa pushed the car door back strongly, providing a wide enough berth to allow him to exit the vehicle. The thrust set the man on the other side to his heels, shifting his weight and disposition simultaneously.

He backed up another step and pulled his hand from his pocket, revealing a knife with a polished handle. "You don't listen so good, holmes. I guess you're not from around here."

"I'm definitely not from around here," Julian said, agreeing on that point as the knife's appearance unnerved him further. "But if that's Felix Calderon's pad right there, then I'm at the right place."

The Latino man from the passenger side had come around to the front, looking to aid his partner with the larger Correa if necessary. "You know Felix, holmes?" he queried. "You Five-0?"

"Nope, I'm an old friend," Julian replied, containing his nervousness as he panned his memory for the faces of both men whom he now knew he recognized from somewhere. "He's expecting me."

"No problem, holmes," the first man said. "Felix is *el hombre*. You tell him we were just watching out for him, okay?" Julian sensed the men's concern now that he had dropped Calderon's name. This jibed with what he'd always heard about Felix, who had Godfather status in Naked City, ruling with fear and economics. His father had spoken of Calderon's early brutality as he built his name, often handling the dirtiest business himself.

"How 'bout you get the fuck away from my door, *holmes*," Julian responded.

"No problem, man," he said as he moved away from Julian, staring at his face in the moonlight as Julian had his own. "I think I've seen you here before, eh?"

"You've never seen me here, *vato*," Julian said, mocking yet again.

"Okay, okay," he retreated in proxy deference to Calderon. "I think he's home."

As Julian passed the men, the latter of the two trained his eyes on him and nodded his head slowly as he made the connection. "It's good to see you again, Governor," he offered semi-sarcastically, as if revealing a secret.

"You remember the governor, don't you, Carlos?" he said to his partner, who had returned his knife to his pocket. "You should." As Julian passed the men and stepped onto the sidewalk his memory arrived on the right vignette, recalling the pair and the beating he'd given them outside the microbrewery with Daniel a few years earlier. With Mario's help, Carlos had just placed Julian as well, but wisely subdued any thoughts of revenge with Felix Calderon's house guest.

Julian thought it might be a good idea for Calderon to walk him back out to his car after their meeting, wondering to what extent the armed men were interested in revenge. As he approached the door and raised his hand to knock, it opened at the hand of Calderon, leaving Julian's fist in the air like a beginning sign language student. "Juliano!" Calderon sang as he beckoned for Governor Correa to enter. "Welcome to my little place.

"I am honored to have our governor in my humble home," he said with the elegant fusion of accent and articulation that made Ricardo Montalban and Fernando Lamas stars. Julian nodded respectfully, uncertain of the appropriate verbal response. The interior of Calderon's residence was much different from the rough exterior. Rich burgundy paint covered the short walls like cake icing and gold ribbon-candy frames surrounded pictures of family members from Cuba and south Florida. Taupe-colored leather couches soft as driving gloves yielded under Julian's weight as Felix settled him to his seat with a wave of his hand. A marble coffee table cut from a single block held a porcelain ashtray and an enormous bird's-eye-burl cigar humidor. The morning's *Wall Street Journal* and London's *Guardian* lay neatly folded next to a stack of mail.

Calderon allowed Julian to drink in his surroundings like Hugh Hefner greeting first-time guests at the mansion, wanting him to absorb the difference between inside and outside, an aesthetic line of demarcation. As he did so, Julian thought that if he'd been blindfolded and brought inside, he would have assumed he was in a lavish hotel penthouse a few miles south of Naked City. Julian peered at the walls around the living room and realized the place was actually two apartments with a common wall removed. In the kitchen, Julian could see an older woman cooking something in a sauce pan and another man dabbing at the dish with a slice of bread as she playfully shooed him away.

"So, Governor, how is the baby?" Calderon began.

"You know you don't need to call me governor. You've known me my whole life," Julian replied, uncomfortable with the formal title in Calderon's home. "Risa is good. She's smart, Felix. I can see it already."

"Children are a beautiful thing," Calderon said as he beckoned to the woman in the kitchen. "I would like to have had them. But a man in my business should not have a wife or children. They can be useful to your enemies and force you to make very difficult decisions, some that are not good for business. Like a priest, I am dedicated to one purpose above all others." His black hair had yet to yield to gray or silver. He was thin and wiry with the look of an aging runner, refined in a way that, much like the décor of the apartment, was incongruent with the scenery of Naked City. Yet Felix didn't look or act like a barrio gangster either. His clothes were subtle and his voice softer than that of most men of his kind. Felix, it seemed, was a man who whispered threats if he need utter them at all.

"We all make choices," Julian responded, waxing philosophical as Felix had. The woman from the kitchen arrived, setting a plate of Cuban churros on the marble table between them. The small, curved pastries covered in sugar looked more like American doughnuts than their Mexican cousins of the same name.

"Eat, Juliano," Calderon offered, while taking none for himself.

"Oh, no thank you, Felix," Julian demurred. "I really can't eat wheat."

"Your father has this problem too, no?" Calderon remembered. "It's hereditary, eh? You have much in common, Juliano."

"I guess we share a few traits, Felix," Julian said. "I just don't know him all that well." A silence cloaked the room as the men waited for the other to speak.

"So, Juliano, I don't see you for a few years and you call me for a favor," Calderon said before pausing, waiting for Julian to affirm.

"Yeah, that's true, Felix," Julian replied uncomfortably. "You know, I just didn't think it was a good idea for me to come down here when I was running and bring any extra attention. I know you and my father were friends."

"Business partners," Felix corrected, a finger raised for emphasis.

"Business partners," Julian agreed, accepting the correction but not the significance as he began his opening statement at the Court of Calderon. "And he always told me you were a man who could get things done, so to speak. I think I need something done, as I mentioned when we spoke on the phone. I just don't think I can solve this problem without your help, Felix. Hayes thinks he owns me, and maybe he's right. But I can't take it anymore."

Calderon sat stone-faced, not reacting to any of Julian's remarks, as if they were not yet sufficient to warrant a response.

"He has no boundaries, Felix," Julian continued, beginning to introduce evidence. "Nothing satisfies him. I have done everything he's asked for and he always wants more."

"But you took his money and his friends' money for your commission race, no?" Felix asked rhetorically.

"Yeah, that's right," Julian said meekly.

"And you needed his help to run for governor, no? He does you a favor, you do him a favor. This is the way the world works, son."

"Yeah, but there's no end to it," Julian argued. "He wants everything. It's not just favors … it's me. He has to control me too."

"Everybody has to work for someone," Felix said as he wet the end of a cigar between his thin lips, sealing the leaves before he lit the stick. "Everybody but me."

Julian put his head down and in his hands, expressing to Felix his frustration and contempt for Hayes. Julian's father had told him when he was a boy that Calderon wielded enormous power in Las Vegas, that he could reach places few men could. But he had always been cryptic about his relationship with Felix and what business had transacted between them after Felix left Havana.

"Felix, *por favor*, I need him gone," Julian pleaded with the humility of a confession uttered by a child to his father. "I can't take it anymore."

"Julian, you want me to kill a man like Frank Hayes?" Felix asked as if he didn't already know that was the reason the governor had come to see him. "Why would I do that?"

Julian considered what to offer Calderon as inducement to terminate his tormentor. "I can make sure your business runs unmolested, Felix."

"I have that already, Juliano," Felix countered pragmatically.

"Well, I can offer you whatever the governor can do for you," Julian said plainly. "That's gotta be worth something."

"Perhaps, but you assume I don't have that in place already," Felix said. "Look around, my friend. I'm pretty comfortable."

"Felix, there's got to be something I can do for you," Julian continued, knowing that if he left without Calderon's promise to help, he was in even deeper waters.

"So you would trade one Papa for another? You know what they say about the enemy you know … he may be better. I could be sitting here with someone else discussing having you killed someday, Juliano.

I don't think that would be better than having Frank Hayes tell you what church to attend."

A chill coursed through Julian's body as Felix's remark indicated he had spoken with Hayes already. Again, Julian's instincts mulled fight, flight, or obey. Felix let the provocative revelation conquer the room and Julian, finally lighting his cigar. The male figure who had been milling about the kitchen entered the living room where Calderon sat opposite Julian, principal and student. He stood between them and once again, Julian raided his memory for the nexus of a man and place.

"Julian, you have met my friend Antonio? Antonio, take a seat next to Governor Correa." Antonio sat down on the leather couch, resting more closely to Julian than men normally do and extending his hand slowly. Julian clasped Antonio's palm and realized this was Daniel's guy, the Cuban jeweler.

"Aren't you Daniel Madison's friend too?" Julian asked as Antonio released his hand. "I think I met you at your store some time ago."

"Yeah, we met," Antonio said coldly.

"Antonio knew your father, Julian," Felix explained, as if that had something to do with his presence at a meeting Julian certainly didn't want anyone else to attend. "You can speak freely in front of him. Antonio's father and my father owned a jewelry store and a fruit stand next to each other in Havana. We came to this country together, two stupid boys with no money in our pockets."

"Hey, that's great," an increasingly uncomfortable Correa muttered in an attempt to wrap things up. "I'm not sure what else I need to cover, Felix. Please just think about any way you can help me with that issue we talked about."

"I'll see if I can come up with anything that can make life simpler, Juliano," Felix replied mysteriously, a verbal accelerant to the flame of insecurity that the reference to Julian's religious conversion had ignited. "I'm sure something can be done to ease the tension."

"Antonio, tell Juliano a little about his father," Calderon said, engineering the discussion. "I'm sure he's curious about life in Cuba, what his father was like, his grandfather, etc."

"Actually, I'm okay," Julian wriggled. "Perhaps we can do this another time. I really should get back to Meredith and Risa. We've got to head back to Carson City bright and early tomorrow, Felix." Julian rose from his seat. Before his head found its apex, Felix's voice raised for the first time, still not a yell but more forceful than any previous utterance.

"SIT DOWN, JULIANO," he commanded. "Do you think we only discuss what *you* want in meetings?" Julian did so immediately, looking at Felix the entire time, reading his mood for what he could and pondering his current position. Not looking at his seat as he descended, Julian found himself even closer to Antonio, their hips nearly touching and the weight of both men in the middle of the couch creating a concave depression that tilted them to each other like lovers in a rowboat.

"So, Antonio, please tell our friend Juliano a little about his father and your experiences with Ramon Del Rey," Felix said.

"There's not so much to say," Antonio started gently enough, speaking directly to Julian, who instead looked at Felix. "Except that he was a son of a bitch."

Julian closed his eyes as the tenor changed, like a gambler who couldn't bear to watch the dealer draw a deuce to make a five-card 21. Clearly, it had been a mistake to come to Calderon, and his father obviously hadn't told him the whole story about their partnership. Now he was in position to inherit the sins of his father from a man who killed for business and had just extolled his virtual immunity from prosecution. "I'm sure he was," Julian agreed, sensing that arguing the point would give him nothing.

"*Callaté!*" Felix ordered again. "This is the part where you listen, Governor."

"And your father's father was a very bad man, Juliano," Antonio said. "He hurt many people and was a thief. A fat, arrogant, dirty thief."

"I thought my grandfather worked for the Cuban government?" Julian weakly offered, mindful of Felix's warning.

"The government are all thieves. That is why we must come to America," Antonio said, raising his voice higher than Calderon's despite sitting mere inches from a sweating Julian. "They steal from everyone … even the poor workers and merchants. It don't matter, they take what they want whenever they want."

"Antonio," Calderon offered gently to his friend, "I believe you are making our governor uncomfortable. Tell him about the Tocororo."

"Juliano, you come in my store a few years ago with Danny," Antonio said. "He's a good boy and he's not going to know nothing about this. And when I meet you I see two things I don't see for a long, long time."

Julian recalled the awkward air of the first meeting at the jewelry store and the strange way Antonio had looked at him then. Unpleasant as it was, it was borderline jovial compared with Antonio's searing gaze now.

"First, I see the eyes of a man I always remember—a man I hate, a man who slapped my father and stole something very precious from *mi familia*. Then I see the very thing he stole.

"And so I know then who you are. That you come from at least two generations of thieves and animals. Julian Correa Del Rey," Antonio accused, blending the generations together. "You cannot lose a name like that in an ocean. It floats after you like shit in a sewer."

"Unbutton your shirt, Juliano," Felix instructed calmly, like a police detective looking for an identifying birthmark on an accused rapist. Julian began to speak and then reconsidered, realizing his control of the state ended at the door into the sovereign nation of Calderon. He unbuttoned the top button and looked again at Felix for instruction.

"Keep going, Juliano," Felix ordered in a more passive tone. "Just a few more." Julian's mind raced with the prospects of where this was headed. Hearing that his father was disreputable was nothing new; his mother had infected each day with that description. And he knew his grandfather had been a Castro henchman, whatever that really meant in application. As Julian unfastened buttons midway down his chest, the plaid polo shirt opened to reveal the object of Antonio's interest dangling from a golden chain.

"There she is," Antonio said gleefully as the diamonds glistened within the yellow ore. "There is my Papa's little bird."

Tears welled in Antonio's eyes and he put his head in his hands just as Julian had done, for very different reasons, a short while before. He wiped his eyes with the heel of his hand and reached forward to gently cup the Tocororo, his palm mere inches from Julian's neck. Antonio gazed up and whispered a soft prayer of gratitude. Julian looked straight ahead like a dog being groomed and resigned to the violation of space Antonio was perpetrating under the color of Felix's considerable authority. Antonio ran his fingers over the golden charm, letting his thumb caress the piece fashioned by his father Diego and remembering the awful morning when he hadn't put the little bird away in time.

He could still hear the slap from Julian's grandfather, Capitan Del Rey, even now and more bitterly recall Julian's father's taunting smile at the doorway of the Rosales Jewelry Store. Here, next to Governor Correa, he could also hear Felix's father encouraging him to always remember his face. Julian's eyes were exactly as he remembered those of Ramon and Capitan Del Rey. He did remember.

Julian's neck betrayed a quickened pulse, and as Antonio's hand grazed his chest he swallowed deeply. The Cuban jeweler raised his left hand to Julian's shoulder and Julian's eyes raced toward Felix, a man he had called upon initially to be his protector. But Felix's expression offered no shelter or empathy as Antonio now had two hands very near his face and throat. Antonio's left hand held Julian's shoulder firmly and Julian braced himself for a punch he expected to come from the right. Instead, he felt a pinch at the back of his neck as Antonio snapped the chain with a yank and freed the Tocororo.

Antonio slipped the charm off the gold rope and tossed the chain back in Julian's lap. Governor Correa was simply shaking his head now and looking at Calderon. His anger was muted only by his fear of Calderon and the Mexican drug dealers looming outside. The luxury of outward frustration, contempt, or other visual display might invoke a violent turn of events that he wasn't willing to risk, whether Calderon had set him up with Antonio or not.

The Tocororo was one of the few things he had of his father's, and in one unpleasant exchange of events he had lost both the charm and his remaining respect for a father he had never met. Worse yet, now he had to wonder what Calderon had said and would say to Frank Hayes. The cat out of that bag might be a lion.

Antonio returned to the kitchen and explained the Tocororo's significance to the woman cooking, gesturing with exuberance, telling her of his father, and Felix's father, and Julian's father, his loving Tia Lita, and his beautiful cousin Eva for whom the charm had been made. The golden bird clearly meant more to him than to Julian, though Julian would never forgive Calderon or Antonio for the manner in which it had been taken, just as Antonio had never forgiven the Del Reys.

"May I leave now?" Julian asked as sarcastically as he thought Calderon would tolerate.

"Of course, you are the governor," Felix replied as if that genuinely had bearing. "This is your state, no?"

Julian buttoned his shirt and exhaled a noise that could only be taken as an acknowledgment of Calderon's sarcasm fused with his frustration and humiliation. As he walked toward the door he remembered the Mexican combatants just outside and considered asking Calderon if he need worry. Remembering how his request for help with Hayes had turned for the worse, Julian opted not to mention the issue. Calderon sat still as Julian breached the door, waiting for him to step just beyond the threshold before speaking over his shoulder to the departing Correa. "Take care of that little girl, Juliano."

"Oh yeah, I'll do that, Felix," Julian answered insincerely, wondering if Felix's words were threat, mockery, or somehow related to his previous remarks about the perils of having a family. He shut the door behind him as he looked out toward his rental. Seeing Carlos and Mario standing in front of his car, he sat down on the steps, considering what lay before him and behind.

CHAPTER 34

"Jay-bird, you gotta pull it together," Craig said, prodding his sleeping partner as the men approached Naked City. "It's almost game time, baby."

"Can we pleeeeeease just go home, Craig?" Jay pleaded as he neared sobriety, but not full strength. "I'm not up for your therapy tonight."

"Nah, let's see it through," Craig said, undeterred. "I've got a couple *cholos* who like to run their mouths when I'm in uniform. They're perfect for this. When you sober up entirely, you're going to be thinking about that dead kid from this afternoon. Let's get a little exercise working on a couple Mexican dealers like that kid's daddy."

"Was his dad even a drug dealer, Craig?" Jay asked.

"Probably," Craig replied as Officer Sheppard sat straight up in the seat for the first time since they'd left the pub. He looked at Craig's service-issue gun sitting between them.

"So, what exactly are we going to do with these drug dealers?" Jay inquired as Craig possessively moved the firearm nearer to himself.

"Let's just go down there and punk them," Craig said. "We'll see if they talk as much shit when we're out of uniform. If they talk shit tonight, they get a beat-down."

"Bad idea," Jay interjected as they turned onto Las Vegas Boulevard and headed north. "They'll make us as cops and phone it in. We'll walk into work tomorrow with Internal Affairs breathing down our necks. That hard-ass Gomez in IAB would just love it if we got a harassment complaint from somebody Latino."

"They're not gonna say shit, Jay," Craig declared confidently. "Both these beaners have priors, and the last thing they want is to have their names better known at the station. They may talk shit, but they're not idiots. I'd be surprised if they don't both have warrants. You think they're going to the station on their own?"

"I still think it's a bad idea, Craig," Jay said for the record. "I don't need this kind of 'therapy' to feel better. Some rain will fall."

"Some rain will fall?" Craig asked incredulously. "What kind of Hallmark-card bullshit is that?"

"Just something my dad used to say when things went wrong," Jay explained. "It just means there's always going to be bad stuff, you know? And that you have to accept that you can't do anything about it."

"In about five minutes I'm gonna show you what you can do about it," Craig said sternly. "Then you can call your daddy and tell him to get a new motto."

As Jay rested uncomfortably in the passenger seat of Craig Peters' small pickup, Julian rose from his own uncomfortable concrete seat and headed for his vehicle. Approaching the rental car, Carlos and Mario turned toward him like valet parkers at the Bellagio.

"Hey, Governor," Mario beckoned, turning Julian's official title into a nom de guerre as he leaned over the driver's-side window and looked menacingly at Julian above the car. "How come Felix don't walk you out?"

"Felix don't like you, holmes," Carlos chimed in before Julian could reply. "If he like you, he walk you to your car. This is a bad neighborhood."

Julian realized Mario had positioned himself away from the front end of the car just enough that it would provide a blind side as Julian attempted to enter the vehicle. The ambush was in place. If he tried to get into his car, he'd be face to face with Carlos and unable to see Mario's movement behind him. Julian had seen them use a blind-side technique on Daniel previously and this time they were armed. He also recognized that they had assaulted Felix's visitors before, having established a code with Calderon about people who mattered and didn't matter exiting Felix's private quarters. And instead of just shaking down small-time hustlers looking for Felix's blessing or forgiveness, they had their own ax to grind with Julian.

Julian surveyed the situation, assuming that physical conflict with the men was inevitable. He knew it would be one against two, like it or not, and the prospects of battling two street thugs armed with knives still seemed a better alternative than returning to Calderon's dangerous sanctum. *I'm gonna have to knock one of them out quickly,* Julian thought, *and face the other one on one.*

To do so, Julian realized his best chance was to come around to the driver's side of the car from the rear, keeping Mario and Carlos in full view. As he did, Carlos shot Mario a worried look, realizing that Governor Correa wasn't following the hastily hatched game plan. Mario nodded a "go ahead" nod and Carlos reached into his pocket for his switchblade. Julian had squared with Carlos, but maintained a five-foot separation from the smaller man.

"Come on, Governor," Carlos beckoned as he held the blade loosely. "It's time for you to get in your little car and go home. You gotta go do some legislation or something, right?"

"Why don't you put your knife down and be a man," Julian goaded. "Isn't it enough that there're two of you little bitches?"

"What, you think this is the Olympics, holmes?" Carlos offered sarcastically. "We ain't in the same weight class either." Carlos turned to Mario to share in a laugh at his retort. As he did so, Julian stepped forward, looking to blast him with a knock-out haymaker. But Carlos turned back sooner than Julian expected and the punch never had a chance to be thrown. Instead, Julian found himself close enough that Carlos could grab his shirt and lay the point of the knife against his abdomen.

The end of the blade hadn't broken his skin yet, but a gentle breeze worth of additional pressure would have its tip somewhere inside him. Julian's back was now against the driver-side door and Mario had come around the vehicle to share in the harvest and punishment.

"You make a lot of money, don'tcha?" Mario asked as he reached inside Julian's pants pockets. "You must have a lot of nice things, *vato.*"

"The Rolex is mine," Carlos declared as he held Julian's right hand down with his left. Julian looked for a window in which to extricate himself, pondering where he could run through the neighborhood to safety if he could get loose. Maybe grab Carlos's knife-hand and swing it into Mario, a Hollywood action-thriller move he'd seen before. He was bigger and more athletic, but they were so close to him and each man had a knife ... and experience with this sort of thing.

Carlos unfastened Julian's Rolex, adding to the governor's jewelry losses for the day. He placed the Rolex in his Dickies pants pocket and smiled with satisfaction at his cousin. Mario had confiscated a money clip and was considering the value of the bills contained within. Satisfied that they had sufficiently cleaned Julian of present value, Mario stepped back and looked first toward his prey and then to his cousin.

"Why don't we take him to your crib, Carlos?" Mario said. "I think your old lady would like to meet the governor, don't you? Ain't she part Cuban?"

"Fuck you, holmes," Mario replied to Carlos's kidding. "She ain't no part Cuban. She's pure Aztec blood, *ese.*"

Carlos looked over Julian, the knife still engaging only the outer-most layers of Julian's epidermis like a fakir on a bed of nails. "Maybe that's a good idea. We can't finish this in front of Felix's. He don't want no bodies getting found in front of his house, 'specially no governor." Julian stood still, held in part by the knife point and by the numbing effect of the night's infernal events. With Hayes about to find out that he wanted him dead, it occurred to Julian momentarily that this might be a better end than worrying about what Hayes was going to do to him.

"Yeah, let's get this off the street, holmes," Carlos agreed as Mario began to turn Julian around. Carlos withdrew the knife from Julian's stomach and moved it to his back as he followed behind the governor trailing Mario. "We'll finish him there and stuff an eight-ball in his jacket."

Another drug deal gone bad," Mario said in a sarcastic voice meant to sound like a stiff white television anchorman. Julian stood still as Mario commanded him to follow. He looked toward Felix's residence to see if his father's former business partner was watching these events. Seeing nothing, he resumed following Mario when Carlos poked him with the knife for not moving quickly enough.

Julian felt the sharp sting of the penetrating blade in his lower back and it angered him more than it hurt. In an instant he decided that as dire as his prospects with Hayes appeared to be, he didn't want *these* lowlifes to determine his fate and sully his daughter's last name in the process. If they were going to kill him, they would do so in an open fight on this street, not in some ghetto hovel where they lived their shitty lives and could manufacture what the police found later.

"Did that hurt, *ese?*" Carlos taunted, as he kept the blade to the governor's back. "It's gonna hurt more when I stick it in your face." An older woman with her hair in a plastic bag had come to the window of the apartment next to Calderon's and was watching the street scene from above. The men walked around the back of the car, following single file with Mario still leading the way. As Julian stepped onto the curb and the blade left his skin for the moment out of lock-step, he veered quickly to the side and kicked Mario across his hip with a powerful blow that sent the smaller man flying.

As Mario fell to the ground, Carlos approached Julian cautiously, the gleaming blade in front of him. Mario cursed loudly in Spanish as he stood back up awkwardly and withdrew his knife as well, joining his cousin as they maneuvered to corner Correa like bullfighters in the final *tercio de muerte*. Julian knew his options were few, and it seemed unavoidable that he would receive a knife wound. With a brick wall behind him, his fate appeared sealed until the screech of tires and the strobe of bouncing headlights gave his attackers pause.

"Co-mo es-tas, assholes," Officer Peters shouted as the pickup landed curbside. Craig and Jay saw only a trio of Hispanic men huddled near a wall and not the battle they'd just interrupted. "Remember me, beaners?"

Carlos and Mario recognized the officer out of uniform immediately, and Carlos swiftly tucked his blade into his back pocket. Mario moved his weapon to Julian's back as the governor stood frozen for the moment, relieved to be out of the fire of the fight, but unsure of the frying pan of this turn of events.

"Yeah, we remember you, off-i-cer," Carlos answered, mocking Craig's *como estas* staccato tenor. "I thought when you go undercover the idea was for nobody to see you."

"Well, we're not undercover, Jose," Craig shouted past Jay and through the passenger window again. "I want you to see me."

"Who's the big spic?" Craig asked Mario and Carlos, assuming Julian was in league with the two dealers. "Is that some new muscle you got in from Chee-wah-wah?" Jay's sobriety had turned to concern, wondering if Peters had done the math to see that they were outnumbered. Neither officer recognized the captive governor in the poor light, nor realized that Julian was a hostage—not back-up. Jay was hoping the disadvantage would end Craig's desire to work over Carlos and Mario.

"That's just a friend of ours," Mario said quickly, reminding Julian of his predicament with a tapping of the knife blade to his back. "He don't speak no English."

"That's a big fuckin' surprise," Craig said sarcastically. "Guess that means he's about ready to work the drive-through window at Jack-in-the-Box. Tell him I'll be there around noon tomorrow to get a Yumbo Yack." Julian looked directly at the officers, hoping they would recognize him and begin the rescue. He'd think of an excuse later, some charitable cause or the like to explain his presence with known drug dealers in the heart of Naked City. But he needed to be subtle as a more obvious move might get him lethally stuck by Mario. So too might the officers leaving without recognizing him.

"What-choo want, Officer Peter?" Carlos asked as he looked at Mario. "Hey, ain't 'Peter' what some white boys call their dicks?"

As Mario laughed behind a stoic Correa, Craig fumed inside the car. The junior high-esque insult wasn't particularly biting or original, but the bravado with which it was uttered chafed at his plan to torment them. It didn't help that Jay had giggled either. Craig unbuckled his seat belt and reached for the door handle on his side. Jay's hand shot out quickly, holding Craig's belt and preventing him from exiting the car. "Bro, you think it's a good idea to take on three of them?"

Officer Peters looked again through the passenger window, mistaking Julian's fixed gaze for something more menacing. "Who the fuck does that guy think he is, Jay?" Craig asked his partner. "He's gonna mad-dog me like he's somebody?"

"Craig, let's just go. Next time we're down here we'll run 'em all in," Jay pleaded. "No good's gonna come from this. It's not even what you expected."

"Fuck that. One's running his mouth and the big one's staring at me like I'm his bitch," Craig replied. "I'm a goddamn police officer."

"Hey, va-to," Craig yelled at Julian over the car engine's idle. "Get the fuck over here." Julian didn't move or speak, unintentionally playing the role of immigrant.

"I told you, holmes," Mario said, hissing the words. "He don't speak no English." Carlos stepped forward in an effort to deflect attention away from Julian. The darkness had hidden Julian's identity thus far, but closer proximity would end the anonymity and prevent them from finishing their plan to execute him.

"I got an idea, officer," Carlos sneered brashly as he neared the window. "Why don't you take your pretty little bitch here home and show her your peter." The old woman's husband had joined her at the sill and the pair watched the street theatrics as if the players were thespians upon the boards. Jay shrugged off the insult and hoped Craig would too. As he turned to gauge Craig's reaction, he noticed the gun had moved from Craig's side to his lap.

"Peter, Peter, Peter-Eater," Carlos taunted, knowing he'd hit a sore spot earlier and picking at the wound like a ruthless boxer on an opponent's eye cut. Jay looked down at Craig's right hand, which softly caressed the contours of the gun, just like the gunslingers in Westerns always did. Craig's hand danced with the permeating vibration of adrenaline, and the last thing Jay wanted was for Craig to point the gun at the men, raising the level of complaint that might come into the station soon after.

Officer Sheppard knew he had to diffuse the situation quickly and to do so would require containing the increasingly agitated state of his partner. As Craig fidgeted with the pistol, Jay looked first at his partner and then at Carlos, who had come to the window, eager to mock Craig yet again.

"Peter, Peter, Peter Eater ..." Carlos began his jeer before Jay grabbed his black sweatshirt and pulled his head into the vehicle. In an instant Jay had hit him twice, the first catching a surprised Carlos with his mouth wide open, increasing the blow's effect. Carlos tried to pull backward, his head hovering above the car window's lower edge, but Jay's grip held and he struck him again, just above the eye. Mario instantly released Julian and ran toward the pickup, the knife that had been against Julian's back now in full view. The elderly couple upstairs watched as the moonlight caught the blade every few steps, shooting light upward.

"You're not so funny now," Jay said to a palsied Carlos, who was now anything but humorous or amused. Jay wanted to punish Carlos to the point of satisfying Craig, to extinguish the dangerous tide of contempt rising inside his partner.

With the distraction, Julian sprinted toward his close-by car, readying his ignition key in his hand as he fled. Carlos was bleeding from his right eye, unable to extricate himself from Jay's firm grip on his clothing through the muck of intermittent consciousness. His head and shoulders nearly filled the small passenger window, delaying Officer Peters' view of Mario approaching, knife in hand.

"Knife, partner!" Craig shouted an alarm.

"Oh, shit!" Jay said as Mario drew near, looking to extricate his cousin. Mario had almost forgotten the knife was in his hand, having held it so long. Carlos, by comparison, was unable to reach his weapon in his present state of pugilistic dementia.

Julian had one foot in the rental when he heard the call of "knife" and turned back to the fray. Through the glass of the truck's windshield he watched Officer Peters raise the gun, the firearm extending beyond the passenger window. Entering the line of fire came Mario, who apparently couldn't see much besides his prone cousin and Officer Sheppard holding him tightly.

"Let him go, holmes," Mario commanded Jay as he reached for Carlos's belt, hoping to pull him free and oblivious to the weapon aimed in his direction. When the shot fired from the gun, it sounded like a cannon to Jay, the truck's cab acting like a woofer.

Julian and the old couple watched as both Mexican men fell to the street just below the pickup. A moment later Carlos had regained some measure of consciousness as his cousin's life was ending. Mario lay bleeding from an artery in his neck that the bullet had severed. Craig set the pistol back down on the seat and walked around the vehicle to where Carlos knelt beside his dying cousin. The blood was entering the street like water from a garden hose, and even in the dim light Mario's once-ruddy skin was clearly lightening. The gurgle of blood in his throat replaced any words he was attempting, and Mario could only hold his head in his hands, letting the end come in the arms of family and friend.

"Is he dead?" Craig asked Carlos, as if they were on speaking terms, while Julian shut his car door and started the engine, stifling an urge to vomit. He could see the trio of men on the street next to the pickup and knew that the gunshots would bring more police. This wasn't a report he wanted to file with the authorities.

Carlos didn't look up—or answer—instead shifting Mario's limp body into his lap. Mario's eyes were fixed upward and unblinking, the small tattoo of a teardrop under his right eye inches from the green-ink tattoo on Carlos's cradling hand. As Craig looked on, Carlos whispered in the empty face of his cousin, *Primo*, I take care of this for you. I promise. I give you justice."

Julian gunned the engine and steered the car toward the corner. As he passed Felix's house he could see Calderon, Antonio, and the cook out on the stoop, watching the tumult. Jay was locked on his partner standing next to the lifeless body.

"Craig, what the hell?" Jay screamed, struggling to grasp the night's fatal impact. "He's shot?"

"He's dead, partner," Craig replied with the calm of an embalmer. "Looks like he took one through the jugular."

"Oh, no. Oh, no. This is baaaaaaad. What are we going to tell Sarge when he gets down here?" Jay asked as his entire body began sweating a coat of ice water, his voice and temper rising commensurate to the trouble in which he'd found himself. "Are you going to tell him we came down here drunk and started fucking with the locals?"

"We're not saying shit to anyone," Craig ordered. "We're getting the fuck out of here. This I don't need."

Craig slammed the door shut and hastily drove from the scene. Carlos sat there solemnly holding his cousin, begging a little boy from next door to fetch Mario's girlfriend and mother.

"Craig, that kid is dead. We have to go back," Jay insisted. "This is a big deal now."

"That scumbag fuck was going to stab you, Jay," Craig said. "I just saved you from getting stabbed."

"Let's just tell Sarge that, man," Jay pleaded again. "We can't just leave. Somebody's gonna give 'em your plates and then we'll have left the scene. Nobody will believe anything we say after that."

"Shut the fuck up, Jay," Craig said firmly as he navigated the exit route from Naked City.

"CRAIG! They're going to give them our plates!" Jay crowed, hoping to implore his partner to return. "We can't run from this."

"My plates are covered in mud, Jay," Craig reported. "My whole front and back end are filthy from pulling the boat out at the lake when it rained Tuesday. Nobody can see shit."

"That other kid knows you, Craig," Jay said. "He knows your fuckin' name."

"You think that kid's going to the police and telling this story?" Craig asked, his voice implying a greater confidence than his body truly felt. "Street dealers aren't witnesses, Jay-Bird.

"Come on, man. Just relax," Craig said positively, as if a tornado had just skipped their town. "This is over."

"You think so? You think Homicide's not going to go over this with a fine-toothed comb?"

"Jay, it's just some ghetto bastard in Naked City," Craig said. "They're gonna find him with a night's sales worth of crack and a knife. You think they're gonna be puzzled as to the motive? It'll be a gang hit or a burn that got even. End of story."

"We should call Sarge," Jay said, mulling the veracity of Craig's remarks.

"No, we should go home and never say anything about this to anyone. If we do, we both go down." Officer Peters stopped at a red light, two lanes over from the governor of the state of Nevada in his rental car. "You know what happens to cops in prison."

Julian had both hands firmly on the wheel, as if inclement weather were at hand. Gone was the expressionless mask he'd worn throughout most of the night, replaced with one forged by the gravity of all that had occurred. He'd come to Naked City to relieve himself of his largest problem and in doing so exacerbated it and left himself in a far worse position than he'd been just hours before. The tears wet on his cheeks blended each stream of discomfiture into a collective fear.

"We've already left the scene, Jay. That's done. There's no turning back now. Can you just keep your mouth shut so that we both get to live our lives as free men?" Craig asked sincerely, bathing the remark in a fraternal tone.

"I thought you said it was self-defense, Craig?" Jay countered. "But yeah, you're right, what's done is done. And I'm not going to jail because of your bad idea. I never wanted any part of this."

"I know you didn't, partner. I'm sorry," Craig apologized, his voice and demeanor parallel to Jay for the first time since they'd left. "It was a bad idea."

Julian pulled his car into the parking lot of the all-night pancake house and picked up his cell phone. As the phone rang at the Madison house, Julian's free hand nervously rubbed the back of his neck and the front, his fingers confirming the absence of the little golden bird.

CHAPTER 35

he distance between Daniel's house and the coffee shop where
Julian cowered in a corner booth afforded just enough time for the
governor to down two black coffees. He knew he wouldn't be sleeping
at all tonight—not after everything that had happened—so the caffeine
wasn't an issue.

The sleigh bells on the glass front door shook as Daniel entered
the all-hours business. The place was small, with the ambient hue of
aging yellow paper, as if the overhead lighting were filtered through
something that compromised its vibrancy. A casino dealer with his shirt
half-unbuttoned read the newspaper over a couple of sunny-side-up
eggs. A homeless man the waitress called Charlie sat in the front booth,
muttering to himself as she handed him a broken piece of apple cobbler.
Through the emptiness Daniel quickly located Julian holding a coffee
mug in both hands as if he were cold. His hair was tousled slightly and
his face pale as his mother had often wished it to be.

It had been well over a year since they'd seen each other, but Julian
looked much older, more thirtysomething than the vital man in his
mid-twenties he'd appeared the last time they had been together. Julian
was always on TV, in the papers, or otherwise in front of Daniel, but
the polished performer from those media was somewhere else tonight.

Julian's call had surprised Daniel. Not just because it had come at eleven
p.m. on a weeknight, but that it had come at all. He'd never told Julian to
go to hell or articulated his contempt after the retraction of the job he'd so
desperately banked on and earned, seeing no upside to an exhibition of
anger with a man who was growing more powerful every day. In truth, his
once-fervent disdain was slowly abating, and when Julian called to say he
needed him immediately, a healthy curiosity blended with forgiveness, sending Daniel to the coffee shop as an enthused Sydney encouraged him to see
if Julian "had any good jobs" for him.

Daniel slid into the brown leather booth as Julian sat motionless, no hand extended in warm greeting nor verbal acknowledgment that he had arrived. He looked down, somewhere near Daniel's larynx, and seemed lost in thought, like an airplane crash survivor with a blanket wrapped around his shoulders. Gone was the manifest bravado of a conqueror, a man who controlled situations and people.

"Julian?" Daniel prodded gently after an awkward half-minute of silence had passed.

"Danny ..." Julian began, now looking at Daniel directly, his eyes still as a man's can be when peering inward. "I saw someone die tonight."

"What do you mean you saw someone die tonight, Julian?" Daniel asked after another pause by Julian indicated he wasn't going to automatically follow up on the dramatic statement.

"A man ... in the street ... he got shot ... and he just died right there," Julian said. "He just bled to death in the street."

"Julian, bro, what are you talking about?" Daniel asked, trying to make sense of the sparse details. "Did something happen to you, man?"

"One minute he was yelling, you know, and then the gun went off, Danny," Julian said. "It looked like it hit him in the throat. That's what he was holding when he fell."

"Jule ... man, we gotta start somewhere ... I can't really follow this," Daniel asked gently. "Where did this happen? Why were you there? Who got shot?"

"It was that kid that sucker-punched you, Danny," Julian said with more clarity than before. "Remember those Mexicans we fought outside the brewery that night?"

"That was like three years ago. Why would you be around those guys again?" Daniel inquired, growing more concerned now that there was some connection to himself.

"I didn't plan it, I was just trying to get some help, you know?" Julian offered, anguished and defeated. "I just couldn't take it anymore. Every day he's taunting me, making me do things I don't want to do, putting me at risk. It never stops. Now he's going to kill me. I know it."

"Nobody's going to kill you, Julian," Daniel said reactively. "You're the governor.

"But I'm so lost, man," Daniel added as he attempted to corral the data into a composite image. "One of the Mexican guys we fought at the brewery has been taunting you, and now he's been shot ... but you're worried that he might kill you?"

"No, no, no," Julian disagreed weakly, rotating the coffee cup on the table top nervously. "I'm sorry."

"It's okay, Julian. I just want to help you if I can. But I don't really understand what's happened here. Maybe we should call the police."

"No!" Julian replied vehemently. "NO POLICE! That's why you're here."

"I'm not a cop, Julian," Daniel said.

"No, but you're my friend, Danny. I need you to help me think this through.

"You're still my friend, Danny?" he asked, hoping it was so.

"Yes, I'm your friend, Julian," Daniel confirmed, knowing that had someone else asked if he were Governor Correa's friend an hour ago, the answer would have been no.

"I know I fucked you over, Danny," Julian said, his eyes moist but short of crafting a falling tear. "I was mad at you and I was wrong. I know you were trying to do the right thing."

"Forget about it," Daniel offered. "I don't think that's the life for me anyway. All things for a reason, you know?"

"It's just that you put me in a bad spot with Frank Hayes," Julian said, attempting to justify his actions as if Daniel hadn't just absolved him. "He's brutal, Danny. He's as bad as it gets, because he's not just vicious, he's smart and vicious. He finds little cracks, and once he gets into you, he owns you. It's like in the movies ... when you invite a vampire into your house and then they can come in any time they want. I know you didn't know what you were doing, but Danny, that was very dangerous for me when you told Martin."

"I'm sorry, Julian. I didn't know much about Hayes then. I just knew that we had all made this pact to protect each other," Daniel said. "But that's behind us. How can I help you right now, Julian? Why did you call me?"

"Because you're the only friend I think I have, Daniel," Julian answered quickly, the words swathed in a humility Daniel had never seen in Julian. "And I know you're honest."

"Thank you, Julian," Daniel said. It felt good to have Julian now value the very thing that had been the instrument of their severed friendship. The acknowledgment from Julian cleansed any rancor that remained and lowered Daniel's guard.

"So, how can I help you?" Daniel asked again, trying not to sound like a retail clerk.

"I don't know … we gotta think things through," Julian said, waving to the waitress and pointing at Daniel and then to his coffee. "Please help me."

"Sure, man. I'm here now. Just tell me what happened and we'll put our heads together. We'll work it out," Daniel agreed, consoling his former comrade while he pondered if there was anything that really could be done considering a person had been killed. The waitress set down a water-spotted coffee mug and poured the steaming brew. As soon as she left, Julian told Daniel the whole story, how he had sought out a Cuban mafioso to kill Hayes and how the Mexicans had been in front of the little house in Naked City. He spoke of Calderon's rejection, the taking of the golden bird from his neck, and the knives against his skin courtesy of his and Daniel's former adversaries. He told of the cops and the Mexicans and how the gun sounded when it was fired by the driver of the pickup. He spoke of the soft thud of Mario's body as it hit the pavement and the awful sound the man made as he choked and bled to death. The only detail withheld was that of Antonio's role in the taking of the Tocororo. Julian couldn't afford to have Daniel torn between him and a family friend. Not after what he'd done to Daniel, and definitely not right now.

"Oh, Julian," Daniel said after Julian finished explaining what had happened. "We've got to call the police right away."

"No!" Julian said sternly again. "I can't do that."

"Julian, you were witness to a person's death, probably a murder," Daniel told the governor. "You have to come forward."

"And say what, Daniel?" Julian answered, his voice rising in tone and pitch. "I'm going to tell them that I was at a known crime lord's home looking to set up a hit on the most powerful guy in Vegas and then I watched a police officer shoot and kill a drug dealer with whom I had a fist fight previously. That won't turn any heads."

"Julian, stuff like this always comes out. There have got to be witnesses. What's the cop going to say about you?"

"The cop has no idea who I am," Julian explained. "They just thought I was another random Mexican. That's not an issue."

"What about the other Mexican? What's he going to say?"

"I don't know, but I doubt that his version is going to mention that he tried to kill the governor before some cops shot his homie," Julian replied quickly. Daniel noticed he was regaining confidence more consistent with the Julian he was accustomed to seeing.

"So, why am I here, Julian, if you're not worried about this getting out?" Daniel asked as he sipped the harsh black coffee. "What do you want from me?"

"I guess I don't know, Daniel," Julian admitted. "After you see something like that—especially after all that happened tonight—you just want to go somewhere or talk to someone stable. I really don't have anyone who's like that for me now. Outside of Meredith, you're about the only honest, real person I know. And, of course, I'm screwing up things with her too." He glanced away, then quickly back again. "I appreciate you coming, Danny. I wasn't sure what you'd say when I called. You'd have been within your rights to tell me to go get fucked."

"You've been there for me too, Julian," Daniel reminded his troubled counterpart. "With the same guys we're talking about tonight. Who knows what they'd have done to me had you not cleaned house."

"I did whip some ass that day, didn't I?" Julian asked rhetorically, a warm smile splashing the grim countenance of his face like a joke in a funeral parlor as he recalled the day he and Daniel routed his attackers.

"So, you're just going to steer clear of this whole thing, eh?" Daniel asked.

"I think I have to," Julian replied. "There's not much that they need me for. There're other witnesses, and those guys were cops. It would just bring dishonor to Nevada for me to come forward." He paused. "I mean that sincerely," he added, knowing he probably should.

"I'm sorry you had to go through all this, Julian," Daniel said, struggling to think of the proper consolation for a friend who had been attacked and then witnessed a street killing.

"Me too," Julian replied humbly. "Everything about tonight was a mistake."

"Well, I hope that life gets a little easier for you, Governor," Daniel said, a lightness gilding Julian's formal title.

"I doubt that," Julian responded. "Hayes isn't done with me. Calderon's going to tell him what I was up to. That seems clear. I'm going to have a war on my hands there, but he's already treating me so badly that I'm not sure it can get worse. Unless he kills me."

"I'm sorry to hear that," Daniel answered. "I wish I could help."

"I wish you could too," Julian said sincerely. "This has been a help. Is there anything I can do for you, Danny?"

"You mean before you get arrested for not reporting a murder?" Daniel teased. "Well, as I was running out the door tonight, Sydney told me to ask you for a high-paying gig. But I think I'm fine, Julian. I'm not making enough to get her off my back, but we're getting by … or at least I think so."

"Danny, if you need something, you call me," Julian said. "I can set you up lots of places."

"Just worry about you for now," Daniel said, hoping it hadn't come out too harshly. A sweet state job from Julian would be a bandage on his marriage, but it would put him back in league with Julian and his many issues. Battling Sydney's dollar-driven complaints sounded more appealing than cavorting with Julian's troubles again. "I'm going to get home," Daniel said as he stood up, extending his hand to Julian. "I'm getting up early with Sofia tomorrow and making her breakfast."

"It's funny that I've never met her, Dan, and that you've never seen my little girl," Julian said.

"Well, maybe someday they'll play together," Daniel offered.

"That'd be nice," Julian said, considering it seriously and warmed by the presence of a man he trusted. "Listen, Danny," Julian said as he placed his right hand on Daniel's shoulder. "I know you can keep your mouth shut about all this, right?"

"Of course, Julian," Daniel replied.

"Swear to me," Julian requested firmly. "Swear to me on your daughter that you'll keep this to yourself."

"Awww, Julian," Daniel lamented, "Does that really mean anything?"

"It does to a guy like you, Daniel."

"Okay, I swear on my little girl," Daniel acquiesced uncomfortably. "Is that good enough?"

"Yeah," Julian said as they walked toward the parking lot. "That's good enough for me."

CHAPTER 36

It had been sixty-two hours since Mario died in Naked City and neither Craig nor Jay had slept more than thirty consecutive minutes. Each man wove the images of the shooting into the uncertainty of their future, wondering if the external quiet of the last two days could hold and allow the fatal night to fade into waning memory. Different as the two men were, each wandered throughout his weekend trading anxiety for panic, jumping when the phone rang, wondering if it would be a call related to the shooting.

Jay had cleaned his gun, his house, and his garage, hoping the consuming effort would clear his mind. It hadn't, and his moral compass wanted desperately to turn him toward the station where he might cleanse himself of the guilt. Craig had waited but half the day before visiting his father to tell him what had happened. He wasn't sure if Jay could be counted on and his father, better than anyone, would know what to do if he couldn't. After Craig poured out the story he waited, expecting his father to explode in the kind of tirade he'd endured as far back as he could remember. At least this time it would be justified.

Instead, his father began his response with an apology, telling his son that he should never have had him in Naked City. Craig wondered momentarily if his own vulnerability had fostered the same in the harsh dictator of the living room where he'd been raised, a boy not allowed to speak when a football game was on television. But the apology had been but preamble to a genuine insult about expecting too much from a son always on the brink of failure. "Asking you to do something right is like asking you to be taller," his father lamented. "This is as much my fault as it is yours."

Craig trimmed the insult from the usable part of the statement, hoping this meant his father would assist him. It did, and Craig was relieved when his father said, in a rare fatherly tone, that things would be all right. The gritty detective stopped short of putting his hand on his son's shoulder or hugging the petrified man before him. That had never been done and wouldn't be done now. But as Craig watched his father transform into the model of efficiency that was his hallmark at the department, he couldn't help but feel a modicum of pride, love even, that his father might now be his champion. When Craig drove to meet his father at his house, his subconscious told him to put his dog Dusty out back, thinking his father might arrest him on the spot and not wanting the black Labrador to destroy his two-bedroom spread.

"You're sure you're not leaving anything out, Craig?" his father said for the fifth time as he drew the scene on a sheet of legal paper.

"You know what I know, Dad," Craig answered humbly, his arms close to his side.

"We've got the vic here passenger-side and the surviving 'spic on the road next to him. The illegal has taken off and that leaves only you and Sheppard, right?" he summarized.

"Correct," his son agreed.

"And here on this side we've got any of a number of possible witnesses." The elder Peters gestured with a black ballpoint pen over the drawing. "But behind you we've probably got nothing, because your back would shield them."

"That's probably true," Craig affirmed softly, deferring to rank, lineage, and aptitude.

"We've got no room for 'probably' here, son," Detective Peters warned. "Is there anyone behind you or to the left that could've seen anything?"

"Dad, there was an old motor home parked behind me and to my left as best I can recall," he explained. "We're good from behind."

"And you're sure that your hand was outside the vehicle when you fired?" he asked.

"Yes. Otherwise it would have been right in Jay's face," Craig said. "He'd have lost his hearing."

"That may be our ticket out of this mess, son," said father to son with a rapport they hadn't shared previously. For a moment Craig wondered if the difficulties with his father were mostly his fault, that if he had just stopped challenging the man who raised him, their relationship might have been better. Craig's humility now was clearly beneficial.

"Walt Brown's got this case over in Homicide," Detective Peters said. "He called me to tell me they're bringing you and Sheppard in on Monday."

"So, you knew?" Craig asked incredulously. "Why didn't you say anything? Why didn't you call me and warn me?"

"You shoot a kid in the 'hood and you've got the nerve to question my judgment?" his father said with a sternness that was second only to his hands in punitive efficacy. "I found out this morning, a couple of hours ago. If I hadn't heard from you today, I would've called you. I can't have you get hung out to dry on this. Not my son."

Craig didn't have the luxury of being offended as he pondered what Brown knew and didn't know. His father explained that Mario's cousin had in fact given investigators the officer's name he knew, and Brown had seen Jay and Craig leave together. Detective Peters added that crime scene investigators hadn't been able to locate the fatal bullet, the soft flesh of Mario's neck permitting the projectile to land somewhere far enough away that it couldn't be found.

Craig knew immediately that the lack of a bullet and ballistics testing took his gun out forensically and that witness reports would be chief among the evidence. With no bullet to match up, any gun of that caliber could have made the fatal hole in Mario. Carlos certainly had no idea what had transpired given the drubbing from Jay. The big Mexican with the car might have seen something, Craig considered, but if they didn't have him in for a statement yet, he was more than likely somewhere on his way back to Tijuana. According to Detective Brown, Carlos had also said the big Mexican's name was unknown to him, that it was just a random guy trying to score a little dope.

"So what do I do, Dad?" Craig asked his father.

"How close are you to Sheppard, Craig?" Detective Peters asked, instead of answering. "Can you trust him?"

"Dad, I think so … but I'm not sure," Craig answered honestly. "He's a pretty good guy. He'll hold up for a while, but I don't know for how long."

"Awhile is long enough," the veteran detective surmised. "Here's what you need to do right now. The only thing they've got is a couple old people who saw a man fire a gun out the passenger side. That's Jay's side. We're going to build your story around that. Jay's the shooter, Craig, like it or not. I'll make sure Walt asks you questions consistent with that line of thinking. You'll come across honest and reliable. If you can keep Jay pushing your old story to deny the shooting completely, he'll come across as the one with something to hide. They'll eat him alive once you tell the 'real' story. Your details will jibe with what Brown and his guys already know from the witnesses. Sheppard will bury himself. To add credibility, you'll need to accept some responsibility. Admit that you let Jay talk you into going down there to harass a few dirtbags. Walt says he was hammered at CJ's, so say he was drunk and you were just pacifying him before you took him home. Tell them he hit one of the 'cans and shot the other. *You* never touched anyone. *You* tried to stop him."

Craig nodded, agreeing to the plot and Jay's demise, wondering if he could sell the ruse to his partner.

"And take that truck and get it detailed and painted TODAY," he said. "We don't need the CSI guys finding anything that rips this story apart. They're going to take that car in and scour it. Those geeks get a new tool every day. Take it to one of those Mexican body shops on Main Street. They do good work."

"We can count on Walt, Dad?" Craig asked meekly, regretting now the way he normally treated his father's friend.

"Yeah, I can guarantee that," he replied with his usual confidence. "Remember the night he had that accident driving home and the college kid in the Jeep died? Remember how angry your mother was that I left that late at night?"

"Sorta … didn't the other guy blow through a four-way stop or something?" Craig recalled.

"Not exactly. Walt was blasted, completely shit-faced when he hit that kid waiting at the four-way. We got him out of a felony DUI by switching the piss at the hospital. He'll do what I tell him."

"Dad, I can't really find the words to sufficiently thank you," Craig said, dismissing the gravity of the betrayal of Jay to enjoy the first real semblance of relationship with a man he'd loathed more than loved over the years. "Thanks for getting me out of this."

"You're not out of it yet, son," he warned. "We've got to make this all work. And you're going to lose your job. I'll make sure of that personally."

The duality of the remarks rekindled a memory of a time when his father had taken stitches out of his forehead when he was a boy. They weren't quite ready to be removed and Detective Peters had stubbornly tugged at the fleshy wound, preferring to force Craig to endure the premature process rather than prove his wife's assertion that the stitches weren't ready. He'd ignored the young boy's yelps and whimpers as he held his head too firmly with his hand. The process had started with a father intent on helping his son, but the detective couldn't stop once he'd begun, even if each black thread pulled upward agonizingly puckered the pink skin like a tent.

"Put some of that stuff of your mother's on it," he ordered as he left the kitchen operating room. "And stop your goddamn crying."

Craig nodded in agreement now, recognizing that the loss of his job was a small price to pay to be out of what would soon be Jay's shoes. Walt would call tonight and he'd get the script down, but first he needed to reach out to Jay and keep him on the team, just like his father had instructed. It would hurt a little throwing Jay under the bus, Craig considered, but he didn't really have a choice. He consoled himself by resolving that he owed this to his father, to prevent tarnish to the name they shared.

CHAPTER 37

J ay buried his car keys in his pocket as he headed into the Metro substation, entering the bustling offices with his breath already irregular. His heart was palpitating like the kids with dope in their underwear when he'd come upon them. Sometimes he could see the blood racing through the neck vein of a lean street kid; other times he simply touched their wrist to feel the pulsing confession.

Jay had noted that Craig seemed supremely confident during their call that morning, and the story he'd crafted sounded like it would work. He was right, without the big Mexican to counter the fabrication, there would be no one to put a gun in either of their hands. As far as anyone could tell, Craig had theorized, the big Mexican might well have been the shooter. Two police officers would certainly assert as much. Jay rebuffed the lie at first, telling his partner that he didn't think he could pull it off. Craig had responded by telling him that his girlfriend was pregnant and reminded Jay of the type of man who had been killed. He had tried to kill Jay too, as Craig told it.

Officer Sheppard sat in his car in front of his home as Craig laid out the story, which prevented Officer Peters from facing murder charges and Jay from being punished for his role as accessory. Craig tried to make it sound like they were in this together and on the same level, as if each had fired the weapon. This was for both of them, he kept saying. And by the call's conclusion, Jay knew his role in keeping his partner off the hook. Craig had made the choice between sending him to prison and telling the truth about the death of a good-for-nothing drug dealer intent on stabbing Jay seem easy to make.

They made Jay wait alone for nearly forty minutes before anyone pierced the maddening silence of the tiny interrogation room. He'd counted acoustical ceiling tiles and then the dots on each of them to pass the time between rehearsals of Craig's story. When Detective

Brown entered with a smile and a Styrofoam cup of water for him, Jay felt a welcome sense of relief. Craig hadn't mentioned that Walter Brown would be conducting the interview, and Jay assumed it would go more smoothly with Craig's father's friend running the questioning. Jay hoped Walt would conduct Craig's interview as well. That would be better for Craig too.

An Internal Affairs officer watched through the two-way mirror as Walt pulled up a plastic chair on the opposite side of the table. Jay tapped his foot nervously as he ran through the outline of Craig's fictional scenario one last time before the curtain went up. "So, Jay, this shouldn't take too long," Walt began innocuously as he shuffled assorted papers on the table. "I just have to sew up a couple loose ends here. You got a few minutes for that?"

"Sure, Walt," Jay said amiably. "Whatever you need."

"Well, why don't you start by telling me what you boys were doin' down there?" Jay told the story as he and Craig had practiced, each false word eroding his self-respect as it was uttered. He told of how they'd decided to go through Naked City at night to see if the same dealers from the day were out and how they had pulled over to check a tire that was low. Walt nodded in assent as Jay continued, challenging nothing and accepting everything. As Jay concluded by explaining that the shot had come from some big, nameless Mexican at the scene, Walt's eyebrows raised in disbelief.

"So, you boys saw the decedent get killed, but you didn't call it in?" Walt asked flatly. Jay realized that with this dubious admission on the record, his career as a police officer was now over. There was no probation for leaving a dying man and the scene. Craig's stupidity had cost him his job and his integrity. He hadn't considered this among the potential after-effects as Craig persuaded him to play ball.

"Yeah, Walt, that was a mistake," Jay conceded awkwardly. "We shoulda called it in. I don't know what we were thinking." Jay lowered his eyes shamefully, wanting this to be the conclusion of his testimony.

Walt paused for a minute while he waited for Jay's eyes to return to his face. When they did, they found a different expression.

"So that's your story?" Walt prodded. "You sure you want to stick with that?" Jay's heart sank, recognizing that Walt wasn't on the team and that he was forced to defend a fictional account of the entire affair. Walt smelled blood, Jay was sure, and he hadn't been prepared for a challenge. He wondered how Walt was going to deal with Craig, his friend's only son, if he doubted Jay's narrative. Craig would tell the same tale.

"Yeah, Walt, that's what happened," Jay said softly, the insincerity of an unaccomplished liar like cellophane on spoiled meat. "We went there just to mess around, and I guess there was a bad drug deal going down or something. Happens all the time in Naked."

"Okay, okay," Walt accepted insincerely as Jay's plastic seat grew more uncomfortable. "Let me look at these witness statements I've got and see how your account lines up."

Walt splayed several pieces of paper on the desktop like an oversized poker hand, leaving most of the context easy for him to view. "I've got a Carlos Gutierrez who says that a cop he describes just like you pulled him into a truck and then beat him unconscious. And I've got a couple of geezers who say they saw a bullet fired out the passenger window and into the person of a Mario Jimenez, who as you recall expired at the scene you fled."

"I believe you did say you were on the passenger side, correct?" Walt queried, securing the important anecdote.

"I was, but I didn't shoot anyone, Walt," Jay answered immediately as he considered his dilemma. He had pledged not to tell of Craig's role, but Detective Brown was putting the gun in his hand now.

"Okay, you didn't shoot anyone," Walt agreed disingenuously. "But we have witness testimony here that says the fatal shot was fired out of the passenger window where you admit you were seated."

Hold firm, Jay thought, wanting to preserve his promise to Craig. *Weather the storm. You can't prove a negative. Don't burn Craig. Don't hang your partner. That's not what cops do.* The thoughts weren't even full thoughts in Jay's mind, more like flashing mental icons that represented something of larger magnitude, like a swastika or a cross. But lies and fabrications weren't Jay's province, and he could tell Walt already knew his story was bunk. In fact, it appeared he'd been expecting Jay to lie.

"So, why'd you shoot the kid?" Walt asked plainly and presumptively. "Was it an old beef from Naked City or did you just have too many in you, Jay?" Walt's tone had become more menacing, like the taunting way he'd gone at him at the bar worsened by some new malice and contempt, retro-justification for a meanness that came naturally.

"I didn't shoot anyone, Walt," Jay reiterated weakly and honestly. "You can ask Craig and he'll tell you the same thing."

"Well, he didn't," Walt said triumphantly, the statement's gravity unmistakable.

Bullshit, Jay thought as he remembered Craig's extended plea for help this morning. *This is their game. Tell one suspect that the other has already rolled on him. Get me to rat Craig out first. Did they forget I'm a cop?*

"I don't believe that," Jay said defiantly. "You're just trying to get me to say something that's not true."

"Why would I want to do that, Jay?" the detective asked. "Why would I want to ruin the career of a good cop? You're a good cop, aren't you, Jay?"

"You know I'm a good cop, Walt," Jay said, the nervousness manifesting in beads of sweat in the chilled room. The manila-colored walls looked like most of the cells at the detention center to Jay, and he wondered who was on the other side of the two-way mirror. Craig had advised him not to bring his union rep, saying that loading up with a lawyer or a union guy made him look like he had something to hide. That sure seemed like a mistake now as Walt peeled away at the story.

"I know that good cops don't go down into the 'hood to shoot citizens," Walt said. "At least your partner was man enough to admit his role in this mess."

"Oh yeah, what was that?" Jay challenged in a hybrid of frustration and courage, hoping to force open the bullshit hand he figured Brown was playing.

"Well, let me get Officer Peters' statement on top here," Walt said as he sipped from the Styrofoam cup, mouthing an occasional word out loud as he re-read Craig's version of the night's events. Brown purposely dragged the moment out as Jay sat wary of the next salvo from the efficient detective. Craig had told him earlier that he was to be interviewed after Jay. As the insufferable seconds passed, Jay grew cautiously confident that he'd called Walt's bluff.

"Well, let me just sort of summarize," Walt said with the lilt of an insult comic as he threw Craig's signed remarks on the brown table in front of Jay as if it were a pair of aces. The paper landed at an angle to Jay, who had to reach and turn it back toward himself. The display of curiosity seemed to invigorate the detective as Jay began to absorb the version of the shooting according to the sworn statement of Officer Craig Peters. Jay had only begun to digest the report, skimming as quickly as he could, when Walt's voice bellowed at a tone uncustomary for men seated three feet from each other. When Jay looked up again, Walt was turned and looking at the wall, as if Jay's response no longer had value, the truth already set indelibly.

"So, you get all hot and bothered that some little kid died at the hospital and you advise Officer Peters that you'd like to have a little revenge. You conveniently get drunk and ask your partner to take you home. Along the way you persuade him to drive your drunk ass to Naked City where you encounter Hispanic individuals such as the little boy's parents standing roadside. While harassing one of the victims—that's the one you hit so hard you broke his eye socket—you decide to grab your service-issue firearm and shoot the other, presumably who was attempting to assist his associate whom you were bludgeoning into unconsciousness."

Jay was simultaneously filtering the parallel of Walt's verbal depiction and the near symmetry with Craig's written remarks. It was Craig's handwriting all right. He'd seen his writing plenty.

"I didn't shoot anyone. Craig did!" Jay exclaimed as he tried to accept that Craig was blaming him. "I never even wanted to go down there in the first place. This was all Craig's idea."

"What was Craig's idea, son?" Walt asked, looking for footholds like a veteran rock climber.

"To go down there and rough up some bangers," Jay answered truthfully now that all bets were off. "I just wanted to go home. You saw me at CJ's, Walt. Did I look like I was up for anything but goin' home?"

"So why'd you beat the kid up if all this was Craig's idea?" Walt followed up, dismissing Jay's question. "All the witness statements say it was you who initiated the violence. No one says Craig did anything like that."

"I was just trying to calm Craig down," Jay said, thinking of how he had tried to subdue his partner by punching the shit-talking Mexican.

"Let me get this straight, you tried to calm him down by beating another man silly?" the detective asked. "Boy, shooting the other kid must have been like a tranquilizer for Craig. He probably slept like a baby later, eh?"

"I didn't shoot anyone, Walt!" Jay tried to explain as panic bled outward. Part of him knew that shutting up was his best course of action, but the blend of Walt's accusation and Craig's betrayal trumped reason. "Craig shot that kid. *He* shot him."

"Son, you've done nothing but lie in here and now you want to bury your partner for something you've done," Walt said. "Why don't you just be man enough to assume responsibility for your actions, for the death of that poor kid, and not drag your partner into this mess you've made for yourself."

"You've got it all wrong," Jay reiterated with a voice that comes from the small hole in the back of a man's throat when he's trying to stifle a burgeoning cry. "I just wanted to go home. That's all."

Jay sat defeated, immobilized by his foolishness in trusting Craig. What would his father say when he called him back in Virginia? What would his mother tell her friends, the same ones she always showed the pictures of Jay in his dress uniform? As Walt droned on trying to procure a confession, Jay tried to think of ways he could extricate himself. The only witnesses to the real events were a man he'd beaten to the point that he couldn't absolve him now and the big Mexican. The latter was now painfully unavailable. Craig had traded Jay's life for his own and now Officer Sheppard's lies in defense of his partner had become the satin lining of his own coffin.

An Internal Affairs officer entered the room once Jay had become unresponsive. Two uniformed officers arrived, crowding the tiny chamber. As they walked behind Jay, he stood up obediently, mindful of the next action.

"Officer Jason Sheppard, you're under arrest for the murder of Mario Gutierrez," Detective Brown said solemnly as a uniformed officer cuffed Jay and removed the contents from his pockets.

"I didn't even have my gun with me, Walt," Jay said to the detective as they led him to the door. The IAB officer followed as Walt stayed behind, dialing a number on his cell phone.

"It's done, Hank," Walt reported from the site of the inquisition. "You can go get some rest."

Jay walked down the hall as fellow officers watched him tread the hallways confined by handcuffs. He looked straight ahead, just as he had in the academy when the training officers screamed coffee breath into his nose and mouth for any misstep. The two officers guided him down the hall like Oswald as they headed toward booking when Craig Peters emerged from a separate interrogation room nearby. Jay tried to speak, but couldn't think of an appropriate greeting for a man who had duped him by convincing him not to betray his partner. Jay's reissue of Craig's prevarication had destroyed his credibility in any his-word-against-mine continuum. Only a governor whom Jay dismissed as a neighborhood dope fiend knew differently.

As Jay approached, Craig's face wore the affectation of a man repulsed by another's failings, selling the picture to the two uniformed officers at Jay's side. Prisoner Sheppard stopped walking for a moment as Craig crossed a few feet in front of him. Craig looked at Jay in synthetic condescension and shook his head. "I'm sorry, partner. I just can't go to jail for your bad idea. I didn't need that kind of therapy."

"Okay, Craig," Jay managed to respond, seeing the full scale of the con. "I guess killing one man wasn't enough."

It was Officer Peters' turn to struggle to reply, the poignancy of Jay's simple utterance articulating all that he had done, and this time the victim wasn't some disposable ghetto dealer. It was a man who was willing to risk his skin to save his partner, who had re-entered harm's way on his behalf. As Jay was led away, Craig knew that for something like this there would be no therapy.

CHAPTER 38

March 2004

It took nine months for Jay's trial to begin and nearly three days for the jurors to determine that Officer Jason Sheppard was guilty of first-degree murder in the shooting death of Mario Gutierrez. The jury divided along racial lines for the first two sessions, leaving the foreman to report on the second day of deliberations that they were deadlocked. A strongly worded note from the judge set the debate in motion yet again and the exhausted jury returned its verdict the next morning.

Officer Sheppard's partner had impressed the jurors with the candor he displayed as well as his tearful testimony as to how he could no longer fulfill the requirements of the job of peace officer after all that he'd seen, having resigned to volunteer with children in at-risk neighborhoods. "I'll find another way to give back," Craig promised as he fielded the District Attorney's softball, his father at ease in a row close to the front of the courtroom.

Craig's testimony sealed Jay's fate as it followed the damning accounts of the old couple and Carlos, all of whom affirmed Jay's violent display and the passenger-side position of the murder weapon. The prosecutor coined the phrase "Mystery Mexican" to mock Jay's pithy defense that a third Latino at the scene could exonerate him. Jay's assertion that Craig was the shooter had also been used as evidence that Officer Sheppard was a man devoid of moral fiber, a person who would put his faithful partner in harm's way to save himself. Craig would shake his head as the state's attorneys scolded or chided Jay, who found himself stuttering on the stand and bewildered by the speed at which everything was happening.

Outside each day, news stations and Hispanic organizations gathered, eager to make the case a cause célèbre. Carlos had become a spokesperson now, fitted in a new suit and rallying for peace and justice in a manner different than he'd promised his dying cousin. At night he'd shed the J.C. Penney pinstripe and Rodney King act and return to his Dickies and tee, doling out dime bags to suburban potheads who sometimes asked if this was the part of Naked City where that cop killed somebody.

Not much had changed for Carlos other than he no longer had to split the take with Mario as the sun came up. Instead, he broke off a few points for Mario's little brother who had followed the family program of terminating formal education at junior high to enter the business. He was going to be a lot of work, Carlos would tell the kid's permissive mother, as Chato seemed most eager to use his gun. "I'm not goin' out like my brother," the boy would declare to all who'd listen, his voice fueled by grief and anger. "Mama don't got no more boys."

Daniel had called Julian twice since the night at the coffee shop, once when Jay began his defense and once when the judge announced that Officer Sheppard would spend the rest of his life behind bars. He knew from Julian's story about the night of the shooting that Jay hadn't been the killer, and he wanted Julian to come forward. The media beating that Jay's parents were taking outside the courtroom was difficult to stomach. Both times Julian rebuffed Daniel, arguing self-servingly that the state shouldn't have to suffer for his mistake. As Julian uttered the familiar refrain he thought of how many times he'd quarreled with his conscience the same way, deciding inevitably not to tell Meredith of any adulterous dalliance taxing his person. She knew anyway, he often thought. The details would only be cruel, an apology impotent.

Same old Julian, Daniel realized as he assuaged himself with the fact that the incriminated cop was at least a violent racist according to Julian's first account. Even still, the notion of the real shooter free and perjuring himself at a murder trial seemed irrepressible, just as Julian's pronouncement of Mike Martin's imminent demise had been before.

But now wasn't the time for a vociferous challenge to Julian, not with his marital life crumbling around him. Sydney was growing more distant each day and Daniel had caught her lying about her whereabouts on multiple occasions. His mind cruelly pictured her in throes of passion with a recharged Zigler as she seemed to be back on the luxury trail again. Of course, Zigler was efficiently calling Daniel once a day, leaving the "I know something you don't know" refrain on his voice mail.

He'd looked up a new purse she'd said she bought at a department store on the Internet, only to find that even the gently used ones sold in excess of three bills. She'd correctly assumed he'd never heard of Longchamp handbags, but had erred in thinking he would neither notice nor be able to research the value. Somewhere money was flooding in and he didn't know from where. He prayed that it was her father, but the manifestation of gift-like booty begged images of a doting paramour of the trust fund variety.

The mood was ripe for infidelity, Daniel feared. Her monetary complaints had emasculated him to the point where he didn't venture an attempt at intercourse, and each morning he took note of the string of days in which she hadn't walked him to the door as she used to, counting two weeks of kiss-less exits and returns. Her amorous aggression in their dating period made him worry that the monster wasn't being fed, at least not by him.

Despite the winter of the bedroom, the Madison residence was far from cold as Sofia filled the home like the smell of baking cookies. Her tiny arms around his neck couldn't replace the absence of attention from the girl he'd married, but they warmed him with the sturdy chords of her affection. Each small achievement—a picture drawn, a letter sounded, an animal she could name—invoked a pride exclusive to fathers. At day's end he still raced home from work to find a beautiful girl waiting, this time in an OshKosh jumper.

Three years of sideways revenues at Daniel's firm had become intolerable to Sydney. She viewed the time since the baby was born as a probation Daniel had failed, his devotion not withstanding. But she wondered if his love for her was abating as it paled now to that which Sofia enjoyed. Sydney would stand in the darkened hallway and listen to him speak to the toddler at her bedside, promising to take her to Disneyland or to get up early so they could run with the pug before he left for work. When he'd leave for the office, the little girl would extol Daddy's happy face eggs or use a made-up word that he had given her like "sillyish."

Sofia sang his songs incessantly as she colored or put together blocks on the kitchen table, driving Sydney to the point of temporary madness. Each infuriatingly repetitive variation that Daniel would sing to the squealing girl she later begged her Mommy to repeat. "That's a daddy thing," Sydney would say dismissively as she cruised a fashion magazine as if it were a portal to a locale more luxurious or opulent.

Some days all they had in common was Sofia, and the only thing to breach the caustic void was a discussion of her health. At least they had that to break the thickening ice, Daniel appreciated, despite the fact that Sofia's allergic outbreaks more than worried them both. They joked through their concern that Sofia was already on the Atkins Diet as she refused to eat bread and other carbohydrate-laden food staples. "How many little girls turn down cake?" Daniel asked his mother at her birthday party when Sofia refused to eat the confection.

As Sofia encountered new things in the spectrum of a growing child's world, allergic reactions were becoming more than occasional. Sydney refused to take Sofia to the doctor despite the rashes and stomach maladies, telling Daniel that it was typical of a girl her age while privately querying her mother as to the cause. "She's just got a tender stomach," Sydney explained to Daniel dishonestly. "But she loves her vegetables, so she's getting what her body really needs. She'll grow out of this."

Daniel wasn't so sure, but the climate of the house told him to pick his battles wisely. And Sydney was right about Sofia eating healthy food and growing. Other than the allergic reactions, Sofia seemed to be a perfectly healthy three-year-old with a penchant for cartoons, a genuine disdain for naps, and the ability to recognize all twenty-six letters by sight.

This morning life at the Madison house was more pleasant than usual as Sydney assisted Daniel in corralling all the StopShot documents he possessed, preparing them to be shipped to the attorney in Atlanta. Daniel had finally let her in on the full scale of what the attorney promised, hoping to soothe her and perhaps keep the gift-bearing wolf from the door. As usual, Sydney had been recharged by monetary prospects. Her father called Daniel a loser the last time they'd taken Sofia to see her grandparents when Sydney hit him up for cash yet again. The utterance wasn't said with Daniel in the room, but it had been said in front of Sofia. Mrs. Banks quickly stifled her husband, fearing that if Daniel were to discover what had been said in the little girl's presence that the Banks' face time with their granddaughter might diminish. Daniel already avoided Mr. Banks when the Madisons visited, spending most of his time in Teena's huge bedroom where delayed adulthood came complete with the latest game system, a plasma screen, and the NFL game package.

Attorney Gillespie had called Daniel yesterday, frothing with optimism and espousing a fallen Scrabble board's worth of legal terms that indicated the pot o' cash once promised was drawing nigh. "We're talking big numbers now, Mr. Madison," he'd prognosticated over the phone as Daniel stared at the Lonchamp purse near the door as if it were another man's underpants. "I just need the originals here right away. Everything you've got. Staglione is eager to settle and keep this out of open court. With your paperwork and a deposition we've got him. You're going to be a wealthy man."

Daniel shared all this with Sydney, figuring that now he had nothing to lose. Earlier, he'd been afraid that a declaration of improved financial prospects might serve to prove his suspicion that she loved his W-2 more than his heart, but now certain of that reality pragmatism suggested he serve her what she desired. It wasn't the life he'd planned, but it was the life he had and in the end Sofia made everything bearable.

In Carson City, Meredith pondered her muddled future, mindful that Julian was chronically unfaithful after yet another disgruntled young girl called his cell phone late at night. She often wondered if he wanted her to know of his foibles outside their marriage as he seemed so disinterested in hiding them, leaving handwritten phone numbers in plain sight on the governor's tidy desk or constantly stepping out to take private calls past business hours. He'd nearly apologized once after a similar episode, expressing a look of sincere regret before stopping short when he thought she'd accepted his non-verbal apology as sufficient. It hadn't been accepted, not by a far cry, but with their little girl just a few months into walking, Meredith had chosen to superficially tolerate his indiscretions while she waited for the right time to exit. Her new friends in Carson City, with more legislative sessions under their couture belts and political husbands of similar ilk, had suggested as much. A political wife does not leave her husband until after his next election.

Between sexual rendezvous, Julian was running the gauntlet between Carson City and Las Vegas at least once a week, blending state duties with Hayes' political errands. Julian had avoided Frank's calls for almost a month after the Naked City episode, not sure what words would follow should Hayes signal his knowledge of Julian's solicitation of his murder. After the altercation with Antonio and Felix it seemed more than likely that Hayes would know of Julian's plan to have him killed. But Hayes had never mentioned the attempt, and it occurred to Julian that Calderon may have withheld the real purpose of the meeting from Hayes, knowing the knowledge gave him control over Julian as well. Calderon hadn't asked for anything, but he had made one casual phone call a few weeks after the melee, speaking to Julian in a fatherly and familiar tone, as if the night in Naked City had changed nothing between them.

He had mentioned everything of import in the seemingly relaxed phone call, vaguely interjecting Hayes' name and the requested murder, the police shooting of the Mexican dealer, and Antonio's Tocororo in sentences like a sous-chef making red sauce, adding each ingredient carefully so it could be ingested. Correa wasn't sure what to make of the call, surprised it had come at all. But there was a purpose behind everything Felix Calderon did, and Julian still placed him and Frank Hayes firmly in enemy camp, even while he served the latter's varied and dubious needs.

Calderon ended the call without purpose or malice revealed. Had there not been the night in Naked City, Julian would have classified the call as one between friends. But there was a purpose, Julian was sure, and it would take time to figure that out. Hopefully, Calderon was going to ask him for something that Julian could do to benefit his business. In that he could ascertain that Hayes might not yet know about his plan and that Felix didn't see the value yet in tattling to Hayes. Perhaps that explained Hayes's unchanged behavior.

There is a peace in knowing your enemy, Julian thought as the call with Felix concluded harmlessly. A dialogue, even one of uncertain intent, kept Calderon and, indirectly, Hayes, somewhere in his field of view. That seemed safer. But just as Julian couldn't ascertain Calderon's present motives, neither could he foresee the disaster heading his way. Hayes and Calderon were potent issues for certain and he'd be wise to monitor their temperaments. But this new trouble would be different—life changing, devastating, irreversible.

Soon enough Julian would have a new enemy, one he'd never expected or considered to be a threat. This new battle would rage differently from those with the willing gladiators he was accustomed to dealing with like Felix and Frank, men who chose a life of combat. This time his enemy would be the one person left he still admired and the only man he considered to be his friend.

CHAPTER 39

August 2004

Daniel had just dozed off in front of a pitcher's duel of a baseball game when Sofia interrupted his slumber with a double-knee dive off the back of the couch and directly into his rib cage. Her brown eyes boiled with mischief as she awaited his reaction. That would take a moment longer as Daniel waited for air to return to his lungs.

"Sofia!" Daniel scolded with the first batch of carbon dioxide. "Baby girl, you can't jump on Daddy like that. I was sleeping."

"You said we're gonna go get a hangaber at Burger King!" she declared with toddler ferocity. "I'm hungry, Daddy."

"Okay, okay, you little criminal," Daniel acquiesced, always amused by Sofia's brashness despite his repeated victimization. Just last week she had poured a glass of ice water on her father, telling him later that she was watering him the way he did the Boston fern by the window. Daniel hadn't been sure if she was conjuring the excuse post facto or not. He grabbed a pair of Nike running shoes under the coffee table and slipped them on without tying the laces. Meanwhile, Sofia collected her backpack, a Barbie in a state of undress, and a soup ladle.

"What's all that for?" Daniel asked as he gathered his brown leather wallet and car keys.

"I need 'em," she said assertively, a pink bow Daniel's mother had made on each side of her head.

"You need a Barbie and a soup ladle for Burger King?"

"Yes ... yes, I do," she responded as if that solved the matter, putting the doll and ladle in her backpack.

"Okay, kid," Daniel said, wondering what else might be in the backpack. "Let's get going."

Sydney's monthly spa day left Daniel with Sofia for the remainder of the afternoon, time he valued immensely both for the duration to be spent with the little girl and for the avoidance of tension that had returned to the household. The attorney had all Daniel's StopShot and V.S.E. paperwork now, every last sheet and disk, but was still ambiguous as to the delivery date of his big check. And Sydney wanted a firm date of delivery.

He couldn't get mad at Gillespie, not even with Sydney breathing down his neck about her needs. The attorney always took his call on his cell phone and seemed genuinely pleased to deliver promising news. Daniel humbly confided to the lawyer his pressing need for settlement, letting his guard down a little and explaining Sydney as best he could. Gillespie proposed that Daniel divorce Sydney now, leaving the StopShot cash out of any divorce proceeding. Daniel declined, telling the attorney that any money he gained from the lawsuit primarily would be spent on Sofia and her future whether he was with Sydney or not. And he hadn't seriously considered leaving Sydney, not yet.

Looking across the table at the three-year-old it was hard to picture her in the context of the future. Daniel always found it odd how he could never really remember exactly what the baby girl looked like at six months, a year, or two years, each image replaced by her present appearance. Going forward seemed just as difficult, and at best he grafted her face onto iconic scenes from movies where blushing brides danced with crying fathers at their weddings.

Sofia had dismantled her hamburger as she always did, discarding the sesame buns and folding the meat over like a taco. Her hands were covered with ketchup, cheese, and a solution of fluids likely to be banned for human consumption. Between burger bites, the little girl tossed in fries like a farmer with a wood chipper, her tan legs swinging gleefully under the table.

"You're doing pretty good there, Sofe," Daniel said. "Maybe Daddy will get you a dessert."

"I want that! The ice cream," Sofia declared as she looked at a tabletop ad for cheesecake covered in strawberry sauce. "Can I have that, Daaaadddy?"

"If you finish all your hamburger you can," Daniel agreed. "I'll get you some of that. It's called cheesecake, not ice cream."

"I don't like cake," Sofia reminded him.

"It's not really cake. They just call it that. It's more like ice cream."

"Then why don't they call it ice cream?" she asked through a mouthful of fast food. Daniel hadn't really studied the nomenclature of cheesecake well enough to aptly respond to a three-year-old's inquiry. Instead, he simply responded, "It's marketing," and headed to the counter to purchase a cheesecake slice for Sofia. She seemed satisfied with that answer.

In between repetitions on the indoor playground Sofia downed the cheesecake, using her fingers to dab at the sweet graham cracker bottom. It pleased Daniel to please her and he noted that today she hadn't asked for his help in climbing up the stairs to the first boldly colored slide-tube. After a half hour of "We're going to leave in five minutes" warnings, they finally did so under Sofia's pursed-lip protest. Daniel realized as he strapped her in the car seat that she probably had no idea what five minutes meant, leaving her confused as to whether her playground time had been shorted. She was never happy to leave a play area, or to go to bed, or even to be denied a piece of candy. *Such is the way of the three-year-old*, Daniel thought, while noting the genetic similarities to her mother. If he ever hoped to keep her from becoming as entitled as Sydney, he'd best find a way to tell her no occasionally.

I'll start that plan tomorrow, Daniel procrastinated internally. He had just slipped his seat belt over his shoulder when Sofia announced that her tummy hurt. He checked her in the rearview mirror and noticed that her cheeks were still red from the exercise in the play area. "We'll be home in a minute, Sofie-girl. We can lie down until you feel better."

"I don't wanna take a nap," Sofia responded reactively.

"No nap, baby, just a little rest," Daniel explained as he drove home.

"We'll put on a cartoon." Daniel guided Sofia into the living room, minus the mischief and playfulness that had been a part of their previous exit. Sofia seemed tired and sluggish and didn't fight Daniel as he laid her on the couch.

"My tummy hurts bad, Daddy," Sofia said weakly as she lay on her back. Her eyes seemed ready for tears, but unable to finish their manufacture.

"I know, baby girl," Daniel acknowledged as he considered what next to do. He began to raise her shirt upward so he could caress her tummy with his fingertips the way she liked, only to find her stomach horribly bloated, like the starving children in the famine relief commercials.

This is bad. Don't panic in front of her, Daniel thought. *Gotta get a hold of Sydney.*

He wondered if this had happened before and been kept from him. If so, Sydney might know some home remedy like a glass of milk or an Alka-Seltzer. But Sydney left her cell phone on the kitchen counter, warning Daniel not to bother her during her "me time" today. Sofia's breathing seemed to be labored now and Daniel's concern intensified. Her stomach was as taut as a basketball and, most disconcerting, she had begun to drift into a hazy state of consciousness, no longer complaining or immediately responding.

Daniel cradled Sofia in his arms and rushed her to the car. Ten minutes later he carried her into the emergency room. A nurse instantly took the little girl into a back room and a flurry of medical personnel hooked her up to every hose, oxygen mask, and monitor available. Sofia's brown eyes peered weakly at Daniel as the NASCAR pit stop activity ensued, never leaving his gaze as he clutched her icy fingers.

Daniel's father arrived and was again fighting nurses to enter a hospital room where Sofia lay. Daniel had called him en route, needing someone to tell him his girl would be all right. "Let him in!" Daniel yelled in a voice that came from the panic inside him. A moment later his father held his warm hand as he held Sofia's. Through the foggy breathing mask she mouthed "Papa" and smiled the faintest smile at the man who fed her candy when no one was looking.

"She's going to be fine, son," Mr. Madison offered, the lack of any rationale rendering the remark comfortless. "Sofia's a strong, strong girl."

Sofia did seem to be gaining a more normal color as the nurses surrounded her like elves, prodding, adjusting, and telling their patient how big a girl she was. Sofia seemed to like that and was abiding their pokes and prods much better than Daniel would have expected. Or maybe she was just that weak, he considered.

When Dr. Springfield entered the room, Daniel felt both worry and relief. She put her hand on Sofia's forehead, simultaneously checking her temperature and affectionately greeting her little patient. The doctor's strawberry-blond hair looked soft and maternal, and a brief smile directed at the Madison men said, *I understand and I'll take care of her.*

"What's wrong with her, Doc?" Mr. Madison could no longer resist asking.

"I'm not sure yet, sir," she replied politely as she continued her examination. "But Sofia's not in immediate danger. Her vitals are fine now. Everything is under control." The simple words resonated through Daniel's being, washing away tension and replacing mortal fear with concern of a lower caliber. His father squeezed his shoulder as he had since Daniel was Sofia's size, an affection never outgrown or unwelcome.

"I'm suspicious of an allergic reaction given her symptoms, maybe even food poisoning," the doctor said as she surveyed Sofia's protruding abdomen. "What has she had in the last hour?"

Daniel felt a swell of guilt as he described the fast-food consumption he'd given his daughter. "But we give her a ton of veggies all the time. She's got a real healthy diet."

"Don't worry about it, Mr. Madison," she said sweetly. "I take my little boy to the fast-food places once in a while too. An empty-calorie meal's not so bad every now and then as part of a broader, more nutritional diet." Dr. Springfield appeared to be massaging Sofia's thin legs as her fingers gripped and re-gripped the girl's tan skin. "Have you ever noticed her muscle tone's a little soft?" she asked Daniel.

"Not really, Doc," Daniel said honestly, having nothing to compare Sofia's body to but other adults.

"Ellen, have the lab run these tests on her blood too. Tell them I need the results stat," Dr. Springfield told the nurse, scribbling additional instructions on a clipboard. "Fellas, just pull up a chair and relax," she said warmly. "She's out of harm's way and we're going to find out what little bug's inside her."

"Thank you, Doctor," Daniel said shaking her hand, appreciative that she had brought the risk down to something bearable. The burning in his own stomach abated once she'd done so.

"I've got a few stitches to sew up on a repeat offender down the hall," she explained as she looked down at Sofia. "Gotta wear those helmets when you get bigger, okay?"

"O-kay," Sofia said audibly, the breathing mask retired for the moment.

"I'll be back just as soon as the lab gets those results to me," Dr. Springfield said.

Daniel's cell phone rang just as the doctor left the room. He reached quickly to extinguish the loud ringer when he noticed his home phone number on the caller ID.

"Syd, honey ... Sofia and I are at the hospital. She got sick. Real sick," Daniel explained. Mr. Madison could only hear Sydney's garbled voice growing louder and Daniel's expression became more angered than consolatory. "Are you even going to ask if she's all right before you start bitching at me? I had to bring her to the hospital, Syd. Her breathing was slowing down and you were out getting a massage."

Mr. Madison pressed his palms downward as he encouraged Daniel to take it easy. "Look, I'm sorry," Daniel offered, wanting to avoid exacerbating the difficult circumstances. "Can you please just get down here? Sofia can use her mommy right now. We're in the emergency room at Mountain View Hospital. We're just waiting on the blood work."

The strained voice echoed loudly from the phone again and Daniel thought seriously about hanging up, thinking that Sofia didn't need this now either.

"How else are they going to find out what's wrong with her unless they do blood work, Syd?" Daniel asked incredulously. "Look, I gotta go. Just get down here with your daughter."

Daniel turned off the phone and looked at his father. "She never even asked what was wrong, if it was all right now, nothing. She's just pissed that I brought her to the hospital. I guess she figures we can't afford this either."

"Another time," Mr. Madison said wisely. "Put out the hottest fire first. Let's find out what's ailing my granddaughter now. You can deal with Sydney when you're more calm."

"You're right, Dad, you're right," Daniel agreed as he picked up a *People* magazine to read to Sofia. "Let's see what Brad Pitt is doing this week, shall we?"

"O-kay," Sofia agreed, riveted as usual on a doting Daniel.

By the time Daniel and Sofia had rendered an opinion on red carpet gowns in their third issue of *People*, Dr. Springfield had returned. Sydney walked in simultaneously, carrying a bag of Taco Bell in with her.

"You stopped to get something to eat, Sydney?" Daniel asked.

"Mrs. Madison? I'm Dr. Springfield," the doctor interjected shrewdly before Sydney could reply. "Let me tell you what we've found out about this little princess."

"So, I think that she's going to be just fine … over time," the doctor began, the mixed bag flushing Daniel's stomach with acidic tension once more. "And I do think the lunch you got her at Burger King had a big part in her reaction," she continued as Sydney shot Daniel an incriminating look. "I think your Sofia is a celiac," Dr. Springfield announced.

"Oh my God. Oh my God," Mr. Madison began chanting.

"It's serious, but very manageable," she said, defusing the elder

Madison. "It's not 'Oh my God,' stuff, but we have to get it under control right away. Your daughter is extremely malnourished."

"I don't know where you went to school, Ms. Springfield, but I feed my little girl a very well-balanced diet," Sydney roared. "She just doesn't like bread."

"You misunderstand, ma'am," the doctor explained. "And perhaps I could've said that better. She's not getting the full benefit of the food you are giving her. She's a celiac, she can't consume gluten. And I graduated from Johns Hopkins."

"What's gluten?" Mr. Madison asked quickly, his emotions on a roller coaster.

"It's basically wheat," Dr. Springfield said. "But it's not an allergy. It's an auto-immune disease that makes it very difficult for her to effectively digest other nutrients. That explains her poor muscle tone. That cheesecake you gave her today had a graham-cracker crust made from wheat. That's probably what set all this off."

"We're suing Burger King," Sydney advanced.

"Well, they really didn't do anything wrong, Mrs. Madison," the doctor responded. "It's a genetic trait and it can pop up any time. We still don't know all we need to about the condition, but it's very easy to control. And we're finding that a very large portion of the population are celiacs. There's a lot of gluten-free alternatives for her diet moving forward."

Daniel's mind was spinning like a roulette wheel, trying to process where he'd been confronted with the symptoms of wheat intolerance before. "Dad, you ever had trouble with wheat?" Daniel asked his father.

"You ever had a meal in my house without bread or pasta, Danny?" he answered.

"I think my mom's uncle had something like this," Sydney offered in a tone far more affable than exhibited previously.

As Sydney filibustered the possibility of a celiac uncle, Daniel's body turned rigid. He stared at Sofia, her color improved but the fatigue of the episode inhibiting her expression and movement. The genetic condition remark had registered somewhere inside him and struggled to breach the surface like a newborn whale. He did know someone who couldn't consume wheat, who wouldn't eat a breadstick or a cracker or have a beer. And as he looked down at the baby girl he called his own, he could see that person's eyes.

CHAPTER 40

Daniel drove toward the Madison home with Sofia nestled under a blanket in her car seat and his mind racing. A cruel nexus had arrived as he stared into Sofia's eyes and noted their similarity to Julian's just as his mind delivered the memory of Correa's past refusal to consume gluten in beer and bread. He explored the past for opportunities in which Julian and Sydney could have been intimate four years ago.

It must have been God interceding, Daniel thought, that Sydney and he drove home separately. Sofia was still very weak and the doctor said she would likely be so for several days until the villi in her small intestine recovered from the gluten. After all she'd been through, she needn't see Mommy and Daddy have an epic argument during the car ride home.

It was unbearable to think she wasn't his child. He'd held her from that first moment as his own and pledged to be her protector and father. Throughout her three years Sofia had become a reason for his existence, a panacea for all things adverse, and the ready bandage for his and Sydney's frequent troubles. Faced with the prospect that she might not be his blood, he couldn't begin to contemplate the ramifications. It was as if four individual pieces of music were playing at the same time, each a woeful dirge.

Sydney knew something had broken inside Daniel as he gathered Sofia and headed to the car silently, leaving her and Mr. Madison behind like gas station attendants met on a road trip. She was sure the genetics discussion had been the cause, and she had a private car ride home to plan her course of action. She'd dreaded this day, hoping to avoid it, and searched her mind for a way to reconcile the revelation of another's fatherhood. Nothing was certain yet, Sydney considered, and she had Daniel's deep love for Sofia on her side. Every day that had gone by was to her advantage, tethering him to the little girl just as she had planned.

Sydney entered the residence treading lightly and expecting to be assailed at the threshold. Instead, she saw Daniel seated by the window in a darkened living room, the sunlight filtering through the wooden blinds making Daniel's face look like a horizontal bar code. He didn't acknowledge her at first, looking out toward the street at nothing in particular. It was the kind of feeling for which words had not been made, Daniel pondered, thinking that a singular dimension of description was wholly insufficient.

Sydney moved cautiously throughout the home, tiptoeing toward Sofia's room where the girl lay sleeping, spent yet peaceful, and mercifully unaware of what the man she called Daddy was confronting. Sydney set her purse down next to the couch and moved closer to Daniel, careful not to get too close. "I know we need to talk, Danny," she said meekly.

"'Bout what, Syd?" Daniel said without looking her way. "The doctor said Sofia's going to be fine now. It's good to know my little girl's going to be okay."

"Daniel, you're jumping to conclusions," Sydney suggested in a passive voice that he hadn't heard since their first year together.

"Sydney, I'm as close as I've ever been to completely losing my mind right now," Daniel warned. "If you try to bullshit me or lie, I'm going to blow my—" He paused, ending the forthcoming threat halfway, holding something back.

"I won't lie. I won't," Sydney pledged, her face confirming most of Daniel's suspicions.

"Am I her biological father, Sydney?" Daniel asked.

"I don't know," Sydney replied feebly, the acknowledgment entering him like a scalpel without anesthesia. All Daniel could do was close his eyes and shake his head like Officer Sheppard had at sentencing. It was as if a boulder had fallen from a rocky ledge, landing on him in soft sand, the weight enough to hold him in place but insufficient to kill him instantly.

"I'm not sure, Danny," she offered somberly, tears spilling from her light green eyes. "It was only one time—just that once."

"It was Julian, right?" Daniel asked inevitably.

"Yes," Sydney affirmed with a solemn nod, upholding her honesty pledge for the moment despite the dangerous set of events the admission might foster. "It was election night and we just sat there by ourselves drinking and then we drove home in a limo and then he—"

"Stop!" Daniel ordered emphatically, incapable of suffering the lurid details. He pictured as much as his mind would allow, Sydney's powder-blue dress sliding off her slender body and Julian with his tie loosened and his muscular arms around her frame like Fabio on the cover of a romance novel.

Then he remembered where he was when it had transpired, sitting in a hospital as his friend and mentor had the white sheet pulled over her head. "You did this to us on the night that Annie died, Sydney?"

"I never planned it, Daniel," Sydney said, offering her best excuse.

"You think that makes this any better?" Daniel said, turning to look at her for the first time. "Who's going to tell that sweet little girl that I'm not her daddy?"

"Danny, slow down … why do we have to tell her anything at all? Nothing's for certain," Sydney pleaded in utter humility. "There's every chance you're her daddy … you and I had sex the night before I was with Julian."

"Stop it, Syd," Daniel insisted. "Julian has the same fucking wheat allergy Sofia has. The one the doctor says is genetic. I'll get a blood test, but Sofia's eyes tell me it's a foregone conclusion that she's Julian's. She's got Julian's eyes."

Sydney said nothing.

"I guess that's better than her being Clint Zigler's," Daniel noted. "So now I know what he's been babbling about all this time."

Sydney's face paled and her expression solidified in a ceramic, hardened pose, the new evidence of the genetic trait destroying the gray area on which she'd counted. "I never told Clint anything about this. He probably had me followed. He does that. And I didn't know that Julian had that wheat allergy thing. I wasn't sure if Sofia was his, Danny. I wasn't."

"But you knew that there was a strong likelihood she wasn't mine," Daniel sniped back as his temper rose again. "So, you just dupe me into being the fool. William Banks can't have his little whore knocked up with no one to claim her, right?"

"I'm not a whore, Daniel," Sydney responded feebly, mindful that she was due some rancor of this ilk. "I didn't know whose she was for sure and I didn't plan any of this. I would never do this to you on purpose. You have to believe me."

"No, I don't," Daniel said. "What I have to do is figure out what to do about Sofia … how I fit in now. Maybe I can be the fun uncle who comes over once in a while."

"Daniel, you are her father," Sydney insisted through silver tears. "She lives for you. I don't even compare to you in her eyes and I'm her mother. I need you now, and Sofia needs you." Her hands were clasped tightly atop her blue jeans. "We need you."

"Nah … I don't think so," Daniel said, dismissing her attempt to entangle Sofia with herself. "You don't need me. That's been made very clear."

Sydney looked puzzled by Daniel's rebuke, never having endured its display previously. Her eyes stayed fixed with his, as if she could wear his defenses down with the intoxicant of a stare. She wanted to walk over, to turn his shoulder outward and rest within his arms. Nothing about Daniel right now suggested that might be well received.

Daniel started to rise, placing his arms on the seat and pressing downward. Stopping half-way, he settled again and looked at Sydney once more. "You know, when I was just a kid full of acne and insecurity and a desperate desire to be somebody's someone, watching guys like Julian use and discard the girls I'd dreamed of, girls who came to me as their friend after they'd been hurt, I prayed that someday I might have someone like you for just a moment," Daniel explained in a voice a decibel above a whisper. "Just to know what it was like to feel your beauty, to feel so good about myself that I could be with someone like you. I prayed to have that moment. I really did.

"And I met you and it was like you washed any self-doubt I'd ever had away. I wanted to walk into rooms and have people see me with you. I wanted to call you my girlfriend in front of my friends and to hear your first name with my last name. Everything about you made me feel good about myself. Now, most days you make me feel like I'm a servant about to be fired, as if I'll never be good enough to make you happy … and I know I never will," Daniel acknowledged for the first time, accepting what he had long known to be true.

Sydney knew it was true as well, but the very fact that Daniel seemed to be pulling away made him more desirable than he had been in ages. She often thought of leaving Daniel, of finding someone who could treat her as she was accustomed, but she had never considered that he might leave.

"I'm gonna go, Sydney," Daniel said calmly, his energy for anything more momentarily arrested.

"When are you coming home, Danny?" Sydney queried through a stream of soft sobs.

"When? The better question is *am* I coming home. And I don't think I am."

Daniel went into their bedroom and threw tomorrow's clothes into a bag. His wallet lay next to their wedding picture on the dresser, and a flash of that day seared his memory. He remembered how elated he'd been to marry Sydney and to watch his father dismiss Zigler in splendid fashion. He recalled what it felt like to stand next to her that day, to enter into the promise of marriage with a woman he couldn't stop thinking about. As the chapel's pastor recited the rote ceremony for the seventeenth time that shift, Daniel had prayed silently, holding Sydney's hand in his and making a promise that he would never pray for anything like her again. As he turned to leave the bedroom, Sydney stood in the doorway holding Sofia. The narrow openings between the baby girl's eyelids told Daniel that Sydney had awakened her, presumably to weigh on his decision to leave.

"You woke her up?" Daniel accused, angry that she'd roused the girl so shortly after the stress of the hospital visit.

"She wanted you," Sydney said, breaking the vow not to lie.

"Good morning, Daddy," Sofia said, confusing her awakening from a nap with a new day.

"Good morning, angel-baby," Daniel said sweetly as Sydney shrewdly executed her plan to keep him home. If she could make it to nightfall using Sofia to keep him home, she could come to him in the bedroom, offering herself in a way he had never denied. She'd fall asleep against his bare chest afterward and lay her leg across his body, the intertwining inescapable and redeeming. If she could just weather the first difficult hours as the revelation pierced most acutely, perhaps she could hold onto her husband.

Sofia rubbed her eyes and Sydney lowered her to the floor, hoping she'd go to her daddy. She did so and Daniel bent on one knee to receive her. "I don't like Burger King," Sofia decried, connecting the hospital and her lunch together.

"Well, we'll never go there again, will we?" Daniel said as the never in his reply bristled Sydney.

"You wanna take Brandy for a walk?" Sofia asked, still thinking it was morning instead of sundown.

"No, Sofie, Daddy's gotta go away for a while," he said, the last few consonants almost inaudible.

"Why?" Sofia asked simply.

"I just have to go do some things," he said, each word an excruciating ember of guilt. Damn Sydney for putting them through this, he thought.

"O-kay," she allowed sweetly. "I'm gonna watch a cartoon until you come back."

"All right, baby," Daniel said as he brushed her face before turning to send daggers toward Sydney.

"Daniel, please … please don't go," Sydney pleaded. "Stay through the night, see how you feel in the morning about everything."

"No, Syd," Daniel countered with resolve. "I'm leaving."

"Tell your father goodbye, Sofia," Sydney ordered, sending a pawn to the middle of the chessboard.

"Bye, Daddy!" Sofia said, her voice weakened but as yet unencumbered by the truth of the day or the poignancy of the moment. Daniel had started toward the door, passing Sydney as if she were a fence post. As Sofia's goodbye resonated, he turned and walked toward the couch where she now rested.

He leaned over the back of the sofa and draped his arms across her chest, her light brown locks next to his blond hair. "I will always be your daddy," he whispered, so softly that Sydney could not hear the words and be comforted at all by them.

"O-kay," Sofia agreed, oblivious to the significance of the affirmation.

He closed the front door of the house and fell into his car. Rage and despair battled for possession as Daniel guided the vehicle out of the quiet peace of the neighborhood where he believed he had started a family. It would be the last peace he would know for quite some time.

CHAPTER 41

The car radio was already tuned to a talk station as Daniel sped away, and a conservative commentator was rattling on about a liberal politician's hatred for the military. Three red lights later, the local news reader had begun a daily recap at the top of the hour.

"State officials toured a Las Vegas charter school today, and Governor Correa took time during his visit to Southern Nevada to read to a group of young honor students," the voice declared to Daniel's chagrin. *"The governor again implored the Legislature to pass a measure reducing class sizes and increasing college preparatory courses available to minority students."*

"We've got to make sure that there's a level playing field for all our kids ... whether they're new Mexican-Americans or fifth-generation Americans," Julian's voice boomed in sound bite-ready excellence. *"If this city and this state are to continue on their path toward becoming one of the great locations in the world, a reinvestment in our youth isn't just a social responsibility, it's an economic necessity."*

Daniel's fingers grasped and re-grasped the steering wheel like a medieval butcher ringing a goose's neck. Throughout the disaster of the day, Sydney's close proximity had made her the face of his anger, delaying the contempt brewing for the man who had bedded his girl and likely fathered his child. Sydney's hands were indelibly soiled by her role, but Julian's were too. Now hearing Julian utter his cliché-laden refrain, innocuously dropping words that signaled other events for Daniel like agita flash cards, his emotions were assembling in a crescendo of fury. He couldn't strike Sydney, not and remain his father's son, but thoughts of vengeance swelled within him.

As he pulled in front of his parents' home, Julian's assorted offenses were aggregating like tributaries to a raging river. There was Julian's betrayal of Mike Martin, his withdrawal of the job offer, and his role in letting Officer Sheppard go to prison for a crime he didn't commit. Every time he saw Jay's elderly father on television, inarticulately pleading his son's case to anyone who'd listen, it fostered a guilt he couldn't deny. Julian might be the one who witnessed the murder, who could tell the real story that would put the right man behind bars and the right man beyond them, but Daniel knew the truth as well. He too was holding a man's life in his hands, incarcerating him via a pact with a man who had fathered an irreconcilable discontent in his own life.

From the street he could see his mother cooking in the kitchen, unaware that her youngest granddaughter was not a blood relation. Today's news would hit his mother and father like Earth-bound meteors, potentially wrecking a devotion to a child they thought looked like this aunt or that cousin from back East. Since Sofia's birth Mr. Madison hadn't started his calls to his son as he had before, beginning each communication now with "How's my girl?" and subsequently nourished by each small detail. Mrs. Madison carried a small baggy with little mints or raisins, regularly greeting Sofia with something from her kitchen. Sofia would sit on her broad lap, snacking and playing with the costume jewelry Daniel's mother favored.

Damn her, he thought again, lamenting that Sydney's actions would resonate further yet, crushing two loving grandparents who had bought the lie in full. Again his thoughts returned to Julian, a target he could hit in ways he couldn't with Sydney. Daniel knew Julian had to be confronted for what he'd done, and his mind was losing its ability to make clear-headed choices, each visiting option clouded by his present torment. Daniel teemed with a need for vengeance, engulfed by the sheer torture of all that had occurred. As he walked into his parents' home, his boyhood home, he did so fractured in ways he had no chance of explaining.

"Hi, honey." Daniel's mother greeted him warmly as she stirred the contents of a sauce pan. "Can I fix you a plate?"

"No, thanks," Daniel replied, thinking he might never eat again, his churning stomach acids better suited for metallurgy. "Where's Dad?"

"I'm sure he's in his chair watching a ballgame," she answered with the suggestive derisiveness forty years of marriage to one person breeds. "How's your baby girl?"

"She's fine now, Mom," Daniel answered, seething, bleeding, burning at the question. His mother didn't know anything about Julian and Sydney yet, and today wasn't the day to tell her. He passed through the narrow kitchen and rounded into the den where Mr. Madison sat comfortably in his boxers watching a fight on a cable channel. The big man more than filled a reclining chair and curled up like a hound dog in the wide seat.

"Hey, son," Mr. Madison said as Daniel came into view. "Have a seat. This kid's a great middleweight. He'll have the title soon."

"Can't do it, Dad," Daniel answered, declining a normally accepted invitation to watch a fight with the old man. "I've gotta use the bathroom."

"You might want to wait a few minutes," Mr. Madison warned in jest. "I was just in there."

Daniel couldn't begin to appreciate the humor and yield the usual laugh. Instead he entered the bright blue bathroom and passed immediately through to his parents' connecting master bedroom, closing the door from the den behind him. He looked around the room for the wooden box he sought, denying the gaze of his grandparents peering down from pewter frames on the bedroom walls like angels of intervention. The box had been moved from its usual place and he needed to find it, to take the contents with him to his next destination.

He knelt at the foot of their bed like a child preparing to offer a nightly prayer, pulling the edge of the quilted comforter upward to reveal the cherrywood box. He rested it on the end of the bed and opened it, staring at the old Smith & Wesson and a handful of bullets. The anger boiling within him allowed a moment of peace to venture to the surface, issuing Daniel a sample of a better day and time when he and his father had gone out into the desert and shot beer bottles like gangsters battling over a moonshine route.

He remembered feeling like a man that day, tiny moustache hairs only arriving a few months before. They'd finished the afternoon with a giant hamburger at Wendell Street Pub, debating the merits of quarterbacks and kids in the neighborhood. His father always used amiable windows of opportunity to offer guidance and advice, leveraging the mood of fonder moments to foster a receptiveness to advice for which teenage boys aren't often known.

Daniel loaded bullet after bullet into the empty gun, assigning a violation or betrayal authored by Julian Correa for each round. His hands shook and sweated, exuding panic and a lust for revenge that governed his thoughts and actions. As he rose from his knees he turned to see his father standing in the doorway of the bedroom and bath, watching his son load a firearm unused for at least a decade.

"What are you doin', son?" Mr. Madison asked, reasonably troubled. He stood there bare-chested, comfortable in his own home yet unsettled by the scene before him.

"Don't ask, Dad," Daniel said, unable to look at his father. "There's something I've got to do."

"Son, there's nothing you've got to do that that thing is going to help you with," Mr. Madison replied. "Just put it back."

"I can't do that, Dad," Daniel said, refusing a directive from his father for only the second or third time in his life. Daniel rose to his feet and tucked the handgun in the back of his pants like he'd seen guys do on television. He walked toward Mr. Madison, standing at the only exit, and tried to put his head down in a way that would prevent him from seeing his father's expression.

"Put it down, Daniel," Mr. Madison commanded. "And tell me what the hell is going on."

"Sofia's not mine, Dad," Daniel said, his voice trembling. "She's Julian's."

"No ..." Mr. Madison answered in shock, his mouth falling open momentarily.

"He's not getting away with it, Dad," Daniel tried to explain. "He gets away with everything, but not this time."

"Son, no ... you put that gun right there on the bed," Mr. Madison implored. "We'll find a better way to handle this."

"No, Dad," Daniel defied. "I'm leaving. That son of a bitch is in town and I know where he's staying."

"There's no gain in it, Daniel," his father instructed, compassionate and firm. "Give me the gun." Daniel didn't, instead pressing forward as he attempted to pass his father. As he did, his father reached and gripped his arm around the bicep.

"Let me go!" Daniel shouted in exasperation, jerking his arm from his father's grip, the recoil sending his father tumbling to the bathroom floor. Daniel could only look down at his father, seated awkwardly on the cold linoleum, an expression of despair a banner across his rugged face.

"Dad ..." Daniel began, awash in guilt among the red-hot rods from his other emotions. "I'm so sorry."

Mr. Madison didn't respond right away, dealing with a complexity of his own turbulent feelings. He couldn't help but consider Daniel's previous admission that he'd come ever so close to killing himself back in college. And now he had a gun and an enormous motive.

The old man sat speechless, the news and exchange with Daniel too much to manage effectively. Daniel reached to give him his hand, to help return him to his feet. Mr. Madison just shook his head and held his arms across his bare legs, pausing in introspection before he spoke to his son. "I've always tried to save the best part for the end," Mr. Madison began. "I've always worked all day so that I could spend the evenings having a good meal with your mother or doing something with my family. That's the reason I worked as hard as I always have, Daniel.

"And I worked my whole life to make sure that your mother and I were comfortable, that we had a little money set aside so we could stay in this house as long as we're able and that we had a little extra if you ever needed it. But one day you wake up and realize you don't really matter, that you're just an old man whose legs don't work like they used to. You just have to accept that it's somebody else's turn to run the show, to do all the things you used to try to do. So, you take a look around and understand that your time has passed, that you didn't really save the best part for the end."

"Dad, it's not like that," Daniel said, looking down at a man he looked up to. But Daniel lacked the momentary strength to properly assuage his father, to set him upright and tell him what he meant to him, what he had always meant to him. Right now his focus was on making someone pay for the way he was feeling, to redeem his losses in vengeance. He needed to grab Julian and pound his face until he bled, to bludgeon him for everything and now for his father too, because he was sitting on a floor considering his existence in ways he never should. Daniel left without saying another word to his father and mother, returning to his car with the gun and his vengeful intentions. His mother had gone to his father as he left silently, leaving the saucepan on simmer and checking her husband for bruises.

Julian's Las Vegas home was a small, well-appointed cottage on the eighteenth green of a developer's perfect golf course. He'd received the luxury home for the price of a regular off-the-course three-bedroom, a kickback from a developer for blessings he'd engineered when on the county commission. Big windows offered emerald fairway views and suffered errant golf ball breakage from time to time, leaving Julian's alarm company to nearly ignore alerts sent from the home. Daniel assumed Julian would grant him entry when the guard called from the gate. With the secret of the Naked City shooter still under wraps, Daniel figured Julian still held him in good stead.

He didn't know what he was going to do once he got to Julian other than it had to make him feel better, at any price, and that Julian would finally know that Daniel hated him. No guile, charm, or insincere promises would steer Daniel from his intent to harm him. No confession or melodramatic appeal could thwart him.

Daniel wondered if Sydney had called Julian to tell him that the truth was out, that Daniel knew of the tryst and had left her. But that would require a selflessness that Sydney lacked, her disregard now putting Julian in harm's way as it had Daniel. He wasn't sure if Julian had any idea Sofia was his daughter.

The guard made a brief call to the Correa residence and welcomed Daniel into the gated community. "Governor Correa arrived a few minutes ago," he reported. "I let him know you're on your way, Mr. Madison."

"Thank you," Daniel said as he fidgeted in his mind for words to use with Julian. "I'll just be a little while."

Daniel parked on the tree-lined street and aimed for the front door. As he turned past an ivy-covered pillar Julian stood waiting in a blue dress shirt and khaki pants with his sleeves rolled up, his standard pro-letariat costume for union events. The fifty-dollar Cuban cigar betrayed the act as he walked toward Daniel.

"Danny-boy! To what do I owe the honor of your presence?" Julian asked, sincerely pleased to see his onetime friend and confidant. Daniel manufactured a warm smile as Julian reached out to grasp his hand. The first punch knocked the cigar from his mouth and sent Julian staggering.

"What the fuck, Daniel?" Julian erupted, his face smarting from the direct hit. His surprise delayed his response and Daniel lunged forward, tackling Julian onto a cast-iron patio table and hitting him again, just below the eye.

"What are you doing?" Julian screamed, completely unprepared for the assault. Julian tried to hold Daniel's wrists, attempting to contain his smaller foe. But Daniel was striking Julian with the vigor of a father who had lost a child, a husband who had forfeited his wife, and a man who had knocked his own father to the ground. It more than made up the size difference for the moment.

Julian covered his face, hoping to prevent another head shot until he could eject Daniel from on top. Daniel wanted to knock his teeth down his gubernatorial throat, to leave him bleeding on his porch. The gun rested awkwardly against the small of his back, the tight brown belt holding his jeans and the firearm tightly. Julian was reaching upward awkwardly, clawing at Daniel's face. As a finger entered Daniel's eye socket the smaller man turned rightward and the table gave way, throwing them both.

The fall felt oddly slow to both of them, as if they were falling through water. But when they landed, their bodies had rotated and Julian was on top, his size difference governing the fracas much differently than a moment before. Daniel knew he couldn't move a man of Julian's size from the bottom and took solace in the fact that Julian's face looked much like he'd hoped it would, bleeding from the nose and below those familiar dark brown eyes. It would be his turn to take the blows now, but none would compare to those suffered throughout the day. Those had little chance of healing.

"What THE FUCK is wrong with you?" Julian bellowed as he held Daniel's hands to the concrete.

"You fucked her," Daniel said in a voice calmly inconsistent with his present position.

"Who did I fuck?" Julian asked, causing Daniel to smirk at the significance of the sincerity of that remark. Correa had done this so often that Sydney didn't register immediately.

"You fucked Sydney, you piece of shit," Daniel explained crudely, wanting to get to the gun digging into his back.

"She told you that?" Julian asked, remarkably civil despite the condition of his face.

"And my little girl is your little girl," Daniel said in mock sarcasm, as if it amused him to share the problem with Julian. The back of Daniel's head was bleeding from the fall and the weight of two grown men driving him into the ground. Julian stared at Daniel as he pinned him down, pondering whether to lie or own up to the accusation. Sydney had told him during her pregnancy that she might be carrying his child and confirmed it once the little girl was born.

"She wasn't your wife then, Danny," Julian reasoned, releasing Daniel's wrists. "She was just some chick I got drunk with one night. There's been a hundred like her since. It wasn't personal."

"It was personal to me," Daniel said. "And I've been raising your daughter."

"I've done my part, bro," Julian admitted, panting heavily. He eased off Daniel slowly and carefully, backing away as he released him. "Your wife has been hitting me up for cash for over a year now. You should be thanking me."

Daniel stepped back, contemplating another run at Julian. So, Sydney had known all along and she'd been profiting from it while she chastised him for his earning impotence.

"What do you want me to say, Daniel?" Julian asked. "Saying 'I'm sorry' isn't going to be enough for you." Daniel reached behind his back, locating the gun caught in the top of his underwear. He could shoot Julian now, take this horrible man from the world, avenge his honor and prevent others from this sorry state of being. But he pictured his father sitting there on the hard bathroom floor, and he thought of Officer Sheppard's dad, meekly trying to explain his son's good character and innocence to the ravenous media. That wasn't a check he would write for his father to cash.

"Does anything matter to you, Julian?" Daniel asked rhetorically. "Can you ever not fuck up everything around you?"

"No," Julian answered honestly and succinctly. "This is who I am." Both men were battered, bloody from the punches and the fall.

"That little girl is amazing," Daniel explained, the words crushing him internally. "She deserves better than you."

"Then you raise her," Julian replied. "What the fuck do I need with another problem like that?" Daniel knew he meant it and couldn't care less about the girl whose paternity had set all this in motion. His payments to Sydney were hush money, not support. Maybe Amber was the smart one.

He glared at the governor, the irony of Julian devaluing the very thing that had brought Daniel to his door nearly unbearable. It was as if Julian was throwing the antidote for a rattlesnake bite over his shoulder as Daniel lay stricken. "Who do you even care about, Julian?" Daniel challenged.

"Go fuck yourself, Daniel," Julian countered, growing tired of Daniel's attack. "You've got your own problems."

"Only the ones you've brought to me," Daniel shot back.

"Oh, yeah? How 'bout that little stock scam you were running at that pump-and-dump outfit, ripping old ladies off for their life savings?" Julian asked. "What's it going to be like to go to jail?"

"What the fuck are you talking about?" Daniel responded indignantly. "All I ever did was write press releases."

"And those press releases made old people drop their savings on that pig of a stock you guys were touting," Julian said, thankful to have mud on both their clothes. "Who the hell do you think has kept your ass out of all that shit over there? Your name's all over everything. I've been getting calls about that V.S.E. racket for months."

Daniel wondered why his attorney hadn't mentioned anything about regulators busting V.S.E. How could his lawyer not know about this?

"I've been protecting you because I thought you were my friend. I vouched for you, told the attorneys calling me to lay off, that you're *my* guy. I've kept you out of everything so far," Julian said indignantly, his hand against his chest for emphasis.

"It's hard to believe you'd protect anyone but yourself," Daniel replied. "I never did anything wrong there, and if you did anything to keep me out of harm's way, you did it because you were afraid I'd be connected to you somehow. It might hurt your next election, right?

"How do you do it, man?" Daniel continued. "How do you just say everyone and everything is mine and I'll just use what I want whenever I want? How do you fuck your friend's girl and never think twice about it? Or lie, cheat, and steal to get everything you have and still feel good about yourself? And how do you leave that poor cop there locked up in prison getting his brains beat out in the shower—or worse—and not go to the police and clear him?"

Daniel paused for a moment, short of breath from the battle and the oration. "And how do you look at the little girl you've been raising and feel like you deserve to be her daddy?"

"I don't," Julian said solemnly. "I never do that." Julian paused, considering the veracity of that admission. He thought of how he'd come in the other night from yet another affair, kissing his daughter on the cheek with the same lips that had been engaged in less honorable actions a half-hour before. "Why don't you get the fuck out of here," Julian suggested firmly. "Or did you have something else you wanted to say?"

"Nah, I'm done," Daniel said, hoping his father would forgive him. "You're on your own, Julian. Don't call me, don't call Sydney, don't call Sofia. If you do, I'll go to Frank Hayes and tell him what you were doing in Naked City. I may not be her daddy, but you're not going to be either. I owe her that."

"You don't want to do that, Danny," Julian said in faux confidence, Daniel's threat jabbing his Hayes-related ulcer. "You think Hayes would let you just walk away after you drop that knowledge on him ... let you run around telling people all about it? We're in the same boat." Julian let Daniel walk ten yards or so away before he lobbed another salvo. "I'd expect to do a year or so, Danny," he offered, sniffling blood through his broken nose. "Your boy Staglione's gonna serve you up."

Daniel didn't acknowledge that Julian had even spoken as he took his father's gun out of his pants and pushed it under his car seat. On any other day the remark might have been enough to set him off. Today, it just barely ranked.

CHAPTER 42

Daniel wasn't sure where to go after he left Julian's house, mindful that home wasn't an option. And with the duress he'd put his parents through earlier, it seemed compassionate to steer clear of their place, at least for the night.

It had felt good to pummel Julian. He thought he'd felt Julian's nose break with one particular blow, and the crooked angle of the bridge after the fight confirmed as much. That was especially satisfying, to mar a man who used his good looks as a spear point. Even still, the feeling had been superficial and fleeting, insufficient to quash his deep-seated despair. Julian's confirmation that Sydney had always known Sofia's true father didn't anger him any more than the first revelation had, but it did make him feel like a rube and servant.

Daniel reached for his cell phone as he drove, thinking Fred or Al might be good to have a beer with tonight. He needed something familiar and stable, predictably loyal. That described them both. Fred answered his phone on the fourth ring, his breath labored from something taxing. "Somebody move the phone a little farther from the couch, Fred?" Daniel chided, figuring that Fred was actually lifting furniture or climbing a fifth floor of stairs somewhere. Fred's girth and fitness were favorite targets of Daniel's, and the men exchanged insults in fraternity the way dignitaries handed out wreaths and medals.

"Is your mom still asking about me?" Fred returned fire, still panting. "I'm supposed to come back over Monday when she gets her Social Security check."

"Seriously, what are you doing?" Daniel asked as he drove aimlessly.

"You don't want to know," Fred warned insincerely, daring him to ask. Daniel didn't respond right away and in the silence could hear the moans of adult theater coming from a television near Fred. The increase in volume told Daniel that Fred was turning it up so he could hear.

"Bro, why would you answer the phone while you're doing that?"

"You called me," Fred reminded him, as if Daniel should have foreseen the interruption.

"You're a sick bastard," Daniel replied, amused as usual at his old friend's behavior. It was exactly why he had called him. "So, whenever you're done with your date, you wanna meet me at Wendell Street Pub for a beer? I've had a long, long day."

"Yeah, me too," Fred answered. "I hate my job. When you goin' down there?"

"I was thinking of going now, before it gets too much later," he told him. Daniel's phone beeped, signaling another caller. He saw the Private Caller display. "Hey, Fred, I'll see you down there. I gotta take this call."

"Hi, Clint," Daniel greeted.

"I know something you don't know," Clint uttered for the two hundredth time.

"I doubt that," Daniel said, relieved that Clint didn't hold anything over his head anymore. Clint paused at Daniel's unexpected reply, unsure what to make of the change in Daniel's voice. He had called so many times, only to hear Daniel quietly hang up, that a response sounded like a firecracker in a shower stall. Daniel could still hear Clint breathing, mulling his response. "Anything else you want to say, Clint? Or do you have to get back to mopping the VIP room?" He heard a click and Clint was gone, the first time Daniel could recall that he had run Zigler off via the phone. Clint probably was checking his sources to see what had happened to give Daniel the confidence to declare that he knew the answer to Clint's perpetual riddle, and if Sydney was now available.

That was of no concern to Daniel this night as he scrolled through his phone directory to find Al's number. It'd be great to see Al right now, and he knew that Al and Fred would get along. Catching Al's voice mail, Daniel left his former co-worker a message as he parked outside the Wendell Street Pub.

The pub was bustling, much busier than usual, Daniel thought, but for some reason the lone pool table was unoccupied. He headed for it like a real estate speculator, tossing his keys on the green felt in claim. He looked around the room for familiar faces, an old classmate, a neighbor, someone from this phase of his life. The panoramic view afforded nothing of the sort until Fred opened the front door.

He found Daniel instantly, illuminated by a slightly swaying pool table light and stopped to grab two bottled beers once he saw Daniel was empty-handed. This was Fred's element, it was clear for all to see, and he thrived in the simplicity, the genuineness of a place in which a guy like Julian Correa or a debutante like Sydney Banks would not allow themselves to be seen.

Fred cradled two longnecks in one hand and high-fived an older man sitting at the bar for nothing more than wearing an Oakland Raiders T-shirt. He handed the beer to Daniel and stared at him, asking a question with his gaze.

"What?" Daniel asked coyly, delaying the inevitable.

"You know what," Fred persevered. "You don't call me to get a beer anymore unless something is wrong, so let's have it. You interrupted my movie night."

"Yeah, that's why I didn't shake your hand when you got here," Daniel countered. Daniel's face let go of the brief smile it held and he looked at his feet for a moment, summoning the words to explain what had happened and preparing to describe the most difficult and humiliating day of his life. As he looked up, Al's gargantuan body stood in front of him.

"You need something, big fella?" Fred checked territorially. Al looked down at Fred, dismissing the semi-challenge as large men learn to do. Daniel disarmed the situation by grasping Al's hand warmly and introducing them to each other. That was good enough for Fred, who offered Daniel's beer to Al.

"I'm glad you're here, Al," Daniel said. "I need to tell you both something and now I don't have to do it twice." He knew that he'd also need to call Mike Martin soon. He began to describe the revelation of Sofia's true father and how it had become known. Daniel told them how he had left Sydney and Sofia, unsure of his future role with the latter and how he'd had the blow-up with his own father. They listened silently, both men completely surprised to hear of the turmoil in the life of their most stable friend. As Daniel detailed his attack of Julian and the resulting broken nose, both Al and Fred seemed to calm somewhat, as if something they would need to do had been crossed off their list.

"Dude," Fred said compassionately, a single syllable loaded with a wealth of sympathy.

"I can't believe it," Al said, shaking his head. "What are you gonna do, man?"

"I don't have any idea," Daniel said honestly. "I don't know where I'm staying tonight, I don't know where I'm going tomorrow, and I don't know what to do about that little girl. I do know that I love her more than anything I've ever loved."

"Well, start there, I guess," Al said quickly. "Sofia didn't do anything wrong. She doesn't deserve to lose her daddy."

"Fuck that, big man," Fred declared. "My boy's not going back to Sydney."

"I didn't say that he should," Al replied, clarifying his point. "I'm just saying that I don't see any reason why his relationship with Sofia should change."

Daniel was watching the exchange intently. His own thoughts were so clouded that he viewed the dialectic of two of his friends debating his future with great interest. Perhaps something in this would help him choose his path. He also thought about Sofia, lying in her bed after all that had happened today, going to sleep tonight without a kiss and a prayer from her daddy for the very first time. He wondered if she had any idea that he wouldn't be there in the morning and what Sydney would say when he wasn't. *Damn her,* he thought yet again in the simple way a man's mind can torture him with repetition.

Fred was now advocating Daniel getting full custody and making Sydney pay child support, arguing the merits of that course of action as if it were possible. Al was respectfully listening, having decided not to engage Fred any further on the subject. Al turned his head toward Daniel and noticed that he had checked out of the conversation and was looking around. "Let's get you a beer, stud," Al suggested as Fred turned to rack the balls on the table for a game of cutthroat.

"I'll get it," Daniel deferred appreciatively. "You keep an eye on Fred." Daniel made his way to the bar and away from the subject, taking an empty spot next to where the waitress made her runs. He noticed a sleek black leather purse to his left as he awaited the bartender. With the seat empty next to him he assumed it had been left by a recently departed patron. He raised his hand to get the bartender's attention, holding the purse in his other hand for safekeeping. As the bartender emerged, so too did an attractive young blond woman with her eyes trained on the purse.

"Goin' somewhere with that, Rambo?" she asked accusingly, noting Daniel's soiled clothing.

"Is this yours?" Daniel replied in embarrassment, quickly handing the bag to the woman with her hand on her hip and her eyes fixed on Daniel.

"Yeah, that's mine," she said as she quickly took it from him, taking her seat back at the bar.

"Look, I just saw it sitting here abandoned and I was going to give it to the bartender before someone walked away with it," Daniel tried to explain as he studied her form. She looked about his age and had short-cut hair that framed her face like a flapper, the kind of hairdo that only women with spectacular eyes can get away with. Daniel couldn't quite make out her eye color. It was somewhere between blue and green under the neon, but the shape of them made their color incidental, even with her brow furrowed in disapproval at his possession of her purse.

"Well, I suppose if you were trying to steal it, you would have walked off with it instead of standing here like a schmuck with a purse in your hands," she said. "And I probably shouldn't have left it sitting here. There was a girl next to me who I asked to watch it while I went to the powder room. I guess she had to go."

The bartender handed Daniel three drafts, and he looked at the girl, hoping she might apologize for the near-accusation. She wasn't looking at him anymore, having turned back toward the bartender to order her own beverage. This gave Daniel an opportunity to look her over, surveying the girl's relatively short skirt and muscular legs. Her arms were ripped too, like she might be a physical trainer or runner.

She looked out of place at the aging bar, like an oil painting at a bus stop. Wendell Street Pub seemed to always be in shades of brown, where a baseball glove or burlap might hide effectively against a wood-paneled wall. The pub had never been known as a place where attractive women might be found, in fact it was infamous for their conspicuous absence. But her demeanor indicated an ease, a cool even, that said she was comfortable in the venerable dive. Daniel hadn't come here all that often since he'd been married, but he was guessing she wasn't a regular.

The woman turned, as if she'd felt his gaze physically subside at her tan feet. "Thank you for saving my purse, Rambo," she offered, extending her hand in pithy appreciation and forgiveness. He wasn't sure if she was mocking him, but he accepted her soft hand as he stared at her eyes again. The black eyeliner framed their unique shape, defining them further, as if they were meant to be appreciated from a distance. "I'm Lynn."

"Danny," he said quickly. "Nice to meet you."

She let go of his hand first and turned back to the bar as her dirty martini arrived. He wanted to say something else to her when Fred poked his cheek from long distance with the chalky-blue tip of his pool cue, leaving an azure mark on his reddening face. Lynn brought her hand to her mouth and giggled, and Daniel laughed too, the shared amusement all but dispelling the acrimony of their previous exchange. "You better get those beers back to your boys," she said through a full smile of glossy pink lips and perfect teeth.

Daniel wiped the blue chalk dust with his hand and gathered the three beers as he grinned a goodbye. As he returned to Al and Fred and the likely continuation of the Sydney/Sofia/Julian discussion, he thought about how those few minutes with the nightmare of his day off the front burner felt good. Lynn had been a most welcome, albeit brief diversion. Al seemed to sense that Daniel had had enough of the debating of his troubles, seeing a closer version of his old friend returning to the pool table with beers in hand and a smile. The strange incongruence with the day's events made Al think that Daniel might make it through this period of change, even if much was still unsettled. Daniel had told him of the college suicide consideration once, and the Sofia paternity issue seemed more significant than the problems he'd battled back then.

Fred knew his current role too, following Al's lead and giving Daniel a simple and jovial night out among his pals while the world of chaos orbited malevolently outside. They shot pool for another hour before Al and Fred encouraged Daniel to join them at their apartments for the night, for a week, for as long as it took their friend to regain his balance. Daniel politely declined them both for now, hesitant to leave the sanctuary of the first place he'd been better than miserable all day. He pledged to give them a call in a while, once he'd decided what he wanted to do. As he re-racked the balls for a little time-wasting practice, he noticed Lynn still seated at the bar.

Al and Fred shuffled out of the pub along with most of the other patrons for the evening. A few dedicated slot addicts waited for the deuces to line up and coins to drop as Lynn sat silently, giving questions to the answers of a *Jeopardy* rerun on a small screen above the back bar. She turned his direction as he was racking the balls for a game against himself. His mind had returned to pondering his options, choices that forever affected the little girl blissfully at rest under a pink fleece blanket on which Daniel's mother had embroidered her name.

He knelt to retrieve a disobedient cue ball from the return and nodded a request for her to come over and join him for a game. She smiled and gathered her martini glass, walking over to the pool table. "I hate this game," she announced benignly. "It was invented so guys can look down girls' shirts."

"If you have a turtleneck in your car, I'll still play you," Daniel kidded, thinking how different she looked standing up with a frame to match the splendor of her face. "Or I can just turn my head when you shoot."

"No need to do that, Danny," she said, using his name. "I'm used to a lot more than just you seeing me in a lot less than this."

"What's that mean?" Daniel asked in a rising voice, eager to hear her answer as he visualized the remark.

"I'm a dancer at—" she started.

"Ohhhhhh," Daniel said, wanting to prevent her from having to make an uncomfortable admission.

"No, not 'Ohhhhhh,'" she corrected. "I guess you have to clear things up when you say you're a dancer in Las Vegas. I'm a *real* dancer ... classically trained in ballet, jazz, tap, etc. Not table, lap, pole."

"Ohhhhhh," Daniel said in acknowledgment, uttered in a slightly different tone. "Because I have a whole bunch of dollar bills in my wallet right now."

She laughed a little and grabbed the stick from his hands. "Can I break?"

"Absolutely," Daniel replied. "So, how'd you get into dancing?" he asked, inviting her to tell him more about herself.

"My mom started me, basically to get me out of the house so she could do whatever she wanted to do. My dad and her split up when I was little and things were never great at home. And I just fell in love with dance," she said as she circled the table, considering her striped options. "It was the only place where I controlled my own destiny, where it didn't matter that my mom wasn't reliable or how poor we were. On the stage, I was the same as the kids who lived in the suburbs."

She looked at him as she twisted the blue chalk around the tip of the stick. "Sure, the rich kids got picked up in nice cars while I sat outside and waited for an hour for my mom to come get me from wherever she was. But once I got to the point that none of them were better than me, I knew that this would always be my life. When I had nothing else to be proud of, when I was the kid with the worst outfit and the mom who never paid the studio bill, I could still look across the floor and know I was better than them. And they knew it too."

They shot pool terribly for three more games with little concern for skill or score, revealing details about themselves as they traded shots. At one point Daniel realized that his wedding ring was still on his finger and that this bright woman surely must have noticed. The quandary forced him to consider his changing life yet again, the truth of the day venturing in and out like a personal storm cloud. He hadn't addressed his marital status as the chemistry with Lynn slowly built from its dubious beginning. It wasn't in him to flee into the restroom and remove the ring, only to come back with the white circle that proved he was married ... and a liar.

It was funny, Daniel thought, as he watched how gracefully the dancer moved around the table with a stick in her hand, that their conversation thus far had been so non-flirtatious and human, as if it were a chat with Al or Fred. Well, maybe not Fred, he reconsidered. He hadn't flirted as interested men normally do, using entendres or offers for drinks to signal interest and test the waters. Instead, they had kidded about the various characters still entrenched at the watering hole, the music on the pub's stereo, and their parents. She had come out at eighteen from a small town outside Kansas City, thinking that NASCAR weekends and marrying the local insurance salesman weren't the reasons she'd spent all those hours at the barre of the dance studio. Her confidence and savings account hadn't allowed her to try Broadway straight off, and a friend with a full tank of gas was headed to Las Vegas where Lynn's maternal grandmother had moved a decade before. A small bag packed and a goodbye note to her mom later, she crossed the Missouri/Kansas state line headed west.

Daniel loved to watch her talk, the way she completed each sentence with a punctuating expression. Her hands moved about as her story did, gesturing with a grace and precision that confirmed her profession even while seated. Despite the climate of infatuation, the disastrous day had rendered difficult any consideration of future romance for Daniel. Nothing was resolved in his life, and fewer than twenty-four hours before he'd had no thoughts of leaving his home and family anytime soon. At the very least, Lynn was a perfect escape from the day.

Perhaps he was aggrandizing the merits of this woman before him, he considered briefly, crafting her in the image of Sydney's opposite. Lynn was at least as beautiful as Sydney, he was sure of that, but she didn't seem to know it as she sat with him this night in his dirty shirt and jeans. There was no sense of entitlement or expectation, no condescension to his working-class roots from her loft as a showgirl and raw beauty. And this was a woman who'd earned her status. She had trained and built a career from proverbial and literal sweat, rising to the top of a profession without a father's name or money.

The conversation wandered from subject to subject as both exchanged opinions on whatever came up. Lynn was intrigued by Daniel's responses and was testing her own views against his in gauging queries. They spoke like prisoners in solitary confinement who carve away at the rocky wall between them for years, desirous of human interaction and finally reaching each other.

Daniel and Lynn found themselves contemplating how very much they had in common, not just from their humble roots, but also in their views of the world at large. At one point Daniel shook his head after she had shared with him how she cares for her aging grandmother, a woman her own mother refused to help. Lynn was living in the dismal old neighborhood near the pub where her grandmother had moved, the old woman needing a rent she could cover with her meager retirement. Lynn had discovered her grandmother living in squalor once on a visit, the one-bedroom house reeking of the cat's untended litter box and a woman whose bad hip prevented regular showers.

Lynn moved in immediately, painting the walls white the first day and playing music tracks of Patti Page on her computer as Granny rocked placidly near a window with her ancient cat on her lap. Each night she'd drive back home from her production show on the Strip, pulling the blankets out of the closet and sleeping on the old velvet couch in the living room.

Tonight she'd stopped off for a drink at the nearby pub as her castmates headed to a glittering nightclub, mindful that morning meant counting out blood pressure meds and calling the insurance company to find out when the long-promised asthma machine would arrive. As she spoke, he thought of his father on the floor in despair, Lynn's commitment a stark contrast to the biting image ... and to Sydney.

Lynn ended her account of family duties minus self-pitying emotion, like a weatherman accepting the inevitability of rain without malice or regret. "Isn't it hard to have to do it all?" Daniel asked, wondering if he could do the same and as well. "You didn't ask for that gig."

"Oh, there're days I wanna go Kevorkian. She can be an ornery old broad," she said with a sparkle that equaled a wink. "It runs in the family."

Daniel desperately wanted to tell her of his plight, to share his tale of woe and explain Sydney and Sofia, Julian and his father. He wanted to see what she thought he should do, this stunning, empathetic woman who came to a bar he used as a human electrical ground. But he couldn't bring himself to contaminate the benevolent discourse with the cancer of recent hours. *Why do I meet her now,* he asked himself in self-pity, *on the worst possible day?*

She had asked him about himself, genuinely interested, yet averting any question about his marital status or the ring on his left hand. There had been no caress or exchange of touch between them, despite the rising awareness of their unique connection. The conversation went on for hours until the bar was empty and the newspaper guy delivered the daily papers. The opening of the tinted front door brought in morning sunlight and the glow washed over Lynn's pretty face, illuminating her green-gray eyes.

"It's weird, you know," Daniel said. "How much we have in common."

"You can dance?" she said, teasing him like a childhood friend.

"Well, no, and you don't ever want to see that," Daniel replied. "I mean everything else."

"Yeah," she said with a lowered voice of acceptance, signaling that she recognized it as well. "I was thinking the same thing."

"It's just weird," Daniel explained. "Not in an eerie way or anything— just how much of what you've said tonight are things I've already thought about, or how I see things too. Pretty specific stuff. I've long figured that I'd bring my mom and dad to live with me when the time comes. And you're already sort of doing it."

She nodded an agreement, appreciative of his appreciation. "Well, my crazy Aunt Susan would have an explanation for this," Lynn offered, reaching forward to take his hand over the bar top.

"Do you believe in reincarnation?" she asked as if preparing to tell a government secret, a little embarrassed by the question.

"Oh, I don't know," Daniel answered, his body teeming from her grasp in a way women completely underestimate. "I don't think I believe that this is it, that it all ends here. I do think of myself as a Christian, maybe by default.

"Well, one day my aunt was discussing the prospect that this life isn't the end for us, that we are an energy of sorts and that this existence is a vessel. I know it sounds a little weird, but it's an interesting thought."

"Go on," Daniel encouraged, unknowingly squeezing her hand a little.

"So, if you look around and realize that the number of people in the world continues to grow, really that the earth's population has exploded over time, and you believe that our energy persists somehow, you have to wonder if somewhere along the way a soul divides and becomes more new beings. And now I'm sitting across from you and I feel like if 'Fire and Rain' comes on the jukebox, that you probably love that song too. It makes me consider my aunt's idea that two different people just might be part of the same original soul."

Lynn looked at their hands together and back at a riveted Daniel, the sleepless night opening a portal to receptiveness that his usual pragmatism might dismiss. "Fire and Rain" was on a CD in his car that he'd made for himself just a few weeks before.

"Yes, my aunt is a little nuts and, no, I don't have a bunch of candles and incense lit all over Granny's house, but I'm sitting here holding your hand thinking how much it feels like I'm touching my own skin, as if our lives are from some common provenance."

"I was thinking the same thing," Daniel said honestly, a little over-whelmed. "I don't think your aunt's crazy at all."

"No, she's definitely crazy," Lynn confirmed with a gentle laugh. "Those are different stories for a different day. But everyone has some-thing to say, and sometimes the crazy people are the only ones willing to say the stuff that other people will laugh at.

"So, Rambo, I think I'd better get back home," she announced. "Granny's gonna call me a trollop if she's up when I walk in."

"I'll forge a doctor's note for you," Daniel kidded, thinking of any way to delay her exit. She leaned in and put her cheek against his cheek as he put his arms around her, holding her in a way that shouted, "Thank you."

Lynn pulled back slowly and looked at her friend. "I know that you've got a lot to work out, Danny," she said presciently. "But I'm go-ing to write my name and phone number on this napkin and tell you that when the clouds are gone, you should give me a call.

"Take your time and get back to good," she instructed with a gentle kiss on his neck. "I have so enjoyed meeting you."

"Good night, Lynn," he said, holding the napkin as she gathered her pocketbook and strode toward the door. He folded it and put it in his wallet behind a picture of Sofia.

CHAPTER 43

"**S**quirm here," the gossip columnist answered his phone. "What's your story, morning glory?"

"Oh, I've got a doozy, Squirm," Clint Zigler began enthusiastically, his hands sweating profusely.

"Another famous fella getting a little too frisky again at the Unicorn, Clint?" Squirm asked in the over-the-top manner that was as much his trademark as his funny flattop and math teacher horned rims. Even the kids fixing copy in the newsroom mocked the caricature of a guy who spoke in headlines and used alliteration liberally.

"Not exactly," Clint said, carefully measuring what he gave this human megaphone. Zigler and Squirm bartered often, with Clint supplying juicy tidbits from the strip club that Squirm would use in his column in exchange for being kept out of the news himself. Zigler loved the irony of anonymous tips buying anonymity. Today, however, Clint wasn't trading tit-for-tat. He was getting in on both sides of the deal as the release of the story itself was payment.

"Well, what if I was to tell you that Governor Correa has a baby out of wedlock with a prominent local businessman's married daughter?"

"Gregarious Governor Beds Businessman's Beauty," Squirm ad-libbed a headline, answering Zigler's question. Squirm saw himself as a champion of the everyman, armed with a sewing needle made for popping beau monde balloons. But his journalistic due diligence usually amounted to taking notes when a tattler called him directly, accepting the call as sworn testimony and encouraging its furtherance by eschewing attribution. A little grease on the street gave him hot tips on impromptu celebrity marriages or run-ins with the law as cab drivers and bouncers called the Squirm-line when someone or something happened. His column was widely read from its prominent positioning in the city's largest paper, and though most people ingested it with a grain of salt firmly in hand, any individuals named therein were assured that their dirt was in everyone else's living room.

"That's a great headline," Clint praised, pleased that Squirm was all over it. "So, the girl is Sydney Banks, daughter of William Banks, and she's married to some local loser named Daniel Madison. She and Julian had a fling a few years ago, but she's been fooling the Madison moron all along. That idiot's been raising Correa's little girl the whole time thinking that she's his."

"Ooooh," Squirm effused like a preschooler with a pinwheel lollipop. "This is going to be a big one."

"Yeah, I figured that you'd like this story," Zigler said. "This is even better than that Dennis Rodman deal last year."

"Oh, that was good too," Squirm fondly remembered. "He's good for business. To tell you the truth, I get a Correa tip about once a month. But how many times can I run a story about him nailing some little tramp or getting a b.j. on a golf course? Now, when the mattress is a respected businessman's little girl ... that's a headline."

"Whatever," Clint said, a little uncomfortable with Squirm disparaging Sydney given that his motive in all this was to get her back. "So, you'll run it?"

"Of course, of course, Clint," he agreed, already writing the dirty words in his head. "You'll have a credit with me too."

"I want it all out there. Everybody's name goes in this, Squirm," Clint said. "Correa, Madison, and Sydney ... even the kid. Everybody takes a hit on this one."

"That's not a problem," Squirm happily agreed. "The more names the better from my perspective. It adds color. Tell me something, what did our man the governor do to piss you off, Clint? You seem almost hostile. This one's personal, eh?"

"I've never met him. I'm just not one for immorality," Clint said with a straight face as he parked his new Ferrari behind The Unicorn. "People need to be accountable."

"Well, thanks again for the tip, Clint," Squirm parted in gratitude. "Stay tuned for the fireworks."

Fireworks were exactly what Zigler wanted, hopeful that the public humiliation would exacerbate Sydney and Daniel's issues, permanently end their marriage, and leave Sydney vulnerable to his pursuit, a white knight of a different armor. He also wanted to make sure Correa and Sydney didn't wind up together, mindful that Sofia created a uniting entry point for them. He knew Sydney well enough to assume she'd likely blame Correa as a seducer when the questions came from all sides. That would end any possibilities with Correa, he hoped. Clint wasn't quite sure why he couldn't give up on Sydney, though he ranked her unavailability at the top of the list of reasons.

The next morning Squirm's column was the talk of coffee shops and water coolers alike as business people and politicos buzzed about the governor's first documented extramarital affair. This wasn't a minimum wage waitress or lap dancer he could dismiss conveniently. Sydney Banks came from a family of import, credibility. The news media gathered in two locations immediately, besieging the governor's office and the Madison residence seeking reactions to run at five p.m.

Sydney's mother had called before sunrise, her morning tea steeped with the bitterness of the respected family name so salaciously sprinkled among the embarrassing text of Squirm's column. Worse yet, this meant Sofia was half-Latino, a fact Mr. Banks would suffer worse than Daniel's dismal tax return. Sydney was forced to call up the story on the Internet, her newspaper lying in the driveway at the feet of a cluster of reporters. She quickly pulled the blinds in the kitchen, shutting out inquiring minds and the scalding light of the new morning. Sofia had risen as well and was furiously checking the master bedroom, the bathroom, and the shower for her daddy, just as she had each morning since he'd left two weeks before.

Sofia's mother's mind raced, pondering what her reaction would be when the microphones were inevitably thrust in her face. Should she deny the tryst and lie? Then again, she considered, these fifteen minutes of fame might make her a local star, a siren who could woo a man who would be governor. This would confirm her allure, setting her above her classmates who had married more affluently than Sydney had with Daniel. She'd be Cleopatra anew with Caesars Palace in her dominion.

She wondered what Julian was saying to his wife right now, if this would forever sever their union and set him loose again. Would the humiliation of it all force him away from Meredith and their own little girl?

What's in my best interest? she contemplated as always while the newsmen knocked on the door every ten minutes like insatiable bill collectors. Maybe Julian would call and they'd work it all out. Maybe they'd even decide to be together … for their daughter's sake … united by the scorn and the little girl who fused their blood. She assuredly didn't love Julian, but she couldn't see herself alone with a child to rear, forced to go back home to her parents or take a job again. Maybe Julian could be a long-term solution. Daniel hadn't come running back as she'd expected and would only say, "Hand the phone to Sofia," whenever he'd called over the past few weeks.

Life with a man she didn't really love might be all right amid the splendors of the Governor's Mansion and the spoils that went with it. She'd done the same for less with Daniel for years now—as had her mother, she suspected. Her mother told her once after Mr. Banks' latest tirade that she "didn't love her father so much as she understood him," intimating an arrangement of a practical nature that fell short of a love affair. Sydney knew Julian could never be trusted, but first ladies usually didn't expect their husbands to be faithful, she reasoned. Perhaps she'd have a paramour as well.

Sofia was eating a rice cake, shedding crumbs from the kitchen to the living room like Gretel as she followed her pacing mother. Sydney settled on the couch with her legs pulled up and crossed, holding the cordless phone in her hand as she considered calling Julian. Julian always answered her calls halfway to frustrated, knowing that each conversation was a brand of extortion. Of course, Julian never called and offered support for Sofia of his own accord either, comfortable with Daniel being the sightless pack mule.

A staffer briefed Julian on the dubious news the moment it had come out, waking him as he lay with his back to Meredith. Julian sat upward in the bed, trying to respond generally so that Meredith would stay in the dark as the sun came up. He pulled on the same pair of trousers he had thrown over the back of the chaise lounge near the bed the previous night, grabbing a clean shirt from the closet, and heading to the hallway where the newspaper rested on a Queen Anne end table.

The headline read just as the staffer had stated, a bold declaration of his paternity and infidelity. This was something Meredith would be unable to ignore. The news would come as no surprise to her, as she was already forcing him to wear a condom on the rare nights they were intimate. But her shame was no longer private, and she would now be the lady at the cocktail party who generated whispers and faux pity. Objects at altitude make far better targets.

Soon, her daughter, Risa, would be the daughter of a son of a bitch, a politician who screwed constituents and his family with equal disregard. Julian could solve the former by tending well enough to the donors who secured his fortune, but Meredith was a different matter. He couldn't count on her to do the Tammy Wynette thing. Not anymore.

Julian pored over Squirm's ramblings with interest, each sordid detail arousing him. He figured Daniel had dropped a dime to Squirm given the way things had ended after their fight, until he reached the part of the column where Squirm called Daniel a low-rent hack in what must have caused the gossip columnist to don a lightning-proof suit as he penned the line. Maybe Sydney had done it, Julian wondered, seeing how the more he learned about her, the more he knew they were very much alike. It would be like her to seek attention of any variety just to get her name in the papers.

Julian walked a green mile back to the bedroom, hoping to grab a tie and shoes before Meredith fully awakened. Instead, he found her hanging up the phone, her eyes wet and her ivory cheeks now crimson. He stood at the foot of their bed like a prisoner being sentenced, as if the time had already passed for explanation. Meredith's face confirmed that she had received an informative phone call.

"I'm gonna say 'I'm sorry,' Meredith," Julian began, hoping to take the teeth out of her attack before she could utter it. "I know that's not worth a lot to you. I haven't been a good husband and you deserve better than this. I know I've embarrassed you."

"My father's reading that column right now. My mother just called to tell me," Meredith said solemnly, wiping at her tears. She turned and stood beside the bed in her cotton pajamas, looking directly at Julian. "How are you going to explain this to Risa?"

"She's not even two years old yet, Meredith," Julian replied, sans the humility of his opener. "I'm not telling her anything."

"I don't mean now, Julian," Meredith said virulently, her voice gathering steam. "I mean later on when she wants to know why you destroyed this family."

"What's that supposed to mean?" Julian asked, already well aware of the answer.

"It means that I won't be embarrassed as your wife anymore." Meredith brushed past him and toward the bathroom's shower. "This was the last time."

Julian didn't turn as she passed him, letting her go along her way in the massive master bedroom of the Governor's Mansion. *This went better than expected,* he thought as he heard the shower knobs squeak the release of warm water over his wife. Apologizing right away and using all the words she would like to have heard had been the right move, truncating her response and keeping the rancor to a minimum. Perhaps she'd cool down in a few days as she always had. But he knew the aggregate of his affairs was pushing Meredith away in a back-and-fill pattern, two steps forward and one step back on a path to her final departure. He couldn't be certain as to what would be her deal-breaker. It may well have been today, though he would have expected a more explosive response were it so.

There was no time for marital woes today anyway, not with a dangerous meeting with Hayes ahead of him. Julian saw Squirm's revelations as a superficial annoyance compared to the risk of Hayes and the floating sword of his meeting with Calderon never mentioned by his perennial foe. Hayes was pissed about another matter, one that fell far short of murder, and Julian was headed to the principal's office to get his swat. Frank had asked Julian to intercede again on behalf of The Unicorn and the elder Zigler, needing a bill killed in the Assembly that would further tax strip clubs statewide. Julian privately dismissed the request despite accepting it from Frank, deciding that this chore would be the first one he'd deny him. Wanting to wean himself from Frank, he figured that being unreliable was the most efficient method. If Hayes couldn't count on him, it would force him to tone down his requests after a period of predictable and repeated tirades.

Hayes would always have a leash on his self-styled governor, but Julian was already thinking of not running for re-election and going into the private sector where he could cash in on the "Gov." in front of his name. Cushy board of directors spots paid fat passive revenue. Following that course meant he wouldn't need Hayes anymore, not if he wasn't running. Frank would have to find a new lackey.

Julian walked toward his private office in the mansion, expecting Hayes to be lurking outside, tapping his watch impatiently. Along the way, his cell phone vibrated in his pocket. He recognized the number instantly, somewhat expecting Sydney's call. She'd probably have her hand out again, Julian assumed, leveraging the risk of her talking to the press in exchange for his sending a thicker envelope this month.

Approaching his office he could see Hayes seated within, at home in the governor's high-back leather chair with his feet on the marble desktop and holding a wooden baseball bat in his hands. Julian quickly hit ignore on his phone and sent Sydney to the purgatory of voice mail.

CHAPTER 44

aniel walked into Mike Martin's apartment eager to spend a little time with his friend and to ask his advice on dealing with Squirm's exposé. Mike, of all people, would know what to do with this breed of crisis management.

Martin maintained an apartment on the east side of town, enjoying a rent far beneath his income strata. Daniel had been there often and teased Mike frequently, calling the retreat his "dorm." It definitely could pass for one. Though the place was clean, "eclectic" and "cluttered" might be the most benevolent adjectives a compassionate surveyor would choose in describing it. The walls were free of any décor and the furniture seemed to be a composite of hand-me-downs and won't-let-gos blending into a discombobulated assembly that could serve as preamble to a Martha Stewart suicide note.

Nonetheless, icons of the genteel Mike Martin were sprinkled throughout like rhinestones on denim. Over the back of a ragged La-Z-Boy hung a blue blazer that Daniel saw as the man's signature look, while a Bocelli compilation rested on a coffee table. On the laminate breakfast bar dividing kitchen and living room a bottle of '91 Chianti sat patiently, awaiting Martin's release of Tuscan-red perfection.

Mike welcomed Daniel in and directed him to the living room, a warm handshake lingering long enough to convey sympathy. Martin read the paper each morning the moment it hit the porch, maintaining a life on Eastern time despite being domiciled out West. It was yet another foot-kept-in-the-door for Martin, a subtle refusal to fully sink Las Vegas roots. Daniel figured the understated apartment was much the same, a reticence to commit to the area until he was sure this place wanted him too. In many ways, the faded Red Sox cap on the back of the old couch confirmed as much.

"Can I get you a coffee?" Martin asked as he took a seat across from Daniel on the ancient recliner.

"No, I'm good," Daniel said, needing nothing else to accelerate his pulse. "I had a cup at Al's before I got the news. Thank God my dad already knew about Sofia. It would have killed him to hear it this way."

"At least there's that," Martin said, acknowledging the gravity of the news. Mike didn't have a bullshit gear that spun events such as this. He'd move on to resolution mode for certain, but he wouldn't feed his friend bullshit.

"How can I help you, friend?" Martin offered as Daniel's eyes reviewed Squirm's column for the tenth time. He'd brought it with him and set the clip on the table.

"What should I say to the media?" Daniel asked. "My dad says they're even calling *his* house."

"I wouldn't say anything," Martin advised. "You're not the governor, you're not the cheater ... you're the guy that got his world turned upside down because of all this. You don't owe the media anything."

Daniel's mind had wandered away from his own question, thinking how it had been two weeks since he'd seen the little girl with whom his day had always started. Sydney was almost an afterthought compared with the absence of the precocious child, a lost hubcap on a totaled sports car. He called each day, avoiding and ignoring any comment or query from Sydney and refusing to introduce any of their troubles into his conversations with the confused little girl. Sofia always asked where he was, when he was coming to see her, and where her papa was too, each question torturing the man she called Daddy.

Daniel deflected each biting question, moving on to subjects of lighter grade. He could hear Sydney feeding Sofia questions in the background, using the little girl to try to determine where he was staying and his present mood. Daniel didn't want Sydney to know he was staying with Al, hoping the mystery of his whereabouts bothered her some. Sofia's patience with the separation seemed to expire yesterday when she cried into the phone about him not playing with her. In response, Daniel instantly pledged to come back to his own house for the first time on Saturday to spend the day. Sydney had been more than agreeable to his return, hoping to corner Daniel with a conjured contrition and best effort toward reconciliation.

Of course, that had been before the Zigler/Squirm release which changed the landscape. Even so, Julian's lack of response to her voice mails made Daniel the clear choice for Sydney. And despite the public and private morass, Daniel still intended to see Sofia tomorrow.

"So, have you thought at all about what you're going to do with your wife and Sofia now?" Martin asked gently.

"I'm done with Sydney," Daniel answered quickly. "I've spent the last few years looking over my shoulder for that little Zigler jerk, consoling myself that Sydney would never do that to me. All the while she already had fucked around with someone else, maybe with him too. I won't spend my life in that mess, asking each day if she's still faithful. But I can tell you that the two weeks without Sofia have been the worst of my life. I'm truly lost without her."

Daniel brought a hand to his face, embarrassed that his voice was breaking in front of Martin. Mike wasn't sure what to do with no sound remedy in the air and in possession of another piece of bad news to give a man already under duress.

"Will Sydney let you see her?" Mike asked, trying to focus on the one thing that might make his injured friend feel better.

"She'd love for me to. I've resisted so far because she's trying to leverage it into me spending time with *her*. I have no interest in that. None. But Sydney's got a wedding to go to this weekend with her mom and Sofia can't go. One of her entitled friends is getting married at Turnberry, and of course Syd doesn't want Sofia around to keep her from having a good time. So, I'm gonna 'babysit' and spend the day with Sofia."

"Mike, I can hardly wait. I swear I'm gonna hug her for the first ten minutes."

"Aaah, that's good, Danny," Martin said, locking in the positive as he pondered the best way to give Daniel the difficult news he'd been holding. Mike moved over to the couch in an effort to console Daniel, creating the opposite effect in his friend who read the move as a bad news pretext.

"I've got something to tell you," Mike said from close range, hating himself for the timing of the revelation. "You're not going to be happy."

"Well then, you picked a good day to tell me," a defeated Daniel answered. "It's tough to fall when you're lying on the floor."

"You sure you're up to another piece of bad news?" Martin asked, second-guessing his choice to tell Daniel today.

"You think I'd be better off walking around wondering what it is you need to tell me? Go ahead, Mike. Let's get it over with."

"The StopShot money is all gone, Dan," Martin reported. "There's nothing there."

Daniel leaned his head backward on the couch and stared at the ceiling as if it were a fresco. The StopShot money had been his 'new start' hope chest, a way to create a new life for him and Sofia.

"I looked into it like you asked me, Daniel. A guy I went to law school with is in the attorney general's office in Georgia where that lawyer you've been speaking with is based," Mike began, his voice bothered by the guilt of each revealing word. "He's not even an attorney, man."

"What?" Daniel said with what emotion he had left. "I've been talking to that guy Gillespie about everything, Mike. I sent him all my records. He's the class-action guy."

"No, he's not a class-action guy," Martin corrected. "He's Staglione's partner. Once my buddy in the AG's office told me that they had no record of an attorney in the state under that name, I took the liberty of hiring an investigator we use for background checks to look into everything. Gillespie and Staglione have worked at least a couple of these pump-and-dumps together. They're a team. Gillespie is a broker who lost his license in some boiler room scam back in Brooklyn."

Daniel just stared at Squirm's column on the coffee table as his financial chariot incinerated. This was money he had hoped to use to buy Sydney's favor in remaining Sofia's daddy. He'd planned an adoption that would make it all permanent and invulnerable to Sydney's moods and mercurial whims. But without the StopShot windfall, his bank account was little more than the soon-to-be-due house payment at Sydney's place.

"There's no easy way to say this … they set you up," Martin continued. "All these guys wanted was more time to get the money all out of the country and into numbered accounts. The whole act with this Gillespie guy was just a ruse to delay you from going to the real authorities and having them freeze their assets. And you gave him all your records too, right? Even the originals?"

"I did that early on. I never doubted him. I have nothing left. I have been hearing 'just a few more months, Mr. Madison,' for nearly three years," Daniel said. "What can we do now, Mike?"

"I think we oughta leave it alone," Martin said solemnly, mindful it wasn't the answer Daniel wanted to hear.

"Leave it alone?" Daniel asked in respectful indignation, careful not to misdirect his anger toward a man who had gone the extra mile to help him. "The authorities have to be interested in all this. I'm the guy who can tell them everything that Staglione and StopShot had going."

"I don't think you want to do that," Mike said gently, trying to cloak his advice in some affection. "It appears Staglione's got your name on everything, from what you've said to me and what I can see online. When the SEC gets involved and they spend the dollars it takes for an investigation, they need a collar. If your old pal Staglione's fled to some non-extradition country and the money's with him, they might just look for an easy fall guy. You don't want to be that guy."

"I didn't do anything wrong, Mike," Daniel said plainly as he remembered Julian's remarks to the same effect. "Not one thing."

"I know you didn't," Martin said sincerely. "You're the most honest kid I know. I'll never forget what you did for me. But sometimes you gotta just walk away with your good name and look at the road in front of you."

"You talking about Sydney or Staglione?" Daniel said in sarcastic truth.

"Maybe both, brother," Martin answered humbly, realistically.

"Julian said that the SEC was already looking into this, into me," Daniel said.

"That was probably Gillespie's work too," Martin theorized. "Staglione probably just had Gillespie get word to Julian somehow to make you damaged goods, to keep Julian from helping you. My guys would know if you or Staglione were already being looked at. I think you're clear if you just leave well enough alone.

"So the bad guys win? I get nothing and they walk away clean with everyone's money?"

"I'm not so sure they really win," Martin said. "Guys who live like they do, who comport themselves this way, can't confine their avarice and immorality just to business. They cheat on their wives, lie to their friends, and have no meaningful relationships with anyone. A guy like Staglione probably dies alone somewhere in a big house with pictures of things, not people, on his walls. He doesn't win."

"Maybe you and I can go back together to Boston and open a consulting firm. We'll start all over, eh?" Martin kidded in a way that wasn't entirely kidding, wanting to punctuate the discussion in optimism.

"Yeah," Daniel said agreeably as he contemplated Martin's suggestion and thought of what still kept him here. "That might be nice."

"I've given myself one more shot at the senator or I'm outta here," Martin confessed for the first time, the depth of Daniel's trouble making his personal despair easier to speak about. "He needs to help me be a candidate. He owes me that."

"I hope you get what you want," Daniel replied politely, too emotionally barren to give Martin's issues real consideration. He was thinking that this time tomorrow he'd be with Sofia again. She'd be sitting in his lap, putting ridiculous barrettes in his hair and bursting with laughs rich in paternal calories. He wondered how he could swiftly pass the hours of this day into the next, afraid of each waking moment between

Squirm and StopShot and the Sofia antidote tomorrow. The trauma of the day made clear that he needed to be her father no matter what it took. Nothing else mattered now and he knew he couldn't live without her.

CHAPTER 45

"**Y**ou're in my seat, Frank," Julian said in annoyance as Hayes rested comfortably behind the governor's desk. Julian wanted to move on from the fiasco of the Squirm column and the terse exchange with Meredith, but he couldn't. He knew that this was serious, a harbinger. His meeting with Hayes wouldn't start from a place with emotional balance.

"Am I?" Frank asked in faux incredulity. "Sorry, about that." Frank maintained his occupancy of Julian's seat despite the acknowledgment, forcing Julian to take the visitor's place opposite. Frank withdrew his feet from the top of the desk, placing them on the floor as he smacked the baseball bat into his open palm. Julian could see the wooden bat was covered in dark blue signatures and that it seemed weathered and aged.

"So, let's get going with our chat, Frank," Julian said irritably, wondering why Hayes had brought a bat into his office. "I'm guessing you're aware I haven't had the best morning so far."

"Yeah, I heard something about that on the ride in today," Frank responded coyly. "Of course, I never believed a word of it."

"Hmm, mmmn. What do you need to talk about, Frank?" Julian asked again, growing angrier that Hayes was screwing with him from his own seat. Hayes' very presence unnerved Julian, like nitroglycerin sitting on the desk in a shot glass, an explosion just one tap away. He already knew Hayes was mad about the strip club legislation, but he wasn't going to bring it up first and give it added weight.

"There's much to talk about, Julian," Hayes cajoled. "But first I brought you a gift." Hayes changed his grip on the baseball bat, sliding his hands down toward the thin end and pointing the bat toward Julian, like Babe Ruth calling a home run shot.

Julian laughed an insincere laugh at the mock threat, reaching to take the fat end of the bat. As he pulled it toward him, Hayes playfully jerked it back a little before completely releasing it to the governor. Julian looked over the bat, scanning the signatures for names he recognized. There were more than a few—Mickey Mantle, Joe DiMaggio, Billy Martin, Yogi Berra, and other New York Yankee luminaries.

"Those are the 1951 New York Yankees, Julian. It's Joe D's game-used bat from the World Series," Hayes explained. "Mantle's first year, DiMaggio's last. You don't see much stuff with both of them on it. I guess they didn't really like each other. But that was one of the greatest professional teams ever put together. Despite their differences, despite the drinking and the whores and the distractions, that squad did what they had to when it was game time.

"And they became legends, immortals," Hayes said with a flamboyant wave of both his hands. One long strand of his silver hair was out of place, dangling over his tan forehead.

Julian wasn't sure what to do with the gift, assuming it must be a Trojan offering. However, having expected a Hayes tirade over his failure to honor the most recent strip club request, the valuable bat was most welcome. He also gathered Hayes's metaphor, and it reminded him to tell his captor that he wouldn't be running for re-election. He wouldn't be on *his* team anymore.

"Thank you, Frank," Julian began politely enough. "I've always respected what the Yankees have done even though they only win because they have the most money to spend on players. They buy their championships."

Frank grinned subtley at Julian's rebuke and moved to his next line of discourse. "It appears your influence with the Assembly wasn't as effective as we had hoped. Now I've got a nasty old man who pays me a lot of money very, very angry. He's actually taking it very personally that this bill passed, says it might put him under."

"He says that about anything that doesn't help his business," Julian countered. "Life goes on. Sometimes in business you gotta take your lumps."

"Yes, that's true," Frank agreed. "But if he isn't getting value out of what he pays me, then it stands to reason that he'll stop paying me. You wouldn't want that to happen to someone who has helped you get this far, would you, Julian?"

Julian glared at Frank, irked by the pleasantries and insincerity. Hayes was baiting him, acting demure and subordinate for as yet unclear reasons. "Actually, I really don't give a shit either way, Frank," Julian said, tapping the bat in his own palms now. "I don't care about Zigler, The Unicorn, what they pay you, or the New York Fucking Yankees. I'm done here."

"Oh you are, are you?" Hayes asked, preparing to remind Julian how totem poles and chainsaws got along. "Perhaps you forget how things work in the real world, my friend? Are we back to the place where I have to threaten you?"

"What are you gonna do to me, Frank?" Julian said with the confidence of a hang-gliding cancer patient. "You gonna send some hooker to sit at my table and take a picture? I could fuck that broad in a daycare center and it wouldn't change anyone's opinion of me now."

"It might by the time you need to be re-elected," Hayes countered confidently.

"I suppose that's right," Julian conceded, his voice even and composed. "But I guess you and I haven't talked much lately—which, of course, I sincerely regret—'cuz I'm not running again. I'm out, done, finished," Julian concluded, each word a triumph of independence. "I really have been meaning to tell you."

"Oh, no you're not. You'll be done when term limits say you're done," Hayes replied, his voice rising much higher than Julian's. "I didn't spend the time, money, and political capital necessary to get your greasy ass this far to have you walk out in your prime, son."

"Hopefully you can learn to come to grips with disappointment," Julian responded in a way that bordered on taunting. "Maybe there's a twelve-step program for control freaks out there."

Hayes was thrown off his game by Julian's revelation. Ringmasters are accustomed to there being only one whip.

Julian wasn't thinking especially clearly either, the gravity of Meredith's disdain and the ubiquitous scandal column gnawing at him like insatiable termites. Hayes was receiving that redirected enmity, which was furthered by the governor's enduring contempt for him. His verbal fray with Meredith just moments prior would be the loose pin in a grenade built from years of Hayes's abuses and violations.

Another lock of hair had fallen from Hayes's normally coiffed perfection, as if the hairspray stood with Julian. Julian could tell Hayes was disturbed by his announcement that he wouldn't be running—and by Julian's newfound defiance. Frank tried to rock in Julian's non-rocking chair as he composed himself, wanting to look unshaken and cool. His initial objective of finding a way to assuage the elder Zigler had fallen off the agenda now as he tried to think quickly of how to maintain his indentured servant.

Julian enjoyed the pause, looking at his tormentor with his eyebrows raised in exaggerated expectation. It was an odd and overdue feeling for Julian to feel some power with Frank Hayes, even if the dangerous man was still seated in his chair.

"Are we done here, Frank?" Julian asked Hayes, whose face had taken on the look of someone different from the man who had boldly entered with a baseball bat in his hand.

"Give me the fucking bat, Julian," Frank ordered, loudly enough that Julian's secretary poked her head in the open door.

"We're good, Carol," Julian said. "Frank's just getting ready to leave. Have them bring his car 'round front."

"Absolutely, Governor," Carol obliged.

Julian was basking in his autonomy, enamored with its display and bridled only by the asterisk of the meeting's precursory events. His conversation with his wife had been both the catalyst to this moment and the boundary of its pleasure.

Frank rose from his seat, buttoned his black suit jacket, and stood arm's length from Julian as the empowered governor looked out the window toward the grounds. Julian let Frank stand there for ten seconds longer than would be polite before turning to meet the man who had tarred the road to the mansion in which they both now stood.

"Frank, do me a favor," Julian began decently. "Why don't you get the fuck out of my office."

It was Frank's turn to utter a startled laugh and feign momentary disregard. "You think you get to tell me what to do, you little spic?" Frank said in boiling animus, deeply unsettled by Julian's provocative demeanor.

"Yeah, I think that," Julian said as he stood to meet Hayes, a full head above his older adversary. Hayes gritted his teeth and reached to poke Julian in his chest with a rigid index finger. Julian held the vintage bat in his right hand as his left swiftly caught Frank's encroaching digit, gripping it tightly and pulling it upward so aggressively that the break in the metacarpal was audible. Frank's face reflected the pain of the broken finger evidenced by its crooked contortion and the bone's eerie crack. Julian released it only so he could put his hand around Frank's warm neck, gripping it with the restraint of a torturer, not a killer.

Julian was shedding years of hatred and shit-eating into one explosive moment, vomiting all that he'd been forced to consume. Reason was gone, displaced by vengeance and despair, the two currents forming one undeniable stream of malevolence. "I said get out of my office," Julian reiterated as he released Frank's throat, widely spaced fingerprints changing from white to red as the blood crept back into the soft flesh.

Julian looked at his vindictive left hand, raising it to his own face and spitting in it as if he were striking a deal in Deadwood. As Frank held his broken finger in his unbroken hand, he watched Julian swirl the saliva over the Hall of Fame bat, smearing the signatures into one unintelligible memento of Correa's independence. He flipped the ruined bat at Hayes's feet like kindling, looking at the battered man as if Hayes was surrendering to MacArthur on the *USS Missouri*.

Hayes picked up the bat and tucked it under one arm, as if it still had use somehow. He looked at the new Julian and told his nerves to ignore the pain in his finger long enough to utter a parting note to his once-obedient pupil. "Well, I guess you're right about not running for governor again. You've certainly lost my support."

"I expected that when I broke your finger," Julian needled.

"Of course you did," Frank agreed. "The question is whether Felix Calderon will endorse your career choice." Calderon's name sent a shiver through Julian as Hayes toyed with the revelation that Governor Correa had long feared.

"You know they say that man is a killer," Hayes continued, attempting to look unfazed despite the throbbing pain in his hand and his increasingly disheveled appearance. "I'm afraid I'll have to report today's events to him at our usual coffee on Monday. It won't help that he hated your father."

With that Hayes exited Julian's office, beaten, provoked, and angered more than he had ever been. The last time he'd been bested like that had been in childhood, a beating by an older kid in a school bathroom in which he was physically overmatched and defeated, humiliated with his face shoved in a urinal.

Julian and Frank were thinking the same thing as they walked in different directions from the battlefield of the office: that Julian's refusal to run for re-election had simultaneously rendered him useless and free ... two attributes that would give Frank Hayes and Felix Calderon no reason to let him live.

CHAPTER 46

Julian's intemperate triumph was as short-lived as it was cathartic. Sending Hayes away with his hand and manhood in disrepair had been long overdue in Julian's mind. But he knew immediately afterward that it was both a battle won and a dramatic escalation of the war. Frank's confirmation that he and Calderon spoke often—and obviously had discussed Julian's solicitation of Hayes's death—let Julian know that he'd best be on guard from both dangerous men. Frank probably had known about the desired hit since it had been requested and was plotting with Calderon how to make use of Julian while he was still useful. Julian assumed that this was why Hayes never mentioned the scheme, realizing that to acknowledge the death plan would be to broach a subject for which there was no resolution, bringing Julian and Hayes to the irreconcilable point they found themselves at today far earlier.

Hayes had milked Julian for as long as he could, even if it meant that his revenge for the requested hit would be served ice cold. Julian was confident that a man like Hayes would never let him walk away unscathed. Frank's vengeful plans to politically assassinate Mike Martin and a dozen others like him told Julian that Hayes would come back guns a-blazin'. And none of his previous targets had physically injured him as Julian had so brazenly done.

It also concerned him that Hayes couldn't use his normal reputation-killing tactics, as Julian's history of moral turpitude would provide him a shield of redundancy and inoculation. Calderon didn't seem the type for subtleties either, Julian considered, and remembered how his father had told him of Felix's proclivity for slashing throats from ear to ear. That seemed a stronger prospect than sending a wanton lass to provoke some tawdry intercourse for public release.

He could attack Hayes first, he considered yet again as he next realized the only man he knew who handled that kind of work was

Calderon. The governor's job didn't exactly afford much access to street thugs and hit men like those who had worked the Miami neighborhood where his life had started.

Julian figured he was safe in the Governor's Mansion and more so up north than in Calderon's home turf in Las Vegas. He could lay low for a long time, delay the inevitable attack until he could figure some way to save his skin or broker a deal. Needless to say, everyone was a potential threat right now and his private meetings should remain exclusive and infrequent.

Governor Correa sat quietly—not peacefully—on a velvet bench in the long hallway between his office and the residential area of the mansion. It was the first time he'd ever done so, always having been in a rush down the corridor in one direction or the other.

It's beautiful, he thought, noting the intersection of crown molding, subtle paint, and a metal sconce on the wall. Nothing elaborate, just simple elegance and geometric symmetry. He remembered once last month when Risa stood on the bench where he now sat and he'd rushed to grab her before she fell to the hardwood floor. It felt odd then, that moment of fatherhood amid a preponderance of parental drive-bys. He did love Risa, wanted the best for her, but didn't have the emotional depth or desire to play the daddy role believably.

Julian remembered a girl from college that he'd dated for the better part of his senior year. She was smart and beautiful, working her way through school as a nanny for a doctor's family. Julian could never really seem to fulfill her, to say "I love you" or to demonstrate the sentiment in any way beyond the bedroom. Things were going well enough, he thought, though the girl he derided as "needy" seemed to be pressing him emotionally, wanting some vocal confirmation of his regard for her. He'd tried to explain alternatively that he cared for her, that he was content and happy with their college relationship but refusing to commit to an "I love you," even though he did. When he found her parting note, he scanned through the gentle beginning where she praised his qualities and what she loved about him. Soon, she segued to her explanation, forgiving him completely for falling short of what she needed in her mate.

"Not everyone has the same size heart," she'd explained as Julian read an articulation of the condition from which he knew he suffered. "It's not that you're a bad guy, or even not a good guy. Your heart's just not big enough for me or anyone else."

Julian balled up the letter and threw it in the closest trash can. An hour later he picked it up, unfolded it, and placed it neatly in a drawer where he kept his passport and birth certificate. Someday he figured he'd use it to explain who he was to someone else.

He knew exactly where it was in the bedroom where Meredith had received the most recent piece of news about his failings. Maybe now was a good time to read it again, to see his shortcomings as a father and a husband and a human as his unavoidable destiny. He was but a captive on a ship called *Free Will*.

He left the seat and headed to the bedroom, wanting to speak with Meredith again. Maybe he could tell her what had just happened with Hayes and she would sympathize. Meredith always sympathized. He found the door cracked open. As his hand began to push the door he could hear Meredith speaking in a talk-cry-talk pattern.

"What will Dad say?" Meredith asked through a sniffle. "Will he be mad?"

"I *have* tried to work it out," Meredith answered back.

"I know, I know," Meredith agreed. "But I don't want Risa growing up with this, building an expectation for her own relationships around a man like him."

Julian paused in the doorway, listening to his wife unravel to her mother.

"I have to, Mom," Meredith said defensively.

"Then you come live with him."

Meredith was pacing the bedroom, the old corded phone tethering

348

her to the nightstand like an umbilical cord. Her back was to Julian and his eyes were trained on her. "Mom, I'm gonna go. You and I aren't going to agree on this no matter how long we talk. I'm sorry that you disapprove of what I'm doing." Julian wondered what that meant exactly, his turbulent day leaving all things possible.

"It won't be right away, but I'm going looking for somewhere to live tomorrow," she continued, answering Julian's unasked question. "I'm coming back to Vegas with Risa."

"She's fine, Mom. She doesn't know anything at this age. We're all flying down first thing tomorrow and Julian's going to watch her in the afternoon while I meet with the real estate agent. I asked him a week ago for something else. I'll just use that time to look at houses with the Realtor."

"I love you too, Mom," Meredith cried softly. "Please tell Dad to try and understand. This is what's best for me and Risa. I tried, I *really* tried."

Julian went no further, turning to look down the hall from which he'd just come. He knew there was no reason to seek Meredith now, mindful of how difficult it was for her to tell her father anything that might lead to his disappointment. He didn't have to see her to know that she was sitting on the bed, blaming him for the awfulness of the call she'd just made. He returned to the bench, having no desire to work on the obligations of the office, and sat with his shoulders to the wall.

Risa emerged from the door, dragging a wagon behind her that made more noise than a small wagon should. She still wore the night's pajamas at midday, a clue that Meredith was way off her normally clockwork routine. The little girl spotted her father alone in the hallway and let go of the wagon handle to walk toward him. She didn't say anything as she climbed onto the bench and sat next to him, her shoulders to the wall as his were. He waited a second before he reached to take her hand.

"I'm sorry, Risa," Julian said, having exceeded his personal best for apologies in a single turn of the earth. She looked forward still, as if the words weren't words at all. "I'm sorry that I'm not the daddy you deserve and that I make your mommy sad. I'm not a very good daddy."

Risa turned just enough to look up at her father, her hand inside his. Julian took the look for acceptance, maybe even understanding. He wondered how much she looked like Sofia and if the sisters would someday know each other. Meredith emerged from the bedroom in search of Risa and spotted her on the bench with Julian, her heart labored by the rarity of that image and the difficulty her choices would soon make its recurrence.

"There you are, honey," Meredith said to Risa. "Let's get dressed, little lady."

"Daddy," Risa said, indicating a desire to stay with Julian.

"That okay with you, Julian?" Meredith asked in a tone that Julian knew was both undeserved and cover for the plans she was making.

"Sure," Julian said as he and the toddler sat oddly still, their hands still clasped. "I've got nothing to do today," he said, as if his schedule was all that kept him from spending time with Risa prior.

"Go get ready and I'll sit here with Risa," Julian offered.

"All right," Meredith agreed suspiciously, lamenting the tease of normalcy that Julian often sprinkled. "Give me fifteen minutes to pull myself together."

"Take your time," Julian replied as he began to digest the only choice he had left. Sitting with Risa now, Julian knew it was time to do the right thing.

A day later and across an expanse of Nevada that generally offered less botany than a moon landing, Daniel was thinking the same thing as he arrived at the little home he'd purchased. Sydney's car was parked angularly in the driveway, as if to prevent another from parking close to her vehicle. Daniel strode toward the front door with his house key in one hand and a backpack of Sofia's favorites over his shoulder. He doubted Sydney had replenished the home's supply of strawberry fruit roll-ups.

Daniel put the key in the lock, tapping the door courteously as family members do at one another's homes. The key barely turned and Daniel realized the lock had been changed on the home for which he'd empty his checking account again next week. Sydney answered the knock and leaned to kiss him on the cheek. He allowed it, telling himself he'd avoid any hostility with her as best he could, wanting to spend the day with Sofia and to make clear his intentions to remain her father. With the StopShot money gone from expectation, he knew that he'd have to plead the case on merit—and whatever else would serve Sydney. He hoped Sydney would be accommodating, seeing her daughter recharged by the return of her daddy, and would welcome his interest in a child he'd raised, not fathered. As he lay restlessly in bed the previous night, he contemplated the desperate times of his past, the troubled first year of college, the death of Annie, and other dark moments. Nothing seemed to compare to the absence of Sofia. Not having her in his life seemed unendurable.

Daniel managed a gentle "Hi" to Sydney while he looked for Sofia. As his eyes surveyed the home from kitchen to living room, she pounced from behind a chair, having intended to hide and make him find her, then lacking the patience once she saw him. "Daddy!" she screamed in unfettered joy as she leapt at him like a tiger cat. He caught her and pulled her against him so tightly that he flushed air from her little lungs. She laid her head down flat against his shoulder as daughters do when they are content. His eyes grew moist and he knew his nose would be running soon.

"She looks good, Syd," Daniel offered in a way he knew she would accept as a compliment.

"She's pretty good," Sydney agreed. "She sure misses you."

"Yeah, I can see that," he replied. "I miss her too. I thought maybe we could talk about that."

"I'd like that," Sydney agreed, hoping this was the beginning of a successful reconciliation that would allow him to return and support the little girl. She'd planned her remarks just as Daniel had. Sofia immediately began to ravage the contents of Daniel's backpack, pulling out a few items before urgent curiosity called for a dumping. Sydney led Daniel to the couch by the hand, using contact like a cocktail waitress enhancing a gratuity.

"So, I've been thinking about Sofia, Sydney," Daniel began. "And she really is my daughter."

"I'm glad to hear you say that, Danny," Sydney said.

"Great," he said blandly. "I do want to be her dad, to be in her life. I think that's what's best for everyone."

"So, you'll be moving back in?" Sydney said suggestively, not logically. Her desire to re-hook Daniel had been increased by five successive calls to Julian that he'd avoided. It had rung two or three times before it went to voice mail each time, telling Sydney that he was ignoring her.

Daniel paused, wanting to tread the invisible line between surprise and expectation. "I don't think that's what's best for anyone," he said.

"Well, we're a package deal," Sydney countered the rejection, having prepared for this contingency.

"Syd," Daniel said, unfurling his own Plan B. "Why would you even want that? You weren't all that happy before … before the whole Julian thing went down. Don't you want to be around someone who makes you happy?"

She didn't. That had never been high on her list. It was more about survival now and keeping what she had. Sydney would look for a different rock in the river later.

"I'd like to adopt her," Daniel continued. "This will take a load off of you and keep her as happy as possible. This is what Sofia wants, and I can guarantee Julian won't oppose it." Sofia had eaten at least two fruit roll-ups as the adults focused on each other and was tearing at a plastic bag of cinnamon bears she had no hope of breaching.

"Not interested," Sydney dismissed like a corporate lawyer. "We're a package deal, Danny."

"Yeah, you said that," Daniel responded as nicely as possible while thinking that he wanted to scream that this entire mess came from *her* indiscretion.

"Look, Daniel," Sydney said in a quasi-professional tone. "We can make this work, keep this family together, and get back to living a normal life." She reached for his hand again. Sydney fashioned puppy dog eyes and lowered her head so she could look upward. "We can make this work, baby."

"Not interested," Daniel said, returning to the business decorum. She did look beautiful in the dress she'd purchased for the wedding. It reminded him to cancel the credit card they shared.

Sydney considered his immobility in her negotiation and leaned away from him. "Daniel, my father's attorney says you're a stranger as far as the law is concerned. You have no parental rights to Sofia. That is, unless you're my husband."

Sydney thought to herself that she didn't want it to be like this, to have to threaten him with Sofia. But when she'd asked her father what Daniel's rights were, he'd made it more than clear that she couldn't come home, that he was too old to have to deal with a three-year-old under his roof.

Daniel didn't have much else to throw at her, though he didn't want to let the discussion end this way, without a deal in place to keep Sofia in his life. Nothing mattered more. He couldn't see himself back among the carcinogens of the failed marriage, inflamed by the proven dishonesty and the perennial threat that would be her outside his field of view. He wasn't so sure he even loved her anymore. His affection for his bride had become a broken vase, glued back together, but fractured and cracked beyond all usefulness, its only beauty from afar.

Sofia was back in his lap now, to Sydney's delight, requesting his assistance on her cinnamon bear emancipation effort. Sydney could see that Sofia's general demeanor had improved immensely since she'd confirmed he would spend the day with her today. Part of Sydney hated

Daniel for that, too, making her second best in her own daughter's eyes.

"Sydney, let's just talk about this later," Daniel retreated, seeing the impasse and wanting to spend the time with Sofia while Sydney went to her wedding. Deep inside he knew she wasn't likely to give in, to let him have Sofia without her in tow.

"Well, you know where I stand, Daniel," she said authoritatively. "I hope you'll do what's best for Sofia ... your daughter. I'll be back later."

Daniel didn't respond, a dark feeling of futility sinking deeper and deeper. He couldn't come back here—not with this woman—but he couldn't see a life without the beautiful little girl sitting on his lap.

He and Sofia played for hours, and Daniel had been forced to wash his face three times in the extra bathroom to remove the makeup she'd put on him. If he could only bottle her laugh, he thought, he could make their time apart something manageable. But in just a few hours the recess would be over and Sydney would be back in the home with her impossible ultimatum.

Sofia was bordering on exhaustion, played out and weary on the couch in the living room. He thought she might fall asleep right there as he looked down at her. The time apart and the time together today had all but eradicated his once-acute despair over not being her biological father. He had to find a way to keep her. He *had* to.

Daniel wandered through his home like a tourist, more pacing than anything, while Sofia rested in front of a cartoon. Eventually he found himself in their bedroom. He looked at the hardwood bedroom set and the bed itself, the one on which he'd erroneously believed they had conceived Sofia.

He remembered that first night in Sydney's room when she had confessed to telling him an untruth to lure him there and he had kidded her about starting the relationship with a lie. Daniel knew he could never trust her and that he couldn't be the kind of father Sofia deserved in a relationship of that sort. The hopelessness was overwhelming him now, even with Sofia just outside the bedroom door and down the hall.

Did he have to choose between being with Sydney and not being with Sofia? Was there any other way out?

Maybe this was how Officer Sheppard felt, sitting there in the front row, receiving the life-ending verdict for someone else's crimes while the true offender pondered dinner plans. Something inside him suggested that he throw cold water on his face to jolt himself a little. He walked into the bathroom and stood at their sink, a mirror above the faucet. Above the chrome hot tap and nestled into the edge of the mirror a business card had been placed for safekeeping.

The Unicorn Gentlemen's Club. Clint Zigler. Owner.

Daniel wondered if Clint had been in his house or if Sydney had been in Zigler's, and his blood began to warm. This was a preview of life again with Sydney, days and nights ravaged by the union of her weakness and his strong memory. He knew he couldn't do it, that he could never accept her ultimatum to live with both of them here or somewhere else without Sofia.

Daniel dried his face and walked outside to his car where under the seat his father's loaded handgun still rested from the day he had taken it to Julian's. As he carried the firearm past Sofia and headed back into the bedroom, it was clear that a desperate Daniel wasn't going to accept either of Sydney's options.

CHAPTER 47

Daniel put the handgun in the small fireproof safe he kept under his and Sydney's bed and set the key back above the door jamb into the bathroom. He refused to put Sofia in his car with a loaded weapon inside. Daniel gathered enough clothes to last a few days as they headed toward his parents' house. Neither Daniel's mother nor father had said anything to their beleaguered son about how hard it had been not to see the little girl, but he knew they too were stinging from her absence.

Before Daniel and Sofia left, he stood in the bathroom staring at Zigler's business card and it occurred to him to simply take Sofia and leave. He realized there was nothing to keep him from doing just that. He *was* her father.

Squirm's column wasn't a court order. In fact, if there was an opposite of a court order, it would be Squirm's column. Sofia's biological father had been officially changed by no one, Daniel noted, and so far Julian Correa seemed an unlikely candidate to willfully advance his responsibility. What Daniel and Julian and Sydney knew about Sofia's father was as yet scientifically substantiated, leaving Daniel's name on the birth certificate as the prevailing document of Sofia's paternity. Sure, Sydney could try to get Daniel and Julian to take a DNA test, Daniel thought as they traveled, but neither Julian nor Daniel would be in a hurry to oblige her.

And so, a father and his daughter would be spending a few days with the little girl's grandparents until he decided his next move. Sydney would likely explode upon re-entering the empty home and call his cell phone to threaten to put all her father's riches and legal associates into play. But while she sent those slow wheels into motion, he would be with Sofia and leveraged by nothing more than his affection for the little girl with a new fruit roll-up habit and a strong disdain for Burger King.

His mother and father greeted Sofia enthusiastically, wrestling for her time and attention. Daniel unpacked the small bag in his old room and put Sofia's pink blanket on his bed where he'd sleep next to her tonight. On the battered nightstand he'd used since he was a boy, he set his phone and wallet. Daniel kicked off the running shoes he was wearing and looked around his old room, smiling at the still-hanging posters commemorating the interests of a young college student.

He could hear Sofia's high-pitched laugh, offered at a piercing decibel only available when little girls are chased and think they are getting away. As he put his hands behind his head, he superficially considered the possible battle with Sydney. He knew she'd only fight him as long as she thought he might still come back to her. Today would prove that wasn't going to happen, and he still had faith that she might simply concede and not oppose his conviction to be Sofia's father. In the end, it made her daughter happier, gave her child support, and perhaps most importantly, a babysitter every other week. A single mother could use that.

The only potential problem could be Julian's re-entry, though gauging by Julian's remarks when they fought, it seemed unlikely. Even still, it was the one Achilles' heel in his new plan.

Daniel fell asleep on his bed and Sofia's blanket, sleeping restfully for the first time in months. Twenty minutes later, he awakened as the old bedroom door creaked, expecting Sofia to be the intruder. Instead, his father stood with a solemn expression, his mother two steps behind holding Sofia.

"Julian's dead, Daniel," his father told him as he wiped the blur of sleep from his eyes. "He took his own life while he was here in Las Vegas today. It just came across the television."

Mr. Madison knew most everything about Julian, the early speeches, the fight at the brewery, and the betrayals of Martin and Daniel. He also knew his son well enough to add, "I'm very sorry."

Daniel sat breathless, grasping Julian's death ineffectively. He wanted to cry right there, to mourn his old friend, and to stand up and say good things about him now. But reason crept in, reminding Daniel of what Julian had done to him and others, chewing at his natural response of grief and pity ... and loyalty. As he and his father talked about it, while Julian's oldest child painted watercolors with her grandmother, Daniel realized that Julian's death nearly guaranteed his retention of a parental role with Sofia. With Mike Martin's help, it might even come to a quicker resolution. Maybe Sydney and Daniel could find a way to be friends again, the divorce behind them and united platonically by Sofia's best interests.

His father politely exited the room, telling his son to take as much time alone as he needed. Soon his phone rang and it was Sydney, telling him the terrible news of Julian's suicide without inquiry as to Sofia's whereabouts. Daniel realized she wasn't home yet and hadn't realized that he had the little girl elsewhere. When it was his turn to speak, he told her that he'd taken Sofia to his parents' house and braced for her reaction. It didn't come as he expected, and it appeared Sydney saw in that remark not a violation but an opportunity to stay out a little later. He realized Sydney's habit of disappointing him did sometimes have an upside.

Tomorrow Daniel would speak to her about Julian and Sofia and how he would remain her father. He'd ready some language from Mike Martin about how cases can drag on forever and how without a real father to contest his fatherhood, how difficult it would be for her argument to prevail. It might not all be true but it should be enough to have her set down her sword.

Daniel looked at the picture of his grandparents on the nightstand and remembered how very young he'd been when they both had passed. He could still hear each of their voices in his head if he tried. He reached for his wallet and opened it wide, taking out two of Sofia's pictures and setting them next to his watch and keys.

He withdrew a swatch of white napkin with a phone number scrawled on it and set it on his lap. Daniel took the phone and entered Lynn's number, striking each key as if it were the code to a bank vault.

CHAPTER 48

October 2005

The courtroom was packed, as was the hallway outside and the sidewalk beyond the courthouse doors. Everyone, it seemed, wanted to hear the final words of the late Governor Julian Correa read aloud. A governor's suicide note only intensified interest in the already explosive subject of the introduction of new evidence regarding a murder committed by a police officer.

Former officer Sheppard sat quietly in the front row of the courtroom as Daniel Madison entered from the foyer, the same expressionless glaze upon Jay's face as during the announcement of his guilt and sentencing. His hair wasn't as short as before, and clean cut wouldn't be a fair assessment any longer. He'd bulked up considerably, and Daniel wondered what a police officer had to do to get by in prison. Sheppard looked harder, colder … more like former officer Craig Peters.

Daniel was uncomfortable from the moment he'd entered the room, yet eager to share the contents of the letter Meredith had given to him. She had stood there waiting for him to open it after she turned it over still sealed, hoping Daniel would allow her to view Julian's last earthly thoughts. Daniel couldn't help but note her disappointment when the brief letter never mentioned her. The bailiff returned to Daniel Julian's red-stained note, withdrawing it from an evidence bag in which it had been stored since the forensic team verified both Julian's blood and handwriting. There would be no question of its authenticity.

Jay's defense attorney began to query Daniel as to the letter's provenance, confirming for the judge that it had been obtained from Julian's widow, who had found it at his side. Daniel nodded and affirmed out loud each of the expected questions as they were asked, his eyes moving from person to person in the courtroom. Daniel couldn't help but note Sheppard's mother, alone and just behind her son, her husband having died of a stroke a few weeks before. Unlike her incarcerated child, her face was a multitude of expressions indicating anticipation, anxiety, and raw grief. Daniel unfolded the letter as the lawyer asked him to read it to the court. With the release of a deep exhale, he began.

> *Daniel,*
>
> *By now you know what I have done with this life, that I have squandered all I have been given or loved. I know most will see my choice as weak and selfish, but for the first time in my life, it's neither. The time has come for me to at last be accountable, and to pay restitution for my grievous faults with my own life. Everyone is better now.*
>
> *I want you to know that you were the only friend I ever had, the only person I could not corrupt. I think a part of me grew to loathe you for that, Danny, for being a person I cannot. At least you can be that person for your daughter, Sofia. I am very pleased that you are her father and I ask that you someday forgive me enough to introduce her to my daughter, Risa. They should know each other.*
>
> *I could apologize for all that I have done to you (and others) but that would be a phone book, right? Instead, I want to leave this life by paying a debt to you that is long overdue. I know you will do what is best with this letter once you have it.*
>
> *Some time ago I was in Naked City meeting with a former associate of my father's named Felix Calderon, who can verify that I visited his home. Upon leaving, I encountered two armed Hispanic men, and as we argued, two off-duty police officers approached us.*

Daniel paused to take a drink of water. As he did, he noticed Sheppard aware for the first time. He seemed to have found consciousness and was waiting for Daniel to continue, pleading with his eyes. His mother was squeezing a Kleenex behind him, as if her grip leeched hope from the tissue.

There was an angry exchange of words and one of the Hispanic men approached the officer's vehicle from the passenger side. Immediately, a punch was thrown by the officer I now know as Officer Sheppard, and soon the second Hispanic male charged the truck with a knife. Seeing this, the driver of the vehicle that I today know as Officer Peters drew a gun, leaned past Sheppard, and fatally shot the second Hispanic male. I was standing fifteen feet from the front of the truck and had an unobstructed view of this event. Because I was embarrassed by my presence at the scene, I chose once again to ignore what is right and just, and to not report this incident as it occurred. I offer my deepest apologies to Officer Sheppard and his family, to the community, and to you, Daniel, for not rectifying this travesty earlier as I could have done.

Your friend,

Julian

Jay Sheppard was looking up, presumably in search of his father's face. Nearly everyone else in attendance was wide-eyed or mouth agape, trying to grasp the magnitude of the former governor's confession. The inarticulate officer convicted of murder had been telling the truth as detectives and prosecutors lined up to condemn him. Sheppard soon would be released and there would be no talk of a new trial … at least not for Jay Sheppard. The next morning Craig Peters would be arrested at the Mexican border about the same time that detectives Walt Brown and Hank Peters were turning in their tarnished badges.

As Daniel exited the witness stand and walked past the man Julian had just exonerated, Jay reached beyond his counsel and shook his hand. In Jay's grasp, Daniel felt a lot like he had the day a promising young candidate first read his speech at the Working Women event, the last time he had been proud of his friend Julian Correa.

CHAPTER 49

January 2007

"**M**y tie looks funny," Mike Martin said again, looking critically at himself in the mirror. "Danny, should I change the tie?"

"No, Mike," Daniel replied as he adjusted the knot for no reason. "It still looks great."

"I asked you that already, eh?"

"Just a couple times," Daniel said with a smile. "You can ask as many times as you want if it relaxes you before your speech."

"I'm gonna blow it. I know I am," Martin said in uncustomary nervousness.

"Mike," Daniel began sternly. "You've got it down perfectly. You have the note cards and it's a short speech anyway, because it's twenty degrees out there. Remember, you've got the job now. This is the inauguration, not the campaign trail."

"The tie does look good," Martin at last agreed. "Good call."

Daniel laughed to himself at Martin's unusual discomfort, his polished New England veneer shelved in earnest concern for what he would become in a few short minutes. Mike remembered the day at Boston Harbor when he had all but given up hope of ever reaching a position of this import. When he spoke with Daniel then, he'd concluded that the system was not built to reward men like them.

But Mike Martin won the governor's election in a landslide. The real battle had been the primary but Frank Hayes and his cronies hadn't had the time they needed to position and groom their own man as they had Julian, having expected him to run for re-election. Instead, they'd tried their best to recruit Lieutenant Governor Prescott, who had finished Julian's term after his suicide. It had been an uneven effort at best with a less malleable Prescott, a man whose family money gave him some immunity from Hayes. Martin had beaten the incumbent with backing from the senator, who knew that to not support Mike yet again would be to make him an enemy. And Martin had campaigned tirelessly, working precincts north and south as no gubernatorial candidate had done since the advent of concrete.

Meanwhile, rumors of Hayes's subterranean dealings with Governor Correa had been leaked by politically motivated investigators, causing donors once in Frank's camp to withdraw their financial support. Squirm was good for something.

Hayes knew it before anyone else, that his career as a power broker in the growing city had seen its zenith. The unsuccessful primary against Mike Martin would be his last. Golf outings would soon be just for golf.

Martin certainly wasn't Julian, being neither manipulative nor seductive. But he was genuine and approachable, smart and comforting, with an "older brother" quality, as Daniel called it. He'd hired Daniel full time for his campaign, making him director of communication at a pay rate that let him leave the mediocrity of his very small business. That helped make the years since Julian's suicide the best of his life. It didn't hurt that he and Lynn were now engaged and living together, along with her granny, in the small home he'd once occupied with Sydney. Lynn had painted everything white there, too.

Sydney Banks quickly married a wealthy lawyer twenty years her senior. Daniel had heard from one of his and Sydney's remaining mutual friends that the new marriage was being haunted by a familiar name. Clint Zigler was somehow being fed enough hope to breed the special brand of harassment that Sydney's new husband was now enduring.

Sydney visited Sofia every other weekend, and when Daniel told her he was moving nearly the length of the state away to be Mike's chief of staff, she offered little protest, having slowly weaned herself from Sofia as the months turned into years. Sofia seemed to have little expectation of her mother anymore, growing taller and closer to Daniel each passing day. A stranger had even said recently that she looked like her daddy. She certainly talked like him.

In Sydney's void, Lynn had become Sofia's willing caregiver, tending to Granny and Daniel and Sofia in a way that she had found fulfilling. When a knee injury ended her dance career a year before, she moved seamlessly to the household's top position.

Martin adored Lynn, greeting her with a sincere kiss on the cheek each time since their second meeting. He knew the effect she'd had on his friend Daniel and her care for everyone under the Madison roof gave her the status of due reverence he assigned only to his own mother. Sofia and Granny were now bonded in a way that Lynn was sure added years to the aging woman's life. One day when Sofia fell asleep on her lap by the window, Granny looked at Lynn and said plainly, "It ain't about blood, it's about love." Lynn knew it already, having fallen for the bright little girl with the dark Cuban eyes just as Daniel had when the delivery doctor handed her to him.

Martin was standing outside now, eager to get to the inauguration and blowing warm air into his cold hands. Daniel was amused by his mild distress and knew that Mike would settle down when it was time to take his place on the podium. A moment later, Al Morris entered, his enormous frame clad in a gray suit that made him look like a linebacker on NFL Draft Day. He walked toward Daniel and Mike, warning them that they had two minutes until the oath of office would be adminis-tered followed by his speech.

"Tell me again why we hired a guy with no political experience?" Martin asked Daniel, teasing more than testing.

"Because we can trust him with anything," Daniel replied. "The only other guy I know like that cannot be around sophisticated adults with-out dropping the f-bomb."

"Oh, you mean Fred," Martin acknowledged. "That guy's a lotta fun. Let's get a beer with him when we get back to Vegas next week."

"I'll set it up, Governor," Daniel said happily.

"Mike, it's time," Al called out. "They're playing your song." Daniel reached to shake Martin's hand and Mike gripped it tightly before pulling his friend into a tight hug.

"I know it's cliché, but we've come a long way, eh?" Martin asked.

"Yeah," Daniel agreed. "You know, we wouldn't have ever built this kind of friendship had we not both met Julian Correa."

"That's true," Martin said, remembering how Julian's treachery had built their trust. "Despite what he did to us, I'm proud of him for what he did at the end there. He didn't have to do that."

"I know," Daniel concurred, the thoughts of Julian's suicide still painful. "It's hard to believe that as he was preparing to kill himself, he took the time to write an account of what really happened at the shooting. He made it right." The thought of Julian and his suicide note reminded Daniel that he must someday introduce Sofia and Risa to Amber's child.

"But enough of this dark talk. Go give 'em that speech you wrote, stud," Daniel ordered.

Martin headed toward the podium with his tie crooked. He accepted the oath as his mother looked proudly on in the dress he'd bought her for the occasion, her own life fulfilled by her son's attainment of his life objective. Governor Martin grasped the edges of the lectern, his burly arms conveying both strength and stability. The bare trees of the Nevada winter kept the horizon visible and snow-covered mountains stood witness to the beginning of his term.

"I won't make any new promises today as I stand here now as your governor. Instead, I simply assure you that I will keep all those that I have already made. Each campaign speech and mailer sent out to you is a contract for which I expect to be held accountable.

"Over the past few years I've learned so much about being a leader that I believe with certainty I can provide to the state of Nevada the stewardship it has long deserved. I will represent this state with character and dedication, looking to her interests and needs while enhancing her many attributes and opportunities. And I say in earnest that I've learned these things not from my political peers or the deep-pocketed power brokers who make campaigns and candidates.

"No, I've learned more about leadership by watching good fathers and good husbands, good mothers and good wives, in witnessing men and women for whom justice is a lifestyle and loyalty their greatest weakness. I know that there's much to be done. You will find me just inside those doors doing the very best I can."

Daniel hadn't written a word of the speech or edited a syllable. It had come from Mike entirely, his unvarnished thoughts and hopes melded into one sentiment. He hadn't read it with the guile of Julian Correa, Daniel thought as he remembered the day Julian made his listeners swoon, but Governor Michael Martin meant every word.

Daniel looked over the crowd from his vantage point near the stage. Lynn's short blond hair stood out among the earth-tone jackets of the winterized attendees. He couldn't help but smile as he watched her slide a scarf from her neck and wrap it around Sofia.

CHAPTER 50

February 2007

The suitcase looked like someone had tipped a general store on its corner and poured the contents into the carry-all. Vitamins, pens, cough drops, aspirin, and candy joined blue jeans and work boots among the clutter. In a velvet bag nestled into his shirt pocket was the primary reason for the journey to Havana. This item, he promised Antonio, would not leave his possession.

Antonio knew he could not personally risk a return to the island where he had been born, not with a family here in Las Vegas and a business that had but one true jeweler. Instead, he decided to use the man who called himself *El Caballo*—"The Horse"—preferring the term to mule. Antonio had watched him run the gauntlet to and from Havana for several years now and was confident he could successfully carry his package. El Caballo's real name was Edgar Cervantez and he made a living taking everyday American goods to those in Cuba who cannot find such luxuries behind the wall of an embargo.

El Caballo would travel to Canada, where U.S. jurisdiction and forbiddance of Cuban travel ended, taking the longest of routes northward to turn again and go south. This was among the reasons that he charged American families so much to take their relatives such inexpensive items. He slept a little on the last part of the flight into the island and arrived fresher than he'd expected. His contacts in Havana met him quickly, helping with his bags and paperwork, eager for the items he brought them, too. Today it was Jim Carrey DVDs with Spanish subtitles for the Mexican market. World peace always starts with *Ace Ventura, Pet Detective*.

His cousin guided him to an old truck they would use to make deliveries, moving from neighborhood to neighborhood around the city like a drugstore Santa Claus. El Caballo noted how the lucky receivers of the American gifts seemed as pleased by the thought that their American cousins still cared for them as by the soap or penicillin.

Cervantez had brought a half-dozen small suitcases and bags with him and they were down to the last delivery, each man wiping his perspiring brow with a white handkerchief whenever the truck stopped and the open windows transferred no moving air. Nineteen fifty-four Chevy pickups rarely have the benefit of freon.

He and his cousin quarreled as to which direction was quickest to the last address on the list where the most important delivery was to be made. Antonio seemed to think the home was closer to town than it appeared to be. Eventually they arrived, climbing a dirt road to a small residence built a few inches from the roadside.

Seashell wind chimes sang from the tiny porch as his cousin loudly shut and re-shut the door to the old truck until the door closed. El Caballo reopened a package and gave his cousin a deck of cards from the Bellagio Casino in Las Vegas as payment for his chaufferring him to the farthest house on their journey. He took the velvet bag in his hand and rang the doorbell.

A woman appeared, cautiously looking through the small window and asking what they needed. El Caballo wanted to see her entire face, to make sure this was the person to whom he had been sent. He mentioned Antonio's name and the woman's dark eyes broadened in a surprise that bordered on shock. She looked down at the suitcase and agreed to open the door, warning both sweating men that they could not come in while she watched her grandson.

El Caballo gave her the case and explained that it had come from Las Vegas, from her cousin who wanted him to say that he never forgets about her. She opened the case and put her hand to her chest, the small gifts not small when much of the world is kept from your island. She sat down on the threshold and surveyed the contents, thinking that the aspirin would prove especially useful on days when the humidity tormented her arthritis. Her silver hair was pulled neatly back and seemed as thick as a woman's hair can be, albeit devoid of the color that had once made men beg her Uncle Diego for permission to seek her. Cervantez let her review the gifts, telling her his opinions of some of the American candies or music that had been included.

He reached into the velvet bag and presented Antonio's gift to her, the gold chain rising upward like a swaying cobra, link by gleaming link until the golden Tocororo hung from its lowest point. El Caballo passed it to her smoothly, as if awarding her a prize that she had won. She had never seen it, of course, though her uncle had spoken of it on nights when drinks of rum and lime liberated his memory.

Her courier signaled his departure with a handshake and a nod of his head, nearly leaving without passing her the note that Antonio had handwritten. She hadn't spoken since the golden bird had come to lie against her tan chest, silenced by the surprise and emotion of the unexpected package. As El Caballo left in the noisy truck, her brown-black eyes quickly read the brief letter.

Eva,

My father had this little bird in his store and I lost it for him. It has taken me forty-seven years to get it back. No one was as good with gold as my father. He made this beautiful little bird for you with the diamonds from your mother's wedding ring. They are not the best diamonds, but they are your mother's diamonds.

Your cousin,

Antonio

The End